PROJECT
VORTEX

MICHAEL CICCARELLI-WALSH

Project Vortex

Book Two in The Zoboros Series

Copyright ©2023 Michael Ciccarelli-Walsh

Cover designed by Momir Borocki

Table of Contents

For Dylan, who gives the feedback only a brother is honest enough to provide.

Prologue

The stamps and cheers of the crowd shook the hallway as Ristin slipped out the backdoor. He smiled. It used to be that he could stick around after his shows and mingle. No longer. The audiences had gotten too big, too ravenous.

And it had happened almost overnight.

He laughed to himself, wishing he had discovered the secret sooner. He'd tried everything over the cycles to break through: new instruments, new songs, new arrangements, new bandmates. But it turned out the only thing his act had been missing was his powers.

Outside, he felt the same electrifying energy permeating the night air, but not because of his show. Firecrackers popped, music blasted out apartment windows, and young people paraded through the streets with banners marked with a great golden triangle.

The Zoboros are back. Any person born with powers was considered one. Their golden symbol had spread across Vasilia like a virus these past few weeks. Now the capital planet of the Republic was screaming for change, screaming for powers to be legal again, and all because two Zoboros in a faraway city had stood up to an army of—

"Hey Floater!" A hovercar zoomed overhead, everyone inside shouting Ristin's new stage name. He hadn't come up with it, of course, nor did he like it very much, but somehow the rest of Vasilia had made it stick. He gave his fans a wave nonetheless and they cheered.

He found even more fans waiting in front of his apartment building, as usual. Sometimes he appeased them with autographs and pictures, but right now he only had a few minutes to spare before he had to get across town for another set.

Besides, the vaxum was wearing off.

He pulled up the hood of his jacket and slipped into the neighboring alley. A few weeks ago, he would never have dreamed of taking the fire escape up 112 stories, but now that his secret was out, it was the easiest thing in the galaxy. He aimed his hands at the ground and let the familiar thrum of energy pulse through. He felt the weight around his feet evaporate and he began to float in his own bubble of antigravity. The bubble climbed higher with his propulsion. He passed window after grimy window and waved at any neighbors who were still awake. Most waved back. The rest of Vasilia might know him as "Floater," but here he was still Ristin.

He opened his window and tugged the pull chain of a nearby lamp, but no light came. Typical. It didn't matter; he knew where he was going. He climbed into the dark and dank apartment and felt his way around. His feet crunched through wadded papers covered in rejected lyrics until he reached his destination: the grand piano. Arguably the only thing of any real value here. He remembered how long he had saved for it; now he could buy a hundred and still make rent.

But he had found a better cause to invest his money in.

He reached under the piano and felt around, but found nothing. What? He activated the light on the communicator he kept strapped to his wrist and searched underneath the piano. Nothing. Panic set in. The next venue would be packed, and these larger crowds had been giving him anxiety. He couldn't just face them and perform, not without—

"Looking for this?"

Ristin spun around, his communicator's light landing on a slender young woman seated on his couch, the bangs of her dark hair casting shadows over her hazel eyes. She wore a confident smile as she waved a small packet of blue powder at him.

"Toss it over, Mila," said Ristin, holding out his hand.

"Aren't you going to offer me a drink first?"

Ristin rolled his eyes. He hated her visits; they were never a good sign.

"Come to my next set," he said. "They'll put you on my tab."

Mila shrugged as she rose off the couch. "Not really my scene." She waltzed past the guitars that Ristin had meticulously hung on the wall and let her fingernails strum over their strings.

"I don't have time for this, Mila."

"No, you don't." Her smile turned to something wicked.

"What are you talking about?"

"In about sixty seconds, the IDF is going to march through your door."

"The ID…" he trailed off, staring at the vaxum still clenched in her hand. "I— I have a prescription!"

"Not about *that*, you idiot." She stepped close to him, tantalizingly close, her breath upon his neck. "You and I are still fugitives, you know."

"Not anymore." He took a step back. "We're coming back. There's legislation that—"

"Won't pass," she finished. "They never intended it to. But you fell for it, like all the other idiots on this planet. Only you flew around on stage for *everyone* to see."

Ristin told himself that she was lying; it was in her nature. Things really were changing for Zoboros. Besides, the movement had grown too big to be stopped. Even the IDF would have a hard time controlling it.

But the heavy footsteps clunking down the hallway told him otherwise.

"Are you in or out, Ristin?"

In or out. The ultimatum called back memories of another life, a servant's life. One he'd been freed from when his rescuer had asked him the same question.

Ristin hushed his voice. "I thought he was dead."

"In or out, Ristin?!"

The door came crashing down. Troopers clad in heavy blue armor stormed in, their machine guns aimed.

"FREEZE!"

Mila vanished into thin air. Ristin aimed his hand at the grand piano and it lifted off the ground. The troopers turned toward it, giving Ristin the moment he needed to fling the piano at them and send them tumbling back out the door.

"IN! I'M IN!" he cried.

An invisible hand grabbed his own and led him out the open window. The fire escape shook violently beneath his feet. Below, a sea of blue helmets were coming up to greet him.

Although he still couldn't see her, he felt Mila grab onto his back. Then he realized – he couldn't see himself! Not while she was touching him, at least. The sensation frightened him.

"Get us across!" she ordered.

Ristin stared at the adjacent building, then down the 112-story drop. A modest height in Vasilia, but more than enough to turn him to jelly should a stun bolt zap him in midair.

With a gulp, he leaped, Mila pressed against his back, and together they floated slowly over the thin abyss between buildings.

"Can't you fly any faster?" she said.

"It's not really flying, I can only—"

A blue bolt whizzed past his cheek. He veered. More stun bolts launched from the fire escape, lighting up the abyss, searching for their invisible targets.

"Why are they doing this?!" cried Ristin, but Mila didn't answer.

They climbed onto the neighboring fire escape, the clatter of their feet against the railing drawing more stun bolts toward their position.

Mila smashed open the nearest window and pulled them both through. A family of Nurranos screamed from their dinner table and ducked beneath it as stun bolts peppered their small apartment and filled it with smoke.

Ristin crawled behind Mila, dodging shards of glass. A few of them still managed to nick his arms, but he ignored the pain and the blood. Right now his sole focus was escaping.

Mila kicked open the door and led them to the elevators, where she pushed the up button.

"What are you doing?" he said. "We have to go down."

"They'll be waiting down there. Trust me."

Ristin didn't like the position she was putting him in. If her plan was to float slowly from building to building, their escape would be disappointingly short. But she had managed to get them this far, so he didn't argue the point any further.

The elevator took them up to the top floor. There, Mila led him up a ladder and onto the roof, where a man stood beside a tarp that flapped in the night breeze.

Ristin aimed his hands at the man, but Mila squeezed his arm. He glanced at her, saw the concern in her eyes that told him this mysterious man was a friend. He relaxed, but when he looked again the man had disappeared.

"Look out!" cried Mila, pushing him. A blaster bolt sizzled into the floor where he had been standing. Not a stun bolt, but a kill shot.

Mila dove for cover. Ristin did the same as smoke bombs burst across the rooftop.

"Who's there?!" he cried, aiming his palms toward the smoke. A figure flashed in and out of sight. He sent his powers in that direction, but missed.

"Ristin!" cried Mila.

He turned. A figure landed before him. It was tall and clad in armor, but not the bulky trooper armor he had seen in his apartment. This was thin, made of silvery metal, and much more dexterous than the traditional uniform. The face of his assailant was hidden behind a mask shaped like a skull, with a green visor that blinked as it assessed its surroundings.

"What do you want?!" demanded Ristin.

The attacker only pointed a finger at him.

Ristin released his powers. The attacker started to float, then aimed its wrists at the ground and fired two grappling hooks that reeled it back down.

Before Ristin could react, the attacker caught him by the throat. As his airway closed, Ristin stared dumbfounded into the visor, trying to discern the face behind it, but all he saw were spots as his lungs cried out for air.

The right side of the visor flashed red. The attacker reached out with its free hand in that direction and caught an invisible hand. A zap of electricity shot through the attacker's glove. Mila reappeared, screaming in a cloud of electricity, and then collapsed. The knife she had been trying to drive into the attacker's neck clattered beside her.

"Mi…la…" Ristin choked, his eyes rolling back.

In his blurred vision, another figure emerged. At first, he thought he was just seeing more spots, but as it approached, he realized it was the man in the cloak again.

The visor flashed red. The attacker released Ristin and reached for its new opponent, but the cloaked man caught the attacker's hand in his own. Electricity pulsed through, but it was the attacker who shook violently this time, smoke pouring out through the seams of its armor until finally it went limp.

The attacker collapsed in a heap. The cloaked man reached down and hoisted up Ristin with what felt like the strength of five men. Ristin found the cloaked man much taller in person, thin, but with a powerful, harrowing presence. He knew that presence. It didn't matter that the man's face was concealed in the shadow of the cloak; Ristin could recognize his old savior anywhere.

"They said you were dead," he whispered.

"Good. I prefer it that way," answered Taranis, his voice like ice.

Chapter 1

Welcome to the Team

"Wake up, wake up! They're almost here!"

Kano, forgetting he was on the bottom bunk, snapped up at the sound of Makoto's high-pitched voice and clunked his head.

"Can't you knock?!" he cried, a lump rising from his forehead.

"No time, they've already landed!" Makoto grabbed a dirty flight suit off the floor and tossed it into Kano's lap.

"Wait, by *they* you mean…?"

Makoto nodded.

Kano leaped out of bed and threw on the nylon suit. He checked himself in the mirror – he looked older, sporting the Republic's blue and white colors, much older than he had when they'd been recruited a few weeks ago. His signature mophead had been buzzed off on their first day aboard the *IDFS Dormarch,* and his scrawny limbs had inflated with muscles from their daily training sessions. He was a soldier now, or at least a soldier in training, and he doubted even his adopted mother back home would be able to recognize him.

Snores rumbled from the top bunk. Somehow, Jaden had slept through the wake-up call. It was a talent of his, a talent which no amount of noise or nudging could conquer, so Kano grabbed a pillow and smothered his best friend with it. A few moments of silence, and then Jaden thrashed back to life.

"I'm up! I'm up!" he cried, tossing the pillow away. "What's the big deal, anyway?"

"They're here," said Kano as sailors and soldiers began hurrying down the hall, all likely headed in the same direction.

Jaden burst from his sheets. "You mean—?"

"Just hurry and get some clothes on!" exclaimed Makoto as he rushed into the crowd.

Kano followed his adopted brother as quickly as he could, though Makoto was tough to keep up with. A Nurrano, Makoto had a stronger, leaner physique than most Humans. He weaved seamlessly through the crowd; the only way Kano could follow was by keeping an eye out for the distinctive red and black diamond pattern of Makoto's skin, which became harder to find as the distance grew.

The harder Kano pushed himself, however, the more everything ached: arms, shoulders, knees, ankles…. Kano didn't even know he could be sore in his ankles. Their new training regimen was teaching him something new every day.

Jaden caught up with him, still struggling to pull on his flight suit. Much like Kano's mophead, Junior's mane of blond hair had also been buzzed off, and Jaden hadn't been quite the same since.

"I hope they don't suck," he muttered bitterly.

Kano blinked. He hadn't even considered the possibility. He'd been so eager to see Captain Carmichael's promise fulfilled: the one he'd given them weeks ago when he'd first recruited them.

"My friends, I'm building a team."

Those words had echoed each day in Kano's mind. To him, it was more than just a promise of new teammates or companions; it was a promise that Kano would meet others like himself, others with powers both terrible and miraculous at the same time.

Today, Kano would meet more Zoboros.

As he passed a porthole, he slowed, entranced by the flicker and flash of hyperspace. It cocooned their speeding ship, swirling around them in an infinite vortex of yellows and blues. Kano wondered how many stars and planets lived within each swirl of color, all just waiting to be explored.

But would they ever accept me? He still felt the sting of rejection from Famora, the city he had called home his entire life; the city that had cast him out as a traitor the moment he revealed his powers. And since then, he'd learned that people almost everywhere harbored a distrust of Zoboros, the military most of all. It was not long ago that the Zoboros had been at war with the Republic. Many of the people on this ship had either served or had a parent serve in that fight, and they would not soon forget it. Kano could tell by the glances they gave him and his friends, even here among the crowd, that they hated him. He suspected it was not excitement that drew the crowd toward the new Zoboros recruits; rather, it was fear. They wanted to see the new faces so they would know who to avoid.

They passed under a hydraulic door at the end of the hall and the claustrophobia fell away, replaced by the clamor of half the *Dormarch*. They had entered the Transitway, where the entire ship opened before them, its ceiling twenty stories high, arching over two raised railways that moved sailors and supplies across the length of the ship on bullet trains.

Kano had often asked how long the ship was across, and he always got a different answer. Thirty miles, fifty miles, but he believed it was even bigger than that. He recalled the chill he'd felt that night when they had first approached the *Dormarch* in the space above his homeworld. Its shadow alone had covered the city of Famora in darkness. Even the other ships surrounding it looked like mere flies buzzing around it. Blue and shiny, the *Dormarch* streaked across space like a mighty spear about to be thrust into the unknown. It was the pride of the Interplanetary Defense Force; the fiercest starship ever assembled by the Republic to protect it from any and all threats.

Too bad it wasn't there when Famora needed it.

The crowd flowed into the hangar bay. Hundreds of ships sat dormant here, but only one had attracted the onlookers: a gunship, smaller and a bit more beat up than the average model. It was the *Pincer*, the ship Carmichael had used to rescue Kano and his friends from Famora.

And now it would deliver the next batch of Zoboros.

Kano and Jaden nudged their way to the front of the crowd, where Makoto was already waiting for them. But they were still missing two of their members.

"Where's Li?" asked Kano.

"Here," came a voice that made Kano's heart thump a little faster. Li stepped out of the crowd. She was a Nurrano like Makoto, but her skin twinkled with a gold-silver pattern that Kano had a hard time taking his eyes off. She sidled in close with them, her green eyes staring inquisitively into Kano's, wondering why his stare kept lingering.

"It's ok to be nervous," she said. "This is gonna be our new team, after all."

"Right, yeah," said Kano, refocusing on Carmichael's ship. Akio was still unaccounted for, but the mysterious creature had a habit of disappearing, so his absence absorbed little of Kano's attention.

The door to the *Pincer* opened in a blast of compressed air. The ramp lowered. All eyes were on it. From the smoke emerged Carmichael in his usual three-piece suit. Kano noticed it looked big on him now. Since their arrival, the captain had been steadily ramping up his physical training, and now after his short trip to collect his other Zoboros, his gut had retreated to nearly nothing.

What Kano found more surprising, though, was the absence of Carmichael's trademark smile. That made him nervous.

The crowd craned their heads in anticipation. Any moment, the new Zoboros would emerge.

But when the smoke cleared, no one came.

Everyone began whispering. Some had started to file out when someone cried out, "Wait, *look*!"

Something padded up to Carmichael's feet. Something small. Something hairy…

"Oh my goodness, come here!" cried Li. She raced to the end of the ramp. A corgi came bounding down toward her, tail wagging and tongue dangling out. It snuggled right into her arms and she squealed as though her entire life had been building to this moment.

Carmichael marched past her, his head bowed.

"Captain, how come you never told us you had a dog?!" exclaimed Li.

Carmichael continued walking without a word. The team glanced at each other. This behavior was very un-Carmichael-like. It took Eines, Carmichael's trusted pilot with the snazzy handlebar mustache, to answer Li's question as he too stepped off the ramp.

"He doesn't."

"Then whose dog is—?" Kano's question was cut off by a horrible shriek.

Everyone turned to Li as she scrambled back. No longer was a corgi sitting across from her, but a Human about their age, tall and lanky, with shaggy brown hair hanging in curls around his head.

And he was naked.

The crowd let out a collective groan and dispersed while the corgi-turned-man howled with laughter.

"Of all the Zoboros, we had to get the worst one," muttered a sailor.

Kano didn't even register the comment; he was already making a beeline for the naked creep as his powers channeled into his fists.

"Who do you think you are?!" he shouted.

Instead of running, the newcomer beamed at him and gave a bow. "I'm Chenji the Changeling," he announced. "And you're the Hero of Famora!"

Kano froze. *Hero?* His hands began to shake as the shockwave he had prepared struggled to escape. He burned it away in small, controlled vibrations like Cera had taught him, reducing it to an imperceptible breeze.

Chenji read Kano's confused expression instantly. "You don't know, do you? It's all over the news."

"We don't get much news out here," sighed Jaden, using one hand to block his view of Chenji's bottom half. "And why are you naked?!"

"Well I can't make the clothes transform with me, now can I?" Chenji shrugged, innocently. "One moment…" He transformed into a songbird and sailed back into Carmichael's ship, leaving Kano and his friends to glance nervously at one another. The others seemed focused on the nudity, but Kano was more concerned about the "Hero of Famora" part. He certainly didn't feel like a hero. If anything, he felt like the villain, for he had been the whole reason that Taranis came to Famora and caused so much destruction. Sure, Kano had ultimately been the one to face Taranis, but that had happened deep within the insides of one of Famora's platforms, unseen by the public. So why had he been deemed the hero?

Chenji emerged from the ship, Human again. He was dressed in a flight suit this time with a communicator wrapped around his wrist.

"The whole galaxy's seen this," he said, punching a few holographic keys on his communicator. A video projected onto the floor. The team stepped cautiously closer to Chenji for a better look, all except Li, who remained at a considerable distance.

The video had been taken from within a crowd, though it was unclear where. It wasn't until the cameraperson pushed to the front of the crowd that Kano realized what they were about to watch.

The memory came flooding back into his mind. *The Trampoline*. The platform beneath Famora. It was normally a quiet spot, but on this occasion, it was filled with a hundred troopers. Kano saw himself in the video, held at knifepoint by Novak, Hendricks's right-hand man who had betrayed them and attempted to kidnap Kano. But the plan had failed. Kano recalled the cold steel against his skin, and the feeling of frozen horror as a hundred machine guns aimed in his direction. There was only one thing standing between him and certain death, and that was Junior, who was trying to mediate between both sides, still pretending to be an ordinary civilian.

Then it happened. A flash of the knife, a blast of fire from Junior's palm, and a gasp from the crowd to let everyone know that Junior's secret was out.

The video ended in a clamor of screams and panic, but Chenji was smiling nonetheless.

"Zoboros everywhere saw you and Hendricks Junior stand up to those troopers," he said. "They started coming out of the shadows in mobs. Protests, riots – it was beautiful to watch!"

Kano shook his head. He had never intended to cause any trouble. He was just trying to stay alive, and now some poorly shot video was causing *riots*?

"Where's all the protesting happening?" he asked.

"Everywhere, my friend!" answered Chenji. "And now there's talk about making powers legal again."

Kano needed to sit down. What did all this mean? Had he just sparked an actual change? That certainly hadn't been his intention. A part of him felt exhilarated to think there were people out there, people like himself, who looked to him as a hero.

Yet that word still sent a shiver down his spine. His mind filled with the images of debris, ambulances, bodies…everything that had been lost in Taranis's attack on Famora. Everything he should have been able to protect the people from.

"What happened to the rest of Carmichael's team?" asked Li, snapping Kano back into the present conversation. "Did they stay behind to protest?"

Chenji's smile faded. "Not exactly."

The team leaned in, awaiting the answer.

"When the Zoboros movement started to get out of hand, the IDF cracked down," said Chenji. "Carmichael had been keeping us all in safehouses. The IDF claimed we would be safe, but the others I was staying with didn't believe it. They started running away. I tried to do the same, but they found me."

"Who found you?" whispered Li, her words barely audible.

Kano turned to her. Her hands were shaking, and her face growing pale, as though something awful was bubbling inside her.

Chenji glanced around the hangar to ensure no one else was close. "The Lusitani," he whispered. The word carried a strange weight to it, though Kano had no idea what it meant.

But Li clearly did, because she ran out the hangar door crying.

Kano raced after her out of instinct, past sailors and supply bots amid the bustle of the Transitway, and finally caught her at the quiet entrance to their barracks.

"What's wrong?" he asked.

Her reply was a gasp, a sob, and the tightest hug Kano had ever experienced. As he held her there, the pieces started coming together. The IDF crackdown, Zoboros on the run…this had all happened many cycles ago. Li's grandmother Nobara had told him about it, and of the only thing that could make Li hurt this much.

"They're the ones who took your family away," he said. It wasn't a question.

"They're Zoboros killers!" she cried, sobbing into his shoulder.

"That's impossible. No one's powerful enough to just go around killing Zoboros, even other Zoboros."

Li sniffled as she tried to compose herself. "The Lusitani have weapons designed to counter different powers. The IDF claimed they were disbanded after the war, but that was a lie!"

Kano felt a chill. He looked around the crowded Transitway, suddenly more wary of who might be here with them. "Have you seen them before?" he asked. "What do they look like?"

"Death," she whispered, and abruptly retreated into the barracks.

Kano stood alone, processing. He knew the IDF had developed some sort of countermeasure for the Zoboros, something that had allowed them to win the war, but he had understood it to be a weapon, one so terrible that it had only been fired once in order to end the war. But a team of trained Zoboros killers? That sent a chill down his spine.

There was more to this story, he knew it. And he also knew there was one member of their team who had been alive to see what happened all those cycles ago.

Kano entered the barracks and approached a door that was smaller than the others – the perfect size for a Jakari.

"Open up," he whispered.

Silence. Kano suspected Akio might not even be there at all. The creature had been known to sneak around. He went to tap on the door when it whooshed open. The blue creature stood there, no higher than Kano's waist, its overlong arms hanging down at its sides, and its bulbous black eyes staring up suspiciously. "If you come to talk about new recruits, I am *not* interested."

It's good to see you too, thought Kano. "Well then maybe we could talk about where you keep wandering off to at night instead."

Akio's scaly face morphed into a scowl. "Get inside, boy of thunder."

Kano ducked his head as he squeezed in. It wasn't actually a cabin, but a broom closet with a hammock strung between two service carts and a few empty buckets cluttering the floor. Kano flipped one over and seated himself on it. He eyed the Jakari carefully before speaking.

"I learned a new word today, and I want you to tell me what you know about it."

"If it is word your girlfriend say in hallway, I would prefer not to," replied Akio.

"She's not...so you *do* know about the Lusitani—"

Akio dove onto Kano and cupped his mouth with a cold hand. "Many ears on this ship, boy of thunder."

Kano scratched his head. Why would Akio care who was listening, unless...?

"Are they here?" he whispered. "On the *Dormarch*?"

Akio nodded.

"Where?"

"Why you want to know?"

"So I can find out why they're hunting us again."

Akio folded his arms. "They are killers designed to destroy you, and you think you can face one? Interrogate one? Many are programmed from birth to be unbreakable. Even if you overpower one, it swallow its own tongue before talking."

Kano sank. He didn't have even the shadow of a plan, just the white-hot fury at the thought of these assassins on the same ship as his friends.

"Did you ever face one?" he asked.

Akio stared long and hard at Kano. "I served one."

"Served? But you're a Jakari. You fought for the other side until you…" Kano trailed off. He realized where this line was taking him, but he couldn't get himself to believe it.

"Until I found new master," finished Akio.

Hendricks. Akio had sworn a life debt to Kano's old protector, though Kano had never learned why. Hendricks had perished on Famora with many of his secrets untouched, but his final order to Akio had been to protect Kano, so now the "boy of thunder" found himself with a Jakari assassin constantly in his shadow.

"But why?" asked Kano. He didn't want to believe that Hendricks was a Zoboros killer, but Hendricks had been such a mysterious figure that Kano had no evidence to refute it. "How could the man who saved so many Zoboros also be their executioner?"

"He had change of heart."

Kano racked his brain. Hendricks had been infamous for his cold heart and unyielding resilience; what could have broken his conviction so completely?

"It was his son, wasn't it?" Kano found himself saying. Junior was a Zoboros too, as Kano had learned, there on the platform on that fateful day. Surely that would have been enough for even Hendricks to reject his creed?

"The Zoboros power passes through blood," replied Akio. "Blood Hendricks himself did not possess. It was a woman, boy of thunder. A woman who changed him."

"Who?" pressed Kano. He sensed fear in Akio at the question, something his Jakari protector never displayed.

"I am forbidden to speak of this."

"Why? What happened to her?"

"It is forbidden!" snapped Akio. Shame filled his face at this outburst, and he retreated into his hammock.

Kano rose. He wanted to say more, to ask more, but he knew there would be no getting through to Akio now. He turned, and the hydraulic door opened for him.

"My master learned not to trust either side," said Akio suddenly. Kano stopped. "That lesson cost him everything. Make no mistake, boy of thunder. You are no safer on this ship than you were on Famora."

Kano nodded and left. He had sensed it before, the creeping feeling that something about their stay here wasn't right. But now he knew the truth: he had enemies aboard this ship. Many of them. Probably more than he and his friends could overcome.

He wondered where Junior was right now.

Chapter 2

Mogaddu

Junior awoke to the blue and yellow swirl of hyperspace.

Ugh.

He had been staring at the same mind-numbing vortex for days on end, waiting for his destination to appear on the radar. There wasn't much else to do in the cramped escape pod; he could barely even move. He'd spent the journey with his long limbs tucked in around the controls, his head bent forward so that it didn't bang against the low ceiling. His muscles were stiff and achy. His body shivered from the cold of space; previously, he'd be able to light a fire in his palm to warm himself, but he had lost the strength to do even that. He had lost weight too, often forgetting to eat without the sun to give him any sense of daytime.

Cassius had warned him that space could drive a man mad, but Junior had thought that only applied to lesser men, weak men. Now, staring at the infinite loop through the windscreen, he was beginning to see why. Visions of the past sometimes appeared in the vortex – visions of ancient markings and secret meetings, of floating buildings in a city that seemed a lifetime away, and of a masked man driving a sword through his father's chest.

Junior slammed his fist against the control console. The whole pod shuddered. He clung to the console, praying that his one outburst hadn't thrown him off-course. He wished Cassius had let him stay on the cargo ship a while longer, but to have routed that ship any closer to his destination would have drawn attention from the IDF. And attention was something Junior didn't need any more of at the moment. He would have to take his chances with the pod, which – based on its constant shaking – seemed ready to burst into a thousand pieces across the cosmos at any second.

Everything about this mission was reckless. Every choice he made was met with obstacle after obstacle, and every obstacle had been a clear reason for him to turn back. But one thought kept him going. One thought had driven him to the farthest reaches of the galaxy.

I need to find my mother.

The radar pinged. His face lit up, almost in disbelief. He was close now. He placed his hand on the lever. "*Pull too soon and you'll lose too much velocity,*" Cassius's voice echoed in his mind. "*Pull too late and you'll fry in the atmosphere.*" Escape pods like this one were ill-suited for atmospheric reentry – they were meant to be picked up in space by a passing ship. He couldn't risk a pickup; his face had become too recognizable after Famora. He would have to take his chances in the atmosphere.

Ding-ding-ding-ding. It was almost time. His grip tightened on the lever. With his other hand, he drew a pin from his pocket – a triangle, with three arrows pointing toward its center. It was no larger than the tip of his finger, yet it held all the weight in the galaxy. It was the last thing his father had given him before being struck down by Taranis, and it had gained him entry onto the cargo ship. With any luck, it would gain him entry with the Orlovs too.

A red light pinged above the viewport. He kissed the pin for good luck and tucked it in his coat pocket. The red light began to flash. He spotted a dot drawing closer on the radar.

Every fiber of the pod began to rattle. His instincts told him to pull, but Cassius's warning kept his hand steady. He would give himself to the count of three.

One.

The dinging became so rapid that he could barely distinguish one sound from the last.

Two.

The pod jolted, as if struck by a wave.

Junior didn't wait for three. He pulled.

Hyperspace vanished, replaced by a giant, gray mass that was hurtling toward the pod.

SHIP! Junior threw all his weight against the throttle. The pod dipped beneath the incoming vessel. Bits of metal popped against the windscreen, singeing it as he dove. He looked up as the ship passed overhead, wondering why it hadn't adjusted course for him, only to find its engines dead. Blast holes gave Junior a clear view inside the hull. An IDF medical frigate…an older class too. A relic of the Battle of Mogaddu.

Junior eased back. He was here. Only he didn't see the planet through the windscreen, just more ghost ships…hundreds of them. He flushed. It was an asteroid field of pure debris.

And he was coming in too fast.

He jammed on the throttle, hoisting the pod over an incoming transport. A frigate waited behind it and he dove, the ceiling of his pod scraping against it. He kept maneuvering, up and down, left and right. With each ship, another took its place. He had no time to distinguish what models they were or what side they fought for; every second brought a new projectile that could easily tear his puny pod to bits.

Junior checked his radar. It said he was caught in the planet's gravitational pull, but he still couldn't see it. By now it should have been filling his windscreen, but all that waited beyond the oncoming debris was the blackness of space.

Light edged along the blackness. Something wasn't right. Junior squinted. There were no stars ahead, no space. What he was staring at was something else entirely…

A Poterian dreadnought.

He yanked the throttle in tight. The pod groaned, arcing higher and higher as the nose of the dreadnought closed in. *A little more, a little more*, he thought. The pod was at a ninety-degree angle now, pressing Junior hard against his seat as he climbed up the face of the behemoth. Even at this angle, he couldn't see the top of it. It was so tall…taller than a mountain.

The pod scraped along the jet-black surface of the Poterian monstrosity, spraying sparks against the darkness. Junior swung the pod side to side, dodging the ship's rudders that stuck out like thorns. Each maneuver lost him momentum, and each second brought Junior closer to collision. Soon it became clear: he wasn't going to make it.

Then he saw it: a gaping hole in the face of the dreadnought, larger than any cannon shell he had ever seen. He dove through it, praying it wasn't a dead end.

It wasn't. The hole led into the Transitway. IDF ships had them too, but not like this. Not this massive. Whole frigates floated inside it, some still docked, surrounded by clouds of their own debris. Junior dipped and weaved through the wreckage. The pod was slowing, but the projectiles were still coming in fast. Control monitors and broken wings slammed against his windscreen, each impact making Junior clutch the throttle tighter.

Hold together. Sunlight twinkled in the distance. Another hole! It gleamed out the side of the ship like a beacon. Just about every object imaginable floated in his way – crates, munitions, fuel tanks – but he kept steering straight for the hole, praying his pod could squeeze through. He drew a deep breath as he closed in. The pod rattled even harder. *Come on…come on…*

With a jolt, the pod scraped through the hole and sailed out the other side. Junior fell back in his seat, his relief quickly turning to awe. Debris no longer obscured his view. All that stood before him was a planet. A planet the color of blood.

Mogaddu. The birthplace of the Zoboros, if the legends were true, and the place they had sought refuge after the war. His mother had gone on the pilgrimage long ago. Whether she was still here, whether she had made it at all, Junior intended to find out.

The planet kept expanding in the windscreen, its features becoming more defined. Crystal blue oceans rounded the edges of a great red continent. Fingers of green cut through the land. Forests. Junior had seen a tree once, when he was younger, at the Orlov Mansion on Famora. Those Orlovs were dead now, but he would find many more of them here on Mogaddu. That ancient family considered this their homeworld, and many of its most powerful members still retained land holdings, even after all the destruction the Poterians had brought here.

The Poterians were beasts from a distant part of the galaxy, separated from the Republic by a rift in space that legend held no ship could navigate through. But the Poterians had found a way some twenty cycles ago and brought with them the might of their empire. It was here on Mogaddu where the IDF had destroyed the Poterian fleet in a miraculous victory, at the cost of everyone who fought in that battle.

Though the Poterians were long gone, there were plenty of other things to be concerned about. The planet had become a lawless outpost since the Republic abandoned it after the war, making it a hub for gangsters, thieves, and fugitives along the outer reaches of the known galaxy. Cassius had advised Junior to meet at the rendezvous point and stay there, and Junior, being alone for the first time in his life, was inclined to listen. He adjusted his trajectory a few degrees, lining himself up with the rendezvous as it blipped on his radar.

The pod jerked. Junior checked the porthole beside him. Smoke. Lots of smoke, billowing out the left engine. He spotted where debris had clipped it during his entry and cursed to himself.

The throttle fought him as he pressed deeper into the atmosphere. He tugged with all his might, but the pod started veering wherever nature willed it. Left, right, then in circles. He started to feel nauseous.

"Come on you stupid piece of—!"

He heard the engine sputter and die.

Shit.

The pod dipped toward Mogaddu at an awkward angle. The wrong angle. He pulled the throttle, but it did little to change his trajectory. He was in gravity's cruel hands now.

Flames sparked along the windscreen; at first small, then larger, growing to eclipse Junior's entire view. He checked the speedometer: 28,000 mph. Too fast. He killed the remaining engine, but that barely slowed him down. Gravity was doing all the work now.

"Punch the green button if it starts gettin' hot," Cassius's instructions returned to him. Heat normally wasn't much of a problem for Junior, but in this situation, it was easily enough to smother him from existence if it breached the hull. He punched the green button and

formula burst across the exterior of the ship, dousing the flames and covering the windscreen in a thick foam.

The foam lasted only a second before the wind whipped it away. Junior could see it all now. He was so much closer than he had realized. The grassy hills rolled across the landscape; the red soil glistened with the morning dew. As he rocketed along, the grass began to give way until all that was left were dunes. Wind brushed upon them, carrying clouds of red from one dune to the next. It was so mesmerizing that, for a brief moment, Junior forgot he was crash-landing.

An alarm blared. "Entry speed too high" came the readout. Nothing he didn't already know. He punched the forward thrusters. They flared before him, their force slamming his chest into the throttle. The ground was closing in beneath him, and still he was coming in too hot.

The pod clipped the top of a dune, tossing up a cloud of dirt. It gave him an idea. He released the bottom rudders, and they caught onto the top of the next dune, and the next one, skipping him along from dune to dune, each impact slowing his momentum. He killed the thrusters and the pod began to tilt. The rudders caught the next dune and dredged into it, allowing him to skate down the surface until the pod finally, mercifully, grinded to a halt.

Junior sat there for a minute, heart pounding, chest heaving, as he slowly accepted the fact that he was still alive. His neck throbbed from whiplash, his ribs ached from being banged against the throttle, but he had made it. For the first time ever, he had arrived on a new planet.

He checked the radar. The rendezvous point wasn't even a blip on the map anymore. He had to zoom out over and over again just to find it…2,000 miles away…

"Dammit!" He ripped off his restraints and punched the hydraulic release. The door above him burst open with a blast of compressed air. He grabbed his pack and clambered out, taking in the warm, dusty air of Mogaddu – a welcome change from the stink of his pod.

All around him, great red dunes rose and fell across the landscape. The rising sun was just cresting over them, casting hard shadows into the valleys between. If he could get to the top of one, he could get a better lay of the land, maybe even find civilization.

He hauled himself over the side of the pod. He touched down on a foot restraint, but it snapped beneath his weight and he landed on his back against the sand. It puffed around him as he groaned, his back now adding to all the other aches and pains that played like a chorus across his thinned body. He had half a mind to just lie here. The sand was so soft. So warm. Not like the bitter cold of space. He watched the little grains roll beside him with the passing wind.

The grains began to roll faster. Junior felt it: the wind getting stronger. A shadow fell over him. He looked up. A freighter hovered above the dunes, bulky and rusted. He couldn't place the model. All its parts were mismatched – the hull of an IDF frigate, the wings of a Poterian transport, a phantom engine that likely came from a stealth fighter…this freighter had been scrounged together from the wreckage.

Scavengers.

Their presence could only mean one thing. Junior leaped to his feet and raced for the pod, but it was too late. The freighter already had it in its tractor beam. The pod rose out of the ground, sand pouring off it. Junior reached for the underside latch that would open the cargo hold, but the latch slipped through his fingers as the pod lifted out of his reach.

"NO!" he screamed. That was the cargo hold where he had stored the disassembled parts of his precious speeder. He summoned all his power to his fist, but all that formed was a sad, tiny fireball. He stepped forward to throw it and his knees buckled, and before he knew it, he was on the ground again, his sore muscles refusing to move. All he could do was watch as the freighter's shadow rolled away.

He laid there for a while with his face in the sand. Stranded, defeated, *weak*. If only he'd stayed in the pod a little longer, the scavengers would have taken him too. They may have also attempted to eat him, depending on what kind of scavengers these were, but at least he would have had transportation.

His thoughts turned to Famora. That silly floating nightmare; how eager he had been to leave, to find a new world that needed the help of someone like him. The help of a hero. And for a moment, he had been a hero. He had saved the lives of many who had found themselves within

Taranis's crosshairs, and even helped to defeat the masked man.

And in return, they had labeled him a fugitive.

The ground grew hot beneath the desert sun. It wasn't the deep desert; patches of grass still managed to survive out here, but he wouldn't, not in his traveler's garb. Cassius had given him a thick, wooly overcoat that concealed him from neck to toe. It had been a blessing in the cold of space, but here it meant death. He stripped down to his combat nylons, the same disgusting pair he had been wearing since his battle with Taranis; they had originally been white, he noted, but now were dusted coal-black from all the exhaust fumes aboard the cargo ship. He tossed the overcoat aside, picked up his pack, and started up the nearest dune on shaking legs. His vision blurred in and out, and the weight of the pack bared down unnaturally hard upon his back. It may have been because the gravity was different here. Junior leaned toward that theory rather than the alternative: that he was simply too weak to haul a meager forty pounds up a hill.

By the time he reached the summit, he fell back to his knees upon the sand. Sweat dripped from every pore, sticking his nylons to his skin. He drew his canteen from his pack and kicked it back. All he got was a splash of tepid water, and then nothing. He tossed the canteen into the sand, cursing. He had rationed only for the journey through space; the desert had not been a factor then. He was supposed to be resupplied by the Orlovs in Drezdan; they were probably waiting for him there now. But would they still be there when he finally escaped the desert?

If he escaped the desert.

From the top of the dune, the landscape took on a completely different appearance. He hadn't realized upon reentry, but the land he had crashed upon was a graveyard. Not of bodies, though, at least not that he could see. Much like the atmosphere, this place was filled with the corpses of ships. Large and small, they dotted the landscape, some half-buried in the sand, some freshly plucked out and gutted by scavengers. Junior drew his binoculars from his pack and scanned over them, searching for a decent alcove from which to escape the blazing sun. He spotted something else though, moving across the sand, and quickly.

A hovercar.

It zigzagged through the shadowy creases between the dunes, a dust cloud trailing in its wake. The convertible was heading toward a Poterian frigate whose nose was submerged in the sand, the rest of its massive frame leaned up against an adjacent dune.

Junior zoomed in on the driver. He could only see the back of its head, but he noticed the wires running from it and the thin, metal arms that jerked the steering wheel with absolute precision.

A bot. Perfect. Bots were programmed to assist all lifeforms, so long as the request didn't violate any Republic laws.

He skated down the side of the dune, watching as the hovercar came to a stop in front of the frigate. An outpost, Junior assumed. Hopefully it held the supplies he needed. If not, he could count on the bot to get him to the next outpost, wherever that may be.

Every step caused his vision to blur more. His destination was becoming a beacon in a narrowing tunnel, but he kept going. This might be his only ride out of the desert, and he was not going to miss it. He dug deep into his pack, past the stun baton and what little food rations he had left, to the pouch he had taken from his father's room. Getting the pouch had been no easy task. The IDF had kept his home under careful watch after the revelation of his powers, but the IDF didn't know about the secret passages his father had built in and out of their floating home. Nor had they known about the pouch his father had hidden for him in case of emergency.

Junior unzipped it. Jewels and coins glinted inside, all currencies for different places across the galaxy. Junior had no idea what the Mogaddans would take; he drew out the cyos for now – little gray coins, the simplest ones, accepted in most places. He tucked the pouch back in his pack and continued on.

The wind threw sand in his face. It puffed and swirled in the air. The effect was enchanting, and Junior's dehydrated, delirious mind clung to the images it played before him. Symbols appeared in the swirling sand, ancient symbols that belonged to an ancient mask. The mask began to glow with electricity. He felt the skin where its electricity had once touched pulse and spasm. He yelped and fell to his knees. When he looked up again, a woman's face floated there, with long dark hair and orange eyes. His eyes.

"Leave this place," she whispered.

"Mom…"

"Leave it." The wind washed her visage away and flung the sand straight into his eyes. He fell to his knees, struggling to find her again as his eyes watered. All he could make out was a thin figure standing over him.

"Mom?"

"I would certainly hope not," said a voice that sounded like it had spoken through a tin can. Metal fingers wrapped around Junior's collar and began dragging him toward the hovercar.

What's the command? thought Junior. There was a phrase that, when given to a bot, would oblige it to fulfill any lawful request, but Junior's mind was spinning in circles. He needed help…he needed…

"Assistance!" he blurted. "Assistance needed!"

"No shit."

Junior blinked. Bots didn't talk back. They were cheery and lovable; sarcasm wasn't in their—

Icy water splashed over his face. His mind surged back to the present, all his instincts awake and alert once more. He gazed up at the bot. It didn't have the traditional red eye like the ones on Famora. This bot had a visor running across its round face, with a red dot that swung back and forth across the visor like a pendulum.

"What kind of bot are you?" he asked.

"The kind that doesn't like being called that word," the bot answered, brandishing a pistol in Junior's face.

Junior scrambled back. He raised a flaming fist, but the bot already had its other arm aimed at him. Formula sprayed from the bot's arm and doused Junior's hand, neutralizing his power.

"How did you—?"

"Relax fleshling, I know what you are." The bot tapped its visor, which Junior assumed ran some sort of facial recognition. "What brings you all the way from Famora?"

"Personal business," said Junior flatly. Bots had masters. Someone else was surely listening to their conversation.

"That answer ain't gonna get you a ride," said the bot. "Of course, you're welcome to ask for a ride at old Hoberachi's Inn, but the new management may not be too accepting of your kind." The bot motioned toward the downed frigate. A being stood by the entrance; what kind, Junior couldn't say. Its face was concealed by a breathing apparatus that hissed and clicked.

"I'll cover my face. They'll never know I'm a Zoboros."

The bot laughed. Junior wasn't sure he had ever heard a bot laugh before. "No, see, the Del Clorans don't like *any* being, powers or not, unless it's their own kind," it said. "I'm only allowed in because they don't consider me a being at all. Their loss, though." The bot walked around the hovercar and began digging through the trunk. "I could use your help with a little project."

"What kind of a project?"

The bot lifted a rifle out of the trunk. "Robbery."

"Are you crazy?" Junior glanced back at the Del Cloran guard, who was already scrambling inside to warn its friends. "I'm not looking for trouble."

"Then you crash-landed on the wrong planet," said the bot, tossing a pistol into Junior's hand. "The Del Clorans stole one of my boss's assistants. He'd like it returned before the Del Clorans hack into its programming. Help me, and I'll get you back to civilization."

"It's a little early to be making enemies on Mogaddu," said Junior.

"The Del Clorans made an enemy with you the moment they stole your pod," said the bot.

That lit a spark inside Junior. He rose. "And are these the same Del Clorans?"

"Only one way to find out."

Junior followed the bot toward the inn, pistol in one hand, the other engulfed in flame.

"You got a name?" asked Junior.

A Del Cloran aimed a rifle out a window, but the bot shot it between the eyes before it even fired a round.

"T8. And I'm the best friend you'll ever make on this goddammed planet."

Chapter 3

The Sim

The canyon was quiet. Too quiet.

Kano peeked over the boulder that he and his friends had been using for cover.

"What do you see?" whispered Makoto.

"Nothing," he replied. It was just a snaking path to the bottom, where it forded a river that ran over the brown earth at the heart of the canyon. He didn't dare follow it, though; they had no idea what might be hidden behind the patches of cacti that lined it. He kept scanning for any signs of movement. It was hard to tell, with the air shimmering from the heat of the sun. The *simulated* sun, he should say.

"Why hasn't anything gone wrong yet?" asked Jaden. "Something always goes wrong by now."

Kano had the same concern, though he didn't want to be as vocal about it. If these simulations had taught him anything, it was that the morale of the team was brittle, and it cracked even faster if he was the one to panic. Still, he knew that, somewhere out there, Carmichael was crafting their intricate demise.

He brought his wrist communicator to his lips. "Chenji. Come in Chenji. What do you see?"

No response.

"He should've been back ten minutes ago," said Akio as he loaded a rifle about twice his size.

"Good riddance," muttered Li.

Kano frowned. They had been counting on their newest member to provide some aerial reconnaissance. It was an advantage they'd never had before, but they only had it as long as Chenji didn't get shot out of the sky.

"Over there!" shouted Makoto.

Kano, Li, Jaden, and Akio peeked eagerly out from their cover.

"What is it?" asked Kano.

"Carmichael added a second sun this time," he said, pointing up. "Did anyone else notice that?"

The team observed a beat of silence.

"Makoto can do recon next," said Akio.

"Enough," said Kano. "We need to spread out and find the Artifact before the Greavenaughts find our position."

"They probably already know our position," said Jaden, shuddering at the thought of those bloodthirsty green beasts. "The only question is: how will Carmichael throw them at us this time?"

Kano looked again to the suspicious cacti, then to Li.

That was all the signal she needed. Her hands began to glow. She aimed them toward the nearest patch. The cacti stiffened ever so slightly at her touch, then relaxed, ready to commune with her.

"These aren't individual plants," she said, her eyes glowing white. "They're all connected through the canyon, but I'm not sensing disturbances anywhere."

"Oh, there'll be a disturbance, honey," said Jaden. "Trust me."

A twig snapped. Akio was the first to spin around, firing up the canyon as he did. There was a sharp cry, and then a big green warrior wrapped in a thick animal hide collapsed on the path.

They're here! Kano sent a shockwave rocketing up the canyon. It blasted away the boulders that the Greavenaughts had been using for cover. The creatures dove into the nearby cacti, their thick scales protecting them from the needles. But that couldn't protect them from Li. She aimed her hands in their direction. Cactus arms snapped around the Greavenaughts and hugged them close.

"How long can you hold them?" asked Akio, picking off trapped Greavenaughts with his rifle as they tore their way through Li's trap as if the cacti were made of paper.

Li replied with a simple shake of the head as she strained to keep the Greavenaughts contained.

"Let's move!" said Kano. He hadn't been comfortable giving orders when they'd first started the simulations, nor had he been designated their leader, but he'd discovered over the weeks that they all listened to what he said anyway. At least when they were in danger.

The five of them sprinted down the path while blaster bolts pounded the trail around them.

"We're too exposed!" cried Jaden.

Akio pulled the pins on two smoke grenades and tossed them back. A smoke cloud formed, but a breeze rushed in and conveniently blew it away. Too convenient. Kano wasn't sure, but he thought he heard Akio curse Carmichael's forefathers.

Blaster bolts neared them once again. Kano knew they would need more cover, and fast, but then he realized – cover was something he could provide.

He skidded to a stop and turned to face the oncoming horde. Dozens of Greavenaughts were pouring down the slope now, many more than Carmichael usually sent after them. Kano launched shockwave after shockwave toward them. At this distance, his powers would do little to hurt the Greavenaughts, but that wasn't his intention. Each blast kicked up more dust, making the path harder for the Greavenaughts to navigate.

Jaden was far ahead while this was happening, unaware that Kano had stopped, but very aware that a large number of pebbles were now rolling down the slope. He glanced back and, seeing his friend blasting the hillside, immediately activated his communicator.

"Kano!" he barked. "*Stop!*"

"What's wrong?" asked Kano. But when the ground trembled, he realized his mistake.

Dirt and rocks tumbled past his feet. Then a boulder dislodged from the ground and barreled toward him like a wild bull. He dove out of the way, his face landing uncomfortably close to a patch of cacti.

"Avalanche!" he cried.

The others picked up the pace, but there wasn't much they could do against a force of nature such as this. Kano rushed to catch up with them, but his body was drained from all the power he had unleashed. Pure adrenaline fueled him now.

He saw the river at the bottom, a possible salvation if they could cross it, but it was still so far away. And beneath his feet, the earth continued to shake.

We're not gonna make it, he realized.

"This way!" shouted Makoto, well ahead of all the others.

Kano looked where his brother was pointing; there was an alcove just off the path, hopefully strong enough to shield them from the coming landslide. He angled toward it, still well behind the others as they slid one by one into the alcove. Then he heard the *crunch*. The earth crumbled toward him in a great wave. The dust caught him first, filling his lungs. He felt the ground rocking beneath his feet as certain death closed in. A death he had incited with his stupid idea!

"Come on!" cried Li. "HURRY!"

"I'm trying!" screamed Kano, though he wasn't sure if they could hear him over the thunder of the landslide behind him. Everything shook so violently that he lost his footing. He slid the rest of the way, his feet skidding through dust until he fell into the alcove.

His friends pulled him away from the edge, and he watched as a mass of brown earth and rock poured over the entrance. The landslide kept coming, occasionally accented by the cry of a Greavenaught that had been caught in its rush, until the entire entrance was covered and all the sunlight had been stolen from the recess in which they sheltered.

Five pairs of lights ignited from each of their combat suits. They stared at each other, all caked in brown dust.

Akio shrugged. "Could be worse."

Outside, the rumbling ceased. Kano approached the blockage at the entrance and placed his hand on it. "I think I can dislodge it," he said, but Li knocked his hand away.

"No! No more shockwaves," she demanded.

"Well, what do you suggest?" he asked, folding his arms.

"There is path here," answered Akio. Everyone turned and realized that the darkness stretched on into a cave.

"What horrors do you think Carmichael has waiting for us in there?" asked Jaden. It was the question on everyone's mind, and Kano could tell it was making them all anxious.

"Come on," he said as he started down the path. "There's only one way to find out."

In the past, Kano hadn't been the one to take the lead. But since he'd faced Taranis and felt the sting of that maniac's electricity against his skin, not much fazed him anymore. At least, not in the Sim.

"Wait," said Akio, climbing onto Kano's shoulder. "We are not alone." He pointed a long finger toward the cave wall, where Chenji laid amid the rocks, his eyes closed.

"Is…is he dead?" asked Makoto.

"You can't actually die in here," said Jaden, giving Chenji a nudge.

Chenji roused. "Is it over already?" he yawned, stretching himself out as though he'd just slept all his troubles away.

"Over?!" blurted Li. "You were supposed to warn us that they were coming up from behind!"

Chenji laughed. "If I had spotted them, they would've just gone a different direction."

"And then we would have known about it," said Kano flatly.

"It's adorable that you still think you can win," said Chenji, shaking his head. "I played this game a hundred times back on Vasilia. I'll let you in on a little secret: it's rigged so you always lose. The sooner you realize that, the sooner you can relax and just let the game play out."

Kano turned to his team, expecting backup. Instead, they just stood there, downcast. After long weeks of constant losing, Chenji's words only validated what they already suspected.

"Well, we haven't lost this one yet," said Kano. He started down the pitch-black path, willing to take it on alone, but hoping he wouldn't have to. He felt Akio climb onto his shoulder, rifle at the ready. A good start. Soon Makoto caught up, followed by Li, and finally Jaden, who grumbled the whole time about how much he hated working in the field.

Even in complete darkness, Kano felt his friends around him. It gave him strength to know he had friends who would fight beside him. Who would do anything for him.

Until he remembered what it could cost them.

The darkness seemed to creep in closer. All these weeks, he'd thought he'd done the right thing by bringing his friends with him; that being aboard the *Dormarch* had made them all safer. But Akio had shattered that illusion. Now nowhere was safe. Not while they were in the possession of the IDF.

"Look out!" cried Makoto, killing the light on his suit.

"What's wrong?" asked Kano. His light landed on a fat, yellow lump that laid limp over a rock just ahead. The lump squealed.

Corcuses! Kano fumbled for the light switch on his suit, but was too much in a panic to find it. Akio struck it for him and covered them in darkness.

Everyone stood frozen as more squeals rang out through the cave. There had to be dozens, even hundreds of the giant insects lying around. Slowly, the squeals subsided, and the team let out a collective breath.

"The hell was that?" whispered Chenji. Everyone jumped, just now realizing that he had been following them. There was a pause. "It sounded like you guys were in trouble, so I thought it'd be more interesting to tag along."

Kano nodded, though Chenji couldn't see it. "Those were corcuses," he said. "And don't worry about whispering. They're deaf."

"But they hate light," added Li, "so I suggest you switch on your infrared."

Kano smiled to himself, detecting in Li's voice a hint of animosity toward their lazy newcomer. He put on his infrared goggles, and the cavern appeared before him in a topographical map of red lines. A sea of lumps rose and fell across the cavern floor. A nest. Typical of Carmichael. Kano tiptoed along, careful to dodge the lumps that, while deaf, could certainly feel…and also eat his face off.

"Look to your right, boy of thunder," said Akio.

Kano turned. He saw a whole pile of lumps sleeping on top of each other, so many that their pile rose almost to the ceiling. And that's when he saw it – a staff protruding from the top of the pile, wooden and uneven in its carving. It didn't seem valuable in any way, but it also seemed terrifically out of place.

"Do you think that's it?" asked Makoto. "The Artifact?"

They had never gotten far enough in these simulations to see it. Finding the Artifact wasn't the only objective programmed into the Sim, but it was one of the most difficult, and it was the one Carmichael kept picking for them. Kano suspected it was because the captain saved all the best tricks for this simulation, and so he didn't want to get his hopes up just to be caught in another one.

"It is," said Li, mesmerized by the sight even through infrared goggles. "I recognize the shape from one of Nama's books. It belonged to a great king once. A *Zoboros* king."

"Sounds like a winner to me," said Jaden, "but there's still a giant pile of corcuses that we gotta address here."

"Li," said Chenji. He tapped her shoulder and she jumped out of instinct; his very presence having left her on creep alert. "Sorry," he said. "I just wanted to ask: can your powers soothe people to sleep?"

"What?" she asked.

"I can help you reach the Artifact, but I need to touch one of the corcuses to do it. Can you soothe it so it doesn't attack anyone when I make contact?"

Li looked to her friends, surprised, then nodded.

Chenji leaned over the nearest corcus. He motioned for Li to go first. She placed her hand over the slimy critter and allowed it to glow, then quickly cupped it with her other hand so the light didn't escape. Still, a little slipped through, and the nearby corcuses answered with a few grunts, but nothing more.

Chenji placed his hand on the corcus. "This might get weird," he warned.

His head snapped back. His hand shook against the corcus, his fingers digging into its flesh. The creature stirred, groaning, and Li pressed harder with her powers, numbing the creature as best she could while Chenji's fingers squished beneath its skin.

They all watched through their goggles as the red lines that made up Chenji expanded into a fat lump, the seams of his combat suit ripping in places as it stretched with him.

"I think I'm gonna be sick," groaned Makoto.

Kano watched, both fascinated and disgusted, as Chenji slithered away. He checked on Li; she had successfully subdued the corcus which Chenji had copied, but she still sat beside it, frozen.

"Are you alright?" he whispered, leaning down beside her.

"I'm fine, it's…" she trailed off, processing.

"It's what?" pressed Kano.

"When I connected with the corcus, I didn't just feel it. I felt Chenji too. He was in pain."

"I'd imagine a transformation like that hurts," he said, unsure what else to make of it.

"It wasn't physical. It was something deeper." She lowered her voice. "I think he needs help, Kano."

He nodded, though inside he had no idea what to do. Li had healed plenty of people before, including himself when he was at his most desperate. For her to be that concerned meant something must be seriously wrong.

It also meant Chenji probably wasn't the one who should be completing the mission.

Kano was about to call him back, but Chenji had already scaled the pile of corcuses, the squish of his slime echoing through the cave as he reached for the Artifact.

What happened next happened too fast. With his massive corcus jaw, Chenji clenched the staff between his razor-sharp teeth. There was a spasm on contact, a squeal, and then Chenji was tumbling down the pile of corcuses, writhing, his body transforming back into his Human self.

His squeals turned to screams. His thrashes struck the surrounding corcuses. They squealed, at first a few, but then a whole chorus as the pile was awakened. The next thing Kano knew, the floodlights had switched on, blinding him. He ripped off the goggles in time to see a yellow blob sailing toward him, row after row of teeth ready to consume his face.

He flinched as the corcus burst before him into a harmless cloud of pixels. The cave turned to pixels too, and the canyon. Suddenly the whole landscape was fading away in the air, until all that was left were six frightened trainees and a giant room of pure white.

A slow clap echoed from up in the rafters. Everyone looked, shielding their eyes from the floodlights as a silvery speck floated down toward them. It was angelic to look at, but they all knew that this was no angel.

Carmichael, on his silver disk, touched down on the white floor. Control boards surrounded him, blinking and blipping, each with hundreds of knobs and levers at his disposal. But the crown jewel (and it really was a crown) was the helmet on his head, so bulky that Kano wondered how the captain kept his balance while wearing it. Dozens of wires sprang from it and fed into the control boards, allowing Carmichael to bring the darkest creations of his mind to life for everyone to not only see, but experience in their full, diabolical glory.

"What did you do to the new guy?!" shouted Jaden. He pointed to Chenji, who remained on the floor, shaking, his once suave face now pale and contorted, his lips a deep blue.

Carmichael removed the helmet and stepped off the platform. He knelt beside Li, who was already running her glowing hands over Chenji, and checked the changeling's pulse.

"He's in shock," said Li.

Carmichael nodded. "And his heart rate is up. Cera!"

"Already called it in," she said.

Everyone turned. No one had noticed Cera come in. Her boots clicked toward them, her blonde hair trailing behind her in a long, immaculate streak. Carmichael's first lieutenant, she carried an authority in the way she walked – certainly enough to command Jaden's attention – and made even stronger by the way she so easily hoisted Chenji back onto his feet.

"What happened to him?" asked Kano.

"The Artifact exacts a toll," answered Cera, without really answering the question at all.

Kano noticed the staff slung across her back. *It was real*, he realized. Nothing from the Sim ever remained except for him and his friends. So why had they chosen today to plant a real object in it? And why had that object harmed Chenji but not Cera?

"How are you feeling?" asked Cera, inspecting Chenji.

He replied with only a nod, the color still drained from his face.

"Will you take him to the infirmary?" she asked Li.

"I'm alright," said Chenji, shrugging away from Cera's grip. "I'm going back to my cabin."

Cera looked to Carmichael.

"If that's what he wants, he can go," said Carmichael. "The rest of you stay with him. Make sure there are no lingering effects."

Chenji stumbled toward the door on shaking legs. Kano and the others followed, Li remaining close to Chenji.

"Kano, stay here," said Cera.

He froze. What did she want from him? Normally he enjoyed Cera's company. A Zoboros herself, she had taught him much during their lessons, and had the patience of a saint no matter how many times he fumbled. There was something about that staff on her back, though, which made him uneasy.

"What suit size are you?" asked Carmichael.

"I...I'm not sure," stammered Kano, confused. "I've never owned one."

Cera drew out a tape measure and began measuring his arms and neck. It sometimes frightened Kano how in sync she and Carmichael were, almost like they shared the same thoughts. "One of your old ones should fit," she said to the captain.

"But why do I need one?"

Cera smiled. "You've been invited to a dinner party tonight, Kano."

"With who?" asked Kano.

Carmichael didn't look quite as enthusiastic about it. "The general," was his only response.

General Mezo. She had been there that fateful day on the platform back on Famora, her troopers all standing behind her, training their weapons on Novak as he held Kano at knifepoint. Kano's life had been in her hands in that moment, and Kano still questioned whether she'd have sacrificed him in the crossfire had Junior not intervened.

But what did she want with him? And why tonight? As he stared at the staff, he began to suspect a connection between the two. Something was at play here; something Carmichael didn't plan on sharing with him.

"Don't worry, Kano," said Cera, placing what she thought was a reassuring hand on his shoulder. "We'll be there with you the whole time."

"Perfect. Can't wait."

Chapter 4

Casus Belli

"You are without a doubt the *worst* friend I could've made on this planet!"

The convertible hovercar sped over dunes as tracer fire pounded the sands in their wake. T8 steered while Junior stood on the backseat and heaved fireballs at the scavenger ship that was hot on their tail.

"Just cover us for a little bit longer," T8 called back.

Easier said than done. Junior launched another fireball, but the scavenger ship easily tilted out of its way on its disproportionate wings.

Junior's gaze fell on the mangled bot that they had recovered from the inn. It sat lifeless against the backseat. Unlike T8, this bot looked like the ones that Junior was used to seeing on Famora. It had wiry arms, a hoverpad base instead of legs, and the signature single red eye, which had been pulverized by bullets. Given its current state, Junior wondered whether recovering it was worth the trouble at all.

Sand sprayed into the convertible as tracers landed alongside it. Junior dove onto the backseat and held the dead bot over him for whatever shred of protection it could provide.

"Hey, that guy's worth a lot more than you, pal!" shouted T8.

"I doubt that!" Junior shouted back, wishing that his speeder hadn't been stolen.

The tracer fire ceased. Junior poked his head up and saw the scavenger turning around.

"That's it?" he asked. "But they practically had us!"

"The Del Clorans wouldn't dare bring their firefight out here," said T8.

Junior glanced around, but all he saw was more of the same red dunes. "And where is here, exactly?" he asked.

"Taipa Kanani territory."

Junior froze. *Vipers*. He'd heard the stories: the Taipa weren't just a gang. They were the one all other gangs paid tribute to. The one that made sailors fear certain trade routes. The one that very few people ever crossed and lived to tell the tale. Junior had checked weeks ago to make sure that the Taipa were far away from his rendezvous point.

Unfortunately, so was he.

"I'd move that to your inside jacket pocket," suggested T8, pointing to the exact pocket where Junior had hidden his money pouch. "Harder to steal when it's right in front of you."

"I'll burn their hand if they try."

"DON'T!" blurted T8, the red dot on his visor pinging back and forth more quickly. "Do not let *anyone* know that you have powers."

Great. Another place that hates us, thought Junior. It took him back to that fateful moment on the Trampoline, the one that had made him famous, or so Cassius had told him. He remembered the crowd and the sting of its jeers and threats. Those had been his neighbors, the very people he was trying to protect, yet still they hated him for what he was. He'd been forced to spend his final days on Famora in hiding because of them, because of the powers that he'd once believed to be a gift.

"Do the people here know my face?" he asked.

"Them and half the galaxy," said T8, its wiry fingers fishing through the glovebox. Amid a mess of spare parts and loose rounds of ammunition, the bot dug out a mask made of ebony. Or really half a mask – it only reached down to the tip of the nose. Embroidered in the wood were two golden Suns – the mark of the Taloans. A peaceful people, they wore these masks on mission trips as a symbol of their homeworld. To be given one was the highest honor, and to lose one was the greatest shame a Taloan could endure.

"How'd you get this?" asked Junior. He flipped it over and found some dried purple blood on the inside.

"Don't ask."

Junior found he was liking this new companion less and less. "How far can you take me?"

"It's just a few more klicks to *Casus Belli*. From there you can find transportation – *if* they don't steal your pouch first."

My mother picked a quality planet to land on, thought Junior. He stared out at the graveyard of ships along the sands. They were more plentiful now, at times obscuring the red earth. Whole frigates laid like beached whales along the dunes, some IDF, some Poterian, and some gutted so completely that it was hard to tell which side they had fought for.

What was clear to Junior, however, was that the battle had been concentrated here. Or in the atmosphere above, where Admiral Carmichael had made his surprise attack against the Poterian fleet. Like everyone else, Junior wondered what truly happened in that battle. He'd never understood how a fighting force a fraction of the Poterians' size managed to defeat them, especially considering the vast superiority of Poterian tech.

Junior rose in his seat. There was something on the horizon…something *covering* the horizon. He recognized the spikes rising from it.

Another dreadnought. This one was even larger than the one in the atmosphere, or at least it seemed larger, perhaps because it was exposed against the landscape. A hundred dunes had been flattened under its belly, and its shadow stretched for miles along the desert sands. Its bow, half pressed into the earth, looked like the face of a slumbering beast. Rust had browned its once jet-black surface, and hundreds of hovercars swarmed around it like flies as they picked at its enormous carcass.

"Is that…?"

"*Casus Belli,*" said T8.

Junior eased back as they fell into the shadow of the dreadnought. How anyone could have built something like this was beyond him. Equally confusing was how anyone could have downed it.

T8 drove them up the spiked surface, dodging hovercars that poured in and out of the many holes in the ship's hull. The traffic had no order to it; everyone just steered as they pleased, honking constantly as they weaved around each other.

"Are all these people Taipa?" asked Junior.

T8 shook its head. "Most people here are just smugglers, fugitives, or any other rat who prefers to live as far away from government control as possible."

"Sounds like the IDF would have a field day out here."

"Not if the Taipa keep bribing the right people. Besides, then they'd have to clean up the mess they made in their battle. It's much easier to just let the sand bury it."

T8 brought them to the top of the ship. From here, the dunes looked like mere ripples along the distant surface. They angled toward a massive crater in the hull and T8 lowered them through it.

Junior leaned over the side. Lights beamed far below, thousands of them, scattered among the many low-lying buildings. He couldn't believe it – an entire city tucked inside this ship, hidden from the harsh desert sun. As they drew closer, the stench of diesel and bareno smoke assaulted his nostrils. The buildings took on irregular shapes, as if the whole community were one elaborate abstract painting. And everything was built out of junk: sheet metal, supply crates, rotted plywood, broken sections of ships – the streets were lined with edifices constructed from the debris. Lightbulbs had been strung up haphazardly between the buildings, their wires dangling over alleyways that their dim glow failed to dispel. Junior saw all manner of people in the streets – Humans, Braimen, Galanads, Nurranos – but none of them seemed to be going anywhere. They just hung around on stoops or in shops. But when the hovercar passed, they made sure to give Junior and T8 a long, warning look.

"You sure you couldn't drop me off at another outpost?" asked Junior, adjusting his Taloan mask.

"You'd find the same aivin shit there," said the bot. "But here you have Sladek's Den."

"Who's Sladek?"

"The first crime lord to set up shop inside the mighty *Casus Belli*. Great guy. Made a fortune here until the Taipa took over. Don't worry though, he's still around."

T8 pointed to a skull on a spike overlooking the city entrance.

Junior rolled his eyes. T8 was starting to sound like the superstitious sailors in the Famoran Dockyards. The Taipa liked to make themselves sound scary, but he doubted half the stories he heard about them were true.

They were coming to the central part of the city; Junior could feel it. Lights glowed in the near distance, brighter than anywhere else, summoning everyone in the city toward it like a beacon. Chatter echoed through the narrow streets, hundreds of voices all shouting and cackling at once. Soon the buildings fell away and

Sladek's Den folded out before them in three wide rings, each one progressively lower. Along the edges of each ring sat hundreds of selling carts covered in fabrics, foods, spices, plants, perfumes, jewels, and other treasures from untold reaches of the galaxy. As Junior looked from one to the next, he gulped, realizing he would have much more ground to cover than he'd expected.

"Look for Brinkborne," said T8, seeming to read Junior's thoughts. The bot landed the hovercar in the centermost circle, among a hundred other parked vehicles. "The shopkeep is an acquired taste, but he's a Famoran. He might be able to help you."

Junior stepped out of the hovercar and slung his pack over his back. "What if he can't?"

"Then figure something else out. What do I look like, your mother?"

No, but you've brought me one step closer to finding her. Junior made his way toward the first ring of Sladek's Den as T8 flew away. As dangerous as the bot had made this place seem, Junior began to realize that it was the perfect spot to gather information. The people here came from all corners of the galaxy, and many of them had knowledge of where other fugitives may be. Of course, Junior would need to be careful – asking questions about a powerful Zoboros would raise suspicions, especially if his mother had made enemies here on Mogaddu. He'd start by finding Brinkborne. Better to get the lay of the land from a fellow Famoran before diving into its underbelly.

Junior started through the maze of hovercars. He spotted a Kimikan in one of them, its hairy paws digging through the glovebox. When its beady eyes met Junior's, the creature dropped what it was stealing and scurried away. Junior instinctively reached for his coat pocket, then stopped himself. If someone saw where he was touching, they'd know exactly how to rob him. He frowned. These were things he didn't have to think about on Famora.

He climbed the stairs to the first ring. The crowd was thick. People brushed past him right and left while vendors shouted at him from either side of the narrow walkway. The loudest was a Galanad, its six pink tentacles chopping meat, passing out cuts, and collecting money all at the same time. Some cuts it dunked into a fryer with a satisfying sizzle, the oily aroma overwhelming Junior's senses. His stomach grumbled. It had been weeks since he'd had any fresh-cooked food. He stared longingly at the fish and eels hanging from the Galanad's cart, then reminded himself that no fish this far out in the desert could be fresh. He moved on.

Brinkborne, Brinkborne. Most of the carts didn't have signs, and those that did were written in other languages, even other alphabets. Navigating this place on his own proved to be hopeless, so he tapped the shoulder of a short, cloaked figure in front of him, hoping she spoke his language.

"Do you know where I could find Brink—?" Junior froze. The purple face that turned to meet him was half-hidden beneath an ebony mask. The Taloan's eyes narrowed at the sight of his stolen mask, and before Junior could save himself, she scoffed and walked away.

This might not be the best disguise to use. He could worry about finding a new one later; right now, he needed some direction. He kept searching for a sign of Brinkborne when a mechanical rasp filled his ears.

He turned. Two Del Clorans were walking behind him. A few hours ago, he wouldn't have recognized the species, but his brush at Hoberachi's Inn had acquainted him with these insects. Each was tall and thin, and used a breathing apparatus that covered everything on their face except for their big, compound eyes, which they kept mostly hidden beneath a pair of dimmed goggles. The two chatted with each other through a series of clicks, and they each carried jet-black support beams over their shoulders. The kind of support beams that were used on speeders.

Junior's model of speeder.

"Hey!" he barked. The Del Clorans turned and ran. He chased them up a series of stairs all the way into the upper ring where Sladek's Den met the rest of the city. The creatures pushed past the selling carts and ran toward a line of warehouses that overlooked the bazaar.

As Junior pursued, a young Human woman, short and bone thin, stepped in his path. He bulled her over before he even realized that she was in the way, then skidded to a stop. The poor girl laid on her back while the Del Clorans disappeared into a dark alley between two warehouses. He cursed to himself as he helped the girl to her feet.

"Are you alright?" he asked.

Her blue eyes dodged his glance. She had short black hair and matching black nails. Junior only caught a glimpse, though, before she pulled her hoodie in tight and slipped away toward the selling carts.

"I'm sorry!" he called, but she had already disappeared into the crowd. Fantastic. He'd only been here a few minutes and already he'd upset someone. But he had found his speeder, at least part of it, and there were plenty of other parts to be carried. He picked a vantage point that was hidden behind the tarps of a nearby perfume shop and waited.

Eventually, another Del Cloran came strolling along, this one carrying a container of blue transmission fluid. G-grade, the only kind Junior's speeder could take. His fists tightened. He stuck close to the crowd as he tailed the thief. It got trickier when he ran out of crowd at the alleyway, and he had to keep behind corners and the occasional dumpster until his target arrived at a warehouse. But not just any warehouse. It had a sign dangling by a thread out front.

Brinkborne.

A spark flickered in Junior's fist. He would need to have a word with this Famoran. He marched through the door to find his speeder laid out in sections on the floor of a large machine shop. Other speeders and hovercars were arranged in varying states of disrepair, separated by worktables that were covered in tools and parts. Several Del Clorans stood around his disassembled speeder, each drawing their weapons upon noticing him.

"Niet-com, chigamena!" one of them hissed.

"Watch your damn mouth," said Junior, having no idea what the Del Cloran had just said.

"She means 'strength in numbers'," boomed a voice from above. Junior shifted his gaze past the Del Clorans to the top of a stairwell. Eight crab legs clattered down the stairs. The red Bolani they belonged to wiped all four of his hands on his sludge-stained shirt. "Del Clorans like to say that before a kill."

That voice. Junior recognized it. He'd seen this Bolani before. Multiple times, in fact, at the Police Plaza in Famora.

He groaned. Just when Mogaddu couldn't have gotten any worse, T8 had sent him to the cheapest mechanic in the galaxy.

"I'm gonna have to ask you to leave, kid," said Ragar as he scrabbled toward Junior. "I don't want any—" He froze. His three eyes widened with realization, though the middle one wasn't focused on Junior at all, but somewhere off in the middle distance.

"That's my speeder," said Junior. By the look on Ragar's face, the Bolani had already figured that part out.

"And now it's my speeder," said Ragar, drawing a bar out of his pocket. It looked like pure silver, but with individual crystals inside it that twinkled in the light. The Del Clorans were drawn to it like a magnet. "I'm sorry, kid, but that's how it works here."

"Well then, enjoy the window decoration," said Junior, pointing to his incomplete speeder.

"What are you talking about?" asked Ragar, retracting the silver bar from the Del Clorans' reach.

"The booster plugs," said Junior. "You probably thought you could substitute your own, but this model only takes a specific kind straight from the manufacturer. Good luck having them shipped out here."

Ragar eyed the shifty Del Clorans.

"Kime neh johne," one of them said.

"You can too understand his tongue!" barked Ragar. "Where are the plugs?"

The Del Clorans looked at each other with their insect eyes. Finally, one of them stepped out of the shop. It returned a few minutes later with the plugs.

"Those the right ones?" asked Ragar.

Junior realized the Bolani was addressing him. He nodded.

"Good," said Ragar, tossing the silver bar to one of the Del Clorans. She snatched it and tucked it in her pouch. "Now all of you, *scram*!"

The Del Clorans hurried out the door, leaving only Ragar, Junior, and the disassembled speeder.

"How much?" asked Junior. He didn't want to pay for his own speeder, but it was a better alternative than fighting armed Del Clorans for ownership – if only slightly.

"2400 cyos."

"That bar wasn't worth nearly that much."

Ragar chuckled. "That bar was pure calladium, boy, and it's fetching a pretty penny right now...plus I did factor in my finder's fee."

Of course you did. Junior rolled his eyes and reached into his jacket pocket.

But nothing was there.

Frantic, he patted each of his pockets, but there was no sign of his pouch.

"Oh no," Ragar chuckled. "Looks like you're doing the Mogaddan dance!" He mimicked Junior patting each of his pockets.

"I was only in the crowd for a few minutes!" exclaimed Junior. "But no one touched me the whole..." He froze. Someone had touched him. Only for a moment, but in that moment of collision, the girl in the hoodie had managed to steal the pouch right from under his nose.

Ragar didn't respond. He drummed his fingers on his chin, lost in thought. "I take it you can reassemble the speeder?"

Junior nodded.

"And what do you know about the X90 model?" asked Ragar.

"From Erilia? Basic design, but heavier on the bottom. Better for low altitudes, unless you mod the thrusters."

"Can you mod the thrusters?"

"I can mod anything."

Ragar smiled. "Is it overstepping to assume that you don't have a place to stay?"

Junior shook his head.

Ragar nodded toward the stairs. "There's a spare room. Work for me and I'll let you earn your speeder back. But you should know that I'm not very nice, and I—"

"How long?" interrupted Junior.

"I'll decide that later."

"I don't like loose terms."

"Then you won't like Mogaddu." Ragar reached out a sludge-covered hand.

Junior looked at his speeder, then at the shrewd Bolani.

They shook.

Chapter 5

Dinner

Pipes surrounded Kano, all filled with a glowing green substance that illuminated the dark and narrow passageways.

He knew this place. A *clank* echoed from the shadows, the sound of a metal boot striking the steel walkway. He knew who was coming.

He turned, powers at the ready, only to find Makoto emerging from the darkness.

"What are you doing here?!" demanded Kano.

"I came to help. We all did."

"We?" Kano turned to find Jaden, Li, and Akio standing there.

Another clank rang out; this one closer.

"You don't understand, you can't be here," continued Kano. "This is where—" He turned back to Makoto, but his brother had disappeared.

Someone yelped. Kano turned and found his three friends being pulled into the shadows by armor-covered arms, the owners of them hidden in darkness. He hurled a shockwave toward the attackers, but struck a pipe. Green fluid gushed out. It flooded the corridor and dragged Kano away in its current.

"Makoto!" screamed Kano, struggling to keep his head above the surface. "Jaden!"

"Kano!" Li cried out as the current dragged her past him.

Kano reached out to her. For a moment their fingers touched before she was pulled under.

"LI!" He dove under the surface. There was no sign of her in the dark depths. He kept diving, surprised by how deep it went, his lungs feeling ready to burst but he kept pressing, reaching out for her, on and on until—

A gauntlet reached through the abyss and grabbed his hand. Kano knew that gauntlet. He gave a silent scream that came out in bubbles as its owner hoisted him from the depths, the ancient markings in its mask glowing with electricity. Kano tried launching a shockwave, but Taranis kept Kano's arm angled away so that the attack rippled uselessly into the distance. Then the horrible, familiar sting of electricity pulsed through every muscle of Kano's body. He snapped up out of bed and once again struck the bunk above him.

"Gahhh," he groaned, slumping back against his pillow. The sensation was gone, replaced by a tingle in his arms where Taranis's electricity had struck him weeks ago. It was not the first time he'd felt this strange sensation – nor, he suspected, would it be the last.

He rubbed his sweaty forehead, where the lump he had earned yesterday morning was now doubling in size.

Beside the mirror, he spotted a freshly pressed suit waiting for him. A note was pinned to the collar.

This one's yours. Be ready at 0800.
    – Cera

Kano rose and inspected it. The suit was blue, to match the Republic's colors; a little faded, but that hardly mattered. His adoptive family had never had the means to buy him his own, and he could probably count on his fingers the number of times he'd borrowed one to wear. He would be sure to take care of this one.

He checked the time on his communicator: 0755.

Shit. Kano hurried into the suit piece by piece. He'd only meant to take a quick nap after the simulation, but he'd underestimated how exhausting their weeks of training had truly been.

When he tried tying the tie, he quickly realized that he had no idea what he was doing. Thankfully, the hydraulic door opened just as he had three uneven knots strangling at his throat.

"Need a hand?" asked Cera, amusement written on her face. She wore a golden gown fitted to her tall, slender frame, beautiful enough for Kano to forgive her jab.

"As long as you don't make it too tight," said Kano, dropping his hands to his sides.

"I make no such promise," she said, raising her hands. From each hand, a beam of green energy stretched out toward Kano. A hand formed at the end of each beam, with green fingers that clasped around the tie and carefully undid the knots.

"Do you always have to use your powers for this stuff?" he asked.

"Never miss a chance to train."

Kano nodded. Every moment was a teaching moment for Cera, but Kano was more interested in learning about the impending dinner. "Why do you think the general wants to meet with only me tonight?" he asked. It was a question he'd been too afraid to ask Carmichael.

She threaded the tie through the new knot. "I suspect it has something to do with you being the 'Hero of Famora' and all." As she enunciated the title, she jerked the tie tight, digging it into Kano's Adam's apple – a subtle warning not to let the newfound title get the better of him.

"I didn't ask to be anyone's hero."

"You didn't ask for powers either. But here we are. And now you can either run away from this path that's being laid out for you, or you can see where it leads."

"What if I get everyone killed in the process?"

"We all have our reasons for choosing this path. Your friends chose it because of you, but that doesn't make you responsible for their fate."

"And what's your reason?"

Cera looked away. "Come on. We're going to be late."

The energy beams retreated into her hands and she led him down the hall without another word. Kano sensed that he'd hurt her with his question, and so stayed silent for the remainder of their walk to the Transitway. They climbed up the stairs and waited among a small crowd of sailors and soldiers at the train stop, where Kano scanned for any unusual behavior. Any one of these people could be an agent of Mezo's – or worse, a Lusitani. He still had no idea what they looked like, which made him even more paranoid to board a train with strangers.

A bullet train zipped into the station. The doors whooshed open and everyone crowded in. No sooner had Kano stepped on than the doors swung shut and the train rocketed from the station. The jolt caught him by surprise; he grabbed a handrail just to keep from falling over. No one else seemed bothered; for them, this was just another day aboard the *Dormarch*.

Staring out the window, he felt so small. The whole ship whirred by, its thousands of passengers just blurs of blue and white. All cogs that kept this behemoth racing through space. All people who feared the Zoboros.

He caught the eye of another passenger. She quickly returned her gaze to the datapad in her hand. Kano noticed more pairs of eyes shifting off him and pretending to look elsewhere. They all seemed nervous.

They recognize me. But why should that matter? Did they think his plan was to derail the train with a flick of his wrist? Or maybe they thought Taranis would descend on the train at any moment to collect him. That was certainly a fear he shared, however unlikely it may be.

When they reached the next station, all the other passengers hurried off.

Kano sighed as the train charged on. He supposed he should get used to this treatment.

Cera leaned over and whispered, "We're going to change things, Kano. You'll see."

Kano wanted to believe her. He had trusted her so far, despite their less than honest meeting back on Famora, where she'd flirted with Jaden in order to find out whether Kano was the Zoboros she and Carmichael were looking for. She had worked with Carmichael for several cycles now and had gone out of her way to help Kano and his friends acclimate to their new surroundings. Though she wasn't much older than the rest of them, everyone on the team still looked up to her like a big sister. Everyone except Jaden, at least, who just liked looking at her.

A tower loomed in the distance, growing larger by the second. Kano leaned into the window. The Panopticon. He'd heard about it, but never seen it for himself. It was planted right at the center of the railway, with two narrow slits cut inside it so that both tracks could pass through. At the top was a round observation platform with large glass windows angled down toward the railways, giving deck officers a panoramic view of everything traveling up and down the ship.

"I heard the sailors came up with a nickname for that place," said Cera, pointing to the Panopticon.

Kano looked to her expectantly.

She smirked. "The Bitch's Nest."

Comforting. Kano didn't have to guess who the name was referring to.

The train sped into the Panopticon. One moment the *Dormarch* was flashing by in the windows, the next there was darkness. Kano tightened his grip on the handrail.

His own reflection stared back at him from the window, looking so small and alone aboard the train.

Lights appeared along the sides of the train. Kano saw faces rushing by, many faces, all of them waiting on a thin platform. He held tight as they came to an abrupt stop.

"Come on," said Cera. She grabbed him by the hand and pulled him into the waiting sea of bodies. The crowd pressed its way into the train, threatening to drag Kano back inside with it. He realized this could be the perfect excuse to miss dinner; he would just say he got stuck on the train and had to travel all the way back. But somehow, Kano didn't think the general was one to accept tardiness, so he pushed forward.

They found Carmichael amid a small crowd by the elevators. The captain smiled as they approached. "My, we clean up nicely," he said, admiring Kano's "new" suit.

"Thank you for the suit, Captain," said Kano quickly, his nerves kicking in. A dinner party waited upstairs, both its purpose and its guests still unknown to him. Judging by the number of people in full-dress uniform here, the Panopticon was a place for the more important people on the *Dormarch*. What would he say to these people once he arrived? What did they want to know about him? He tried to formulate some questions to ask Carmichael and Cera, but already he was having trouble thinking clearly.

"This is my first time at the Panopticon," he managed to get out.

"Then I trust Cera told you its real name," replied Carmichael with a wink. Cera playfully smacked him on the arm, drawing disapproving glances from some of the higher ups around them.

The elevator doors opened. More suits poured out, their shiny black shoes clicking toward the station. The waiting crowd started forward in a tidal wave of motion. When they corralled Kano inside the elevator and packed in on either side of him, he felt the energy instinctively snap into his fingers. *Fantastic.* His powers liked to creep up at tense and inopportune times. Cera had been teaching him how to vent them safely during their sessions, at least until he gained complete control over them, but it would be hard to do in such a tight space without rousing attention. He resolved to hold them in, something he was getting better at, but only when he felt in control.

Presently, he did not.

Cera must have sensed it, too, because she placed a hand on his shoulder. A small gesture, but it gave Kano the boost he needed to keep the energy at bay, if only for a little while longer.

No one spoke as the elevator climbed. Kano could hear the pounding of his own heart. He wondered if everyone else could hear it too. The air felt thicker here; it made him dizzy. He craned his neck to see how close they were to the top, assuming that's where dinner would be served, but he couldn't see the floor indicator over the crowd. Almost every officer was at least a head taller than him.

If only I were Junior. He thought back to his encounter with the towering cadet on the Trampoline. Where had

Junior gone since revealing his powers there? Did he ever make it to Mogaddu? Kano feared he may never learn the answer to that question.

The elevator stopped. Some people shuffled out; others shuffled in. Cera kept her hand locked on Kano's shoulder, signaling that this wasn't their floor. Kano gulped. His hands kept shaking as the power continued to rush into them. It was getting harder to breathe. He tried adjusting the collar of his shirt. It didn't help.

He felt the tingle of electricity again. Small spasms started in his arm muscles. Then a sensation rode up his spine, one he hadn't felt since…

Lightning flashed through the elevator.

Kano gasped. Everyone looked at him. He stared back at their confused faces. Hadn't they seen it, too?

The door opened and again Cera held him back. More people shuffled off. As they dispersed, Kano realized that what lay beyond the elevator doors was not a hallway, but a familiar series of pipes filled with green ooze, and standing among them was the masked man.

Kano closed his eyes. When he opened them again, he saw a dimly lit hallway filled with well-dressed officers.

"Are you alright?" muttered Cera.

"I— I'm fine," he stammered. He knew she didn't believe him, but she made no attempt to argue the point further.

What's happening to me? The tingling grew stronger the longer he stayed on the elevator. It crawled up his back and down his arms, begging to be released.

"*Find us,*" someone hissed.

Kano turned. The gentleman next to him glanced back out of the corner of his eye, then stared straight on, pretending to ignore him.

It's just in my head, he told himself.

"Find us, find us, find us." The voice was becoming many. *"FIND US FIND US FIND US."*

Kano saw another flash and the doors opened.

He burst out of the elevator and fell to his knees. Others shuffled past, giving him odd looks as he caught his breath. The voices in his head went silent; the only sound now was the tapping of shoes against the tiled floor. The tingling was gone, too.

"How'd you know this was our floor?" asked Carmichael, marching ahead.

Cera stopped and inspected Kano. "We can postpone, if you'd like," she whispered.

Kano shook his head. He wouldn't let these visions get in the way. He'd had them before; he could deal with them now.

Freed from the confines of the elevator, he found he could safely and quietly vent his powers as he headed down the hallway. The space was far wider than any other he had seen aboard the *Dormarch* (except for the Transitway, of course); it was large enough for all the officers to stop and chit-chat as they funneled in and out of the tall, half-oval entrances that lined either side. Most of them didn't look like the officers downstairs. They seemed smaller, younger, far less dignified and, as a result, far more approachable. They each noticed Kano as he passed. He heard whispers, saw a few jaws hang loose.

But it wasn't like his experience in the train car. There was a twinkle in each person's eyes, a sort of nervous excitement bubbling up in them.

"This is where the analysts work," said Carmichael. "They spent months tracking Taranis's moves. Beating him made you something of a celebrity up here."

"Really?" said Kano, puffing his chest a bit.

"Don't get carried away," Cera tutted. "You've still got a lot of work to do before you can parade around in a cape."

"I don't want a cape," said Kano.

"Thank goodness for that," said Carmichael. The captain stopped in front of a short stairway at the end of the hall. Guards flanked either side of it; one of them approached the captain with a datapad in hand. Carmichael placed his hand on the screen. It scanned, then lit up green.

The guard stepped aside. "She's expecting you, Captain."

Carmichael led Cera and Kano up the stairs. "Let me do the talking," he said. "Only speak when asked a direct question."

Kano nodded, relieved to play a minimal role in tonight's performance.

At the top of the stairs was a single door. Carmichael wasted no time in opening it. Kano filed in behind the captain, and found a room far more luxurious than any other he'd seen on the ship. A chandelier hung high above, twinkling with jewels over a great table that ran the length of the room. At the back was an angled window overlooking the Transitway; from this height, the bullet trains looked like mere worms as they sped along the tracks.

Kano didn't look out the window, though. He was focused on the woman seated at the far end of the table, the woman with the cold, gray eyes that he remembered from Famora.

She was also the only other person present.

"Good evening, General," said Carmichael with a salute. "Thank you for the invitation."

"Just Kano," Mezo replied.

Carmichael and Cera stood there, stunned. They looked to each other, then to Kano.

"We— we'll be outside," stammered Carmichael, then he and Cera headed back down the stairs.

Kano watched his only lifelines abandon him. As he turned to face Mezo, time stood still. His heart began to race. He wasn't prepared to face her alone.

"Take a seat," she said, gesturing airily to the one directly beside her.

Kano approached. The room seemed to stretch as he crossed it, the chair she had indicated suddenly miles away. A few weeks ago, he had faced down a terrorist capable of launching a bolt of lightning from the palm of his hand; somehow, this seemed even more terrifying.

He sat down. The chair's leather scraped against his dress pants, its squeals filling the uncomfortable silence.

A server entered and placed a tray of bread and olives before them. Mezo gave Kano a once-over beneath her glasses before turning her attention to the tray. She didn't take a bite though. She just sat there, studying the food.

Should I eat first? wondered Kano. *Should I talk first?* The silence was getting painful. Finally, Kano couldn't take any more. "You wanted to see me, General?" he squeaked out.

"Not me," muttered Mezo. She nodded toward the door.

Kano turned. He hadn't realized there was anyone else in the room, though, technically, there wasn't. A short, stout, holographic man sat in a holographic chair in the far corner. He wore a pair of spectacles so small that they failed to cover the crow's feet behind them. His velvet tux was bright white, the tie tucked and pinned. A cane rested between his legs, topped by a jewel the size of his wrinkled fist.

"Young Master Kano," said the man, rising slowly on his cane. "You seemed to have forgotten the first rule of secret meetings."

"I…I did?"

The man smiled. "You left the door open, lad."

"I…oh." Kano could see to the bottom of the stairs where Carmichael and Cera waited anxiously beside the guards. Kano stumbled out of his chair, crossed the room, and shut it. When he turned, the holographic man was standing in front of him.

"Allow me to introduce myself," he said. "I am Danadas Orlov, patriarch of the Orlov family. I believe you were acquainted with a few distant cousins of mine."

Kano's eyes widened. An Orlov *here*? The ones he'd met on Famora had been some of the most influential people in the city. And the most secretive. He recalled the Zoboros girl, Jacelyn, who they'd kept locked in their house for her 'protection'. Kano always questioned that decision, but he also had to weigh it against the fact that those Orlovs had sacrificed themselves to save his friends.

"Mr. Orlov," said Kano, bowing his head. "I owe your family for—"

Danadas raised a solemn hand. It was all he needed to silence Kano. "It is what we do, lad."

Kano nodded. Unsure what else to do, he extended his hand. Danadas smiled and pretended to shake it with his own transparent one. "A pleasure, Kano. Truly."

Kano returned to his seat, awestruck. The Orlovs on Famora, despite their influence, had considered themselves to be a low branch in the family line. He couldn't imagine how much power their leader held. It had to be significant, though, to gain a private audience with the highest-ranking officer aboard the IDF's greatest ship.

Mr. Orlov's projection fizzled out for a moment, then reappeared in the seat across from Kano. Presumably, he had found a chair of his own from wherever he was remoting in from.

"Quite the stir you're causing, Master Kano," said Danadas.

"So I've been told," said Kano cautiously. He caught a hint of malice in Mezo's expression as she prodded an olive with her fork. This appeared to be a sore subject. "It was never my intention, though."

"But it might yet be an opportunity," said Danadas. "The tale of two Zoboros saving the day against a dastardly villain is proving to be quite a powerful narrative. Hendricks Junior has, for lack of a better term, sparked a flame, and it's bringing young Zoboros out of the shadows in almost every corner of the galaxy."

"And you think that's…good?" asked Kano hopefully.

"It is for Mr. Orlov," said Mezo. "Along with every other big name in the press that stands to fatten their wallets."

"People have been waiting a long time for this, Lana," defended Danadas.

"And they would have kept waiting until it was safer to move toward integration," said Mezo, her face reddening. Kano wasn't sure if her anger flashed at Danadas disagreeing with her, or because the old man had just used her first name.

"It would never be safe," said Danadas. "Better to rip the bandage off now and start moving forward."

"Better for who?" asked Mezo. "For the Zoboros being assaulted on their way to work? Or how about my soldiers, who are being trampled and beaten in the streets trying to stop these riots? Or maybe you were thinking of the entire cities that have been shut down because of the violence that you've 'sparked' with your damned video! I still see only one person who benefits from all this, and he's sitting in this room."

"The news may be grim, dear, but that is the nature of news," said Danadas. "Things will get darker and uglier, sure, but that is because we are faced with a dark and ugly truth – that for cycles we have rejected our greatest gifts." He pointed to Kano, the gesture planting an enormous weight on his young shoulders. "The Zoboros forged the history of this galaxy, my *family's* history. They cannot simply be snuffed out. They are rising, and will once again shape the course of our future."

A memory came to Kano. The Zoboros girl, the one he'd met at the Orlov Mansion, the one who could command lightning. Though she hadn't been an Orlov by blood, the Orlovs had taken her in despite all the risks. Kano hadn't agreed with the extreme way in which they'd sheltered her, but now he was beginning to understand why. They were grooming a new generation of Zoboros, waiting for the moment to reintegrate them into society.

The moment he had inadvertently created.

"I've given you the video," said Kano. "But what more can I offer you beyond helping Carmichael?"

"Why, lad, the worst thing we could do is lose the momentum we've generated. We must fuel the fire, and to do that, we need a poster boy."

"A what?" blurted Kano.

"What Mr. Orlov is *trying* to say," interjected Mezo, "is that this video has made you one of the two biggest faces behind the Zoboros movement. Everything you do, everything you say, can help us calm the storm."

"And I take it Junior is the other face?" asked Kano.

Danadas nodded, leaning closer. "If we hope to win the public over and smooth this transition, it would help to have both our heroes on the stage. Of course, no one knows where Junior has gone…"

Kano could feel Danadas's eyes pressing into him. It was no secret that Kano had aided in Junior's escape. Everyone had asked him where his friend had gone, and though he knew perfectly well, he refused to betray that information. Not when Junior had a chance, however slim, to be reunited with his mother.

"What would you have me do as your poster boy?" he asked, dodging the old man's unasked question.

Danadas eased back, his smile failing to conceal a flicker of disappointment. "Tour you. Small at first, places that are safe, where we know we can get a decent following. From there we'll branch out to less accommodating places, but by then we should have more Zoboros under our belt to—"

"So my friends can come too?" interrupted Kano.

Danadas eyed Mezo for a response.

"Carmichael's plan has failed," answered Mezo. "He believed a team of Zoboros could be assembled to win the public favor, but those Zoboros have disappeared."

No thanks to you and your Lusitani, thought Kano, but instead he said, "You still have the rest of us."

"I've seen the reports from the Sim," said Mezo. "Your friends are not fit for any assignment."

"I disagree," said Kano. "They rescued me on Famora. They've outsmarted and outmaneuvered your troopers multiple times. And they've carried me this far through the impossible trainings that your people created. They'll be ready."

"I admire your dedication, Kano," began Danadas, "but understand that this path puts your young friends in terrible danger. Our people can ensure that they are taken somewhere safe and given all the proper protections."

"I'm sorry, Mr. Orlov, but your family offered us the same protections before," said Kano. "I can't thank them enough for what they tried to do, but they were doomed the moment we went inside their home. My friends will be in danger no matter where you take them. The only difference with your plan is that I won't be there to help."

"What we're proposing is much bigger than yourself or your friends," said Danadas. "You must understand."

"And *you* should understand that my friends are exactly who you need on your tour. If you want to integrate Zoboros, then you need an integrated team to represent that."

"And what happens to your team when a member dies?" asked Mezo. Kano froze, unsure how to respond, so she continued. "The road we will put you on is dangerous. Your very presence in any city will draw assassins and incite riots. We intend to protect you as best we can, and bringing others along will only make our job more difficult. We can take you and only you."

Kano stewed, a fire igniting inside him. He understood her position, but it was clear she didn't understand his. "Then I won't be your poster boy," he muttered.

Mezo's eyes narrowed. "You will do as commanded."

"Or what? You'll throw me off the ship? You couldn't risk losing me to Taranis, and you can't risk losing me to whoever else is out there searching. You need me and you know it."

"But I can make your stay here far less comfortable," said Mezo.

"More uncomfortable than the simulator already makes it? I doubt that."

Danadas chuckled. "I've seen the reports as well. The boy does have a talent for rallying his friends against the impossible. If they motivate him as much as he motivates them, then it would be unwise to separate them."

"I will not entertain the idea of endangering children," said Mezo.

"Most are of conscription age," said Danadas.

"And undisciplined. They're cannon fodder. And for you, Danadas, they're a media disaster in the making."

"We're facing a disaster, Lana. If you want to use my channels to prevent it, this may be our best move."

Kano turned to Mezo hopefully. She stared into his blue eyes, unimpressed. Then she smiled, a devious smile, as an idea began to form. Kano became uneasy.

"If you really believe that you and your friends are capable, I will give them one chance to prove it. Only one."

Danadas leaned forward, enthralled by the drama.

"Just tell me what I have to do," said Kano.

"In three days, your team will be evaluated in the Sim. Succeed in your mission, and your friends become part of your tour. Fail, and they will be sent to an undisclosed location while you travel alone.”

Kano’s heart sank. If Chenji’s claim about the Sim being rigged was true, then this was a losing deal. But as he stared at two of the most powerful figures in the galaxy, he realized this was the only deal he was going to get.

“I’ll see you in three days,” he said.

Chapter 6

The Tattoo

Junior adjusted his facemask as he stepped out of the shop. Some fresh air would do him good, although "fresh" was a generous term in Sladek's Den. The stench of wastewater and rotten food was a permanent fixture in the pit, where it lingered in the hot and stagnant air. Still, it was a welcome change from the diesel fumes that filled Brinkborne.

He'd worked two days straight without any real breaks, except to sleep. It wasn't that Ragar was working him mercilessly; it was because everything that Ragar asked him to repair needed far more work than what Ragar had in mind. The shopkeep didn't care if his speeders fell apart in midflight, but Junior wasn't about to let someone ride out with an engine that had been strung together with tape. If anything, he'd advise them to try a different mechanic – although that assumed there was one more reputable in Casus Belli.

Somehow, he doubted it.

Amid the rancid odors, he clung to the savory scent of fried aivin and kobodi spice. Every day, it rose from a noodle shop one ring below and snuck through his window on the second floor of Brinkborne. He'd been dreaming of it each night, waiting to sink his teeth into it, and now that Ragar had finally offered up a few cyos to him, it was time to indulge.

He descended the stairs to the middle ring, where the noodle shop was built into the edge of the ring itself. There were no windows to see inside, just a chimney to let the steam fill the surrounding air. A Gorv stood by the door like a statue, seven feet tall, its muscular arms folded, its gray face frozen in the grimace all Gorvs shared.

Junior hesitated. Gorvs were the preferred hired hands of the underworld, notorious for both their strength and their discretion. Having one stationed outside suggested that this might not be a noodle shop at all. Junior's instincts told him to turn back, but the rumbling in his stomach told him otherwise.

The Gorv's black, soulless eyes followed him as he approached. They gave him a once-over at the door, and then the creature nodded.

Junior entered. The steam hit him first; it dampened the air and cast a haze throughout the little shop. Then the noise hit him, though there were only a handful of patrons. It was concentrated at a single table: four people sat there, with far more empty glasses between them, laughing and stuffing their faces while other customers gave them sideways glances.

They were an unusual lot: a Del Cloran, a giggling little Kimikan with shaggy brown hair, a Tenu – Human in shape, but with skin the color of blood – and a Nurrano who was about Junior's age. She looked either too proud or too bored to be joining in the others' merriment, opting instead to watch a martial arts match on her datapad. Junior passed their table and took a seat at the empty bar. A Maloran bartender slithered over, its hundred tiny legs tapping across the floor.

"What would you like, humbled guesssssst?" it hissed, its jagged teeth forming into a smile. Junior looked around, but there were no menus. The choices of the day hung above the bar. It seemed dead birds or detached tentacles constituted the two primary categories. He took his chances by pointing at one of the birds.

"Excccellent choice, sir. Just ssssnared this morning."

This far into the desert? Fat chance, thought Junior. The bartender unhooked the bird and slithered through the kitchen door, allowing a thick cloud of steam to plume through.

"Nishen!" it cried from within the kitchen. "Ooshie akten mar!"

There was a clatter of pots, but it was nothing compared to the noise coming from the party behind Junior, who were laughing as the Kimikan climbed onto the table and imitated the bartender.

"Ah yesss, yesss," he said. "Throw me coins and I give you a tap dance, yesss."

The Del Cloran tossed some coins on the table while the Kimikan did a little jig. Junior kept them in his periphery – he sensed this was the group the Gorv was protecting, though the Kimikan and the Del Cloran didn't strike him as all that important. They just seemed like a couple of bumbling thugs laughing and goofing around. It was the Tenu who drew his attention, dressed in a silk suit and top hat. Far too eccentric for a place like Sladek's Den; the kind of outfit that would get you robbed in the absence of a Gorv bodyguard.

"Yesss, your money keeps these hips shaking!" said the Kimikan.

The Del Cloran's drink sprayed out its feeding tube. It coughed and wheezed as it tried to unclog its apparatus, which got a laugh out of the Tenu.

"I think we need another round of drinks!" called the Kimikan.

No one came. The table's laughter died so abruptly that their silence consumed the whole restaurant.

The Kimikan glanced at the Tenu. "Should I go in the kitchen and knock 'em around a bit?" he asked.

"No," said the Tenu, easing back in his chair. "Someone can get the insects for us. You, at the bar."

Junior tensed. His first instinct was to turn around and punch the pretentious Tenu square in the nose, but deep in his mind, T8 was warning him not to draw attention to himself.

"Are you deaf?" said the Tenu. "I said get the bartender."

"Get him yourself," said Junior, keeping his eyes forward.

The Kimikan started toward Junior, but the Tenu held him back. "Relax, Scraps, the Human must be new in town. Turn around, boy. I want to see your face."

Against his better judgment, Junior turned, fighting to hold back the flames that wanted to erupt from his palms. But when he saw the Tenu's face, he froze, for on it was a freshly printed tattoo of a serpent. It ran up his cheek, its open mouth poised to swallow his left eye.

Taipa.

"Why are you wearin' a Taloan mask?" asked the Tenu, chuckling. "You gonna convert me or somethin'?" His cronies burst into laughter, but the Nurrano girl beside him stayed silent, still focused on her datapad.

The Maloran hurried out of the kitchen, fresh drinks in hand.

"I am so sorry, good sirssss! My apologies!" In its rush, the Maloran tripped, smashing into the table and splashing the drinks all over the Tenu's face, which somehow managed to turn redder. The Tenu rose like a specter, his shadow falling over the trembling Maloran.

"Good Mr. Clemens, I am so—"

Clemens, the Tenu, grabbed the bartender by the throat before he could finish and slammed his face against the table.

"Do you know what you just did?" hissed Clemens, pinning the frightened bartender beneath his arm. "Yui!"

The Nurrano, Yui, drew a mirror from her purse and held it up to Clemens without ever looking up from her datapad. Clemens checked his tattoo, inspecting it from every angle.

"Are you trying to sabotage me, Maloran?" He pressed the creature's face harder against the table. "Do you have any idea what this thing means?!"

"Please sir!" it cried. "I wassss just trying to help your friend. It was accident!"

"Oh yeah. Accidents do happen, don't they?" said Clemens. "Scraps, why don't you bring Roger in here?"

Scraps giggled.

"No please, ssssir, don't hurt me! You get free noodles anytime you come!"

"And what would all these people say if I let you buy me out with noodles? No, a better message would be to toss you into the windscreen of a hovercar like the insect you are."

"ENOUGH!" shouted Junior. All eyes turned to him.

Clemens smiled, showing off all his sharp, pearly teeth. He tossed the Maloran aside. "What's your name, new guy?" he asked.

Junior said nothing, his palms warming, ready to strike.

"I'm only askin' so we know what to put on your tombstone," said Clemens. The Gorv entered behind him; it had to bend down just to fit through the door.

"Roger, would you kindly show our new friend out?"

Junior raised his fists as the Gorv approached.

"You'd have to be an idiot to pick a fight with a Gorv," said Scraps.

"I've done it before," said Junior, prompting Yui to look up from her datapad for the first time.

Clemens laughed, a twisted laugh that made Junior cringe with every high note it reached. "You got fight in you, kid," he said, stepping closer. "I could use someone like you. How would you like a job?"

Junior spat at Clemens's feet.

Clemens sneered and drew a pistol from his belt. Junior was about to summon a fireball when the door burst open. A tall, gaunt silhouette stood there, a red dot flashing side to side across its face.

T8?

"Taipa business," said the Tenu. "Keep your mechanical ass out of it."

"No one touches the boy, Clemens," said T8. "Boss's orders."

Clemens frowned. He kept his pistol trained on Junior, thinking. Finally, he lowered it. "Let's get out of here," he said. "The noodles are shit, anyway."

His party shuffled out on command. Clemens stopped as he passed T8, his yellow eyes narrowing. "You best make sure he stays the hell out of my way." He left, his Gorv trailing behind him, its bare feet shaking the ground as it walked.

Junior approached the bot. "Why are you following me?"

"Outside," T8 replied curtly. The bot headed out the door. Junior turned to the Maloran, who stared at him, wide-eyed and speechless.

Junior followed T8 outside. "You didn't tell me you were Taipa."

"I'm not," said T8. "But that doesn't mean I go picking fights with them, especially anyone wearing the Apopis. That serpent is a rare rite of initiation. It means he's wormed his way to an untouchable position, something *you* don't have."

"But he listened to you. Why would—?" Junior froze. There, amid the outside crowd, he spotted her: the girl in the hoodie. Pale face, about his age, and sporting a much nicer jacket than she'd had before she robbed him.

Junior charged. The girl bolted, pushing her way through the crowded street. She was quick, light on her feet. Junior was starting to lose her as she raced around a corner and into an alleyway. By the time he got there, the alley was deserted.

"Dammit!" he shouted, pounding his fist on a wall of sheet metal. Flames licked out, causing the metal to glow red.

"What are you doing?!" cried T8 as it rushed into the alleyway.

"She got away!"

"I don't care! What did I tell you about your…condition?" T8 lowered his volume on the last word.

Junior stood silent, brooding over his lapse in judgment. *Why can a gangster advertise his membership right on his face, but I can't even use my powers here?* he wondered.

"When did she tag you?" asked T8, pointing at his empty jacket pocket.

"Shortly after arriving."

T8 sighed. "I told you to get out of here as soon as possible."

"Well maybe your boss can arrange it," Junior fired back. "Considering he's so interested in my well-being."

"That back there was a courtesy for helping recover his bot. He owes you nothing." T8 turned to leave. "You're on the Taipa's radar now, so don't do anything stupid."

Frustrated, Junior turned away from the bot as it left. Who was this mysterious boss, and why was Junior on his radar? And how did the thief get away so quickly? He searched the alley, but it was no use. He left emptyhanded, unaware that his target was perched across the street, watching the metal on the wall cool where he had punched it.

Chapter 7

The Game Plan

Pixels faded all around them as they caught their breath.

"Again," said Kano, picking himself off the white floor. "We're going again."

"No, just…five minutes," said Makoto. He rolled onto his back and shut his eyes.

"You can't sleep *now*," said Kano. "We only have twelve hours until Mezo's test!"

"Eleven hours actually," boomed Carmichael's voice over the loudspeakers. He floated high above them on his silver disk. "You'll need to rest at some point, team."

"I vote now," said Jaden, wiping the sweat from his face. "If I have to see that stupid canyon again, I'll scream."

"I second that," said Li. This got Kano's attention. If Li and Jaden were agreeing on something, he knew it was bad.

"Third," said Chenji, who laid sprawled out like he was making a snow angel.

Kano looked to Akio, the oldest and most experienced of the group, for an answer.

"Rest would be wise, boy of thunder."

"Amen to that," said Jaden, lying down as well.

"I could use a rest, too," said Carmichael from above. "This machine is a bit draining."

Kano wasn't sure, but he thought he saw Jaden's head perk up at Carmichael's comment. That seemed to be the most enthusiasm he was going to drum from any of them for the foreseeable future, though. Resigned, he headed out the door without another word. If they wanted to give up, fine. It was their residency on the *Dormarch* that was in jeopardy, not his. They might as well quit now and save themselves the trouble.

And then he would be alone.

Kano stopped. He was at the entrance to his cabin. The walk over hadn't even registered for him; it had been more of a blind glaze through a darkening tunnel. He felt weak. His knees shook, his head started to spin. He leaned against the doorframe as his vision started to blur.

"Kano," echoed a voice faintly from behind him. "Kano..."

He felt a cool wave come over him. Some of his strength returned. His knees stopped shaking; his head stopped spinning. He turned around to find Li standing there with her glowing hand hovering in front of him.

"Are you alright?" she asked.

"I'm fine," he said. He tried to look casual by leaning against his door. It whooshed open and he fell inside.

"Come on, let's get you to bed." Li hoisted him off the floor and led him into his bunk.

He laid down as Li held a glowing hand over his forehead. The tension of the day seemed to evaporate into his sheets as a cool numbness took over.

"You don't have to carry the whole world on your shoulders, you know," she said. "Let me help you."

"You won't be able to help me if we fail tomorrow." Kano yawned. Her powers were dimming his senses.

Li shook her head. "We'll find a way. All of us."

His eyes began to shut. "I hope so," he whispered, and then sleep overtook him.

◁◆▷

Water splashed in his face. Kano gasped as he struggled to keep his head above the murky water. He searched above for the sun to keep him oriented, but there was no sky here. Only a ceiling of damp rocks.

A cave? Kano wasn't sure. He felt the current pulling him on to an unknown destination.

Another wave crashed over his head and dunked him under. Water filled his lungs. He coughed and gagged as he fought frantically to find the surface amid a torrent of bubbles. Then he felt a hand grab him by the collar, and all at once he was hoisted up and tossed face down in the sand.

He lifted his head and coughed up water as a pair of metal boots marched past him. He stared up into their owner's mask, angry.

"What do want from me?!" he demanded.

Taranis said nothing. He only looked up.

Kano looked too. A great door towered over them. It climbed all the way to the rocky ceiling some thirty feet above, its stone etched with the same ancient markings as the mask.

Taranis placed his gauntlet on the door. The markings began to glow a bright white.

"What is this place?" asked Kano.

"Home," answered Taranis's icy voice.

Kano placed his hand on the door too. The markings changed from white to red at his touch. The door groaned as if it were…angry. Kano pulled back his hand, but it was too late. There was a flash of light and he felt a great heat come over him in a fiery wave, and suddenly he was falling out of his bed onto the floor.

He laid there sore and confused. These dreams weren't like they used to be. They used to be of a mountain and a man. A man on fire. And Kano hadn't been the only Zoboros to see it; the girl at the Orlov house had claimed to have the same dreams…the same visions. But ever since his battle on Famora, Taranis had taken over those visions, as had water and sand.

Kano checked the time – 1000. Past curfew. Too bad; he wouldn't be able to sleep now. Perhaps Jaden could provide some entertainment.

But Jaden's bunk was empty.

Alarmed, Kano hurried into the hallway. It was quiet. The lights were dimmed – an effort to keep everyone aboard on a standard circadian rhythm. He tiptoed along until he heard faint chatter leaking through the walls. It was coming from Li's room. He tapped on the door. The chatter died. There was a pause. The door whooshed open. Makoto stood there, looking surprised, then pulled Kano inside.

The room had been rearranged. Li's bed was placed in the middle, serving as a meeting table, and Jaden, Chenji, and Li were all sitting around it.

"Look who's back from the dead!" exclaimed Makoto, reassuming his seat with the council. He motioned for Kano to claim the one beside him.

"Game planning, I assume?" asked Kano, sitting down.

"I prefer game *winning*," said Jaden as he tinkered with his datapad, some of its wires hanging exposed out the back.

Kano squinted at the code written on Jaden's screen. Anytime he saw code on that screen, he took it as a bad omen. "What are you cooking up?" he asked, noting the concerned look that Li and Chenji exchanged.

Jaden smiled. "All good things to those who wait."

There was a tap at the door. Makoto opened it and Akio slipped inside. The Jakari waited until the door was sealed before drawing a small metal box from beneath his poncho and tossing it to Jaden, who eagerly connected it to the datapad. Code began flashing across the screen faster than Kano's eyes could follow.

"Is it working?" asked Chenji.

"So far so good," said Jaden, "but it'll take me most of the night to get it operational. Akio, can you make the switch before roll call?"

Akio gave a small bow. "At your service, strange boy of the computer."

"I'd wear that hat proudly," said Jaden.

"Switch what?" asked Kano, feeling desperately behind.

"That box is a neural connector," whispered Makoto. "It takes the signals from Carmichael's brain and tells the computer in the Sim what to project."

"Wait, you mean…" Kano trailed off as it all came together. "Are you hacking into the Sim?!"

"The game's rigged, Kano," said Jaden. "We're just leveling the playing field."

Kano looked to Li. He could tell by her face that cheating wasn't sitting well with her, either. "If we get caught, we lose," he said flatly.

"If we don't use it, we lose," countered Chenji.

"Just because you couldn't beat it doesn't mean that we can't," said Kano.

"And how's that going for you?" Chenji fired back.

"Boys, let it go," said Li.

"No," said Kano. "We're a team here, so we make it a team vote. All in favor of hacking the Sim, raise your hand."

Jaden's and Chenji's hands shot up first. Makoto looked to Kano, then to Jaden, then sheepishly raised his own.

"Come on, Li," pressed Chenji, trying to break the even split in the votes. "Unless you've got a better idea, this is all we've got."

Li slowly raised her hand. As far as Kano was concerned, she might as well have stabbed him in the heart. She never cheated, never lied, and *never* sided with Chenji or Jaden. She was desperate. Kano turned to Akio, the only one not raising his hand.

"Switching connectors is pain in ass," replied Akio. "But this also gives me best chance to stay and protect you, so I change my mind. I vote to hack."

Kano slumped back in his chair, defeated. "What happens when you use the datapad?" he asked, rubbing his forehead.

"If all goes well, things in the simulator won't go quite like Carmichael imagines them," answered Jaden. "I can make the changes subtle though: a missed shot here, a convenient gust of wind there. Easy."

Kano shook his head. "But you haven't even tested it yet. No offense, but I've seen you make bigger mistakes with much simpler equipment than the Sim."

Jaden paused, looking a little wounded. "I'll run whatever tests I can tonight, Kano. We'll be gambling when we try it in the Sim regardless, but like Akio said, it's still our best bet."

Kano looked around the room. It was clear the others weren't going to change their minds. To go against them would only split the team when they needed to be working together.

"If we do this," he began, "can we agree not to activate the cheat until we're certain we don't have another choice?"

Everyone glanced around the room. Heads began to nod, all but Chenji's.

"There is no other choice," said Chenji. "Mezo is giving us this test, which means she had a hand in building whatever simulation we're going to face. We'll get no mercy in there." Chenji's hands began to shake. He tucked them in his pockets.

A long silence fell over them. Kano felt their collective dread filling the air as the weight of the next day pressed upon them. He looked around the room, realizing this could be one of the last moments he and his friends all shared together.

"Wait for my order, tomorrow," Kano finally said. "But when I call it, we're all in."

Chapter 8

The Arena

"Time to close up!" called Ragar from the upper deck.

Junior roused, reminded of the fender that he was in the middle of polishing. He'd lost track of time, which tended to happen in a city with no sunlight. All the hours blended together here, until he couldn't remember which speeders he'd worked on that day or the days prior. All he knew was that a straw mat was waiting for him upstairs. Was it comfortable? No. Would he sleep? Like a baby.

He closed the garage doors one by one. It wasn't until he reached the last one that he spotted a figure staring at him from across the alleyway, silhouetted by the streetlights behind it, its shadow reaching out into the garage beneath his feet.

"We're closed!" he called, placing his hand behind his back and readying a flame, the other hand checking that his Taloan mask was secure.

The figure stepped back into the streetlights, which revealed her pale, weaselly face beneath her hoodie.

"YOU!" Junior charged down the alley. The thief bolted. When Junior reached the street, she was already three buildings away.

She's fast. He chased her into a tunnel. There were only a handful of people around, all late-night shoppers heading in and out of the den. The girl maneuvered around them with ease, never breaking stride as she cleared the tunnel. Junior felt his chest getting tight, his breath getting heavy. By the time he reached the end of the tunnel, she was out of sight and he was winded. He had entered the dreadnought's Transitway. Several railways loomed overhead – what was left of them, at least. Several train cars lay collapsed on the ground. He searched them but found no sign of his target.

A coin landed at his feet. He looked up. The girl was perched on a support beam of the nearest railway. She waved his coin pouch at him. He didn't like that.

Junior grabbed onto the beam and began to climb. The metal was slippery and had little purchase for him, making his ascent slow, and leaving him to wonder how the girl had scaled it so quickly. It wasn't until he'd almost reached her that the girl slid down the opposite side of the beam and continued her run.

"That's it!" Junior heaved a fireball in the direction she was running. His goal was to block her path, but he missed and struck right at her feet, the fireball swallowing her in a plume of smoke and ash.

Oh shit. He slid down the beam and raced over, expecting to find her injured on the ground, but when the smoke cleared, she was gone.

He searched frantically. *How?*

A whistle echoed down the Transitway. He turned. The girl stood in the distance, her arms crossed. She didn't seem to be having fun anymore.

"It's nothing personal," he said, approaching her with his arm outstretched. "Just give it back and we'll forget this ever happened."

She took a step back toward a staircase that descended into darkness. A staircase where anything could be hiding.

He stopped. "You're baiting me," he said. "Who are you working for?"

She pointed to herself.

"Where are you taking me?"

She tilted her head as if to say, "You'll have to follow me to find out."

"Why should I trust you?"

She smiled, then vanished in puff of smoke.

Zoboros! He raced down the stairs, fists ready in case an ambush was waiting, though he doubted that now. There was something bigger going on here for her to reveal her powers to him. But how did she know he was Zoboros too? Was she in league with T8's 'boss'? And what did she stand to gain by bringing him here? The money in that pouch was enough to set her up for a long time.

As he descended the stairs, it became clear that nothing secret was happening below. Distant voices echoed up the shaft, loud and numerous, and he felt a powerful rumble shake the steps at his feet.

The girl was waiting for him at the bottom of the stairs. She stood beside a small hatch in the ground. Before he could ask her any of his many, burning questions, she opened the hatch, and a thousand voices exploded out.

Junior's jaw dropped as he followed her through the hatch, for here they stood high in the rafters above what Junior assumed had once been a hangar. Instead of ships, though, the hangar now housed a massive crowd, all packed into risers that had been assembled along the towering walls. Even more people were crowded along the hangar floor in rows of foldout chairs that surrounded a raised central ring. Junior couldn't make out what was happening in the ring; from here, it looked like two ants leaping at each other.

The girl grabbed his hand. There was a puff of smoke, and a moment later he was standing in the middle of the risers, hordes of people stamping their feet around him.

Junior blinked, trying to wrap his head around that sudden jump through space. It had been so quick, so easy. Could she teleport farther than that? As far as Drezdan, perhaps? That would certainly solve a lot of his problems.

"SEVAS! SEVAS!" someone screamed beside him. Others were screaming it, too, until it overpowered all the other shouts in the arena. He turned his attention back to the ring. He could see the fighters more clearly now: a Human, lying on his hands and knees, blood trickling down his face, and a Nurrano standing over him, her blue and black argyle skin looking somehow familiar.

Another puff and they were standing at the edge of the ring. Junior could practically smell the sweat pouring off the fighters from here. Better yet, he could identify the Nurrano: *Yui*. The girl from the noodle shop. But that meant…

"Well it's about time!" exclaimed a familiar voice. Junior turned, his stomach knotting at the sight of the red face that was approaching him.

"Well I'll be damned!" said Clemens, pointing a long black nail in Junior's direction, his yellow eyes turning toward the girl. "*This* is your mark?"

She nodded.

Mark? All at once, Junior realized what was happening. He glanced back at the ring, where Yui delivered a final punch right into the other fighter's face that knocked the poor Human's lights out.

"This is a mistake," said Junior, backing away. "I'm not here to fight."

Clemens ignored Junior. "What's your wager?" he asked the girl.

The girl answered by tossing Junior's coin pouch to him. Clemens dug his nails inside it, inspecting. A smile creeped across his face.

"That's my money!" cried Junior. "I came to get it back!" He reached for the pouch, and Clemens caught him by the collar.

"You want it back?" Clemens hissed in his ear. "Earn it."

Two Del Clorans passed by, carting the Human away on a stretcher. The Human was barely recognizable, his face swollen from a dozen blows.

Junior shoved Clemens aside and tried to make a break for it, but Roger the Gorv was right there. It caught Junior in its massive paw and tossed him into the ring.

This isn't happening, he thought as he got back on his feet. He needed to get out, *now*. He turned toward the edge of the ring. Posts rose along its perimeter and a field of electricity began crackling between them. On the other side of the electric field, Junior saw Clemens smiling.

Slowly, Junior turned to face Yui.

"Is electricity your weakness?" she asked, her brown eyes sizing him up. "Or are you just scared?"

Weakness? "This is a mistake!" he called to her. "I didn't come here to fight anybody!"

Boos erupted from the crowd. They tossed their food and empty bottles at him. He stepped out of their range, feeling hot under the ears. He just wanted to get out of here. He wanted to go back to the straw mat.

"Your move, big guy," said Yui.

Junior shook his head.

She shrugged and balled her hand into a fist. He took a step back as cold air sprayed out between her fingers. The air turned to ice, and the ice formed into a long spear.

Oh no. Now it all made sense. *This* was why he wasn't supposed to reveal his powers. Why Warp had led him here. Why his father always cursed the Taipa Kanani.

He'd stumbled right into a Zoboros fight ring.

"Does our new challenger have what it takes to melt the Ice Queen's cold, cold heart?" boomed Clemens's voice through the loudspeakers.

Yui heaved the spear at him. His hands shot up and fire erupted from them, blasting the spear apart into steamy chunks of ice.

A gasp ran through the crowd. Yui stared back at him, stunned, her jaw hanging dumbly.

"Cheven Sahar?" she whispered.

"I— I don't speak that language," replied Junior. He heard the same foreign phrase echo through the crowd. All eyes were on him. They recognized him, he realized. They recognized his power from that video Cassius had told him about.

Well, no use hiding it now. Junior tore off his Taloan mask. "My name is Aaron Hendricks Junior!" he exclaimed, turning back to Yui. "And I'm not here to fight you."

"But you have to," she whispered.

Junior shook his head as more boos echoed from the crowd.

"You don't have a choice!" She reached out her hands and an icy wind blasted from them. Junior dove out of the way as ice formed on the ground where he had just stood. She kept turning toward him as he sidled around her, the ice trailing after him. He broke into a run and summoned up a fireball. His accuracy was miserable while running, but he threw it anyway. It burst a few feet away from its target; she didn't even flinch.

"Throw it like you mean it!" she cried. She relinquished her icy blast and tucked one hand behind her back.

Watch that hand, Junior warned himself. He hurled a fireball and she blocked it with an ice blast from her free hand. Then the hidden hand swung out. From it, a curved icicle came spiraling toward him. He dove sideways, but not fast enough. It nicked his arm, which stung and burned as cold blood dripped from it.

He grimaced. He didn't like when people made him bleed.

Yui threw another icicle, but he was ready this time. He blasted fire to one side, launching himself out of the icicle's path. With his other hand, he hurled fireball after fireball, each one exploding at Yui's feet until finally one connected with her chest and launched her into the electric barrier. There was a loud *zap* and then she slumped forward.

Oh no. Junior ran toward her. He hadn't meant to knock her that far. When he gripped her limp arm, he found a pulse. Just unconscious. He sighed with relief, but then he remembered, thousands of people were watching him now. And they were all silent.

He turned to Clemens, who stared wide-eyed at him. Instead of saying something into the microphone, he raised his red hand into a fist.

For a moment, Junior thought that was a kill signal. He half expected a sniper to take him out, or the crowd to come swarming toward him, but then Clemens nodded his head toward his fist. He wanted Junior to do it too.

Slowly, Junior raised his fist up in the air. A sign of victory, he assumed. Victory over the crowd favorite. *This ought to end well*. He braced for whatever objects the crowd would throw at him. By the look on Clemens's face, the Tenu was bracing for the same.

But then the crowd roared.

Chapter 9

The Glitch

It was time.

The team stood on the white floor of the Sim, waiting for the test to begin. Kano looked to his friends. No one made eye contact with him; they were all too focused on checking their gear or calming their own nerves as they prepared for whatever horrors Mezo and Carmichael would throw at them.

"We got this, we got this," Jaden repeated, mostly to himself. He checked for the twelfth time to make sure his datapad was securely tucked in his pack.

We definitely got this, Kano told himself. He needed to believe it, more than anyone else on the team, because if he didn't, then the others wouldn't either.

He would get them to the finish line, whatever it took.

Carmichael descended toward them on his disk, helmet in hand, Cera at his side.

"Today's mission will be different from the ones you're used to," began the captain. "You're to rescue a group of evacuees from a warzone. Find and protect them until their shuttle takes off. If too many evacuees die, you lose. If any member of your team dies, you lose. If the shuttle is destroyed or unable to launch, you lose. Any questions?"

Silence.

"Good," said Carmichael. "Remember, you have everything you need to accomplish your mission." He placed the helmet on his head and ascended. Cera kept her eyes locked on Kano's, a silent reminder for him to keep it together. Kano had heard that she put up quite a fight to join them on today's simulation, but her demand had been promptly denied by Mezo.

The lights faded. The wind picked up. The floor shifted in the darkness. Kano expected to feel the loose grains of the canyon rolling against his feet, but this terrain was different. Harder. He knelt and gave the floor a tap. Metal.

Screams echoed through the darkness, not from his own team, and not from Greavenaughts either, but from the simulated chaos happening somewhere outside their formation.

"Brace yourselves," said Kano. "We've never seen this place before."

But he was wrong. When the light returned, a hundred floating platforms surrounded them, each bobbing and weaving within a twilit sky. Great towers filled each platform, most of them ablaze as explosions rocked the floating city.

That *bitch*.

"Look out!" Makoto pulled Kano out of the way as a falling platform collided with their own. Glass and rubble rained around them. Their platform began to tilt as the weight of the fallen one pressed against it. They tried to run, but the floor quickly tipped beneath their feet, and all six of them began sliding toward the flames.

"Form up behind me!" called Kano. His friends obeyed, Makoto, Li, Jaden, Chenji, and Akio lining up at his back. He threw a shockwave that blasted the burning debris out of their path. It was enough to keep them alive for a few moments more, but it would do nothing to stop them from spilling over the edge and into the abyss beneath the city.

"I don't suppose the Trampoline is still in play?!" called Jaden over the screams of nearby Famorans.

Kano shook his head. "Even if Mezo kept the tractor beams active, they would take too long to bring us back to the city," he called back.

"Check your belts!" said Akio. Kano looked; a grappling hook had materialized there, courtesy of Carmichael. He unlatched it and took aim at an adjacent platform.

Six grappling hooks snagged onto the other platform. Space ran out beneath them. They swung hard over the abyss; Kano held on with all his might, refusing to let the force of the fall sever his grip. After a few wild swings, he and his friends found their momentum slowing.

Akio squeezed the trigger on his grapple first, reeling himself up to the platform. The others followed suit.

"This simulation is all sorts of messed up!" cried Jaden. As soon as he climbed onto the platform, he pulled out his datapad and started the activation sequence.

"Wait!" said Li. "We're still in the game. We can still complete the mission."

"Look at the city!" Jaden snapped back, waving a hand at the many platforms that were either burning, falling, or both. "We'd have better luck finding the Artifact than rescuing anyone from this."

Everyone turned to Kano, expecting an answer.

Focus on the moment. He shook away the shock of seeing his hometown being ripped apart and dialed in on the screams coming from the distance. He followed the sound to the Crossing, a spiraling walkway that led down the full height of Famora, a place he and his friends had been intimately familiar with when they lived here. The evacuation shuttle sat on a platform at the bottom, its engines just beginning their prelaunch sequence. Dozens of people scrambled up its entrance ramp as fire bellowed out of the surrounding buildings, all of them looking like ants from here. It was too far to run or grapple to.

"We need a way to reach the evacuees," said Kano, pointing.

"Use the datapad first," said Chenji. "All it takes is one of us getting shot for the simulation to end. We should even the odds."

"No," said Kano. "It may seem like we're at a disadvantage to you, but for the rest of us, this is our home turf. This is winnable."

That seemed to spark something in the team. Jaden stepped forward and cleared his throat, now willing to play ball. "There's a hovercar over there that we can use."

"Where are the keys?" asked Li.

Jaden scoffed, offended that she would even ask. He nodded to Makoto, who drew a baton from his belt and smashed the driver-side window. Jaden then climbed inside, pried the underside of the steering wheel out of place, and began snapping and reconnecting wires like an artist at his craft. Kano shook his head, wondering how many times the two of them had hotwired hovercars.

The headlights flicked on and the engine roared to life.

"Everyone get in!" said Jaden. They piled into the back and Jaden took off without delay.

As they approached the shuttle, they found the evacuation in chaos. Famorans ran, stumbled, and limped out of side streets and alleys, most of them covered in ash or blood, some too injured to even scale the entrance ramp without assistance.

Kano was the first one out of the hovercar as it touched down.

"What happened?!" he called out. He assumed someone in the crowd could tell him why Famora was in flames.

"The bots!" a young Nurrano screamed as she ran past them.

"Bots?" repeated Makoto.

There was a scream. Two retrieval bots floated toward the team upon their hoverpad bases. They each had a single, glowing red eye, which normally looked adorable to Kano, but for some reason now made them look hostile. Perhaps it was because of the machine guns they carried in their skinny metal arms.

"Die Human!" one of them blurted.

Kano hurled a shockwave that sent one of them sailing into the abyss, while Jaden put a bullet through the eye of the other.

"Sounds like Carmichael's been watching those crummy sci-fi movies again," said Jaden as he reloaded.

"Jaden and Chenji, do a flyover and see if you can spot any more survivors," ordered Kano.

Chenji turned into a bird on command and flew away. Jaden hopped back in the hovercar and drove in the opposite direction.

"Makoto, Akio, I need you to—"

Another scream. Retrieval bots rained down on the ramp, scooping up evacuees in their arms.

"We know what to do, boy of thunder," said Akio, a hint of excitement in his voice. He and Makoto charged up the ramp. Makoto drove his stun baton into the nearest bot and zapped it out of commission. Akio vaulted over Makoto's back, launching himself high enough so his long arm could snag one of the bots as it tried to float away with a child. Akio drew his knife and jammed it into the bot's red eye. It died in midair, releasing the child.

"Nurrano boy!" Akio called.

Makoto dove and caught the child, smiling up as the Jakari vaulted onto the next bot and began stabbing it.

"Where do you need me?" Li asked Kano, her glowing hands waving over each person as they limped by, giving each one a nice boost.

"Stay here with me," he replied. "The shuttle is our biggest lifeline; that's where they'll concentrate their attacks." He paused, thinking. "You might need some plants."

She smiled and drew a vile full of seeds from her belt. She smashed it on the floor and reached out with a glowing hand, the seeds exploding into dozens of leafy green vines, each thick and healthy. More bots swooped toward them and the vines lashed at them like tentacles, trapping them all in a mighty web.

A crack echoed across the platform. They spun around. A ten-story building was tumbling toward them in a wave of crumbling concrete. People screamed. Kano sent out a shockwave that blasted the debris in the opposite direction, leaving only dust particles to strike the shuttle.

"Your training's paying off," said Li.

"Careful," he said. "Carmichael likes it when we get cocky."

His communicator buzzed. He tapped it.

"I picked up a few survivors," came Jaden's voice, "but there's one trapped under some debris. Just north of your position."

"I'm with her now," came Chenji's voice over the comms. "But I could use an assist."

Kano raced around the shuttle as its engines roared to life. He had only minutes before it would be airborne. Fortunately, Chenji was easy to spot when he took the form of a giant, white-haired gorilla.

The gorilla strained as it tried to lift a slab of collapsed concrete off the legs of a Braiman. The Braiman whimpered as Kano knelt beside her, assessing the situation. If Chenji's gorilla form was straining this much, Kano's puny muscles would do little to help. He would need his powers, though at this proximity he ran the risk of injuring the Braiman further.

"Chenji, can you flick the slab up higher so I can get an angle on it?"

"It'll come down fast," cautioned Chenji in a deep ape voice.

"I know." If Kano didn't hit it hard enough, the slab would crush the Braiman's legs completely. He tried reminding himself that she wasn't real, but the terrified look in her tear-filled eyes made that hard to do.

"Throw it now!" ordered Kano. Chenji gave a mighty grunt and shoved the slab however little he could. Kano slid in beside the woman, his power already charged in his fist as the slab swung back toward them. He blasted it at an angle and it tilted back up, almost upright, but still wanting to fall toward them. He rose and blasted it again, tipping it the opposite direction so it could crash down away from the Braiman.

"Thank you," she said through her tendrils, grimacing as she tried to move. Kano saw her legs were broken and bloodied. He motioned to Chenji. The ape reached out its big palms to scoop her up.

But they phased right through the Braiman.

What? Kano saw the blue projector light catching onto the back of Chenji's hand. That's not how the simulated people worked. They were supposed to feel as real as everything else. He jammed on his communicator.

"Everyone, it's a trap!"

Chenji screamed as lightning danced across his body.

A pair of metal boots slammed down where the projected Braiman laid, phasing through her. Chenji convulsed on the floor while Kano drew his fist back, summoning a shockwave, but a bolt of lightning caught him before he could release it, dancing from Taranis's fingertip and sending Kano into convulsions of his own.

It feels real! Like needles stabbing into every muscle. The lightning ceased and Kano gasped, staring up at the metal mask as its grooves glowed with electricity.

"I have the package," Taranis said into his communicator.

Kano tried to throw his fist again, but he was met with another bolt of electricity. He screamed and sank, smoke rising from his chest.

"When are you going to learn to sit still?" asked Taranis, his boots clinking closer. Kano tried to inch back, but his limbs were still twitching, refusing to do what he asked. All he could do was stare at the monster marching toward him.

Suddenly, the metal of Taranis's suit glowed blindingly bright with...*headlights*. A rusty hovercar plowed into Taranis and drove him straight into a pile of debris.

"JADEN!" Kano rose on shaky legs and stumbled toward the hovercar, falling with every few steps.

The driver door opened. Jaden spilled out onto the concrete. Kano fell to his knees beside him and tried lifting his friend off the ground. Jaden's flight suit felt damp. Kano smelled blood.

"This…is this real?" asked Jaden, shaking.

"It's not supposed to be," said Kano, panicking.

A blue glow flared from the pile of debris. A gauntlet reached out and crunched into the hood of the hovercar.

Kano drew back his arm to throw a shockwave, but when the power reached his fist, his muscles spasmed, sending the energy sputtering out at an odd angle that threw Kano back to the floor.

I don't have control. He looked down at his shaking hands. They were useless to him, but if he didn't fight back, the simulation would be lost. And worse, the simulation might actually kill them this time.

"Jaden!" he shouted over the crunch of metal as Taranis dug himself out from behind the hovercar.

Jaden didn't hear him, though, too fixated on the blood trickling from his forehead.

"Jaden, do it!" screamed Kano.

Jaden snapped back into the moment. He reached into the hovercar and pulled out his pack. He dug inside it, but he looked lost, in a daze, unable to find anything.

Kano rushed to his side, pulled the datapad from the pack, and jammed it into Jaden's hand. Jaden looked up at him, his eyes searching for a final confirmation.

The shuttle roared as it entered its final sequence. A metal hand reached out. Lightning launched from it and struck the back of the shuttle with a crack, killing one of the engines.

"Now!" screamed Kano.

Jaden typed away. The screen pinged. Kano looked to the masked man and saw the blue glow drain from his mask.

"I think it's working," he said.

Taranis screamed. His armored body contorted, folding in on itself over and over until he burst into pixels.

Thank goodness. Kano nodded to Jaden. It was over.

Screams echoed from the other side of the shuttle. Kano turned. Li was running toward them.

"Kano!" she cried. "Something's wrong!"

The survivors were running after Li. They screamed in pain and started to collapse, their limbs folding on themselves like origami. Buildings crumbled around them, sending up dust and debris that pixelated in the air, the pixels buffering, freezing.

Cera's voice cried out through their communicators. "Captain, what's wrong?! CAPTAIN!"

Famora shattered into a sea of pixels, replaced by the bright lights of the white room. The disk crashed down beside them and tossed Carmichael and Cera across the floor. Kano caught Cera from her tumble, but the captain continued to roll away.

"Are you alright?!" he cried.

"Carmichael!" she screamed. "Help him!"

Kano turned. The captain convulsed on the floor, drool dripping from his mouth, the helmet still stuck to his head. Li was on him first. She ripped the helmet off.

"Help me roll him on his side!" she cried.

Kano was there in an instant. "Can you heal him?" he asked, trying to get the captain on his side, but Carmichael shook so violently it was hard to get a grip on him.

"There's no healing a seizure," she said, trying to maintain her composure. "We have to let it pass."

Kano looked over his shoulder for help. He saw Jaden standing there, datapad in hand, frozen with horror, an ugly gash still lingering on his forehead.

What did we do?

Carmichael thrashed beside him, his head thumping against the ground.

"CERA!" screamed Li. A green cushion of energy materialized beneath Carmichael's head, absorbing the blows.

The convulsions slowed. A bit of blood trickled out of Carmichael's mouth.

"No, no, no," Li raised a glowing hand over his mouth. The bleeding stopped.

"Is that hemorrhaging?" cried Cera, diving in beside them.

Li shook her head. "The blood was from his tongue. He bit it when he crashed. He'll need to be checked for anything more serious."

Cera nodded, relieved. Kano was too, but also scared. How much damage had they done to Carmichael?

The hydraulic doors flung open. Medics rushed in, checked Carmichael, and carted him away on a stretcher. Kano watched the whole scene as if from another body; as if this was one of his nightmares, and any moment he would be waking up to bang his head against Jaden's bunk.

But Jaden stood right beside him and let the datapad drop to the floor.

Kano felt the eyes of his teammates on him, all searching for something. An order, an idea, a plan…anything to give them some direction.

"Is he going to be okay?" Makoto asked him.

"I don't know."

"Does that mean we failed?" asked Chenji.

"I don't know!"

Everyone took a half-step away from Kano while he processed this. While he tried to understand how everything could have gone so wrong.

Li approached him first. "What happens to us now?" she whispered.

"I don't know."

Chapter 10

The Champion's Club

Junior threw up for the third time that morning.

"Breakfast is ready, party boy," someone snickered from outside the bathroom door.

Junior's stomach growled. He longed for food, but he didn't know if he could hold it down. Besides that, he felt like a knife was stabbing repeatedly through his forehead. As he stared at the bile in the toilet, he told himself he never wanted to drink again.

Then again, last night had been fun…

The smell of bacon crept into the bathroom. His stomach growled again. He sighed, adjusted his indoor sunglasses, and entered back into the Champion's Club.

The clubhouse had looked nice when they brought him up here last night. A full-service bar, giant TV screens, plenty of couches to crash on, and more food than they could ever hope to eat. Now, however, most of the furniture was overturned, the couch cushions stained with drinks, and the staff were methodically cleaning up the trash littered everywhere. In the back, two repairmen were replacing a large window that overlooked the arena. Evidently, someone had smashed a hole in it.

Junior found the other four fighters gathered in the adjacent dining room. They were talking and laughing loud enough to reignite his headache. He considered waiting for them to finish before claiming his breakfast, but they spotted him before he could veer away.

"There he is!" announced Zivo. A Talak, he had a long face that ended in sharp points at the top and bottom. He drummed his six hands against the table like he was announcing the arrival of royalty. "Our one and only Hellfire!"

That name triggered a faded memory from last night. Junior had been chugging a Scorcher while the others chanted it. As they had done for the Ice Queen before, the group had christened him.

Nera motioned toward an empty seat beside her. Junior approached it, his feet sticking to the floor with every step (the janitor was still working his way over with the mop). He did his best not to stare at Nera, though it was hard to contain his curiosity – he'd never met a Norphimian before. She had scaly, greenish-bluish skin and webbings between her fingers and toes. Fins lined her arms and legs, and a crown of spongey red cartilage topped her head. Norphimians rarely left their homeworld (or the ocean), which begged the question as to why she'd chosen to come to this dump of all places.

When he sat, his attention was promptly stolen by the banquet that had been arranged before them. Egg frittata, smoked tentacles, freshly toasted baguettes, buleruck sausage, and, to top it all off, trays of bacon. Junior had never imagined such a breakfast could exist in Casus Belli.

"I can tell you're gonna like it here," said Zivo, his arms amassing food on his plate at record speed. Once satisfied, a hole opened in one of his wrists, and through it he produced a fork and knife. Junior blinked. He had to remind himself that he was at a table surrounded by Zoboros.

Nera waved her hand; water rose from a pitcher and jetted into Junior's cup. "You should rehydrate," she said, cutting herself a small piece of frittata and placing it delicately on her plate. "And some greens to replenish the vitamins you lost."

Junior found it amusing that Nera was the one giving him hangover advice, considering she'd been the only one not drinking last night.

"He's gonna need it," snickered Brivek from across the table. A big-gutted Vosni, he loomed over the table, practically inhaling the food as the servers brought it to his plate. Of all the fighters, it was easiest for Junior to figure why Brivek had come to Casus Belli: his people lacked pigmentation, so a dark city that admitted Zoboros was a natural choice for the one they called the Pale Warrior, though Junior still wasn't sure what Brivek's powers were.

Behind Brivek, Junior noticed a line of statues. Each statue depicted fighters who looked powerful, imposing, and filled with pride.

"The wall of champions," Nera whispered, noticing his stare. "A great honor to be placed there."

Junior found "honor" an ironic word to use in an illegal Zoboros fight ring, but he kept his opinion to himself. Besides, the statues presented a new idea: if he was surrounded by local Zoboros history, then perhaps someone here could help him in his search.

"Who was the strongest champion to pass through here?" he asked casually, hoping no one would pick up the personal motivations behind his question. From what he had gathered, his mother was one of the most powerful Zoboros ever known. If she had fought here, the locals would remember.

Zivo leaned back, giving it some thought. "Maybe…oh I know! Kenji the Kraken!"

"Ohhh, dats a goo one," said Brivek through a mouthful of frittata.

"No, Tsunami was better!" said Nera.

"You're only saying that because he controlled water," Zivo fired back. Brivek nodded in agreement.

"Yui, back me up here," said Nera. "Tsunami or Kenji?"

Yui didn't look up from her poached egg. She hadn't looked up since Junior had joined them at the table.

"Hey Ice Queen, any chance you could warm up a bit?" asked Zivo. "The rest of us lose every once in a while. Get used to it."

"Don't give her a hard time, Zivo," said Nera. "It's not every day you face your *kama*."

All eyes turned toward Junior.

"Her what?" he asked.

"Sorry, her *weakness*," answered Nera. "For every power, there's another one out there that can naturally beat it. You're Yui's kama because your powers can melt her ice, just like she's my kama because she can freeze my water."

Junior nodded with fascination. No one ever spoke openly about the Zoboros, least of all other Zoboros, but here they had formed their own culture, their own phrases, their own way of life. It was exciting. There was so much more he wanted to learn from them…but he had to be careful. They still worked for the Taipa. Say the wrong thing and he could end up in a shallow desert grave.

A server, seeing Junior's plate was empty, put some eggs and toast on it.

Junior drew a cyo from his pocket, one of a handful he'd won from Zivo in a game of nixus last night (before his memory had tanked), and offered it, but the server shook her head and hurried out of the dining room.

Strange. Now that he thought about it, none of the servers had taken any tips last night. And none of them had spoken, either.

"Is there some kind of code here for the staff?" he asked.

The others glanced at each other until Nera finally spoke. "Well, they're not *technically* staff…"

The door burst open and Clemens strutted through, a girl wrapped in each arm.

"There's my champion!" he exclaimed. He pinched Junior's cheeks, exhaling fumes of alcohol in his face. It took every ounce of restraint Junior possessed not to ignite the liquor on Clemens's lips.

Clemens shifted his gaze to the cyo in Junior's hand. "What are you doin' with this?" he asked, scooping the coin in his long nails. "This is chump change, Heatwave."

"I thought we agreed on 'Hellfire'," said Zivo.

Clemens smiled. It was hideous. "Hellfire…I like it. Scary. People pay for scary. Speakin' of pay, here's your winnings from last night." He slapped a fat stack of cash in front of Junior. "I've been gettin' calls from all over the quadrant about 'the Famoran in the fight ring'. I see a lot more winnings in your future, Hellfire."

Junior stared at the cash in front of him, his anger rising. He wasn't Clemens's money machine; he had no obligation to keep fighting for him.

"I see a lot more in my future, too," he said as Clemens headed happily for the door. "Because you're short."

Clemens stopped, his smile fading. "What did you say?"

"That thief of yours bet *my* money," said Junior. "It was worth double what you just gave me, and eight times as much given my odds last night."

Clemens's eyes narrowed on Junior. He looked ready to strike, but held back. He and Junior both knew that the 'Famoran in the fight ring' could leave anytime he wanted.

"I guess you'll have to take it up with her, then," said Clemens flatly, then marched out the door.

The room went silent. Nera waited until Clemens was long gone before she finally whispered, "I advise caution with him. If he gets upset, he might…" She trailed off, staring at some of the empty seats around the table.

"He might ship us to another game master who ain't as forgiving," finished Zivo.

"Why not leave?" asked Junior. Each of them could easily beat Clemens in a fight. What were they so afraid of?

"He has ways of finding us," said Brivek, pushing his plate forward, his appetite suddenly lost. "Once you get cozy with the Taipa, they don't like to let you go."

Junior stiffened. Did Clemens think he was Taipa property just because he got shoved into a fight ring last night? That Viper had to be pretty full of himself to think a tattoo gave him that much power. Then again, he'd only seen one person challenge Clemens's power so far.

"Who controls the bots?" asked Junior.

The others exchanged glances, confused.

"I saw one threaten Clemens," he continued. "It had a 'boss'. Who?"

Zivo grinned. "They say the bots are controlled by a cyborg." Everyone at the table rolled their eyes. But Junior leaned forward, which was all Zivo needed to continue his tale. "They say there's a castle deep in the desert, and in that castle lives a cyborg who makes bots out of the scraps he finds—"

"And sends the bots to steal little children who don't finish their supper," finished Brivek. "I've heard this one before."

Zivo hushed his voice. "Whoever he is, even the Taipa are scared of him. You got a better explanation as to why, Brivek?"

"They could've been programmed by the IDF. Or a rival gang."

"No gang has enough leverage to let their bots roam free in Taipa territory," said Zivo. "I'm telling you, they've got some kind of arrangement with the cyborg."

"Based on what evidence?" asked Nera as she nibbled at her frittata.

"Those bots have been spotted all over the planet," said Zivo. This got Junior's interest. "They're his eyes and ears. I'll bet he has dirt on everyone and everything in Mogaddu."

Including other Zoboros, thought Junior.

"Then explain why no ever sees him," said Nera.

"Because he never leaves the castle," said Zivo. "Many have tried to enter. You can find their bodies rotting around the perimeter."

"Do you know where this castle is?" asked Junior. Everyone turned to him, surprised at his interest. He didn't believe Zivo's superstitious mumbo jumbo, but he suspected there might be some truth behind it. If there was someone with bots patrolling the planet, they might know if his mother had ever passed through.

"I've never been out in the deep desert," said Zivo. "But that land wasn't always desert. In ancient times, it was fertile ground to build castles and kingdoms on. If you get your hands on an old map, you might be able to narrow it down."

Junior needed more than a map. He needed transportation, and for that he needed his winnings. And, if these rumors were true, he would also need a way to slip past castle security.

Fortunately, all these problems could be solved by the same person.

He looked out the new window that the repairmen were adjusting into place. Clemens was skulking around the empty arena, his thief trailing him like a shadow.

"Does she fight?" he asked, pointing. Clemens was speaking to her, and he didn't look happy.

"You mean Warp?" asked Brivek. "Nah. She doesn't talk either. She just hangs around until Clemens has a job for her."

"What kind of jobs?" asked Junior, but before he could get an answer, he saw a red hand slap Warp across the face. Junior rose from his seat, his fists clenched, though he wasn't sure why. That girl had robbed and tricked him, so why did he feel so angry to see her hurt? Perhaps it was because it was Clemens's hand that did it. Whatever the reason, he found himself marching for the door.

"Didn't you want to know who the best fighter was?" asked Yui.

Junior stopped. It was the first time she'd spoken since he'd arrived.

"There's been talk of a new fighter," she continued. "A better one. On Moraban."

Everyone at the table got uneasy at the mention of that planet.

"Who?" asked Junior.

"They call him Calamity," said Zivo darkly. "I heard he kills in the ring."

"They play differently on Moraban," muttered Brivek.

"There's no way Clemens would let us get killed," said Nera. "He depends on us."

"I wouldn't be so sure," said Yui, who Junior now believed was living up to her title of Ice Queen. "Pitting the top fighter on Moraban against a Hero of Famora, now that would be a fight. People would pay anything just to see it, especially if only one came out in the end."

"Well good thing it'll be me," muttered Junior. He stormed off, having no reason to indulge Yui any further. Besides, he wanted his winnings. He checked out the window, but Clemens was alone in the arena now. *Dammit.* Warp had teleported, but where? Junior looked up to the only place he could think of: the rafters where she had snuck him into the arena. He was relieved to see her up there, her feet dangling over the edge.

Lucky for Junior, he already knew how to get there.

When he finally arrived, the metal walkway shook beneath his feet. Warp jumped up, fists clenched, ready to teleport.

"Wait! It's just me," Junior exclaimed.

She saw him and slowly lowered her defenses. She sat down and kept her back to him, sniffling.

This might take some convincing. He sat beside her and let his feet dangle as he tried to come up with something to say. He found himself staring at the ring below, where thousands had cheered him on the night before. Fighting was easy for him; he'd been training for it all his life. But trying to cheer someone up, that wasn't the kind of skill one practiced when they grew up with no mother, no siblings, and a very distant father.

"Where are you from?" he asked, immediately feeling stupid for saying it. She didn't even look at him. *Try again, Junior*, she seemed to say.

He thought back to his last conversation with Clemens. He'd made the Viper angry by asking for his money. Perhaps that's what Clemens had been talking to Warp about.

"He didn't give you the rest of my winnings, did he?"

She shook her head.

"Is he always this stingy?"

She smiled and nodded.

Her smile sparked something inside Junior. He wasn't sure what. "Why does everyone want to stay here?" he asked. "The other Zoboros. Is it really better than going somewhere else?"

Warp thought about it and shrugged.

Figures. Given the conditions most Zoboros faced in a galaxy that didn't want them, a fight ring probably didn't seem that bad, especially when it offered a clubhouse stocked with freshly cooked food.

"I was thinking of leaving for a bit. Do…do you wanna get out of here?"

She nodded insistently.

"It might be dangerous. I was gonna stop by Brinkborne first and buy a—"

She grabbed his hand, and a moment later they were standing in front of the machine shop.

Well, that'll do it, thought Junior as he led her inside. They found Ragar scrambling around the shop floor on his many legs.

"Where the hell have you been?!" he cried. "We've got orders out the ass!"

"Ragar," began Junior, but the Bolani had already hurried past him toward a speeder. "Ragar! I'm here as a customer."

"A what?" Ragar wiped a hand across his face, causing sweat to splatter right on Junior's shirt. "You're broke, how could you—?"

Junior waved the wad of cash Clemens had given him. Ragar's three eyes followed it like a hawk. "I'll take my old speeder back, please."

"W— would you like anything else?" Ragar stammered. With anyone else, he'd have pretended the speeder was worth even more and upped the price, but since Junior already knew the value of everything in the shop, Ragar's only choice was to try and sell him on more.

"Yes," said Junior. "Do you have any old maps?"

Chapter 11

Dock 584

Cera entered the waiting room and waved him over.

Finally, thought Kano. He'd been here for hours. The rest of the team had waited with him for a time (except Jaden, who himself had been checked into the infirmary), but one by one they had wandered back to bed. Li had stuck around the longest, but when she started to nod off, Kano had convinced her to leave. She tried to bring him back with her, but he refused. He couldn't leave until he'd spoken with Carmichael; firstly to apologize, but more importantly to secure the captain's help, as he was the only person who could protect them from Mezo's wrath.

Kano entered the infirmary. Hospital beds lined one side of the room, most of them empty. Jaden occupied one, but he was asleep, his head wrapped in bandages. Kano stared at his friend for a time, the guilt tugging at him.

"They call it depersonalization," came Carmichael's voice.

Kano turned. The captain sat a few beds away, a little paler than usual, but otherwise looking alright. A tremor of relief pulsed through Kano. There was something off about Carmichael, though; the way he stared into the middle distance, disconnected. Empty like the room around him.

"What are you talking about?" asked Kano.

"The simulation. I went through months of training to learn how to control that machine, to control what you see and feel. The most important part of that training was to make sure that no one inside the Sim got hurt. The trick is to distinguish what's real from what's imagined; that way you can pull your punches when necessary. When I created Taranis, though, I created something too familiar, too personal, so that once it appeared, I started to lose my sense of reality."

"And that's why it hurt Jaden," said Kano.

Carmichael nodded.

"And the seizure?"

"No, that was a sensory overload brought on by a couple of nameless hackers."

Kano felt the sting of Carmichael's comment, until he realized the captain was smiling. "I'm sorry about what happened, sir," he said. "It was my fault."

"Never apologize for doing what's necessary," replied Carmichael, looking into Kano's eyes for the first time. "You were right to assume the game was stacked against you. It is winnable, despite what Chenji may claim. But today's simulation was designed specifically to break you, if you hadn't already noticed."

"Because Mezo wanted to make sure that we lost," said Kano, clenching his fist.

"I can neither confirm nor deny her involvement," said Carmichael. "What I can tell you is that by hacking the game, you've made it even easier for her to court martial your friends and have them removed from the ship."

"A court martial?" said Kano, thinking. "But we can appeal that, can't we?"

"Mezo will ensure that it's just a formality. Unlike the simulation, this game is unfortunately *un*winnable."

They lapsed into a long silence, punctuated only by Jaden's snores. Normally, those snores would be a source of irritation for Kano, but in this moment, he clung on to them, knowing this could well be the last time he ever heard them.

He recalled when this same moment had come on Famora. The Orlovs had planned to separate him from his friends forever, and they had almost succeeded. At the time, Kano had thought it was the best solution, that by distancing himself from those he cared about they'd be out of danger. Now, he wasn't so sure. Danger seemed to follow them regardless, and the only reason they had survived it so far was by sticking together.

"What would you do?" he asked Carmichael.

Carmichael leaned closer, motioning for Kano to do the same. It wasn't until they were within inches of each other that the captain whispered, "I already told you, Kano: never apologize for doing what's necessary." The captain grasped his hand. Kano felt something slip into it. A card. He didn't risk looking at it, not when the security cameras were likely on him, but he'd already figured out what it was.

The captain's swipe card.

Kano stuffed it in his pocket. He felt the weight of it there, the power it held. This was a golden ticket, one that could grant him access to almost anything on the ship.

Including an escape vessel.

"Dock 584," whispered Carmichael before leaning back against his pillow. "Creating this team was always my mission. Protect it."

"What if I fail?"

"You haven't failed until you're dead. Everything else is just a steppingstone."

Kano nodded, not wanting to think of what a "steppingstone" might look like. He just wanted off this ship.

"Cera and Eines will be ready for you once I give the signal," said Carmichael.

"What's the signal?"

Carmichael flashed his trademark smile one last time. "You have five minutes, Zoboros." He punched the nurse call button and threw himself off the bed. Nurses rushed over as he thrashed on the floor. All eyes were on him while Kano crept quietly, invisibly toward an awakening Jaden.

"What'd you do this time?" asked Jaden, yawning.

Kano grabbed him by the arm and hoisted him out of bed.

"Hey, where are you taking me?" demanded Jaden, trying to keep his airy hospital gown from climbing too far up his legs as they walked.

"Change of plans." He flashed the swipe card at Jaden, who grinned from ear to ear.

"I suppose you'll need some help rounding up the troops," said Jaden.

"We have five minutes." They raced out of the infirmary and into the hallway, where a bird caught them halfway to the barracks.

"Where are we going, Chief?" cawed the bird in a voice similar to Chenji's.

"Where did you come from?" asked Kano as Chenji perched on his shoulder.

"I'm usually midnight snacking in the mess right now, but I thought I'd fly by and check on everybody. Good thing too, because the captain's not looking too good."

"Don't worry about him," said Kano. "Just stick with us."

"Aye aye, sir!"

They crossed into the barracks, where Jaden made a beeline for their shared cabin.

"The others are this way!" Kano called.

"I need pants!" said Jaden as he disappeared inside.

Kano banged on Li's door while Chenji fluttered over to Makoto's and began pecking on it. Li appeared a few moments later, looking immaculate despite clearly having just been woken up.

"Did something happen in the infirmary?!" she asked, startled.

"Sort of," said Kano quickly. "We've got a ride, but we need to leave now."

Li's eyes narrowed. "Who? Can we trust them?"

"More than I trust anyone else on this ship."

"That's not saying much!" called Jaden, buttoning his pants as he rushed out of his room, his datapad slung over his back in a satchel.

Kano looked into Li's eyes. "You trust me, right?"

She nodded, then reached out her hand toward a potted plant by the sink. The plant rose out of the soil, roots and all, and slithered up the fabric beneath her flight suit, ready to surprise any guard who might come their way. "Insurance purposes," she said.

"That's why you're the best on the team," said Kano. He didn't notice her blush as he banged on Akio's door. There was no response.

"Where the hell is he?" demanded Makoto, who was just emerging from his room.

"Here!" Everyone jumped as Akio dropped from one of the air vents above.

"Where were you?" asked Li.

"Shield girl told me plan," he replied. "Your way is clear."

No one understood what Akio meant until they entered the Transitway and found all the cameras down. The techs and service bots were scrambling to fix them, too preoccupied to notice a group of kids and a Jakari rushing toward the hangar, which was locked at this hour. Kano swiped Carmichael's card and the doors parted before them.

Together, all six of them hurried inside. The hangar was eerily quiet, the lights dimmed, obscuring everything more than a few docks ahead. Chenji swooped high over their heads and surveyed.

"Don't see any guards," he whispered as he fluttered past Kano's ear.

"You won't," said Akio, smiling.

"Where's our ride?" asked Jaden.

Kano pointed to Dock 584. The Pincer sat there, its ramp lowered, Cera standing beside it. She waved at them to hurry.

Through the windscreen, Kano spotted Eines making a preflight check.

It's really happening, thought Kano as they approached. *We're leaving*.

"This is going much better than usual for us," said Jaden as they neared the ramp.

It is. Kano stopped dead in his tracks. He listened. Something wasn't right.

The others kept running ahead, but Makoto stopped beside him, sensing it too.

"Kano!" he cried. He leaped in front of his brother and absorbed a stun bolt that leaped out of the shadows.

"Makoto!" cried Kano. His brother slumped to the floor, paralyzed. The others stopped, realizing the trap they had fallen into.

"Circle up around me!" ordered Kano. They did, taking aim in every direction, but all they saw were shadows between the dimly lit ships.

"Who was that?" demanded Chenji as he morphed into a gorilla and slung Makoto over his shoulder.

Kano had an idea, but he didn't want to say. It was the thing he'd been dreading since he'd learned of it. Dreading even more than he dreaded Taranis.

Because these things were designed to kill enemies like Taranis.

Akio drew his knife and climbed onto Kano's back. "I will be the eyes on the back of your head, boy of thunder. Lead everyone to the ship. Fast."

Kano obeyed. Their circle started toward the ship. All was quiet save for their footsteps. Cera remained planted where she was, knowing that if she left her post, their attackers could cut off their one means of escape.

"No sudden movements," whispered Akio in Kano's ear, barely audible. "At your seven o'clock. Wait for my signal."

Kano didn't know what his target would look like, but he trusted Akio's heightened senses to spot it in the darkness.

"Three taps, then attack," whispered Akio. On the first tap on the shoulder, Kano kept moving as if nothing had happened. On the second tap, he loaded the energy into his palm.

On the third, Li screamed.

Kano threw out his fist and a wave like thunder rolled over the nearby ships. It nudged them out of place, their anchors grinding along the floor in a shower of sparks, but his shockwave found no enemies in its path. He looked to Li. She had her roots out, ready to strike, but whoever she was aiming at dove back into the shadows.

"Keep it together, team!" he called, as much to motivate himself as everyone else.

"Two o'—!" cried Akio as a blue flash whizzed by Kano's head. He felt his little friend go limp on his shoulder, and then Akio spilled onto the floor.

"No!" he cried.

"We gotta make a break for it!" screamed Jaden, abandoning the circle and steering straight for the ramp.

"Jaden, NO!" cried Kano, but it was too late. A stun bolt caught Jaden between the shoulders, and he was down.

"It's just us Zoboros now," said Chenji in his gruff gorilla voice.

"Why don't they just take us out?" asked Li.

Because they're toying with us, thought Kano. These warriors had probably been waiting weeks for this moment. They were going to savor the hunt.

Kano resolved to hurl his shockwaves in any direction that his allies were not standing in, which was easy to do now that their circle had been reduced to three. Ships grinded out of the way, supply crates spilled and crumbled, but not a single enemy appeared.

Until one swooped in right in front of him. Tall and clad in silver armor, the Lusitani emerged before him like a specter. Its mask was in the shape of a skull, with tally marks scratched into it. Though shaped like a man, the warrior moved sideways, like a spider ready to pounce.

Kano threw a shockwave, and rockets flared from its wrists, propelling it out of the way of his attack.

Another Lusitani landed, this one in front of Li. She launched her roots at it. The Lusitani aimed its wrists, and chemical vapor sprayed out of them. Kano could smell it from where he was standing, helpless as he watched Li's roots crumble and die in the vapor.

"*They can counter any power*," Li echoed in Kano's mind.

Chenji, seeing Li defenseless, leaped in front of her and swung his big fist at the Lusitani, but his target dove out of the way. Another Lusitani leaped from the shadows and tossed a round metal ball at him. The ball sprung open into a wide net that pulsed with electricity. The net wrapped around Chenji and he screamed, trying to fight it, but each movement sent a zap that slowly, painfully, diminished his resolve.

Li looked to Kano, her hands glowing white but her roots not rising to her aid, still choked by the chemicals.

"Kano, *run!*" she said just before a stun bolt took her in the chest.

Now there was only one.

"No!" screamed Kano. He looked to the ship, where he realized Cera had been fighting the whole time. Two Lusitani laid unconscious at her feet. Two more were taking turns striking at her. He took a step toward her when another Lusitani dove out of the shadows. Kano threw a shockwave, and the Lusitani disappeared as quickly as it had arrived. When he looked back at Cera, she and her attackers had disappeared.

"Enough!" cried Kano. He raised his fists and stood his ground. He wouldn't run anymore; they had already lost. But he wouldn't go down without a fight.

"Face me!" His cry echoed through the hangar. All had gone quiet. No shadows stirred. No stun bolts came seeking him. He was alone.

Then, a figure emerged from the shadows. Taller than the others, its skull mask was painted red, with over a dozen tallies scratched into it. It marched purposefully toward Kano, its footsteps echoing through the silence.

The Lusitani stopped. Kano readied himself. Then, just when he was about to strike, the Lusitani drew a remote from its belt and pushed a button at its center.

Kano found himself locking eyes with Eines through the distant windscreen of the ship. One moment Eines was there; the next, fire exploded out of the windscreen and the Pincer collapsed in a plume of smoke and chunks of metal.

"NO!" screamed Kano. The shockwave of the explosion hit him before he could throw one of his own and he went sailing back. He rose quickly, his ears ringing, to find the Lusitani still standing there, unperturbed.

"What are you?!" cried Kano.

In answer, the Lusitani drew two stun batons, one in each hand.

Kano stared into the lifeless eye coverings of the mask, the silver of the murderer's suit glowing from the fire raging behind it. Never, not even when facing Taranis, had Kano felt such a desire to kill.

He threw a shockwave, and the Lusitani charged toward it. Kano thought his opponent was crazy; no one ever tried to take his attacks head on, but then the Lusitani dove to the ground and rolled like a ball, letting the shockwave roll over it, never losing speed. Kano stared in shock, so surprised that by the time he had summoned his powers again, the Lusitani was already on him, its stun baton catching him right in the chest.

Chapter 12

The Cyborg

The engine purred as Junior sped over the blistering desert. He smiled. It was a smile that no amount of heat or sand could wipe from his face. His speeder was back, and Mogaddu was his to explore.

Warp clung to him from behind, her hoodie flapping back against the wind. They each wore goggles over their eyes and bandanas over their mouths to keep out the sand, which was getting more and more pervasive the deeper they drove into the sea of red dunes.

She tapped his shoulder and pointed. He saw her mark: a pair of stone columns, one of them toppled against the red sand. He lowered the speeder for a closer look. It appeared to be the top of a much larger structure, long since buried in the sand that it stood on. Junior climbed off the speeder and poked around for any activity, but it was clear this castle had been abandoned long ago.

Just like every other one they'd found so far.

He opened Ragar's map, its frayed edges waving in the wind. Warp crossed out another marker on it. She had been surprisingly on board with the whole expedition, even the part about the deadly cyborg. Junior suspected she was just eager to escape Clemens for a while, which was strange, given that her powers could take her quite literally anywhere she wanted to go. So why did she choose to stick with Junior? And more importantly, why did she choose to stick with Clemens? Junior saw the sun dropping to the horizon and shook the thought away. They still had plenty of ground to cover, and not much daylight left to help them.

"I think we should try heading north," he said, pointing to a cluster of castle markers on the map.

Warp shook her head and pointed toward the horizon.

"We have everything we need to travel by night, don't worry."

She shook her head more insistently, then pointed at him and raised her fists as if she was about to fight.

"What are you saying? That I have a fight tonight?"

She nodded.

It triggered something in Junior. "Well, I'm not going. I didn't sign up for that, just like I didn't sign up for the last one."

She clasped her hands together, begging.

"Clemens doesn't control me. And you shouldn't let him control you either."

She scowled and turned her back on him.

"What? Do you actually *like* working for him? Just because he gives us nice things doesn't make him good. He only does it because he's profiting from us, and if that money dries up, he'll toss us out just as quick as he took us in. You watch."

She crossed her arms and seated herself on the speeder, signaling that she wanted to leave. Junior was mid-eyeroll when he noticed something pop out of the sand, its red eye blinking.

"Get down," he whispered. He yanked Warp off the speeder and pulled her into a cleft in the dune. They watched as the bot hovered toward his speeder and ran a quick scan. Its antenna flashed. More bots emerged from the sand and began grabbing up the speeder in their wiry arms.

"Not again," muttered Junior. He leaped out of the cleft and began blasting away the bots with fireballs. They dove into the sand and burrowed out of sight.

Junior hopped onto his speeder. "Warp, come on! Before they send more." But Warp didn't come. When he looked to their hiding spot, he saw no trace of her.

He readied a flame and searched the surrounding sands for more bots, possibly more capable ones like T8, but none appeared. Just as he eased back, the floor parted beneath his feet. Sand poured through the opening as he and his speeder plunged into the pit. He switched it back into flight mode and tried to steer up toward the opening, but the cascade of sand was too thick; he could barely see the fading sunlight above. Then he realized: the trapdoor was closing!

Bots swarmed in from every corner, dozens of them, their hoverpads buzzing out of doors that lined the rounded walls of the pit. Junior realized this was a connector for them, but where all these tunnels led, he couldn't say. He dove deeper, dodging the many red eyes coming toward him. Lights flickered on along the walls, revealing that the pit stretched on indefinitely. It had once been part of the castle, a tower perhaps, but its stone had been patched together with scrap metal, likely the handiwork of its newest tenant. Junior kept diving, farther and farther, the swarm of bots tailing him growing larger until it eclipsed most of the lights above.

Yet none of them seemed to be attacking him. Just corralling him.

Their boss wants me to go deeper, Junior realized. It was clearly a trap, but he didn't have much choice but to follow. He figured if they hadn't shot at him yet, there was a chance he could still make it out of this.

A bot jetted past him, faster than the others. Instead of a hoverpad, it sported two short wings that glowed with blue phantom energy. Long and thin, it had four spindly arms that it used to wave him on. Junior followed. He noticed it was getting colder the deeper they went – a welcome change from the desert heat. The winged bot headed straight for a hydraulic door in the wall, which opened as the bot neared. Junior glanced back. The other bots had eased off him and formed into a cloud of curious red eyes that watched him as he passed through the hydraulic door.

The door sealed behind him and he landed in what he could only describe as a workshop from hell. A single light bulb hung over a worktable that was covered in the remains of disembodied bots. An arm here, a leg there.

Blades, tweezers, and welders hung precariously over the table like ornaments, twinkling in the dim light. Junior scanned the room. He knew he wasn't alone, but he couldn't see anything in the shadows beyond the table.

The bot fluttered to the opposite side of the table and folded its wings, descending slowly as a mechanical arm reached into the light. It was unlike the arms on any of the other bots – bulky yet sleek, parts of it semi-transparent, revealing the wires running beneath it like veins.

Bionics. Junior had never seen any so advanced. A hundred gears all rotated in a beautifully choreographed sequence, opening a slot in the forearm into which the bot fit snuggly.

"Have any other pets you'd like me to meet?" asked Junior, his voice echoing through the workshop. He kept his senses tuned, listening for any disturbances.

There was a pause before the cyborg spoke in a deep, gruff voice. "Why did you come?"

"You tell me. You're the one who sees everything."

"Don't play games with me, Hendricks. You're the one who picked the most dangerous planet to flee to."

Junior had no intention of giving the cyborg any more information than it already had. "Why did you have T8 following me?" he asked.

"I make it a point to keep tabs on all the Zoboros on my planet."

"So you'll watch us but you won't help us?" spat Junior. "The Taipa are afraid of you, yet you sit back and let them enslave us for sport."

"The plight of your people is not my concern."

"Then why are you so interested in me!" Junior marched toward the shadowed figure, but when he got close, the bionic arm reached up and grabbed him by the throat.

"It's my business to know things," huffed the cyborg while Junior clawed at the arm, its metallic fingers digging into his windpipe. "One thing I've learned is that your people don't fare well on this planet. I suggest you take the next ship off, before Mogaddu kills you."

Junior began seeing spots. Every breath felt like it came through an increasingly tighter straw. He grabbed hold of the arm and let the heat rise to his palm, intent on melting through.

"Gahhh!" the cyborg screamed. Junior felt the pressure release from his neck. He gasped as the bionic arm retreated toward the shadows. Vents opened along its side, spraying its reddened surface with compressed air that caused the metal to hiss and cool.

Junior stared in awe. "Sensory connectors," he muttered. "No one has that technology. No one except…" He grabbed the dangling bulb and aimed it at his host. He had to aim high, for the face towered seven feet in the air. The cyborg was large, husky, with three red pockets in his forehead and two small tusks that edged either side of his chin.

"An outsider," said the Poterian.

Junior stumbled back and collided with a switchboard that had been hidden in the shadows. It sparked to life, activating a line of monitors that played footage of spaceports, marketplaces, taverns, hallways, and more.

"You…you really do have eyes all over Mogaddu," said Junior, igniting his fists. "You're a spy for the Poterians!"

"*Spy?*" The Poterian slammed his metal fist on the table with a clang. "You think the most powerful empire in the galaxy would take back a cripple like me?!" The cyborg hobbled forward on a bionic leg. Junior tried to stand tall but found himself shrinking, at least on the inside, as the giant's shadow fell over him. The Poterian stopped only inches away, his jagged teeth filled with bits of meat. His breath reeked of blood. Junior couldn't help but think of the stories he'd heard in school about how the Poterians ate their enemies on the battlefield.

Battlefield. Something clicked. "You were wounded in the Battle of Mogaddu, weren't you?" he exclaimed. "You were there! You saw it!"

The Poterian eased back. "That wasn't a battle," he muttered. "It was a slaughter."

"Tell me," said Junior. "I want to know."

"Why? What good is that information to you? It won't lead you any closer to Angeline Hendricks."

Junior froze. "How did—" He turned back toward the monitors and answered his own question. "Do you know what happened to her?"

The Poterian shook his head. "Many Zoboros wanted to come here after the war. Few made it."

Junior's heart sank. All this distance, all this searching, and he was no closer to finding her here than he had been on Famora. He sat down on a nearby work bench and was silent for a long time, long enough for the Poterian to turn aside and begin tinkering with his machines.

"What happened to the Zoboros who did make it?" Junior asked eventually. "Where are they now? Did they find the lost city?"

"That city doesn't exist," said the Poterian flatly. "I should know. The Zoboros who came looking for it either perished in the desert or took up with the Taipa." He cast a disappointed glance at Junior. "I'm not sure which one is worse."

"I'm not one of the Taipa."

"Oh no?" said the Poterian. "And how did you pay for your speeder?"

"It was mine to begin with! I did what I had to, nothing more."

"So have many Zoboros who took up with the Taipa."

"I can walk away whenever I want."

An alarm rang out and warning lights flushed the room in red.

The Poterian shook his head. "They seem to think otherwise."

A puff of smoke plumed in the middle of the room.

"Warp!" exclaimed Junior, fearful the cyborg may snap on the intruder. But the cyborg made no sudden moves. He only stared as Clemens emerged from the smoke, holding Warp's hand.

"Just when I thought you couldn't be more of a nuisance," said Clemens.

"Oh, we're using big boy words, are we now, *Viper*?" muttered the cyborg as he busied himself at his worktable.

"Watch your tongue, Sterling," snapped Clemens.

Sterling? Junior had heard Poterian names in school before, and none of them sounded anything like that.

"The boy came here of his own accord," said Sterling, turning his attention back to his worktable. "Take him back if you like. I'd hate to keep him from his match."

"You better not be plantin' no dirty Poterian ideas in Hellfire's head, you hear me?" said Clemens as he prowled around Sterling's workshop like a wolf on the hunt. "This kid's the next big thing. I don't want him distracted tonight."

"I'm not going to the match tonight," said Junior. "Not until I get the winnings you owe."

Clemens cast a dark gaze on him. "I'll give you the winnings when I decide to give you the winnings. Things don't work here like they do on Famora. You play my game and I make you rich. You cheat me, and I'll make Mogaddu your worst nightmare. Understand?"

Junior stared at Clemens for a long time. When he looked to Warp, he saw a desperate look in her big eyes that screamed, *"Don't do anything stupid!"*

Clemens caught his gaze and smiled. "Ah, so you have made some friends on Mogaddu." He stepped behind Warp and wrapped his long, black nails over her shoulders. "I'd hate for anything to happen to them during your stay."

Junior glanced at Sterling, who looked away, as if to say, "I told you so."

"I'll fight," said Junior.

"See! Everyone comes around for the right price." said Clemens. "Come on over here, kid, and don't you ever go runnin' into the desert on me again."

One promise at a time, Clemens, thought Junior as he took Warp's hand. *One promise at a time.*

For a fleeting moment, Junior thought he saw disappointment on the Poterian's face, and he couldn't quite understand why that bothered him.

A puff of smoke, and then he was standing inside the ring, tens of thousands of voices ringing in his ears. He looked around. The crowd was already assembled. They rose to their feet at his arrival.

"Clever trick!" Clemens shouted in his ear.

"What trick?!" he shouted back, straining to hear even his own voice amid the raucous.

"Making them wait."

Clemens and Warp stepped down from the ring, leaving Junior to soak up all the cheers and affection. Goosebumps prickled up and down his arms. The crowd was much larger than yesterday's; he couldn't spot an empty seat in the house. A flush of pride came over him.

They're here for me.

"AND NOW," boomed Clemens's voice through the loudspeakers as the electric field rounded the ring's edges, "tonight's challenger! All the way from Darraden, please give a half-hearted welcome to *Amanita*!"

A Taloan stepped into the ring. She was greeted by a blitz of boos. Short and pudgy, her purple skin was coated in yellowish sores. She wore a flowery dress and a scowl on her face. Junior scratched his head. One of these things didn't belong.

"How'd you end up with such a pretty name?" called Zivo from the sideline, snickering. Junior spotted all his fellow fighters packed in just behind the electric field.

"Not for my looks," replied Amanita in the deepest voice Junior had ever heard. Fluid spewed from her sores and sailed toward Junior. He dove out of the way and let the fluid sizzle and pulse on the floor where he had just stood.

"GO! GO! GO!" cried his Zoboros companions, but they didn't need to tell him that. He was already moving, staying light on his feet, dipping, dodging, searching for an opening as acid sprayed from his opponent's arms, legs, and face. He tried angling a fireball at her, but he was keeping such a distance that she could easily step out of the way of his attacks.

"Why don't you come a little closer?!" taunted Amanita. Smoke rose around her from where her acid had touched.

Didn't plan on it. Junior tried matching his power to the acid, but the liquid extinguished his flames on contact. All he could do was keep moving, keep searching for an opening, and not get melted in the process.

"Use an aerial!" called Brivek.

Junior understood Brivek's plan immediately. If Amanita tried spraying up, the acid would fall back on her face. It was risky, but it was the best plan he had so far. He blasted the ground with his flames and went soaring above his opponent's surprised face. He launched a jet of flame at her. Acid sprayed back to match it, but it never reached Junior. Instead, it rained back down on the Taloan.

Junior landed across the ring, feeling victorious. But when he turned, he found his opponent licking the bubbling acid off her lips.

"Mmm, mmm, mmm," she said. "Tastes like jelly. I wonder what it'll taste like for you?"

Junior shot Brivek an annoyed look. The Vosni shrugged.

More acid came spraying Junior's way. He circled the perimeter of the ring, the acid trailing behind him. At this point, the arena floor was charred up from it and gave off a stench of burned rubber. It overpowered Junior's nostrils. He started to feel lightheaded.

"Enjoying the fumes?" asked Amanita, smiling.

They are nice. Junior shook his head. He was getting delirious, on top of being winded and nauseous. His opponent had complete control of the field, which she kept coating with more acid upon every spin.

Spin. That was it. Junior started to run faster. With each pass, he drew a little nearer to Amanita, feeling the acid coming closer, its fumes growing stronger, but he kept charging. *I either give it all out here, or I die trying.*

The Taloan rotated with him, faster and faster, the frustration visible on her pudgy little face.

"Enough!" she shouted, relinquishing the acid for a moment.

It was the moment Junior was waiting for. He threw a fireball straight down the middle and right into her chest. She sailed back and hit the ground with a *thunk*.

The crowd roared. His friends screamed and stamped their feet. The whole place began to chant, "*SEVAS! SEVAS! SEVAS!*"

Junior racked his brain. Someone had told him what that phrase meant last night during the party. It was Ancient Mogaddan, he had learned; something that was said in the Zoboros duels of old. Back when they fought for blood.

Then it came to him: *spill the life's blood.*

"*SEVAS! SEVAS! SEVAS!*"

Junior approached Amanita, heart pounding, the fumes making him dizzy. He felt like he was outside of his own body, fueled only by the wild adrenaline pulsing through his veins. The Taloan groaned on the floor, nursing the burns beneath her now singed dress. She reached out and released a feeble spritz of acid that fell at Junior's feet and fizzled.

"*SEVAS! SEVAS! SEVAS!*"

Junior felt powerful, superior, like the statues in the clubhouse. The crowd loved him. No crowd had ever loved him before, not even when he was trying to save them.

Now he would show them what he could really do.

He engulfed his hand in flames and clamped them down against Amanita's. He felt the acid pores in her hands sizzle shut on contact.

"*AHHH!*" she screamed, reeling back. "*What did you do to me?!*"

She started weeping, moaning, curling up into a ball as the crowd laughed at her. Junior felt the fumes clear, his head clearing with them, and his gaze fell upon her burned, discolored hands.

He looked at his own hands and snuffed the flames away, realizing what he had done. The roar of the crowd droned out of his ears. All he could hear was his victim whimpering on the floor, and all he could see were the other Zoboros on the sideline, staring silently.

And then he saw Clemens, smiling.

Chapter 13

The Connection

Kano kneeled before the stone door, its ancient markings towering high above his head. He heard the boots crunching across the sand behind him, knew his enemy was coming, but didn't flinch.

"Is this real, Taranis?" he asked.

The boots stopped beside him, but there was no response.

Kano looked up. The mask he saw was shaped like a skull, with tally marks etched into it. He screamed as a gloved hand reached for him.

Lusitani! Kano awoke on the hard prison floor. His back ached. He rose and found a wall of plexiglass standing before him. A few dim lights illuminated the rest of the corridor. He scanned the cells across from his but saw no sign of his friends. Either they were hidden in the shadows or, more than likely, they were already gone.

A pain sprang from his chest, but not because of his injuries. It was the thought of losing his friends forever, of not even getting to say goodbye, of being alone and trapped and...

Drained. It was only then that he noticed the power dampener cocooning his hands. It bound them together at the wrists, its lights pulsing as it absorbed his powers. There would be no punching his way out of this one, no teammates to rescue him. For the first time, he truly had nothing. He hugged the power dampener to his chest and began to rock himself on the floor. He could picture their faces, hear the voices, the voices of each person he'd failed. They'd come here and risked everything just to protect him, yet in the end he couldn't protect them. He sniffled. Tears welled in his eyes.

"They're gone," came a gruff voice. "Get over it."

Kano leaped to his feet. He searched his cell, then up and down the corridor, but he saw no one. Only shadows.

He heard footsteps, uneven, echoing from the cell across from his. He waited and watched as a foot stepped into the light. It was wrapped in bandages. The sight brought Kano back to Famora, to the ship he had been held prisoner on. But Hendricks had come to the rescue then, and driven a knife through the foot of Kano's traitorous captor.

"Novak," muttered Kano.

The former colonel limped into view. Kano tensed. It was the same tall man with the same bald head that he remembered on Famora, but the face was checkered with deep red gashes. Only one eye stared back at Kano; the other was swollen shut.

"I was wondering when I'd see you here," said Novak. He seated himself on his foldout bed. It creaked beneath him. He looked tired.

"What have they done to you?" asked Kano.

Novak ignored the question; he was too busy scratching at a scab on his chin. "You put up quite a fight on Famora. I could've used someone like you."

Kano shook his head. "I'd never join—"

"I know," interrupted Novak. "And I doubt holding your friends hostage helped my case. Still, it was better than what the Orlovs had planned for you."

Kano stepped closer to the plexiglass, a rage igniting in his veins. "The Orlovs sacrificed themselves to save my friends from *your* soldiers!"

Novak looked up with his one good eye. "But did you trust them?"

No, thought Kano, though he didn't dare admit it. The Orlovs had been a strange and secretive family. Li had warned him about their nature, but Kano had only gotten a taste of it before their untimely demise. All he knew was that the Orlovs had planned to take him far away from Famora, someplace where he would likely never see his friends again.

Not so different from what the IDF was doing to him now, come to think of it.

Novak rose and limped toward the glass, relishing Kano's silence. "Good," he said. "You're learning. You may survive this after all."

"Is that a threat?"

"A warning." Novak nodded toward a camera that was angled above their cells. "Don't think this cell changes anything. You've been a prisoner on this ship from the moment you arrived."

"I could've been a prisoner of yours, too. You wanted to exploit my powers just as badly."

"Everyone is looking to exploit your powers, Kano. The question is, what do you want to use them for?"

The question took Kano by surprise. It wasn't often that anyone asked him what he wanted, least of all his enemies. He found he didn't have an answer for Novak.

"The sooner you can answer that question, the better," said Novak. "Because if you keep letting people pull your strings with their talk and their promises, you'll never find your own path."

"Why are you telling me this?"

Novak looked away. "It was once my job to get inside the minds of Zoboros. To understand them so we could defeat them."

Kano froze. "You were Lusitani too," he said. It made sense; if Hendricks had been one as Akio claimed, then surely Hendricks's right-hand man would have followed.

"How did they manage to drag you into the brig?" asked Novak. "Concussive grenades? Camouflage? If it were me, I'd have rolled into a ball to absorb the blast of your shockwaves."

"Why would you and Hendricks choose to become Lusitani?" demanded Kano.

Novak rose. "Because we were trained to believe that the Zoboros needed to be destroyed. But we were wrong. The Zoboros are a part of nature, and our attempt to control them exploded in our faces. Hendricks believed the Zoboros could be kept alive if they were pacified. I believed they should be allowed to move mountains again."

"Like Taranis did?"

"For every Taranis, there's another Zoboros to fight him."

"And leave half a city destroyed in the process," muttered Kano.

"Famora may have been damaged, but you saved it from a worse fate. Your powers *can* be used for good, Kano."

"How can I use them for good if everyone has a different idea of what good means?"

"Make your own damn definition," answered Novak. "And stop caring what everyone else thinks. Your first mistake was to think that you had friends out here. Everyone wants something from you, so take something in return."

"That doesn't sound very heroic…"

"Heroes die. Survivors adapt."

Kano looked to Novak, seeing the man in a different light for the first time. Not necessarily a good light, but not a hideous one either. "How do I beat the Lusitani?" he asked.

"A Zoboros always has the advantage," said Novak. "That's the law that every Lusitani must first accept. Then they learn to exploit any advantage that they can create. Darkness, deception, these were our tools. As long as a Zoboros couldn't engage us directly, we held the upper hand. But if you take control of the environment, then the Lusitani are no more than people in expensive suits."

Two guards entered the corridor.

"Looks like I've said too much," said Novak with a wink. "It was no mistake putting our cells together. I guess they were just hoping we'd have found a more interesting subject."

Kano nodded. Their fortunate cell placement made perfect sense. The IDF had wanted Novak to talk about Taranis and the rest of his organization, but *not* their own Lusitani.

The guards opened Kano's cell and grabbed him by the arms. The time for questions was running out.

"Who do the Lusitani report to?" asked Kano quickly as they pulled him from his cell. "Is it Mezo? Who would've given the order?"

"Goodbye Kano. It looks like this will be the last time you see my pretty face." Novak smiled. There were teeth missing.

"Tell me!" cried Kano as the guards dragged him out of the corridor, but Novak didn't utter another word.

The guards shoved him into an elevator. They ascended in silence as Kano's rage bubbled. He felt weak wedged between these two guards – guards he could easily handle if he had his powers. But with the dampener on, he was just a skinny teenager aboard the most powerful ship in the galaxy.

When the elevator doors parted, Kano recognized his surroundings instantly: the top floor of the Panopticon. But unlike last time, there were no analysts crowding the large hallway. The whole place had been cleared out, with only the echoes of his footsteps to fill the void. The guards led him up the stairs and toward the dining room where he had met with Mezo once before. He steeled himself.

The door to the dining room opened as two guards hauled Chenji out, his feet dragging against the floor, his head tipping forward.

"Chenji?" said Kano. "Chenji?!"

Chenji didn't respond. He just babbled nonsense to himself as he passed.

Kano gulped. He wondered what torture device could be waiting beyond the door, but when they entered, he found nothing new. Just the same long table, the same chandelier overhead, and the same cold, gray eyes staring at him from across the room.

Somehow, though, Mezo was frightening enough.

"What do you want with me?" asked Kano.

Mezo turned her gaze to the guards. "Leave us."

Kano's escort left as quickly as they had entered. When the door shut, a palpable silence filled the room.

"You killed Eines," said Kano.

"He sealed his own fate," said Mezo. "As did your friends, but I can make their stay aboard the *Dormarch* much more comfortable if you do as I ask."

They're still here, thought Kano, though he didn't let his face betray his emotion. Not while he was face to face with the general.

"And if I don't?" he asked.

Two Lusitani emerged on either side of him. Kano hadn't even noticed them in the room.

"Do not test me, Kano." Mezo marched over and inspected him like a slab of meat. It was then that Kano noticed she had gloves on her hands.

"What did you do to Chenji?"

"Nothing he hasn't experienced before," she replied. One of her Lusitani set a long, heavy briefcase on the table. She approached it and began twisting a dial at its center. A lock clicked and the briefcase opened with a blast of compressed air. "Chenji was right though, at least partially. The game was, for a time, unwinnable. At least until he arrived. That's when we started placing the Artifact in it."

"Why?" asked Kano. "Why place a real Zoboros artifact in the Sim?"

"We wanted to see which of you might share a connection with it. I expected you to be the first to touch it, considering your tendency to throw yourself headlong into danger, but Chenji surprised us." Mezo nodded to one of her Lusitani. The masked warrior approached Kano and removed the power dampener.

Kano gasped. A wave of relief rolled over him. Strength returned to his muscles. The tingle of his powers rushed back to his fingertips. He felt whole again. The Lusitani were quick to aim their wrists at him, though. Kano avoided making any sudden moves. He had no desire to experience whatever horrible weapon they planned to counter his powers with.

Mezo extended the staff to him. He eyed it warily, the image of Chenji writhing on the floor of the Sim still fresh in his mind.

"What does this accomplish?" he asked, his hands shaking.

"Everything," she replied.

Kano reached out, bracing himself. The Lusitani inched closer, ready to strike him down if he didn't do as commanded. Kano wanted desperately to lash out with his powers, to punish Mezo for killing Eines and capturing his friends, but curiosity had overtaken his fear. What did the staff do? Why did they want him to touch it? What connection did she believe he shared with it?

He grabbed it and…felt nothing. No pain, no struggle. His heart rate dialed back to normal as he realized that the relic had no effect on him.

Mezo wrenched the staff from his hand, her eyes never betraying the disappointment he knew she felt.

"What was supposed to happen?" asked Kano.

Mezo turned away.

"What does it—" He took a step forward and the Lusitani pressed in on him. He stopped and let them clamp the awful dampener back over his hands.

"Take him back to his cell," ordered Mezo, not daring to look back at him. Kano said nothing as the Lusitani dragged him out the door. He only stared at the staff in Mezo's hand. What was she really after? And why did it mean so much to her?

The Lusitani took Kano back into the elevator. For the first time, he noticed just how many floors there were.

More floors than it would take to reach the Transitway, he realized. Many more. It was one of these lower floors that the Lusitani selected.

"That's not the brig," said Kano.

The Lusitani ignored him as the doors closed. The elevator started, and with each floor, Kano's dread grew stronger. Was this because he failed to connect with the staff? Did they have no further need of him? He kept imagining the elevator opening up into a kill room of some kind, though he wasn't sure what that would even look like. He kept trying to devise a way to escape, but the dampener, in combination with two trained Zoboros killers, made all his ideas seem useless.

The doors opened. Instead of a kill room, Kano found himself inside a small hangar. There was only one ship – a troop transport – and there was no one else in sight. The Lusitani hurried him onboard, where he found a collection of familiar faces waiting for him.

"Kano!" exclaimed Li, rushing over to hug him.

"LI?!" Kano stood there in her embrace, overcome with shock as Makoto and Jaden joined the hug. Chenji sat in a corner, still shaking, and Kano saw a small smile cross his new friend's face.

"But…the Lusitani…?" Kano stammered. When he turned around, one of his captors ripped off her helmet and let her blonde hair spill out.

"You think we'd give up on you that easily?" asked Cera.

"I thought they captured you!" exclaimed Kano.

"They certainly tried," said Carmichael, ripping off his own Lusitani helmet. "Are we ready?"

The door to the cockpit opened. A familiar Jakari sat eagerly at the controls. "I've been waiting a long time to fly again."

Akio flipped the control switches one by one, each making his grin grow wider. The engines sparked to life and the transport began to rise.

Kano stared out the window as the floor beneath their transport parted. The vacuum of space opened before them and the transport lowered them out of the *Dormarch*.

"But they'll detect our escape," said Kano. "They'll shoot us down!"

"Relax Kano," said Cera. "We have plenty of friends on the inside."

"What friends?" asked Kano.

Carmichael smiled as he activated a holographic communicator in the wall.

"We're on our way," said the captain proudly.

A holographic man appeared before them, a jeweled cane held in his wrinkled hands.

"We'll be expecting you," said Danadas Orlov.

Chapter 14

A New Challenger

The fighters sat in silence, as they had been in the hours since Junior's fight with Amanita.

"Sevas." Junior muttered to himself. He could feel others staring at him, could feel their fear and pity permeating the air in the clubhouse. But who were they to judge him? They'd been a part of this scam for cycles, beating up their own kind in the ring time and time again. And what would they get for it? A statue? It wouldn't even belong to them; it would belong to the scumbags who profited on their blood. Every game they won was just another loss for the Zoboros.

And that's how the Taipa wanted it.

Junior grabbed the nearest chair and flung it halfway across the room. It landed with a crash. The others stiffened but didn't say a word. What could they do? After witnessing what he had done in the ring, none of them wanted to be next.

It was Yui who had the courage to speak first. "Why did you come here?" she asked.

Junior turned to her, surprised by the question. "I have my reasons."

"We all do," said Nera. She hugged her long legs and placed her chin on her knees, lost in her own memory. Of everyone, she'd seemed the most shaken since Junior's fight.

"My planet was starving," said Brivek. "When I heard the Taipa paid well for fighters, I signed on. Never had a real fight in my life, but I figured I'd fake it till I made it."

"I got my start in the circus," said Zivo, growing two batons out of his wrist and juggling them. "They accepted me there. One day a Viper came to our show and made me an offer. I thought it was a one-time gig, but in three cycles I've never left Mogaddu."

"I came because I wanted to use the powers I was given," said Yui, encasing her hand in ice. "If this is how I have to do it, then so be it."

Junior thought for a long time on that. The thought of a Zoboros fight ring had always disgusted him…until he had become a part of one. Until he'd heard the cheer of the crowd and known what it felt like for people to celebrate his powers, even if that celebration came at the expense of his people.

"This doesn't have to be the only way for you to use your powers," he said.

Everyone looked to him expectantly. The phrase *"Cheven Sahar"* echoed in his mind. It was the name, he'd learned, that the ancient Mogaddans had once given their Zoboros savior. A savior who never came. It compelled him to continue.

"This planet is the birthplace of the Zoboros. Our home. The Taipa have no claim here. And they don't have our powers, either. We're stronger than they are."

"Be careful," said Zivo. "The Taipa have more influence than you think."

"And more muscle," added Brivek.

"We have a Zoboros who can teleport us literally anywhere we want to go," said Junior. "We have more advantages than they want us to think."

"Warp is Clemens's right hand," said Zivo. "We can't trust her."

"I trust her," Junior fired back, surprised by his own comment. As he recalled, she'd robbed him during their first encounter.

The door burst open and Clemens strutted in, his fingers adorned with shiny new jewelry.

"That's my boy!" he exclaimed, oblivious to the somber air that choked the rest of the room. "Amanita was undefeated until tonight. Leave it to the Hero of Famora to clean her out!" Clemens knelt down and kissed Junior on the head with his sticky, purple lips. He turned his smile to the others, only then to read the room.

"Who died?" he asked. "Come on! We *all* won tonight. Pop some Konos! I'll have them send some girls down just for you, Hellfire."

Junior rose, ready to call Clemens out when someone else blurted, "We don't want your damn party!"

"Who said that?!" Clemens's good humor evaporated instantaneously. He scanned the room for the culprit. Even Junior looked, expecting it to be Zivo or Yui.

But it was Nera. She was on her feet, fists clenched at her sides.

Clemens marched toward her, his black shoes clicking. Nera dodged his yellow eyes that watched her so coldly. "Tell me, Nera, since you feel so compelled to form an opinion, what exactly is it that *you* want?"

"I...I want..." she stammered, still unable to meet Clemens's gaze. She started shaking.

"*I, I, I,*" taunted Clemens. He grabbed her by the red cartilage that crowned her head. Junior could tell by her expression that it hurt. He readied a flame behind his back.

"I..." Nera trembled. Her voice was barely audible. A tear streaked down her face. "I want to go home."

"A little louder, so your friends can hear you."

"I want to go home!"

"Hear that, everybody?!" shouted Clemens. "Nera wants to go home. Back to her family's lovely underwater estate. Oh, but one small problem. Her family won't take her back, will they? Because sometimes even the most powerful families run into a little trouble. Thankfully, when that happens, there's people like me around to buy up their daughters at a discount."

Nera cried out. It was something feral; a war cry from deep within her gut. She charged at Clemens, but the Tenu didn't flinch. Instead, he snapped his finger. Yui rose from her seat on command and stood between them.

She blocked Nera, the look in her eyes warning Nera to stop.

Zivo and Brivek were on their feet now, but not to help Clemens. If anything, they looked ready to pounce on him. But Clemens sensed their anger and decided to feed on it.

"How about you, Zivo?" said Clemens, approaching him. "I see you already have your batons out. Why don't you give us that old routine of yours? How did it go again? Kick, step, pivot!" Clemens smacked Zivo across the face.

Brivek stepped forward, and Clemens cast his vengeful gaze upon him.

"Oh, did you think I'd forget my favorite one?" He reached out and patted Brivek's pudgy cheek. "Had it not been for me, the IDF would have zipped you up in a bag just like the rest of your family. Do you know what kind of experiments they do on their Zoboros prisoners?"

Brivek turned away from him, his pale face turning somehow paler.

"The galaxy is cruel, and I am your protection from it," said Clemens, stepping right into Junior's face. Junior stood his ground, staring down into those sick, yellow eyes. "I can give you glory like you never imagined."

"I don't want your glory," said Junior. Every instinct told him to hurt this man. It was only the memory of Clemens's threat against the other fighters that convinced Junior to turn and walk away.

"Well it's coming whether you want it or not!" Clemens called after him. "Your next fight has already been arranged. Another undefeated. A Morabani."

Junior stopped. Nera gasped. Zivo dropped his batons. Yui watched Junior closely.

"You've been entered into the greatest fight of our time," said Clemens. "Everyone will come to see it. And when it's over, they will worship you…if you win, of course."

Junior knew now he couldn't deny Clemens's fight. Not unless he wanted to see the Taipa inflict further damage upon his fellow fighters. Fighters who were more broken than he'd realized. It was clear they hadn't chosen this life, at least not entirely. This really was the best hand they'd been dealt.

So far.

"Think on it, Hellfire. If I see you here in the morning, I'll assume you've committed to the fight." With that, Clemens left, and silence once again filled the room.

"You…you're not actually going to fight, are you?" asked Nera.

Junior sat down and began to think.

"You can't!" said Brivek. "The Morabani will kill you. And Clemens won't try to stop it. I know it."

"No, he won't," said Junior. "He'll be too distracted. If the crowds are going to be as big as he claims, him and his security detail are going to be extremely preoccupied during the fight."

The others began to perk up. They sensed Junior was onto something.

"What are you saying?" asked Zivo.

"I'm saying I'll fight," answered Junior. "I'll put on the greatest show they've ever seen. And while I fight, you all make your escape."

Chapter 15

The Palace

Akio jammed on the brakes. Everyone braced as their transport lurched out of hyperspace. Kano was slammed against his restraints, the whole weight of the ship seemingly pressed against his back. A moment later, it settled. The team looked to one another, bewildered, as the vortex of hyperspace vanished from the windscreen, replaced by a sea of peaceful stars.

"You were supposed to pull the left lever first," said Carmichael to Akio.

"You Humans need lesson in ship design," Akio grumbled back.

Kano emerged from his seat, shaken but excited. He hurried into the cockpit for a better look, but from this distance their destination was a mere pinprick in the vastness of space – a faint red glow in the dark.

Mogaddu.

He drew a deep breath. This was birthplace of the Zoboros; the place that Taranis called "home". It would also be the first planet he ever set foot on.

The transport rattled once more. Sparks flashed across the windscreen.

"What is that?" he asked. They were close enough now that he could see Mogaddu's outline and what appeared to be an asteroid field surrounding it.

"Debris," answered Akio. "Do not worry, boy of thunder. We are not flying through it."

Akio veered them off-course, letting the little red planet dip out of view.

"What are you doing?" demanded Kano.

"The rendezvous isn't on Mogaddu," said Carmichael, pointing. Kano had to squint to see what the captain was referring to. A tiny speck floated beside Mogaddu, though as they neared, that speck quickly filled the windscreen, forming into a blue orb flecked with spots of green.

A moon. Kano knew nothing about Mogaddu's moons, but he saw that Jaden's eyes were wide with recognition.

"You know this place?" Kano asked him.

"You remember The Place at the Edge of the Moon?" said Jaden. "That's a code for the Orlovs, who base all their operations from a single moon. *This* moon."

They stumbled forward as turbulence reclaimed the ship.

"Everyone, back in your seats!" ordered Cera.

Kano claimed the seat across from her and strapped in as more sparks flashed across the windscreen. He noticed she was fidgeting with her nails, which was unusual for the normally poised and confident Cera. In fact, she'd been acting strange the entire journey. He'd tried striking up conversation with her a few times, but had been met with short, unenthusiastic answers. He'd assumed she was processing the death of Eines; he and the others hadn't had much time to get to know their former pilot, but Cera had been closer to him. Even so, Kano sensed a nervousness in her, something that went beyond grief. One look at Li, and he knew that she sensed it in Cera too.

Fire blazed across the windscreen as they dove into the moon's atmosphere. Everything shook. He gripped his armrests tight, the G-force pressing against his head, and prayed that Akio was skilled enough to get them safely through reentry.

The pressure suddenly released from his head as the ship began to settle. The flames evaporated away, replaced by a vast, blue ocean in the windscreen. His jaw dropped. He'd never seen so much water in his life. The ship leveled just above the surf, riding with it. Kano watched the waves below crash over each other in a way that was oddly graceful. A few tiny islands broke up the otherwise endless stretch of blue, but there was one that caught Kano's eye. It was coming up in the windscreen, and by the way Akio was slowing them down, Kano could only assume it was their destination. The island formed a perfect circle, almost too perfect, with white sandy beaches rounding its edges. A layer of fauna filled its interior, so rich in greens, reds, and oranges that it looked like someone had wrapped the whole island in a bouquet. And at the center of it all, sprouting from among the trees, was a palace unlike anything Kano had ever seen.

And I thought the Orlov Mansion was big. This palace was fit for kings and queens of old, its white stone a glowing beacon beneath the intense tropical sunlight, its dozen spires stabbing high into the bright blue sky. Kano rose from his seat and pressed up against the window glass as they sailed over the palace grounds. Akio yelled at him to move, but he didn't notice. He was too focused on the long pool that was reflecting the belly of their transport as they passed over it. The pool gave way to a courtyard large enough to fit a hundred transports, its surface made entirely of shiny marble. It was here that Akio stopped and lowered the ship.

Kano sensed excitement in his teammates, too. They began unstrapping their restraints and hurrying toward the exit well before the ship had even touched down. That is, everyone except for Cera, who joined Carmichael by the controls. Neither spoke. The captain simply patted her on the shoulder.

Not wanting to intrude, Kano joined the others at the liftgate as they waited and wondered. Was this to be their new secret home? It certainly wasn't inconspicuous, but Kano was confident there would be plenty of places for them to hide. Not to mention, the palace would be a huge upgrade from the *Dormarch*.

The door opened with a blast of compressed air. Kano stepped through, and was caught immediately within the choking grasp of the sun. It surprised him. He'd spent his entire life in the controlled atmosphere of Famora, and since then had spent his time on air-conditioned spaceships; the air here was thicker and muggier than anything he'd experienced before. Simply standing in it was making him sweat.

The ramp began to lower, but not fast enough. Makoto leaped down onto the marble some ten feet below, an easy feat for a Nurrano, and scurried about the grounds, exploring every nook and cranny as if they each held some secret treasure. The others hurried down the ramp after him. Jaden led the charge, only Kano quickly realized that his friend wasn't filled with the same excitement as Makoto; Jaden was filled with something else, which he yacked over the edge of the ramp. Li tried checking on him with her glowing hands but he shooed her away. He would deal with his motion sickness from reentry on his own, so Kano continued on toward the palace. It stood a short distance away, looking hazy from the heat rising off the surrounding courtyard.

Three figures approached through the haze. Two were guards dressed in red armor, but not the bulky armor that the IDF troopers wore; this was more fitted, dexterous, and breathable. Each guard had a spear balanced against their shoulder, clean and polished; more for show than actual use, Kano assumed.

A tall woman floated between the guards, Human, with a white silken gown that trailed behind her across the marble. As she approached, Kano realized that she was riding on a small hoverpad.

"Danadas Orlov bids you welcome to Palace Binoshé," she announced with a small bow. "I am Plí

Dalia, stewardess to the great Orlov family. Allow me to escort you inside for some refreshments."

"Don't mind if we do!" exclaimed Makoto as he promptly rejoined the group.

Plí led the way upon her hoverpad. The others followed, though Kano found it hard to keep up as he admired the grounds. Long trails snaked beyond the courtyard, leading into hedgerows and gardens that were bursting with life and color, as though someone had cut pieces of the surrounding jungle and planted them within the palace. It was overwhelming for someone who had never known anything but the metal and concrete of the floating city, nor any ounce of luxury.

"You can fit an entire town in here," said Chenji as he pulled back his shaggy hair, which was already damp with sweat. "Who are these people, anyway?"

"Old friends," said Kano, remembering the Orlov twins with the auburn hair that they'd left behind on Famora. The twins who helped them escape the IDF at the expense of their own freedom. The twins he'd never heard from again.

"And old money, too," added Jaden as he peeked around nervously.

"Older than yours?" asked Makoto.

Jaden flushed. He wasn't one to talk about his family, but it was common knowledge among the team that he came from a powerful one.

"The Orlovs are older than the Uptons by a few centuries," said Plí from her hoverpad. "Though some claim your family sprang from a loose branch of ours. Where do you stand on that debate, Master Upton?"

"Let's not get into politics before we eat," muttered Jaden.

Plí smiled to herself as she led them up the stairs. Makoto's gaze fixed upon her hoverpad, watching as it levitated over each individual step.

"Could I get one of those?" he asked.

Plí chuckled. "Certainly, Master Sasaki. But they are a bit tricky to master. I recommend practicing in the gardens before you try hovering over stairs."

A smile stretched across Makoto's face, one that told Kano that the stairs would be the very first place his brother practiced on.

He noticed Li's face had lit up too, probably because of the gardens. Famora never afforded much in the realm of vegetation; to practice her powers in gardens like these was something she had only dreamed of.

When they arrived at the great red double doors, the guards assumed sentry positions on either side of them. Kano tried to peek through the visors of their red helmets and see who was beneath. Human? Nurrano? Were they Orlovs or just hired hands? Everything around him just filled his head with more questions.

The doors parted at a wave of Plí's hand. Inside, two curved staircases rounded the edges of a grand foyer. Kano found his eyes drawn instantly to the ceiling; it was a glass dome that arched high above their heads. It reminded him of the Archives on Famora, only instead of the stench of mold and decay, the air here carried the sweet scent of apricots. Best of all, though, was the air conditioning, which rolled over him in a soothing wave after their sweaty walk outside.

A fountain burbled in the center of the foyer. A statue of a man stood on top of it, the water pooling at his feet. He wielded a spear that was drawn back for the throw, battle written on his twisted face. Kano found himself focusing on the spear, on the markings etched within it. They seemed disturbingly familiar.

"Welcome, young masters," announced Danadas. Everyone turned. The old man was looking down at them from a balustrade at the back of the foyer, his jeweled cane in hand. "If you wouldn't mind another set of stairs, lunch is waiting for you."

The team followed Plí up one of the staircases toward him.

"Should we have dressed up for this?" whispered Li.

"Don't ask questions when free food is involved," said Chenji quickly. Makoto nodded in agreement, though Li's comment now made everyone acutely aware of how filthy their flight suits were after escaping the *Dormarch*.

They passed through another set of double doors at the back of the balustrade and entered into a dining hall, with several long tables all stretching from one end to the other, each seating at least fifty to a side. The centermost table, though, drew everyone's attention, for it was covered with about every food imaginable: breads, cheeses, briskets, nuts, salads, pies, tarts, fruit bowls, even whole roasted birds lay glistening beneath rows of giant chandeliers that glowed with a hundred candles each.

Makoto and Chenji attacked the table first, wolfing down entire chunks of aivin in a horrifying display of hunger. Li rolled her eyes and started adding to her own plate, sticking mostly to the greener items on the menu. Jaden, still queasy, turned hard toward the nearest bathroom, and Kano, his mouth dried and dehydrated just from walking across the courtyard, went straight for a pitcher of water.

"The heat does take some getting used to," came Danadas's voice.

Startled, Kano coughed some of his water back into his cup. Their host had been standing behind him the whole time. "A lot of things will take getting used to," replied Kano, nodding toward the table. "Assuming you planned on keeping us?"

Danadas turned and held out his arm. "Come with me, Master Kano."

Kano, surprised, took the old man's arm and followed him toward the kitchens, leaving the beautiful buffet behind with sinking heart. Did this have something to do with Danadas's plans to turn him into a Zoboros poster boy? If it was, Kano wished he'd scooped up a few morsels from the table to get him through the sales pitch.

As Danadas hobbled along beside him, Kano could feel the frailty the cycles had inflicted on his old bones. Yet somehow, the man still carried a certain strength and dignity to him. The cooks all stopped their hustling around the kitchen to give a short bow in his presence.

They didn't seem fearful or subservient, though. Rather, they seemed intensely respectful.

Danadas stopped at a door to what Kano assumed was a pantry, but when Danadas placed his hand on a scanner beside it, Kano quickly tossed that assumption.

The scanner pinged red. Danadas gave it a whack with his cane and it switched to green.

"Top of the line model, they told me," said Danadas. "Personally, I'm tempted to go back to lock and key."

The door opened into a short stairwell. As they climbed, Kano began to wonder what other secrets this palace held. Was this to be their hideout if IDF investigators came by? Or maybe there were other Zoboros fugitives already inside, as the Orlovs were known on occasion to harbor.

What Kano found upstairs was not a hiding hole, but a study lined with towering bookshelves, each packed to the brim with actual books. Odd. Kano was used to datacubes, which held far more information than these yellowed pages. Plus, datacubes didn't burn easily, which was something to consider given the fireplace crackling at the far end of the narrow study, just behind Danadas's wooden desk.

As Kano walked along, he noticed an echo in his step. He looked down and realized the floor was made entirely of glass, allowing him to see straight down into the dining hall where his friends were seated around the center table. The study's location now made perfect sense; Danadas had a bird's eye view of whoever he chose to entertain, even when they didn't think he was watching.

From this point of view, Kano noticed something that he had missed downstairs: a giant tree was painted on the center table, its many branches reaching toward the table's edges, some of them so small that Kano had to squint to see them.

"Our family may have its crest," began Danadas, "but I believe that the Orlov Tree is our true symbol. It is what binds our many branches across the galaxy."

"But the tree doesn't have a spear in it," replied Kano, thinking of the Montiquo, the Orlov crest that Jaden had once used to get them into a nightclub. "Your guards all have spears. And the statue in the foyer, with the symbols on it."

Danadas smiled as he released from Kano's grip. "And do you know what those symbols mean?"

"I know Taranis does," said Kano. "He wears the same marks on his mask. The same language."

Danadas hobbled toward his desk, his cane clanking against the floor. "They refer to the Tale of Three Kings. Are you familiar with this one, Master Kano?"

Kano nodded. Li's grandmother had told him the story back on Famora in what felt like a lifetime ago. It was a legend of how the Zoboros began. But that was all it was to Kano. A legend.

"Then you'll know each king left a weapon at the Gate of Iramwerta."

"It was a gesture of peace between each of their kingdoms," said Kano. "So that the gate would…let them pass." Kano froze. The vision of the stone door in his dream flashed through his mind.

"And did you know the Orlovs ruled one of those kingdoms?" asked Danadas. He reached under his desk and lifted out a spear made of fine, silvery metal with the ancient markings etched upon it.

Kano approached eagerly. "Are you telling me that your family is one of the first Zoboros bloodlines?" He observed the spear, but dared not touch, recalling what happened to Chenji. "Mezo had a staff with similar markings."

"The Staff of Amun Ven," said Danadas. "King of the Deserts. It's a rare thing to look upon all three of the ancient weapons in a lifetime."

"Three?"

"What, did you think all swords could wield the power of a Zoboros?"

Taranis. Kano remembered his enemy's sword all too well, how it had channeled Taranis's electricity every time he used it. And when Junior had taken it, the weapon had started channeling fire instead.

Danadas could sense Kano's realization. "That sword belonged to King Niscelles," he said. "The Poterian King. It was a symbol of strength even before it was imbued with the power of the Zoboros." Danadas shook his head. "Strange that Iramwerta would gift the kings the very power they needed to destroy each other."

"You talk about Iramwerta as if it was a living thing."

"Because it is. Or at least, it is something beyond our understanding. It opens and closes when it wishes.

Appears and disappears as it pleases. And never does it betray all of its secrets."

Kano imagined the red glow of the gate in his dreams, and the heat death that had swept over him without any explanation. Had that been a warning? A taste of its power? Then again, he was assuming that Iramwerta was real, despite everything about it sounding more and more like a fairytale.

"One thing I don't understand is why would the city demand peace between the three kings and then make their weapons stronger?"

"They say the power of Iramwerta was not meant for mortals," began Danadas. "That it is a game the gods play to grant us powers that will destroy us. That is the curse of the Zoboros."

Gods, curses, magical artifacts, this was all getting a bit over Kano's head. He tried to focus on his most immediate questions.

"Mezo's staff had some kind of effect on Chenji when he touched it. I don't know why it hurt him, but when I touched it…I felt nothing."

"Your friend Chenji must share ancient blood with Amun Ven to be connected to his staff, and much of it for the connection to be that strong," answered Danadas, looking sadly at the spear. "Mine is unfortunately far fainter."

"What kind of connection? What does it do?" Kano recalled how powers could be passed between generations. Could the same be said for the connections to these Zoboros artifacts?

"I could tell you, or you could try seeing for yourself." Danadas motioned toward the spear. "Our family is vast, Master Kano. Let's see how much of our blood you carry."

Kano gulped. Him, an Orlov? He'd never considered the possibility. His own parents had possessed no known powers, and Kano had found it impossible to find much information on them or the rest of his family line. Could this spear help him unlock that secret? He reached for it despite the memory of Chenji thrashing on the floor, despite all his instincts telling him to stop. He took it in both hands, and suddenly the world was whirring past him. He was flying over a river, then into the river. The water crashed around him, yet he didn't feel wet. He just kept diving deeper in a bubble of the spear's creation. He swam through caves and darkness until finally he landed on a sandy shore. The stone door towered before him, its ancient letters lighting up with gold. It parted at the middle and light surged out, blinding him, warming him, and then…

He let go of the spear and realized he was falling.

Danadas caught him before he hit the glass floor. Kano felt a sudden strength in the old man's bones.

"Did you see it?" Danadas whispered.

"Y-yes."

"And a path. Did you see a path?"

"Through the river."

"It is as I thought," said Danadas, wonder in his eyes as he beheld Kano.

"Does this mean I'm an Orlov?"

"More than an Orlov, Master Kano. You just might possess a stronger connection to Iramwerta than anyone else in our family."

Our family. Kano had never had a true family, a family bound in blood. And now suddenly he was a part of the most powerful one in the galaxy.

"What do we do?" he asked.

"We act." Danadas turned toward the fireplace, its embers casting shadows beneath his wrinkles. "My time is near its end, Master Kano, and I fear I leave my family worse off than when I first assumed control. Much like the rest of the galaxy, we are weak, divided, and a shadow of our former strength. We need something to rally behind."

Kano deflated. "So you're still set on making me your poster boy?"

"More than that!" exclaimed Danadas, spinning around to face Kano again. "You must think bigger, Master Kano, if you are to take my mantle."

"Take your—" Kano shook his head, shocked. "But I barely know you. And a minute ago I didn't even know I was one of you!"

"You are young, with many cycles ahead of you. And don't worry, I still have time enough to teach you."

Kano shook his head, stunned. "Teach me what? I mean, where would we even start? I barely know a thing about this family."

"The spear chose you." Danadas lifted it before Kano, his wrinkled arms trembling beneath the weight. "It chose one of only two Zoboros that the entire galaxy happens to be watching. That is no mere coincidence. It is an opportunity. An opportunity to lead our people back to Iramwerta.”

“*Our* people?” repeated Kano. “Are you—?”

“Like I said, there is much I have to teach you.” Danadas raised his hand. Kano felt a familiar tremor, a…*shockwave*, but so gentle, so controlled; it was unlike anything he’d ever produced. He leaped back.

“I never thought there was another…like me.” Kano stared at Danadas with newfound joy. *A master*. Someone who could help him unlock secrets about his powers that he’d never thought possible.

“Before our lessons can begin, I have a mission for you,” said Danadas. “The most important mission we may ever face.” He placed the spear in front of Kano. “I want you to find Iramwerta.”

Kano took another step back, baffled. This old man had dropped a lot of bombs on him, but this might have been the largest of all. “Why me?” he asked. “Why now?”

“Because our enemies are searching for it as we speak. I fear they may be close, and if they find it first, they can unlock powers that would doom us all.”

“Who are our enemies?” asked Kano.

“The ones who attacked your home. The ones who created Taranis. They have no name, but they exist everywhere, even on the *Dormarch*, and I fear perhaps even in my own family. Like us, they want the Zoboros to return, but not as equals. They believe the Zoboros are destined to rule as conquerors and killers, but that is not our way, Master Kano. If you could be the first to step beyond Iramwerta's Gate, and to beckon the others to it peacefully, we could lead everyone toward a better future."

"But how would I get there?" asked Kano. "How do I find a place that no one can find?"

"The spear will guide you. But fear not: you will have help." Danadas nodded toward the door.

Kano turned just as Carmichael entered.

"Mogaddu is a rat's nest," he began. "You'll need someone with field experience to keep you alive."

He motioned behind him. Cera entered. She nodded but said nothing, her mind still seemingly distant.

"And you'll need someone who knows the terrain well," added Danadas. "Someone who's been training for this since the moment she arrived."

Kano heard footsteps. A guard emerged at the top of the stairs. She removed her helmet, and auburn hair spilled out, revealing a familiar, freckled face. Kano rushed over and embraced her.

"Sandra!" he exclaimed.

"It's good to see you too," she said, beaming.

"How did you escape Famora? The IDF, they—"

"All I had to do was make a call." She nodded toward Danadas, who smiled.

"She's proven to be one of the most capable warriors in our family," said Danadas. "There's no one I trust more to aid you on your secret mission."

"Secret?" repeated Kano. "Secret from who?"

Carmichael stepped in. "We've decided to keep your team as small as possible to avoid detection from Taranis and the IDF. However, if the rest of the team were to learn about your mission, it may prove difficult to keep them here in the palace."

"But—" Kano wanted to protest, to tell them how much his friends deserved to know that he was putting himself in danger, but he already knew they were right. If any of them got word of this mission, they would surely find a way to escape the palace and help, even if it meant commandeering a ship of their own.

"Who else knows about this mission?" he asked.

"Just the people assembled in this room, Master Kano."

He gulped. If he accepted the mission without telling his friends, they would resent him for it. But if he did tell them, he risked compromising their chance to stop Taranis from claiming the most dangerous power in the galaxy. He didn't want to imagine what failing this mission would mean for everyone else.

"When do we start?" he asked.

Chapter 16

The Match

Junior waited while Nera wrapped his knuckles in tape.

"You know I'll burn through this stuff, right?"

"It's just for show," replied Nera, avoiding eye contact. "Remember, you need to win the crowd. They decide how it ends. If they like the Morabani and not you, they might demand the match end with a—"

She cut herself off, but it didn't matter; Junior knew what she was going to say. *Death.* It had been on everyone's mind since he'd agreed to the match. And not just his death. If their escape plan failed, they would all be on the chopping block.

He needed to put on a good fight. That was his part of the mission. He cursed to himself. It would be so much easier if they had just enlisted Warp's help, but the others had refused to let her in on the plan. They said she was too close to Clemens.

Junior thought differently.

The ceiling shook. Thousands of feet stamped above the empty locker room in anticipation.

"Are you sure about this?" asked Nera.

Junior nodded.

"You'll have no backup," she insisted.

"I know."

Nera sighed. With the last of the tape finished, she hugged Junior and left.

She'll pull through, Junior told himself. They all would. Besides, it was his job that would be the hard one.

He made his way into the tunnel, pounding the wall with his fist as he went. This was his moment to stick it to the Taipa. To break the cycle.

And to beat the Morabani.

The noise from the crowd grew fiercer with every step. He felt their voices reverberating through the tunnel. It was the loudest crowd he'd ever heard. Maybe the loudest this arena had ever heard.

He stopped. Someone was leaning against the wall ahead. It didn't take him long to figure out who.

"Did you teleport here just to say goodbye?"

Warp dodged his orange eyes.

"I'm not going to die. Trust me."

She shook her head and turned away.

"Look, if you don't want me to go in the ring, then—" He stopped himself, remembering the others' wishes. But she turned and looked up at him, wide-eyed…innocent…and then Junior found the words just slipping out. "We're getting out of here tonight. Everyone. We have speeders waiting at Brinkborne. If you teleport me there you can—"

Warp extended her arm, her fingers closed around something in her hand. Junior blinked. She was offering him something, but seemed too afraid to show him what it was. She opened her palm slowly, wincing, as if whatever it was would jump out and bite her. Junior didn't understand why until he saw it.

His father's pin.

He snatched the golden triangle from her. "When did you…how did…*why*?!"

She tried running away, but he grabbed her arm.

"Has anyone else seen this? Did you show anyone?!"

There was a puff of smoke and suddenly they were standing at the edge of the ring. The roar of the crowd smacked Junior in the face. His ears rang. His grip loosened and then Warp slipped out of it and puffed away. He made no effort to stop her; he was too stunned by the size of the crowd. All he saw was a sea of faces packed into the risers. It must have been over a hundred thousand people, all on their feet, cheering and screaming like bloodthirsty animals.

"Ladies and gentlemen," announced Clemens into the microphone, strutting across the ring like a peacock in his tight velvet suit. "I give you the pyro boy wonder, the Hero of Famora, and the current Champion of Casus Belli…*HELLFIRE*!"

The answering cheer was laced with boos. *Let them boo*, thought Junior, fire pulsing in his palms. *We'll see what they think when I'm through with the Morabani.*

He glanced at his companions on the sideline. They were heading for the tunnels that led to the clubhouse, pretending they were too sickened to watch their friend's fight, when in reality they were getting into position.

At least, Junior told himself they were pretending.

"And now, his opponent," said Clemens, to which the crowd stamped their feet and drummed their hands on their laps. "All the way from Moraban. You know him as the Smiter of Gods, the unstoppable, unbreakable, undefeated CALAMITY!"

The answering roar shook the very earth they stood upon. Junior's instincts told him to cover his ears before his eardrums cracked, but he held his hands at his sides. He couldn't show weakness against the Morabani. He'd seen the odds – he would need every cheer he could get.

Smoke billowed across the opposite side of the ring. A figure emerged through it, taller than a Human, with lanky arms that hung lazily at its sides. Blue scars riddled its muscular, coal-black skin. The Morabani grinned at the crowd with crooked, yellow teeth as he raised his fist. When he opened his mouth, red cartilage unfolded along its windpipe, and what came out was the most feral scream Junior had ever heard in his life.

The crowd howled. Calamity turned to Junior, arms held out wide as he basked in the adulation of his screaming fans. It was then that Junior noticed something in his opponent – a wildness in the eyes. A wildness he'd seen before in the Dockyards on Famora.

Vaxum. The sailors often used it to stay awake on long journeys. But whatever the trainers had fed Calamity was much more concentrated. That meant that no matter what Junior did in this match, Calamity wouldn't feel a thing.

"Take your positions!" called Clemens.

The electric field crackled to life around the ring. The crowd screamed and stamped with joy. The people on the ground level surged out of their seats and crowded the ring for a closer look. Even Clemens kept close to the electric field, wanting to savor every moment.

"Let's get this over with," said Calamity, cracking all his bones in one orchestral movement.

Junior assumed his fighting stance – knees bent, arms locked and at the ready. He sparked fire in each palm, and its flicker made Calamity's smile even wider.

Yeah, I bet you like the pretty lights you drugged out piece of—

"FIGHT!" announced Clemens.

Junior tensed as the crowd cheered behind him, but his opponent remained loose and relaxed. Waiting.

"*You need to win the crowd,*" Nera's voice echoed in his head. Junior wouldn't normally make the first move, but standing around wasn't going to win him any favors, especially when he needed to take up as much of the crowd's attention as possible while his friends slipped away. He threw a fireball, but Calamity made no move to dodge it. He simply lifted his hand and…

Caught it.

Junior froze. Another pyro? It was only then that he realized many of the Calamity's fans in the crowd were sporting fiery orange and red hair.

Well this should be interesting.

The fireball came surging back, its flames now brighter and bluer. Junior dove out of the way, then released a jet of flame in front of him to stop his momentum as a second fireball flashed across his path. He could feel its heat, far greater than anything he had ever produced. Would it be enough to burn him, though? So far, only Taranis's electricity had been hot enough to do the trick. He preferred not to find out if Calamity's fire could do the same.

He readied a fireball in each hand, expecting Calamity to rush him now that he was off-balance. But Calamity just stood there with a stupid grin on his face. Junior threw another fireball and Calamity slapped it away. He tried again and again, but Calamity deflected every shot, yawning while he did it.

Enough. Junior threw out his fist and sent a jet of flame at his opponent, who absorbed it in one hand and fired it back with the opposite one. It slammed into Junior's chest like a sucker punch and knocked him flat on his back. He laid there gasping, his shirt in smoking tatters, and patted his bare chest. No burns, but definitely bruises. He would need to be careful how much power he threw Calamity's way, because it would come back with added force.

A pair of bare feet bounded straight for him. He rolled away as fire exploded where he had been lying a moment ago. Electricity crackled in his ear. He was getting too close to the edge. Options limited, he dove forward and took a fireball to the chest that dropped him back to the floor.

"Do you yield?" asked Calamity, his bare feet stepping closer, blue flames balanced in each hand.

Junior rose slowly, shakily, the smoldering remains of his shirt falling to the floor. He stared at Calamity, at the blue flames much stronger than his own, at the blue scars from fights much harsher than any he had ever known. Still, he raised his fists.

The crowd booed. Calamity smiled, and for a brief moment his glazed eyes looked to the crowd. *That's it*, thought Junior. The opening he'd been waiting for. He drew his arms back and yanked the blue flames from his opponent's hands. A gasp ran up the risers as Junior hurled the fire back into Calamity's chest and sent his opponent tumbling across the ring.

A hush fell over the crowd. Even Junior stared in disbelief. *It worked.* But it was a small victory. The Morabani was back on its feet quickly, its bloodshot eyes zeroing in on Junior. There would be no more games now.

Only blood.

"Come on!" cried a visiting gangster from behind the electric field. "Scorch his ass, Kazan!"

Kazan? Junior stopped. He knew that name. But where had he heard it before? He had little time to think; a blue flame was already sailing his way. He dove out of the way and kept moving, kept thinking while fireballs burst all around him. *Kazan...Kazan...*

It appeared in his mind's eye – the Taranis report he'd stolen from the Police Plaza in Famora. In it, he'd found the names of Zoboros that Taranis had kidnapped.

Junior hurled a fireball into one of Kazan's and they burst with an earsplitting crack. The two fighters stood there amid the smoke, catching their breaths, sweat steaming off their skin.

"Had enough…*Famoran?*" said Kazan with a grin.

"You tell me, Androssi," replied Junior. Kazan's grin vanished. For the first time, Junior saw fear in his opponent's bloodshot eyes. "That's where you were born originally, wasn't it?" continued Junior. "That's where he gave you your 'freedom' so you could disappear. And what did you do with it? You ran off to your peoples' homeworld so you could become a slave again."

"I'm a champion!" The Morabani summoned a jet of flame and cracked it like a whip.

Now I made him angry. Junior tried dodging the whiplash, but its tail caught his leg and burnt a welt into his flesh. He cried out and clutched his wound. Kazan was holding nothing back now. As the Morabani drew back for another strike, something came to Junior. Another memory from Famora – or rather, the mountains near Famora, where he had fallen to what at the time had seemed his imminent demise. But he'd been able to break the fall using two jets of flame that let him hover above the ground. He'd wondered if he could do more than hover with that trick, but had never needed to try it.

Until now.

He blasted the floor with twin jets of flame. They launched him high over Kazan's head, but he didn't stop there. The crowd gasped as he teetered left and right, trying to control the trajectory of his launch. The higher he climbed, the more he realized that he wasn't just hovering…he was *flying.*

"Congratulations!" called Kazan from the ring. He let his whip fizzle into smoke as two jets of blue flame erupted from his palms. Before Junior could react, the Morabani launched himself up and began hovering level to him.

"It's your move," said Kazan.

Junior pressed harder. The flames pushed him higher, but Kazan followed closely along his smoking path. Junior kept snaking through the sky, the crowd shrinking beneath him. His arms strained; his head felt heavy. He couldn't keep this up much longer. He spotted the rafters and launched for them. His vision began to tunnel. With a last push he vaulted himself over the railing and tumbled across the metal walkway, his flames sputtering and dying.

The spotlights followed him up, illuminating a pair of bare feet in front him.

How is he so fast? was the only thought that passed through Junior's exhausted brain as Kazan picked him up by the throat and held him over railing.

"Kazan…wait…" Junior gasped, trying not to look down at the hundred-foot drop.

"How do you know my name?" demanded Kazan.

"Because…I know you want freedom too…so why do you serve them?"

"I serve no one!"

"Would Taranis…agree?"

Kazan fell silent. He stared at Junior, thinking, while a hundred thousand eyes squinted from below to see what was happening between them.

"This is all I have," said Kazan finally, loosening his grip.

"Kazan, please…" Junior clasped Kazan's arms feebly, his vision filling with spots as a bright blue flame formed in front of him.

Junior braced for the oncoming strike when he heard someone scream. Not from below, but close. From the rafters. Water splashed in his face. The flame disappeared, and his neck slipped through Kazan's fingers.

He was falling, just like on the mountain near Famora. He unleashed fresh jets of flame that licked down toward the incoming ring. The crowd screamed. Junior kept pressing. He was starting to slow. He was gaining control.

A blue fireball exploded against his back. He screamed and crashed down onto the ring, his shoulder absorbing the brunt of the impact. He cried out again, his mind in a whir, pain springing from everywhere, especially his shoulder. Dislocated, he could tell. He tried rolling onto his back to save himself some pain, but the fresh burn there stung even worse, like a hundred hot knives all being pressed into his flesh at once. He rolled onto his belly and laid there, every limb and joint feeling either too bruised, broken, or burned to move any more.

Blue jets of flame licked the floor across from him. The Morabani landed there and marched toward him.

"SEVAS! SEVAS! SEVAS!" the crowd chanted.

Junior tried to summon another flame, but nothing came. His hands just laid there uselessly as he stared up into Kazan's bloodshot eyes. Pain, rage, confusion: they were all written across his opponent's coal-black face as a blue fireball grew larger and larger in his palm.

"SEVAS! SEVAS! SEVAS!"

Fight you idiot. Junior tried lifting himself up, but his shoulder gave out under his weight as a searing pain shot through it.

"I'll deal with your Norphimian friend next!" said Kazan, raising the flame high above his head.

"WAIT!" boomed Clemens's voice.

The crowd booed as the electric field shut down and Clemens rushed into the ring.

"Don't worry, my good people, you'll get your ending. But before we finish Hellfire, there's something I want him to see."

Smoke puffed around the ring. With each puff, another one of his friends appeared, each one looking confused, shocked, and frightened.

Last to appear was Nera. She looked Clemens dead in the eye.

"Snake!" she cried. She whipped a jet of water at him. A puff of smoke and Clemens appeared right behind her, Warp holding his hand. With the other hand, he smacked Nera in the back of the head and knocked her to the floor.

Junior clenched his fist, wanting desperately to burn Clemens for that, but unable to summon the flame. Zivo and Brivek clearly felt the same way, for they took a step toward Clemens, but made no attack. Clemens's gangsters were positioning themselves along the edge of the ring, their guns aimed, the crowd holding its breath.

And all the while, Yui stood in place, watching.

Clemens raised his microphone. "These Zoboros attempted to escape tonight." Boos erupted from the crowd. "It seems they thought they could just abandon their matches. But let's not blame them. They only did it because the Hero of Famora was whispering in their ears, feeding them lies. He thinks the Zoboros should be above us. Should *rule* us!"

The crowd was on their feet, screaming and tossing their drinks onto the ring.

"Liar," muttered Junior.

"But your champions can redeem themselves!" announced Clemens. "The Hero of Famora planned this escape, so now he will reap its rewards." He turned to the other Zoboros fighters. "Kill him, and you may remain here as champions."

"Never," said Zivo, drawing knives from beneath his skin. Brivek stepped up beside him, his skin turning to stone as he assumed a fighting stance.

Clemens nodded to his gangsters at the edges of the ring. They drew closer, weapons ready.

"I'll do it."

The whole crowd turned as Yui stepped forward.

Clemens smiled. "That's my Ice Queen."

"Yui, no!" cried Nera.

Yui marched toward Junior, ice condensing around her hand. He looked up at her, pleading with his orange eyes.

"Is this really what you want?" he asked.

"It's what I've wanted for a long time," she said, but when she looked down at him, she hesitated. The whole crowd watched in silence, holding their breaths.

Clemens drew closer and whispered in her ear. "Sevas, my dear."

"Sevas," she repeated. She grabbed Clemens's wrist. He gasped as ice enveloped his entire arm. The microphone dropped from his hand. With her other fist, Yui smashed Clemens's arm to icy bits.

The crowd screamed.

Clemens fell to his knees amid the shrapnel of his own limb, staring in shock at the frozen socket where it had once sat.

"Sh-sh-shoot her," he gasped, regaining his voice. "*Shoot the fucking bitch!*"

The Ice Queen and company readied their powers. Kazan skated back, trying to avoid the crossfire as the gangsters prepared to unload.

Then something bright flashed above their heads. Sparks rained down from the rafters. Everyone froze. Was it a bomb? Smoke floated down and filled Junior's nostrils.

Not a bomb, he realized. He knew that smell all too well.

Electric burn.

"RUN!" he screamed to his friends, unable to do the same as he lay sprawled on the floor.

"Run?" boomed a voice over the loudspeakers. A voice like ice. "Why run from destiny?"

Junior felt the whole world go cold. He heard the clank of metal boots as they marched down a distant flight of stairs. Thousands of eyes turned to the source as it made its way down the risers, a microphone held in its gauntlet.

"Not much has changed since I last visited Mogaddu," continued Taranis, the microphone pressed right against the mouth slit in his mask. "But this time, I bring the change."

Two gangsters charged up the stairs. They fired at Taranis, but the bullets pinged off his armor, not even slowing his approach. The people around him screamed and ducked for cover. But Taranis could care less for their safety. He grabbed the gun of the first gangster and smashed it into the man's forehead. Then he flipped the second gangster around and snapped the man's neck in one swift motion.

More people screamed. They surged toward the exits, piling in like stampeding cattle as the risers cleared out.

"ZOBOROS!" called Taranis, continuing his descent. "No longer are you slaves! You may take any path you choose. And if you choose mine…you will have vengeance."

He stopped as Clemens's Gorv, Roger, came charging up the stairs. He held out his hand and let the electricity leap from his fingertips, drowning the Gorv in blue bolts until it was down on one knee, groaning. Taranis drew his sword from his belt and cut the head clean off the beast.

The Ice Queen looked down at the wreckage that had once been Clemens's arm. She smiled, and from her hand grew an icy spear. She hurled it into the chest of the nearest gangster, who screamed and tumbled over the edge of the ring.

"Follow me," she said to the other Zoboros as a new spear materialized in her hand. She charged toward the gangsters and blasted them with jets of ice. Brivek charged after her, his stone body blocking the bullets intended for Yui. Zivo followed, swords and axes sprouting from his arms, each swinging with such precision that not a gangster in his path was left standing. Nera ran after them, crying, begging them to stop.

"Wait, don't..." groaned Junior, reaching out helplessly from the floor as he watched his friends slaughter the Taipa enforcers. How could this have gone so horribly wrong? Across the ring, he saw Kazan's trainers running and flailing, their robes ablaze with blue fire. Junior kept crawling. There were screams. Gunshots. The crowd was clearing away. In the stands, he spotted a Gorv gunning down gangsters, its face half-covered in scars. Dimitri. Taranis's pet. Another figure appeared and then vanished beside it. At first, Junior thought it was Warp, but the dual pistols in her hands told him it was someone else. She gunned down gangster after gangster with savage indifference, vanishing and reappearing, vanishing and reappearing...

He reached the edge of the ring and tried to pull himself over but found he couldn't. Not because of his injuries, but because he couldn't get any leverage. Something was holding him back. He pressed harder, but his fingers had no traction. He felt...weightless.

Suddenly, he was rising in the air, clawing at it like a madman until he came face to face with the metal mask.

"Thank you, Ristin," said Taranis.

Junior saw Taranis's accomplice standing a few paces away. A tall, scraggly boy about his own age, looking fearful and wholly out of place in this bloodbath while he kept his hands outstretched in Junior's direction.

"Young Hendricks," hissed Taranis, aiming his sword at Junior's neck. "Look how far your luck has brought you."

"I didn't need luck to beat you the first time." He wanted to spark a flame, but even if he could, the slightest flicker would be answered with a jolt of electricity.

"You're right. You just needed your father."

Junior spat at the mask. Taranis didn't budge.

"I'm impressed by what you *almost* accomplished here," he said to Junior. "Trying to free the Zoboros, it was noble. Inspired. But you made a mistake."

"What's that?" asked Junior through gritted teeth.

"You played their game." Taranis drew back and swung. Junior braced, knowing this was it. The end. He felt something clutch his back and then he didn't feel weightless anymore. He collapsed onto his knees. The screams were gone. The spotlights no longer in his eyes. All was dark except the glow of the Orlov moon. He felt a hand on his shoulder, saw a pale face beneath a hoodie beside him. Then he blacked out.

Chapter 17

The Search Begins

He's back.

Kano shook in his seat as they entered Mogaddu's atmosphere, and not just because of the turbulence.

Danadas had delivered the news of the sighting a few hours ago, and since then he'd been unable to sit still. The tingle crept up his muscles again, a faded memory of his enemy's power.

But why here? There hadn't been any confirmed sightings of Taranis since their battle on Famora. And now suddenly the maniac decided to strut into a packed arena and start an uprising? Did he know that Kano and his friends were here? Kano found the timing suspiciously convenient.

Then he recalled Danadas's warning: *"Our enemies are searching for it as we speak."* That had originally been a reference to Taranis's allies, not Taranis himself. Not a man who was supposed to be dead…if he even was a man. Kano hadn't gotten a good look at who was hidden behind the mask during their last encounter, what many believed would be their final encounter. But Kano always suspected that his enemy hadn't perished on Famora; that someday he would face that monster's electricity again.

He just really wished it wasn't now.

The shuttle descended through the clouds and a sea of red dunes opened before their eyes. Kano tensed. He'd been warned of the dangers of this planet. The heat, the wild desert, and worse: the people, most of them bandits and gangsters, and all of them in search of the hefty bounty that Mezo had so graciously placed upon the heads of Kano and company; as if his face wasn't famous enough already. He had been all too eager to agree to use the disguises the Orlovs had prepared for them. That was, of course, before he'd learned the virtues of scavenger garb, like how the head wrappings were near impossible to breathe through, or how much the wooly overcoat itched, or how heavy the cargo pants were even when the pockets weren't filled with loot.

"Pull in there," Cera ordered, pointing toward a distant mountain that seemed wholly out of place amid the sands.

The Orlov guard who served as their pilot glanced warily at her. His orders came from the family, not a guest who had spent the shuttle ride silent and brooding. "The bazaar is too populated," he said. "Besides, you'd be stuck in deep desert. I'm to drop you at the riverbank."

"The riverbank won't have any intel on Taranis's movements, which we need to know in case we're walking into a trap," answered Cera, to which the pilot only shook his head.

"Taranis has the same destination as us," Cera insisted. "Your sources say he's already on the move, so let's make sure we're not following the same path. Otherwise we put Kano and your master's spear at risk."

The pilot looked to Sandra, who sat at the navigation console, the spear protruding from her scavenger pack.

"Do as she says," said Sandra through her head wrappings.

The pilot steered toward the mountain, only as they approached, Kano realized it wasn't a mountain at all, but a crash-landed ship. His jaw dropped. Not even the *Dormarch* could compare in size to the ship that dominated the horizon. The spikes on its hull told him that this was a Poterian vessel, which gave him an added chill. Not only was his enemy here on Mogaddu, but so were the relics of the greatest enemy their side of the galaxy had ever known. He could only hope the Poterians hadn't remained here after their defeat.

"Casus Belli coming up on the portside," announced the pilot. He lowered the shuttle through a crater in the dreadnought. The sunlight slowly vanished, and Kano's fear grew with the darkness. This was the belly of the beast, the hive in which the most dangerous people on the planet festered. And now they had the added pleasure of visiting when Zoboros–Taipa relations were at their worst.

His hands began to shake. *You didn't even tell them.* His friends were probably waking up right now wondering where he was, but Danadas and Carmichael wouldn't tell them. He couldn't help but think what would happen if the mission went sour, which seemed much more likely now that they had entered a city of fugitives. What would happen if he died or was captured? Would they tell his friends what happened? That he'd run off and robbed them of any chance to protect him? That had been their whole reason for coming. He felt sick.

He hurried straight to the restroom, ripped off the head wrappings, and doused his face in cold sink water. He stood there for a moment and stared in the mirror as water dripped from his chin. He didn't recognize the figure that stood before him; it looked so bulky with all the wrappings and pads that came with a scavenger's outfit. And none of them matched, of course. If they did, anyone on Mogaddu could make him for an imposter.

Something tickled his wrist. Not the spasms caused by Taranis's electricity, but something *moving*. He pulled back his glove and a dilepede crawled out, its hundred legs rowing their way up his hand. *How did that get all the way out here?* He flicked the critter out the door and down the hall.

He splashed more water on his face, thinking that the Orlovs needed to do a better job cleaning their disguises, and when he looked up, Chenji was standing behind him in the mirror, no longer a dilepede, and naked as usual.

"Oh for the love of—"

"Can I borrow some clothes?"

"No!"

"But you clearly have enough to spare."

"Chenji!" Kano hushed his voice and checked that no one else was in the adjacent hallway. *"What are you doing here?"*

Chenji shrugged. "I wanted to see Mogaddu."

"Well maybe you can take a trip sometime when there isn't a terrorist on the loose."

"Gimme some clothes."

"We didn't pack any extra disguises," said Kano. "All we have are flight suits. You'll be made the moment we step off the ship."

"Then I can be your personal aivin." Just like that, Chenji morphed into one, flapped his wings, and set his talons delicately upon Kano's shoulder.

"I don't need an aivin!"

"You sure?" he cawed, checking the mirror. "I think it really adds to the image."

"Just stay here. The pilot will bring you back to the palace."

The ship shook, tossing them both to the floor.

What the hell could it be now? Kano ran back to the cockpit, Chenji still on shoulder, and found Cera and Sandra hurrying the opposite direction.

"What is that?!" shouted Sandra, pointing at the aivin.

"Ignore Chenji," said Cera, shaking her head as she continued down the hall. The others scrambled to keep up.

"What's going on?" asked Kano.

"The scavengers swarmed us the moment we lowered into the bazaar," answered Cera. "It seems the Taipa don't have control of anything anymore. We're getting off now before they tear the ship apart."

"It sounds like it'll be safer to stick with you," Chenji whispered in Kano's ear.

"Fine. Just please don't poop on me."

"No promises."

Cera led them into the cargo hold, where the liftgate was already lowering for them. Outside, anarchy had swept over the bazaar. Hundreds, maybe thousands, scrambled through the three circular levels of shops and stands to grab whatever treasures and trinkets they could find. Kano saw Humans, Nurranos, Galanads, Del Clorans, Gorvs, and more, all in the mix. Fires roared out of some of the shop windows, and up above dozens of hovercars and scavenger ships circled like vultures, waiting to pick up their friends along with whatever loot they'd found.

The team stepped into the fray, Cera at the lead, Sandra in the middle where her precious spear would have the most protection, and Kano and Chenji taking the rear.

"Where to?" asked Kano as Cera led them deeper into the crowd of thieves.

Sandra leaned back and muttered in his ear. "We couldn't say it in front of the pilot, but this detour isn't for intel on Taranis."

"Then why the hell are we here?!" demanded Kano as a scavenger ship crashed into one of the nearby shops.

"Junior was sighted here yesterday," she whispered. "But we're not sure if he's alive."

Junior. He'd made it after all! When they'd split up on Famora, Kano assumed he'd never see his friend again. But what had happened that made Cera unsure whether he was alive? Kano could only assume it had something to do with Taranis.

Sandra paused, zeroing in on a Nurrano child who was running around with more stolen silver than he should have been able to carry, and caught him by the shoulder.

"Hey, what's your problem?!" shouted the child.

"We're looking for a pyro," she began. "From the fight rings. Have you seen him?"

The child shrugged. "I might've…"

Kano reached in his pocket. He knew this routine well from living on the Westside of Famora. The cyo he tossed the child, though, was met with a frown.

"You kiddin' me? This won't buy me a bowl of noodles," said the kid.

Cera approached. "Tell us what you know and we'll give you the talking bird."

"You most certainly will not!" cawed Chenji, who immediately regretted opening his beak, for the child's eyes lit up with wonder.

"He worked in a repair shop on the second deck!" exclaimed the child, pointing. "Brinka-somethin'. A Bolani owns it, I think." The child reached greedily for his prize, but Chenji flew away in the direction the child had pointed.

"HEY!"

Cera and Sandra raced after Chenji. Kano stopped to dump a few more cyos in the child's hands and then followed his teammates up the stairs.

By the time they reached the repair shop, Chenji was already waiting for them, Human again, and wearing an oversized tunic and jeans that he'd clearly stolen from a nearby clothesline.

"Shop is locked up," said Chenji. "Took a peek through the window, though. No pyro, but it looks like the people inside are having a bit of a dispute."

"Well then we should settle it for them," said Cera. She raised her hand and a razor-thin blade of green energy extended from it. She guided it through the seam in the door, then sawed away until the lock severed.

The door opened. A Kimikan stood on one of the many worktables inside and a Del Cloran sat beside it, checking the scope of its rifle. They leaped up at the sight of the intruders and aimed their weapons.

"We're not looters," said Cera, not even bothering to raise her hands in surrender. "We wanted to speak with the owner."

"The owner is indisposed," replied a snide, slippery voice. Kano heard the click of expensive shoes. He turned. A one-armed Tenu approached, its red face covered in fresh cuts and bruises from the night before. Those weren't what caught Kano's attention though. It was the serpent tattoo snaking between them.

Taipa. Carmichael had warned him about them in the mission brief. He raised his fists, but Cera was already rushing forward with long green arms extending from her own. She used them to grab each of the henchmen's guns and toss them across the room. The Kimikan scrambled after his weapon, but Cera scooped him up in a green hand and flung him out the window. The Del Cloran drew a knife and Cera let her energy arm go limp like a noodle. A hook formed at the end of it, and she swung it over her head and into the side of the Del Cloran's face, severing a tube on its breathing apparatus. Compressed nitrogen sprayed everywhere, and the Del Cloran fell to its knees, grasping desperately to stop the leak.

Cera left the Del Cloran there and pursued the Tenu, who was already running away. She caught him by the torso in her energy hand and flung him onto a worktable in a crash of tools. The Tenu laid there, groaning, as a green tentacle snapped around his neck.

"No…please…" the Tenu gasped.

"Where is he, *Viper*?" she demanded, venom in her voice. "Where's Junior?"

"Cera, stop!" shouted Kano, but she only squeezed harder.

"I…came here askin'…the same question," gasped the Tenu, his face turning purple. Cera sneered, thought a moment, and then released him.

The Tenu gasped and clutched his now redder neck. "I was really hopin' I wouldn't see any more Zoboros today," he muttered.

Cera's green hand turned into a long blade with a thin, pointed tip, which she pressed against the Tenu's nose. "Choose your next words carefully," she said.

The Tenu gulped. "I tried askin' the owner where he went, but the big man won't talk."

He pointed with his eyes. Kano looked first and found the Bolani lying strapped to a nearby worktable. A familiar Bolani.

"Ragar!" he blurted, rushing over. He ripped the restraints off each of Ragar's four limbs. The old crook had cracks all over his red shell. Kano shuddered to think how much force it had taken to inflict that amount of damage on a Bolani.

"Do I know you?" muttered Ragar weakly.

Kano pulled back his head wrappings, assuming they were useless now that Cera had blown their cover anyway, and the Bolani's three eyes, even the lazy one, lit up.

"Ah, my boy!" exclaimed Ragar in a sudden surge of energy. "Back to return my speeder, I hope!"

Kano grinned. "Things got a little shaky on Famora. Would you accept an IOU?"

"Bah!" said Ragar, waving an indifferent hand. "I'll take the rescue as collateral."

"They say you've seen Junior. Is that true?" he asked.

Ragar sighed. "I don't know where he went. Some say Taranis killed him in the ring. Others say he joined that maniac and ran off."

"Do you know where the Zoboros have gone?" asked Cera, her blade still fixed on the Tenu's neck.

Ragar glanced over at his office on the second floor, suddenly serious. "Follow me." He hopped off the table, his crab legs scrabbling a little off-balance. Kano noticed one of them was broken.

Cera looked to Sandra and nodded toward the Tenu. That was all the signal Sandra needed. She drew the spear and held it to the Tenu's neck while the rest of them followed Ragar into the office. There they found their injured host rifling through a stack of large, printed papers on one of his many worktables.

"A few Zoboros came through here looking for him," said Ragar quietly so the gangsters downstairs wouldn't hear. "I didn't have an answer for them, but they told me if Junior turned up, that he should join them at the river. Here, I'll show you."

Ragar unfolded a map of the Mogaddan desert and circled a river to the northeast. Kano read the name next to it.

The River Niscelles.

The image of a river flashed through Kano's mind. The same river he'd seen before, when he held the spear. He blinked, returning to the present, then looked down to the spear in Sandra's hand. He saw a glow in its markings slowly fade.

"If Junior's still alive, the Zoboros there will hopefully have found some information on him by now," continued Ragar. "I should warn you, though. The river is Del Cloran territory, and they don't like visitors. You'd be heading into danger."

"Nothing we're not used to," said Cera. She folded the map and stuffed it in her pack before turning to the rest of the team. "We're leaving."

"Me too," said Ragar. He pulled a duffle bag out of one of his drawers and began stuffing it with his belongings. "Help yourselves to any speeder you like. I keep the keys in the cupholders." Ragar approached a bulky speeder in need of a paint job, its round seat fitted for his many legs. "And if you're ever in the market for speeders, I'll be setting up shop in Darraden."

Always a sales pitch, thought Kano as he watched the Bolani rocket away. *Never change, Ragar.*

"Well you heard the Bolani," said Chenji. "Let's get us some speeders!" He hopped onto one that was slender and clearly built for speed. Kano claimed one as well, not really knowing the difference between the models, and not really caring. This time, though, he did make sure the fuel gauge was working.

Cera and Sandra claimed speeders of their own, leaving the gangsters to lick their wounds. But by the smile on the Tenu's face, it was clear he still had something to say.

"Why don't you take off those wrappings, honey?!" he called after Cera. "Don't think I don't recognize those helping hands of yours!"

"Let's go," said Cera as she started her engine, but the Tenu wasn't finished.

"Let me see that lovely face, Barricade! You always did melt hearts!"

"What's he talking about?" asked Kano.

Cera revved her speeder and launched out the main doors without a word.

Chapter 18

Uninvited Guests

When Junior woke, he found only darkness and pain.

Where am I? His tired mind retrieved glimpses of an arena doused in blue fire, of a struggle and…

A mask.

He gasped and leaped out of the blankets. His shoulder screamed from the sudden movement as if a blade had been twisted inside it. He hissed through gritted teeth and tenderly touched the bandages that now covered it. His arm had been put in a sling too. But who had been taking care of him since the fight?

Metal springs creaked beneath him as he rose. Not the most comfortable bed, but a bed nonetheless. He climbed out despite his body's screams of protest. Everything ached, especially the burn on his back, which kept him stiff as a board as he limped toward the curtains. He drew them back and sunlight blazed in, blinding him. As he blinked away the spots, he found the dune sea stretching out far beneath him. He was in a tower, he realized. Another tower lay below him, smashed against the sand.

Sterling.

Someone stirred. Junior snapped around, the motion sending another sharp pain through his shoulder, and found Warp waking up in a chair at his bedside.

"You brought us *here*?!" he shouted.

She folded her arms and looked away.

"Don't act so insulted. I trusted you with our plan and you betrayed us. You tipped him off and rounded everyone up for him. They would've escaped and been far from Taranis if it wasn't for you!"

She made no response. She didn't even look at him, but he could see she was trembling. He took a deep breath and turned away, not wanting to hammer the point any further. The shouting alone had winded him, anyway.

Footsteps echoed outside. Someone had heard him. He steadied himself, even though he could only raise one fist. He could feel his power channeling through it, though, and that was all he needed.

The door opened. T8 entered the circular room and the blip on its visor began pinging rapidly. Junior assumed the bot was assessing his condition.

"The boss would like to see you now," said T8.

Junior approached the door. Each step sent a new ache up his body, but he grinded through it. That is, until he saw the spiraling staircase that awaited him beyond the door.

"Can't your boss come to me?" he asked.

"He doesn't visit the guest quarters."

"Well then he better get used to it."

T8 stared at Junior for a moment, then jabbed a metal finger into his bad shoulder. Junior screamed and fell to his knees.

"The boss doesn't like to be kept waiting, either."

Junior clenched his fist, a little fire flickering in it, but he held his temper. Better to save his limited strength for the Poterian.

Warp tried to help him up, but he shrugged her off and started down the stairs. He let his rage fuel him. It dulled the pain, if only slightly.

"Wait here," he told her, assuming there would be no need for an escape. If Sterling had wanted to kill him, it would have happened already. But what did the Poterian want? His people weren't known for charity. Junior knew this hospitality would come at a price.

It only took him a few steps on the staircase to realize how weak his body actually was. Already, he was working up a sweat. His head started to spin, but he kept pushing, drawing deep breaths and steeling his mind as though he was a runner in the final stretch. He had to pause and catch his breath when they reached the bottom. He wasn't used to this feeling, this…weakness. He didn't like it.

"This oughta brighten your day, fleshling," said T8. The bot led him out of the tower and onto a platform that hung suspended over the gaping hole that was the center of the castle. Much to Junior's relief, a hoverpad floated there. Long and flat, it fit them both comfortably. T8 steered it down the hole and into Sterling's workshop, where the Poterian sat beneath a single dangling lightbulb with a glass of ice water in his bionic fingers. Junior stepped off the hoverpad and took the seat across from him.

"Drink," said Sterling. A bot promptly served a glass to Junior and then floated away. Only this glass didn't contain water, but a strange, goopy black liquid. Junior looked to Sterling, reluctance written on his face.

"It'll help you heal. Unless you think I plan to poison you."

Junior grabbed the glass with his good arm and kicked back the goopy liquid. It slid down his throat with the consistency of a raw egg, but the soothing effect it had on his dry throat felt oh so good.

"Why are you helping me?" he asked.

"Because the sooner you're back on your feet, the sooner I can get you off my planet."

"Your planet? Last I checked, Mogaddu belonged to the Taipa. Or is it Taranis now? I'm not sure how much I missed while I was out."

"You've been asleep for two days. And in that time, the Zoboros have descended on the River Niscelles and destroyed everything in their path."

"Isn't that Del Cloran territory? I thought you'd be happy to get rid of those insects."

"The Del Clorans are an annoyance. War is dangerous."

"Says the man locked up in a castle?"

Sterling shook his head and leaned back in his chair. He gave some thought to his response before answering. "On Mogaddu, they say it was blood that turned the sands red. Every species and every civilization has tried to claim this land. This was the first time in centuries that no one has fought for it beyond a few rogue gangs. But if you bring the galaxy's attention back to Mogaddu, you risk starting an even greater conflict."

"*Or* I risk bringing the galaxy's attention back to you," Junior fired back. "You, who's enjoyed peace and quiet out here while Zoboros fight as slaves right under your nose. You, whose people started the last war on Mogaddu in the first place."

Sterling drummed his fingers on the table. "Is that what they told you?"

"You crossed the Rift. You declared war on us. It seems pretty straightforward to me."

"Our *emperor* declared war," said Sterling. "But he originally came for peace."

Junior rolled his eyes. He couldn't believe what he was hearing. Almost every family he knew had lost someone to the Poterians. But he was willing to entertain the cyborg's narrative a bit longer. "So what changed his mind?" he asked.

Sterling looked Junior up and down. "It's a shame, boy. You would have been royalty where I come from, just as Emperor Palorex was. But he saw how you treated your Zoboros on this side of the galaxy; how you would treat his people if they brought their powers across the Rift. So he set out to make…corrections."

Just like Taranis wants to make corrections. It made sense swhy the Zoboros had allied with the Poterians during the war. They had offered the Zoboros equality.

More than equality – power. The Poterians didn't see themselves as warmongers; they saw themselves as liberators.

But that still didn't explain why Sterling was helping him. Did this mean the Poterian was sympathetic to the Zoboros? If that were true, he would have done something about the fight rings already. No, Sterling didn't care about the Zoboros fighting each other. It was only now that they were fighting at the river that he seemed to care.

The River Niscelles. Junior knew that name. Niscelles was one of the fabled kings of Mogaddu, one of the first to step through the gate.

"The lost city!" he exclaimed. "You're afraid the Zoboros will find it!"

"I told you, that place does not exist," muttered Sterling.

"Then why protect the river?"

His host sighed. "Because it is the *idea* of Iramwerta that's dangerous. The idea of a place that holds ultimate power is what brought war to Mogaddu over and over again. It drew the emperor here and left his armies buried in the sand." For a moment, Junior thought he saw Sterling's bionic arm tremble. "If the Zoboros are drawn here again, they will be wiped out."

"Or they'll rally and claim a land of their own," said Junior.

"And how do you intend to defend that land? The Taipa's power extends far beyond Mogaddu, and even if you were to ward them off, you would still have others to contend with."

"Like the IDF?"

"Or other Zoboros," shrugged Sterling. "Did you think bringing all these powerful, outraged people together would be peaceful? You bring them to a lawless land and they will eat each other."

"I think we would surprise you," said Junior, though the seed of doubt was already planted. He'd seen what the Zoboros could do under the influence of a maniac like Taranis. And he'd seen how easily they'd fallen under that influence, too. He had been so focused on external threats like the Taipa and the IDF that he'd never considered what the Zoboros could do to themselves.

Sterling eyed him knowingly. "Your fame among the Zoboros will not last. Already Taranis stands to challenge you."

Here it is, thought Junior. "And you want me to use my fame, Sterling?"

"To convince the Zoboros to go somewhere else, anywhere else. There are plenty of planets and continents that you could claim without risk of conflict. I could take you there, where you and your people can figure out your leadership and politics on your own."

"Why do you care so much about this?"

Sterling looked down at his water for a moment as he swirled his bionic finger in it. "We're castaways, Hendricks. No one else is going to watch out for us."

Junior's eyes narrowed. He didn't buy that line for a second. There was something in this for Sterling; something the Poterian wasn't disclosing.

"T8 will help you find the Zoboros as soon as you're fit to travel," continued Sterling. "Until then, keep to the tower."

Junior rose, a million questions still on his mind as T8 ushered him onto the hoverpad. What was Sterling's endgame? Where else could the Zoboros go? And what power did Iramwerta hold that everyone was so attracted to?

T8 dropped him at the base of the tower stairs. Junior stared up the long, winding staircase and cursed to himself. Fatigue had already set in; his body needed more recovery than he was willing to admit. He braced for the climb when he felt a hand on his back. A puff of smoke and he was back in his room.

"Thank you," he said. He lied down in bed, and as he watched the smoke clear away, a thought occurred to him. "How much did you hear in Sterling's workshop?"

Warp shrugged.

Junior interpreted that to mean "all of it." "Why are you still here?" he asked. "You could be anywhere on Mogaddu right now with your powers. Don't you want to join the other Zoboros or something?"

She shook her head.

Junior felt sleep overtaking him as his face sank into his pillow, but he pushed himself to keep talking. "Why did you stay with Clemens so long?"

She turned away.

"I was just curious." He stewed a while in silence before drumming up the courage to ask another question. "Where's home for you?" he yawned.

She mouthed the word slowly so he could read her lips. "Nowhere."

"I'm sorry." Numbness overtook him. He shut his eyes for what he thought was just a moment, but when he opened them again night had fallen. Beyond the window, wisps of cosmos threaded through a million stars.

"Warp, what time is it?" He turned and found her asleep in her chair. He climbed out of bed, groaning, though the pain was noticeably less intense than before. A good sign. His throat was dry, though, probably thanks to Sterling's concoction, so he opened the door and started down the neck of the tower.

"T8, are you down there?" he asked. "I could use a glass of—"

A crash echoed up the tower. He stopped and listened. The patter of feet came from behind. He spun around and saw Warp coming toward him, awoken by the noise. He motioned for her to stay quiet, to which she simply shook her head in annoyance. She didn't need to be reminded to use her default setting.

They crept down the stairs. Voices carried faintly from somewhere within the castle. Junior couldn't place them, but he was pretty sure they didn't sound like bots. He peered over the platform at the base of the tower and down the hole. Light flickered through a window a few floors down. The curtains had been drawn, but silhouettes were moving behind them. Definitely not bots; they lacked the sharp angles. Sterling had visitors, but who? Other Zoboros? Other Poterians? Only one way to find out.

Junior pointed to a large, stationary silhouette in the window, which he assumed to be a desk or table. "Can you get us behind that? Quietly?"

Warp answered by crouching, so he did the same. She took his hand and a moment later they were beneath the dim yellow lights. Thankfully, the object he'd pointed to was in fact a table, with a tablecloth set over it to keep them concealed from the visitors on the other side. It was warm and stuffy in here, and Junior swore he heard a fire crackling somewhere inside.

Footsteps pattered around the room. Junior counted at least five pairs of feet beneath the tablecloth. He couldn't see who they were, but he could make out their voices in mid-conversation.

"Where do you reckon he's gone?" someone hissed.

"I say we check again," said another. Junior recognized this one, though he struggled to pinpoint where he'd heard it before. "I'll bet he buried himself deep in that damn hole of his."

They wanted Sterling, Junior realized. These were no guests at all.

"I'm sure he's got plenty of escape routes down there, too," came a woman's voice. She sounded bored. "Wherever he went, he's long gone now."

"Let's burn the place down, just to be sure," said the familiar voice. Junior felt the heat ramp up as the room brightened, and instantly he knew who it was.

Kazan!

"We need him alive," came a voice that washed over Junior like frostbite. He knew that voice too. He felt his muscles trembling where electricity had once struck them. "He left his ship here. He plans to return, and soon."

"Then I will remain here to greet him," said Kazan eagerly.

"No," said Taranis. "I believe there is another way to find what we seek. My sources tell me we have other visitors on Mogaddu. They've come in disguise, and they carry the spear."

"What spear?" asked another female voice. Junior recognized this one too.

"You let us worry about that, Ice Queen," said the bored woman. "Just don't be in the way if they point the spear at you."

"I didn't plan on it, Mila," muttered Yui, annoyed.

"You hear that, Ristin?" asked Kazan. "Better stay out of the way. Wouldn't want to lose those musical fingers of yours."

"You'll lose more than fingers if you cross any Zoboros that carries this weapon," said Taranis in a tone that commanded silence in the room. "Do not underestimate our enemies."

"So how do we find them?" asked the woman named Mila.

"By following the Zoboros," said Taranis. "They are gathering at the river. Sooner or later, our targets will collide with them."

"I thought you said they were undercover," said Yui. "How will we recognize them?"

"Oh, I'll recognize them," said Taranis.

There was something about the coldness of that statement that sent a chill through Junior. He slipped forward and thumped his head against the leg of the table. The room went silent. He heard metal boots marching his direction. Warp grabbed his hand, and suddenly they were sitting on the desert sand beneath the tower.

Taranis has enemies on Mogaddu, thought Junior. *Ones he recognizes. Ones he hates. Could it be…?*

He turned to Warp. "I need your help."

She nodded slowly. She looked frightened.

"We need to be the first ones to find whoever has that spear."

Chapter 19

The Boy with the Spear

It was late into the night when they finally made camp on a hilltop. Kano had wanted to stop hours ago, but Cera had kept pressing on, leading their speeders deeper into the night. No one dared to raise a complaint during their journey; they were all too afraid to speak up to her.

Kano shook his head as he set down his sleeping mat. Cera was the last person he ever expected to be afraid of. It seemed the longer they stayed on Mogaddu, the colder she became. The Taipa had made it clear that she had a history with this planet. He wondered just what that history was.

The grass crunched beneath him as he laid down. A comforting sound amid all the uncertainty; it meant they were finally leaving the desert behind. He could feel the change in the air, and not just because the sun was down. It was humid here, gentler on the lungs, and the air smelled of the sweet grass growing around him, something he'd never known in the floating city.

"The river is only a few klicks away," announced Cera as she laid down a good distance from the others. "We set out at first light."

"First light isn't that far away," groaned Chenji.

Kano shared his friend's sentiment. His thighs were sore and raw from riding the speeder all day long, and his throat burned from the sand he'd inhaled while riding in Cera's wake. He wanted to capitalize on what little sleep he could get, but his mind was restless. It kept replaying the chaotic scene he'd witnessed at Casus Belli; a scene caused by the local Zoboros. Their anger had turned an entire city on its head, and now that same anger was marching toward the river.

Despite his concerns, the softness of the grass gradually lulled him. He wasn't sure whether minutes or hours had passed, but when he opened his eyes again, the dawn was breaking. Chenji and Sandra slept nearby, but Cera's sleeping mat was vacant. Kano found her seated at the edge of the hilltop with her legs hugged to her chest. He sat beside her, silent, as they both stared at the pink wisps of early light reaching across the sky. Grassy hills rolled across the landscape, a few trees standing among them. He even spotted a flock of birds fluttering overhead. This planet really could be beautiful, he realized. A good home.

But not for Cera.

"Does Carmichael know you came from Mogaddu?" he asked, resolved to get to the bottom of his team leader's struggle.

She nodded. "He's the one who got me out."

They stared at the horizon while Kano formulated his next question. He didn't want to push her away by being nosy. To his surprise, though, she continued talking all on her own.

"My homeworld looked a lot like it does here. Pretty. And quiet. I was the only Zoboros in my village. To them, my powers were a gift. We didn't have much contact with the rest of the galaxy. We didn't know how dangerous that gift could be.

"One day a traveling merchant was passing through. I always put on a show for visitors. I would do this trick where I juggled fruit and then made a slide with my hands that led them onto the visitor's plate." She smiled to herself, but then darkness retook her. "It turned out his merchandise was people. He broke into my home in the middle of the night, strapped a power dampener on me, and stole me from my parents."

Kano stared at her for a long time. "I'm sorry," was all he could manage.

"I was nine when he sold me to the fight rings. I was so scared that I couldn't even summon my powers in the ring. My new owner didn't like that. He had this Del Cloran enforcer who he would send in to beat me when I couldn't perform, and after a few beatings, I started to fight back in the ring. And then I got better at it. And then I got used to it.

"My reputation grew. With each fight, I got stronger. With each beating, I got tougher. They called me Barricade, and after a few cycles, Barricade was selling out arenas. I got so popular that my owner was able to arrange a fight in front of the leader of the Taipa: a monster named Mon Chogorath. My owner said it was the greatest honor there was. But I was terrified."

Kano looked up expectantly.

"When two Zoboros fight in front of Mon Chogorath, only one comes out alive."

There was a long silence before Cera continued. "They blindfolded me and took me to a secret palace in the desert. When they pulled the blindfold, I saw my opponent at the other end of the ring. A little boy, younger than me. But when I looked into his eyes, I saw…nothing. Just emptiness. Like the blindfold was still on him.

"Four Gorvs carried Mon Chogorath in on a palanquin. I never got a good look at his face, just his purple, scaly hand. He waved it and the fight began.

"I had trained hard because I was terrified to lose, but this kid…he *wanted* to lose. It wouldn't have been obvious to someone watching, but I could tell by the way he opened himself up after an attack that he wanted me to knock him down. He wanted it to be over. And when I finally gave in, I heard Mon Chogorath utter one single word.

"Sevas."

Kano felt a chill even though he didn't know what that word meant.

Cera wiped away a tear. "When I looked down, the boy just nodded to me like he was ready. Ready for the end. I created a blade and aimed it at his heart…but I couldn't do it. I wouldn't. In that moment, I saw my real opponent hiding in his palanquin while he forced us to kill each other. I felt ashamed. So I turned to Mon Chogorath and shook my head.

"My owner was furious. He sent his Del Cloran into the ring. It aimed its pistol at my head, and I just stood there, ready to take it. I don't know where I got that courage from, but I think in that moment I just…I finally knew what I stood for. So I stared the Del Cloran down and waited for the shot. That's when I noticed something beneath its goggles. A bluish glow. Del Clorans don't have blue eyes.

"He turned the pistol on the palanquin and fired. There were screams. The Gorvs scrambled to protect their leader. Other Taipa in the audience drew their guns, but IDF agents burst into the room and a firefight broke out. It all happened so fast. Before I knew it, the Del Cloran was dragging me out of the room, and it wasn't until we were safely away that he ripped off the fake breathing apparatus.

"That was the first time I saw Carmichael's face. The first friendly face I had seen in a long time. He held me and I started to cry. I cried because I knew it was finally over."

Kano sat there for a while, absorbing it all. "So Carmichael switched places with the Del Cloran right before the fight?" he asked.

"He was always the Del Cloran. It was part of his deep cover. He'd waited over a cycle for a shot at Mon Chogorath, and I gave it to him."

"You mean Carmichael beat you?!"

"It's hard to understand," said Cera, looking away. "Yes, he tortured me, but he was willing to do what no one else would. He got his hands dirty for a chance to cut the head off the serpent. So many Zoboros could have been saved that day, but Mon Chogorath escaped. That's what Carmichael told me when he asked me to join him. And I agreed because I wanted to do whatever was necessary to protect our people."

"What about the boy? The one you fought?"

Cera shook her head. "He was killed in the crossfire that day."

Kano thought for a long time on that as the sun rose over the horizon. "Sometimes I wonder if our people can ever actually be saved."

"Only we can save ourselves," said Cera. "And only if we stand together. That was the point of this team. And it would have been so much easier if Taranis hadn't come and made an even worse name for Zoboros."

"I don't know about that," said Kano. "It was Taranis that brought us together. And his mission isn't too different from our own. He's just willing to get his hands even dirtier than Carmichael's."

"Carmichael is nothing like Taranis," said Cera flatly. "Taranis has no mercy."

"He does. I've seen it. And people will hate us too if we don't show our enemies mercy. Even the Taipa. Even Taranis."

Cera sat silent. Footsteps crunched through the grass behind them. The others were getting ready. Or so Kano thought. But when he turned around, four bandits were standing over his sleeping friends. He and Cera jumped up and raised their fists.

"No sudden moves," said one of the bandits. A Nurrano, she raised her black-blue hand. Ice began to cover it, forming into a sharpened tip that she aimed down at Chenji's neck.

Chenji stirred. He opened his eyes and, seeing his attacker, morphed into a snake and slithered away.

"They're Zoboros too!" cried another bandit, this one a Talak. He sprouted swords from each of his six arms.

Cera generated her own blades of green energy. "We're not here to fight you! We're looking for the other Zoboros in this region."

"Why?" demanded the Nurrano. She turned her ice blade on Sandra, who had just woken up.

"We'll state our business when we reach your camp," said Cera. "Now let her go."

"I don't know what camp you're talking about," said the Nurrano, inching her blade closer to Sandra's neck.

"Wait!" shouted a Norphimian, pointing at Kano. "That's the other Hero of Famora!"

The bandits gawked.

"Other?" repeated Kano. "Have you seen Junior?"

"Not since his last match," answered the Talak, lowering his swords. "We're not even sure if he's still alive."

"Then take us to the other Zoboros," said Cera. She kept her blades raised, not willing to budge until the Nurrano lowered her weapon as well. "Someone else might know where we can find him."

"We don't know any other Zoboros," said the Nurrano.

"Bullshit!" cawed Chenji. He swooped in as an aivin and landed on Cera's shoulder. "I see a lot of activity to the north. Looks like a training camp."

The Norphimian stepped forward. "Why do you seek the one you call Junior?"

"He's a friend," said Kano. "And if he's alive, we could use his help."

The Norphimian turned to the fourth bandit, a Vosni, who scratched his pale cheek. "I say we take them to the camp," he said. "They might help us find him."

"We don't need to find him," said the Nurrano.

"But if we do, he'd be a big help to our cause," said the Norphimian. "We will take you there. But we have enemies throughout the river valley. You must promise not to tell anyone of our camp or our numbers."

"Your secret is safe with us," said Cera. She watched the Nurrano reluctantly retract her ice blade. Satisfied, the Norphimian led the way down the hill, her allies forming up around Kano's party as they marched for the secret camp. Kano asked them questions along the way; he found each of them easy to talk to, except the Nurrano. Yui was her name, and the others, Nera, Zivo, and Brivek, had all been there during Taranis's attack. They had lost track of Junior, having been too busy fighting their Taipa captors. Apparently, their actions had sparked even more uprisings across the region, and those Zoboros were now converging on the same camp.

The hills turned from grass to trees as they neared their destination. Soon they found themselves in a forest, the brambles thick, the air more humid. Creatures seemed to chirp and caw and squeak all around them from places unseen. Life practically oozed through every crack of the forest. Kano wished Li were here to see this.

Zivo stopped and waved his arms. Kano spotted a lookout perched in one of the trees, waving back. They continued into a clearing filled with tents, supply crates, and smoldering campfires from the night before. Like Chenji had reported, there had been plenty of activity here.

But there was no one else in sight now.

"The command tent," said Zivo, pointing. One tent stood much larger and wider than the others. Even so, it would be a tight space for the number of Zoboros who appeared to be living here. And if training had taught Kano anything, it was to be wary of tight spaces.

Nera pulled back the tent flap. A crowd stood inside, their backs to the newcomers. It was so thick that Zivo needed to use all six of his arms to make a hole through it. The Zoboros crowd seemed fixed on whatever was happening at the other side of the tent, but as Kano passed, their attention quickly drifted toward him. He heard whispers of "Is that really him?" and "How did he get here?" He tried to ignore them as best he could. He needed to think of what he would say once they reached the front and addressed everyone.

The crowd parted between him and the one who they'd been staring at. Kano froze. His face flushed, for seated in the command chair on the other side was a familiar nightmare wrapped in a cloak and mask.

"Kano," said Taranis from his seat. "What a pleasant surprise."

Chapter 20

The Camp

Kano summoned a shockwave to his hand, ready to strike, but Taranis didn't flinch. He simply opened his arms to invite an attack. Cera grabbed Kano and nodded toward the crowd, reminding him that everyone here was under Taranis's sway. Kano stayed himself, fully aware now that he'd walked into a trap.

"Why are you here?" demanded Kano. He noticed another Zoboros standing beside Taranis in a place of honor – a Morabani with a sadistic smile on its face, one that looked eager to see Kano launch a shockwave into the innocent crowd. Exactly the kind of company Kano would expect Taranis to keep.

"I'm here to inspire the troops," answered Taranis, rising from his seat. The crowd backed away, leaving a hole for only Kano and Taranis to fill. Kano held his ground and stared up through the eye slits in the mask as his enemy's shadow fell over him.

"The Zoboros aren't yours to command," he said defiantly.

"No. They're not," replied Taranis, turning to the crowd. "You have your freedom now. You have a choice. Find your own path, or stand with us and take your place in history."

To Kano's horror, the Zoboros in the tent began to nod, their eyes wide with wonder. They really believed Taranis could give them a better life. They had no idea what he was actually capable of.

"Our Promised Land is within reach!" cried the Morabani in a voice that boomed throughout the tent. Many cheered when he spoke. "Every day we come closer to driving the Del Cloran invaders out. Every day we march closer to our true home. And our new visitors have brought us exactly what we need to finish the job."

His eyes fell on the spear, as did the rest of the crowd's. Sandra reached for it, afraid someone might try to take it from her pack, but Cera stayed Sandra's hand and stepped between her and the Morabani.

"This power doesn't belong to you," announced Cera with a strength in her voice that Kano hadn't heard since they'd set out for Mogaddu. "I saw what you did on Famora. I saw what your 'freedom' costs. Hundreds died at your hands, many of them families, *children*. It's not you they should be following, and the rest of the galaxy knows it."

"I do what is necessary," said Taranis. "You should understand that, Cera. Or should I call you Barricade?"

Cera flushed. "Don't you dare try to justify what you—"

"Perhaps we should tell them what *you* did," interrupted the masked man, his metal boots pacing the floor. "You, a champion of the fight rings, should know what complacency buys you here." He pointed to the scars that riddled his Morabani friend's face. "And when the gangs who rule these territories grow bored of their games, what happens then? Will they sell us to the IDF? Or maybe they'll slit our throats in the night and auction off our heads? Whichever's the more profitable, I assume."

Shouts erupted from the crowd. They didn't like that prospect.

"This spear is more than it appears," continued Taranis. "It may offer us a guide to our homeland, to our future. But our guests here intend to use it only for themselves, and I cannot allow that."

The crowd started to grow restless. They inched toward the spear with longing. Kano knew he needed to say something. This was his moment to win the crowd over with inspiring words, but none came to mind. All he could think about was what would happen if the crowd turned on them completely. Already they had sealed Kano and his friend in on all sides. Even Yui from their escort looked poised to fight them for the spear. He drew a deep breath and—

"You're going to get these people killed, Taranis!"

Kano turned. It was Chenji who had spoken, not him.

"Where I come from, people spit on your name for what you did," continued Chenji. "If we follow you, no one else will follow us. We'll face the rest of the galaxy alone."

The crowd looked from Chenji to Taranis, ready for the next volley.

"Is it the galaxy's approval that you seek? Why should we want that from the very people who approved our demise?" demanded Taranis, to which he received many nods and a few cheers. "They would only jump at the next opportunity to wipe us out. But with this spear, we can ensure that our people live on for generations."

He took a step toward Sandra, and she took a step back, bumping into a crowd that had no intention of letting her pass.

"You don't know the power you're dealing with," she said, trembling.

"Believe me, Lady Orlov, I do." Taranis patted the sheathed sword at his side. He held out his gauntlet, waiting.

Don't do it, thought Kano, but already she was drawing the spear, driven by the fear that Taranis's lifeless mask brought out in people. He couldn't just sit by. A rush came over him. He snatched the spear from her and the crowd gasped. He fell to the floor as images flashed through his mind; images of water, and sand, and stone, and fire.

He released the spear. It clunked on the ground beside him. His mind was back in the present. He knew all eyes were on him now. A metal boot landed beside him. He braced, expecting an attack.

Instead, the gauntlet landed gently upon his shoulder. Taranis knelt beside him and whispered, "What did you see?"

Kano shook his head. It had all happened so fast. Even if he had wanted to answer Taranis, he couldn't, especially the part with the fire. That was new, and it felt real.

In fact, he still smelled the smoke.

"FIRE!" he cried, pointing to the top of the tent. Flames were eating through it like paper. The Zoboros screamed and crowded toward the exit, too many people for such a small tent flap.

"Kazan!" barked Taranis.

The Morabani reached out his hand and the fire started rushing into his palm.

There was a scream. Kano turned. Fires had ignited across other parts of the tent. They were spreading quickly. The crowd began ripping new openings in the sides of the tent and climbing out, yet still they weren't funneling out fast enough. The smoke was already choking the air. Time was almost up.

Kano grabbed the spear. It was the only thing he could think to do. Visions flashed through his mind again, but he held on, letting them rush by, letting himself surrender to its power. And once he did, that's exactly what he felt.

Power.

He thrust the spear into the air and a shockwave rocketed out of it like a missile. The lines snapped and the tent launched into the air, its flames snuffed by the force of the wind.

The Zoboros all stood there in shock, jaws hanging open, not even noticing the tent crash down some fifty feet away as they all stared at the boy with the spear.

Kano blinked. He could see the whole camp despite the spear still being clutched in his hand. Had the visions stopped? He wasn't sure, because in the distance he saw a familiar face, one he hadn't seen in a long time, with one arm engulfed in flames and the other wrapped in a sling.

"BASTARD!" screamed Kazan. Everyone turned. Kazan stood beside a ship that had been set ablaze. Taranis's ship, Kano assumed. Kazan pointed his finger at the newcomer. "You will pay for this!"

Junior cracked his neck. "Come and get it, asshole."

Kazan charged, his arms engulfed in blue flames. Junior raised his one good arm. Kano started forward, spear in hand, knowing his injured friend was no match, but a giant green hand beat him to Kazan. It wrapped around the pyro, and Cera let out a vicious scream as she lifted the Morabani and slammed him into the dirt.

"He's with us," she said, pointing to Junior. Kano, Chenji, and Sandra formed up beside her. When Kano glanced to his right, he saw the Norphimian, Nera, standing beside them. The other Zoboros all stood back, unsure which side to take.

"If you follow these Heroes of Famora, they will lead you to your demise," said Taranis to the crowd. He stepped up beside the injured Morabani but made no effort to help his comrade up. "Only I can save you."

"Like you saved the people of Famora?!" said Kano, aiming the spear.

Taranis drew his sword. "Do not test me, Kano."

"I passed your last test just fine." Kano steadied himself, letting his power flow into the spear. It felt strange, like an extension of his body, only it made all the rest of him feel stronger, more connected, more alert.

Electricity crackled up and down Taranis's blade as the masked man spoke. "I still think it a waste to spill your blood, but as I said, I will do what is necessary."

Lightning flashed from the tip of the blade and thunder exploded from Kano's spear. The forces collided in a great clap that threw everyone in the camp back, Kano furthest of all. He tumbled across the grass, ears ringing, too stunned to even register the pain. When he finally stopped, he found Junior was helping him get back on his feet, shouting at him, though he couldn't hear.

"What?!" cried Kano, realizing he could barely even hear himself.

The ground shook. Fire and dirt plumed in the distance from an explosion.

"What is that?!" screamed Kano. He couldn't hear Junior's response, but he could read Junior's lips.

Del Clorans.

Kano looked to the skies. A scavenger ship hovered above them, its cannons aimed in their direction.

Cera leaped in front of them and created a shield wall from her palms. She strained as bullets pounded against the other side of it, her feet digging into the dirt as the force of the gunfire pushed her back.

Through the semi-transparent wall, Kano spotted Taranis marching through the camp, bullets pinging off his armor. He aimed his sword toward the scavenger ship and with a flash the ship's right wing snapped in a blast of electricity.

Zoboros scattered as the ship collapsed in the middle of the camp. Kano heard the crash faintly, but his attention was focused on the mask turning toward him.

"We have to go!" he screamed. He grabbed Junior and Cera, the latter relinquishing her shield, and led them toward the tree line at the edge of the clearing. He noticed many other Zoboros heading that direction too, and then the thought occurred to him.

Had the Del Clorans only sent one ship?

Bullets sprayed out from the tree line. Foot soldiers! Kano could see their breathing apparatuses reflecting their own gunfire. People screamed. Many Zoboros fell. Cera generated another shield in front of the crowd as its members skidded to a stop. Many diverted in other directions while her wall absorbed the bullets, but Kano and Junior remained planted beside her.

"Scale of one to ten, how bad are we doing?" Kano asked Junior.

"Given our track record, I'd say about a seven."

"I can work with those odds."

"Kano!" cawed Chenji, swooping onto his shoulder in his aivin form. "Sandra's trapped!"

Kano spotted her running between the tents. Taranis marched after her while Kazan creeped up from the side. Soon they would have her cornered. He sprinted toward her. Junior shouted after him, warning him to wait, but he could barely hear it. Sandra's grandparents had saved his friends on Famora; he would sure as hell save her here.

The sword was aiming for her, electricity sparking. Kano readied the spear. He didn't know if a shockwave from it could clear the distance in time, but he knew his voice could.

"TARANIS!" he screamed. The maniac turned the sword on him and lightning exploded out of it.

Kano felt someone grab his shoulder. There was a puff of smoke, and a moment later he was standing on the other side of the camp, staring at Taranis's back as lightning flashed over the ground where he had just been standing.

What the hell?!

Kano turned. A girl stood behind him, her dark hair spilling out from beneath her hoodie. She had one hand on his shoulder and her other on Junior's.

"Kano, this is Warp," said Junior. "Warp, Kano."

"Uh…it's a pleasure," said Kano, still disoriented.

The girl offered Kano her hand. He took it. A puff of smoke and they were standing right in Sandra's path. She collided with them, and with another puff they were right behind Cera's shield again.

"What the hell just happened?!" cried Sandra.

"I'll explain later," said Junior. "Where's your talking bird-thing?"

"Did you miss me?" asked Chenji. He landed on Junior's shoulder and beat his wings.

Junior rolled his eyes. He grabbed Cera by the shoulder and kept his other hand on Warp. Kano, beginning to understand the routine, made sure to grab the confused Sandra by the hand. Another puff of smoke and they were deep within the trees, the sounds of the battle far behind them.

"Will someone please explain what's going on!" cried Sandra.

"A teleporter," said Cera, nodding to Warp. "Well done."

Warp blushed.

"Where to now?" asked Chenji.

"Iramwerta," said Sandra. "We're almost to the river. This is our chance to complete the mission."

"I don't know," said Kano. "Taranis and his buddy are too close. What if we accidentally lead them to it?"

"My vote is with Kano," said Cera. "This area is more dangerous than we realized. Let's return to Danadas with the intel we have and make a new plan."

"Well, my vote is with Sandra," said Chenji. "I didn't go through all this crap just to pack up and go home."

"You're not even supposed to be here, Chenji," said Kano.

"My vote stands!"

"That's two against two," said Cera. "Junior, you and your friend still have to vote."

Warp looked around nervously.

"You saved our lives," added Cera. "You have as much right to vote as the rest of us."

Warp looked from one party to the other, rubbing the tip of her shoe sheepishly in the dirt. She pulled her hood in tighter and shrugged.

"Alright, abstained," said Cera. "Junior, you're the tiebreaker."

Junior looked to each of his companions, then to the spear. Kano sighed and braced himself. He knew his friend was a punch first, ask questions later type of guy. That meant the vote was going to be to stay. But as Junior stared at the spear, Kano noticed a change in him. There was something in his friend's expression, not fear but…respect. Like Junior understood the weight this artifact carried, a weight that was amplified by the sound of distant gunfire.

"Taranis is coming for that spear," said Junior. "I say we leave with our lives and figure out a way to beat him."

Cera nodded. "I'll hail the ship." She drew a distress beacon from her pocket and pressed the button.

"Damn," said Chenji, seating himself on a stump. "I really wanted to see the lost city."

"This isn't the end, Chenji," said Cera. "We'll—"

A stun bolt flashed across the brush and struck Cera in the back. She collapsed without another word.

"Get down!" barked Junior. Everyone dropped into the brush and went silent, listening while a girl cackled somewhere in the trees.

"It's the end for you!" she cooed.

Chenji poked his head up, his sharp aivin eyes scanning. "I don't see her," he whispered.

Junior thought back to the fight ring. "She's one of Taranis's. She can turn invisible."

Chenji nodded. He morphed into a giant lizard, six feet long with ten legs, a big scaly head, and no eyes. Quietly, he slithered into the brush.

Another stun bolt flashed above their heads. "Come on out and play!" the invisible girl called. "I promise I won't—"

There was the snapping of brush and then the girl screamed.

"ECHOLOCATION BABY!" exclaimed Chenji.

Kano let out a sigh of relief. But when he saw Cera lying motionless beside him, he started to panic. How would they get her out of here with their enemies closing in?

Lightning flashed. Kano looked up from the brush. The masked man was marching toward their position, his armor and sword stained with green Del Cloran blood, his mask glowing with electricity.

Kano felt the spear slip through his fingers. Junior had taken it and aimed for Taranis.

"Junior, don't!" cried Kano, but it was too late. A fiery jet erupted from the spear's tip, more than Junior could control. It spewed side to side, setting trees and brush ablaze. Kano knocked the spear from Junior's hands and the fire ceased, but now they were trapped in a veil of flames and smoke.

"You think that got him?!" barked Kano angrily.

"No," replied Junior.

Lightning shot through the flames and struck the tree beside them with a clap.

"Warp!" shouted Junior. Warp grabbed Cera and Sandra and together the three of them disappeared, leaving Kano and Junior alone amid the flames.

"She'll be back," reassured Junior, but Kano already saw the silhouette emerging through the smoke. Not Warp's silhouette, but a much taller, thinner one, a bloodied sword at its side. Kano instinctively blasted a hole through the flames and ran through it. Junior followed, waving his hands to keep the encroaching flames away while the crunch of boots trailed not far behind.

"Surrender the spear!" shouted Taranis.

Lightning flashed above their heads. They kept running through fire and brush. Kano checked over his shoulder. Taranis was running now, his armor aglow from the surrounding flames. Even with the mask concealing him, Kano could tell that Taranis was angry, and that made Kano even more terrified.

Junior started hurling fireballs back while Kano led the way. That's when he saw it – the river. It was some fifty feet beneath them, wide and commanding, its crystal blue water rushing along a forested path. Then he realized, there was no path down the hill to it...just a straight drop.

He skidded to a stop. "Junior, look out—!"

His friend, still focused on Taranis, crashed into his back and together they tumbled over the precipice and splashed into the rushing waters below. The impact smacked Kano so hard he didn't know his up from down. Worse, he didn't know how to swim. He fought and flailed and found that seemed to be working. The sunlight was getting closer. He was rising with the bubbles, and then he realized – something was *pulling* him. Not the current, but something in front of him.

He looked to the spear in his hand. Its inscriptions glowed brightly in the water as bubbles pumped all around it. He realized then that he didn't need to swim; the spear was doing all the work! He resurfaced, gasping. The waves tossed him up and down as he rode through the current. He had to fight to keep his head up, searching for his friend. He glanced back at the hill they had fallen from, and swore he saw something splash into the water, but the spear pulled him away before he could get a better look.

"KANO!"

He turned and spotted his friend coming up in the distance, just barely keeping afloat with only one good arm to use.

"Grab on!" he cried, extending his hand as far as he could reach. Junior caught hold and the spear pulled them both underwater, deeper and deeper until they came through a crevice in the rocks along the river's edge and into darkness.

Chapter 21

The Pillar

A cold wave splashed over Kano's face. He awoke on the sand and coughed up water. *Where am I?* A rocky ceiling arched high above him, sunlight peeking through its many cracks. Everything seemed so…familiar. Then the realization hit him.

It can't be. He crawled up the beach, determined to see what had only existed in his dreams, if those had even been dreams at all. They had all felt so real. Could this be a dream now? Somehow, he knew it wasn't. That's when he saw it.

The stone door.

It towered over the cove; the largest door he'd ever seen. Letters of a dead language were etched into it, each one bigger than himself, and each glowing a golden color. The light presumably came from a source behind the door, though, standing here, Kano couldn't help but wonder if some mystic power was the cause of it. This place had that kind of effect on him.

A body laid face down on the beach. *Junior!* Kano hurried over, but as he drew closer, he realized that it wasn't his friend at all. It was a man in armor wrapped in a soaking cloak.

Taranis. But how? He saw the sword still clutched in his enemy's hand, the glow on its inscription slowly fading. The same glow he'd seen coming from the spear. Had Taranis come here the same way that he had? And was he still alive? Knowing Taranis, it was probably a trick. The moment he tried touching the masked man, he'd be shot full of electricity. But a curiosity swept over Kano. All this time, he'd never had an opportunity to look behind the mask. To see his enemy's true face. He started toward Taranis, almost in a trance, his feet splashing through the water as he reached down.

A burly hand grabbed his arm. He jumped back, a shockwave rising to his fingertips, only to realize that it was Junior who had grabbed him. Junior shook his head, and that was enough for Kano to regain his senses. They stepped away from Taranis, Junior keeping the spear aimed at the prone figure. Kano had completely forgotten about the spear, having been so focused on trying to orient himself. He saw Junior wielded it in his bad arm, which now lacked a sling. The bandages on his shoulder were now soaked and in need of replacement, too. Junior showed no sign of slowing down, though, as he aimed the spear, its inscription still glowing faintly, toward the stone door.

"Do you think the spear is a key?" asked Junior.

Kano shrugged. He still had no idea how this door worked. And he was afraid to find out. As he recalled, one of his dreams had ended with the door's inscriptions turning red and blasting him in a fiery heat death. Not something he'd like to repeat.

Something moved in the corner of his eye. He spun around in time to see the electricity spark between the fingers of the rising gauntlet.

"Junior!" he cried.

Junior ignited the spear and swung it toward Taranis's neck. Kano flinched; for a moment, he thought his friend would go through with it, but Junior stopped just inches away from his target, for he found the sword was already raised and positioned to pierce his torso. Stalemate.

"It would be a shame to spill blood on this sacred land," said Taranis calmly.

"Not if it's yours," hissed Junior, resisting every urge to drive the spear forward.

"WAIT!" cried Kano. He pointed to the stone door. Just like in his dream, the letters began to glow red, and emanated a heat so strong he could feel it all the way from the beach. It steamed the water from the sand around them, which was enough to convince the two adversaries to lower their weapons. They watched the door intently, but the color, and the heat, didn't change.

"Drop them," said Kano. Junior and Taranis did, and the red faded back to gold.

"Now what?" asked Junior. "It should be opening now, right? Just like in the story."

"I thought so," said Kano. He approached the door and ran his hand over it, hoping the glowing letters would turn white just like his dream, but they didn't change.

Taranis placed his hand beside Kano's. Kano jerked away instinctively, only to realize there was no threat. At least, not as long as they had the protection of the temperamental door.

"I don't understand," said Kano. "When the kings gave up their weapons, the door opened."

"But those aren't our only weapons, are they?" said Taranis.

Kano stared at him, confused. What was Taranis talking about? Kano knew he had nothing else to fight with except for…his powers. Was that the secret? That to enter the home of the Zoboros, they would need to give up a part of themselves, *the* part of themselves that made this city their home. A few weeks ago, he would have been eager to part ways with his destructive powers, but now he saw them in a new light. Now he knew that he needed them. How could he just get rid of them? Did he need to enter with a power dampener or something? That would make the journey decidedly more difficult.

"This is a bad idea," said Junior. "People who come here never return. We'd only be making ourselves vulnerable."

"We're already vulnerable," said Taranis. "Our powers are insignificant compared to the power that lies beyond this door. If we wish to pass, we must obey its rules."

So Taranis thinks of Iramwerta as a living thing, too, thought Kano. Danadas had expressed similar sentiments. Though it didn't seem like either of them thought of the lost city as a person; rather, it was an entity, an energy, but with its own thoughts. Its own feelings.

Feelings that apparently could get hurt.

Kano focused on the inscriptions in the stone. They must have been a message, maybe instructions of some kind. He turned to Taranis, who seemed to understand his unspoken question.

"It's a riddle," said Taranis. "It reads, 'I am gone at the start and return at the close. But while I am here, nobody knows'."

"The Zoboros?" suggested Junior. "Nobody knows that we're here."

"Zoboros weren't around when the door first opened," said Kano. "It has to be something else." He thought back to the three kings. They must have solved the riddle. But why didn't their story mention anything about a riddle? That seemed pretty important in retrospect. Unless the answer was hidden somewhere in the story, but all it said was that the door opened once the kings made…

"Peace!" exclaimed Kano. "It's gone when a war starts and returns at the end, but no one really thinks about it once we have it, I guess. What's Ancient Mogaddan for 'peace'?"

Taranis looked up to the stone door, addressing it. "Vasil."

The letters on the door turned from gold to white. Taranis kept his gauntlet fixed upon it as a thunderous crack bellowed from the stone. Suddenly, he collapsed.

Kano knelt beside him. "Taranis? Taranis?" he whispered. Taranis roused slowly and sat upright, shaking his head as though he'd just woken from a deep sleep.

"It's your turn," said Taranis.

"What are you talking about?" asked Kano.

"To touch the door." Kano didn't take his meaning until Taranis held out his gauntlet and snapped his fingers together.

No spark.

Kano turned to Junior, frightened. Was that it? Just touch the door and lose your powers? Would they ever get them back? And what dangers waited on the other side? By the expression on Junior's face, the same questions were on his mind, too.

"I won't do it, Kano."

"We have to."

"I'm not making peace with the man who murdered my father in front of me!"

They felt the heat as the letters started to glow red again.

"There'll be another time to deal with that," said Kano. "But if you want to find your mother, then we have to get past this gate."

Junior stared at his masked enemy. His powerless enemy. This was his moment; it would be suicide, but if he struck now at least he knew Taranis couldn't stop him. He'd be doing the galaxy a favor…

"Your father was an honorable man," said Taranis. "And he'd advise you to listen to Kano right now."

"Don't tell me what my father would or wouldn't do!" Fire sparked in Junior's fists, the heat from the door rising to match it. All was silent, Kano too afraid to speak. Taranis just sat there, staring through the holes in his expressionless mask, accepting whatever fate Junior would choose for him. That, or he was just confident that Junior wouldn't take the shot. And if that was the case, then he was right, for Junior relinquished the flames and the door glowed white once more.

"Don't mistake this for forgiveness," said Junior. He placed his hand upon the door. There was a rush of energy and he slumped forward. Kano was already there to catch him, but Junior stood his ground. It took just a few moments for his strength to return to him.

He snapped his fingers, and just like Taranis, no power came.

Kano gulped. It was his turn. He placed a shaking hand on the door, unsure what to expect. He felt a rush, like the wind had swept through his insides and then exited through his fingertips. He fell to his knees and sand kicked up around him. And…that was it. Even without trying to use his powers, he could feel their absence. Feel the emptiness.

A mighty groan echoed through the cove. The white glow of the Mogaddan letters faded and the ground began to rumble. Kano took a step back. A seam opened down the middle of the stone wall. *This is it.* Air screamed out; air that had been trapped there for an untold number of cycles. The two halves of the door parted, each dredging sand as Iramwerta opened before them.

Kano rushed through the opening first. There he found himself at the top of a hill looking down upon a city of stone. It was real, the lost city, standing right in front of him, yet he felt…disappointed. He wasn't sure why; he'd had no idea what the mysterious Iramwerta was supposed to look like, he just hadn't expected anything this bleak. The buildings were all as jagged and colorless as the rocks surrounding them, and hardly any of them rose more than a story or two off the ground. He supposed an ancient city would have lacked the technology to build the kinds of structures he'd grown used to seeing in Famora, but it didn't change how hollow Iramwerta felt.

There was one spot, however, that caught his attention: a temple at the city's center. It towered over the rest of the city, its face a giant staircase leading to the top, where a great pillar reached toward the rocky ceiling above. From here, the pillar looked like a candle, its top aglow thanks to an orb of light fixed upon it. Kano had no idea what the orb was made of; all he knew was it was the only clear light source this deep underground, but it glowed dimly, sadly, as though it had died with its city.

Taranis started down the sloping path toward Iramwerta, leaving Kano and Junior to stand there, unsure what dangers lurked along the shadowy path. They looked to each other and nodded, a silent pact to make sure that they both got out of this alive.

And a pact to trust nothing Taranis said or did.

As they approached the city, Kano swore he saw something rushing through the lanes between the crude buildings. It looked like water, but it didn't flow like water. It was too frenetic, moving in all directions rather than sticking to one, clear path. Nervous, he tried summoning his powers into his palms, just in case, only to be reminded that they were gone.

"What the hell is that stuff?" Junior whispered to Kano.

"People," Taranis called back, somehow able to hear him.

Kano squinted. *Impossible*. There would need to be hundreds of people, maybe thousands, for those streets to be filled the way they were. But how could so many survive underground without access to food or even a decent amount of light? It wasn't like they could grow any crops down here. Were these people Zoboros? And had they been trapped behind the gate all this time?

A closer look only raised more questions. When he entered the city streets, Kano found people of all species bustling between shops and selling carts, only there was something wrong with them. They all looked faded, semi-transparent, many of them phasing through one another. Their clothing varied greatly too, some wrapped in fine silks and linens while others wore furs and pelts. These people looked like they had been plucked out of a history book…from every chapter of a history book.

Kano reached for a nearby Braiman, but the little gray creature phased through his hand.

"They're projections," said Taranis without looking back, his focus locked on the temple ahead. "They don't know we're here."

"Projections?" repeated Kano, searching for projector lights. "But who controls them?"

"I wouldn't ask *who* so much as *what*," replied Taranis.

"Quit speaking in riddles," said Junior. "What's creating these holograms?"

"I said projections, not holograms."

"Projections of what?" demanded Junior.

"Projections of time." Taranis pointed to a faded being that walked on four stilt-like limbs. "That's a Kimu. They've been extinct for over a thousand cycles. And yet here they are, walking among us."

Kano paled. He'd never seen a creature like that before to refute Taranis's claim. But, if it was true, how was it possible?

"Are…are they trapped here?" asked Kano.

"No. They are merely reflections of the past," answered Taranis. "Time has folded on itself here."

"What does that even mean?" asked Junior. "And how do you know this?"

"There's much you have to learn, as do I." Taranis nodded toward the temple. "Come, and we may find answers together."

Kano sensed a change in Taranis. Despite the mind-bending nature of everything around them, the masked man seemed calm, contented, like being here in this place somehow brought him peace. Kano couldn't say the same for himself. The projections were making him more and more uneasy – he noticed their behavior changing the deeper they ventured into the city. Many looked frightened or angry. Some were weeping. Then he noticed many of them were running, all in the direction of the temple, their bodies less transparent than before. Kano and Junior looked to Taranis, both expecting an answer.

"We're witnessing history," said Taranis. "More recent history."

"What happened?" demanded Junior, his eyes frantically searching the crowd. "And how recently?"

Taranis didn't respond. He just kept walking.

Kano looked to Junior. They could both tell that something bad had happened here, it was written on the semi-transparent faces around them. But he knew Junior was searching for a very specific face.

His mother's face.

The crowd thickened as they reached the foot of the temple. There were too many projections to sift through now, and many of them had turned violent, throwing their hands out to use their powers on an unknown enemy. But who was that enemy, and who had won?

Distracted by his own thoughts, Kano jammed his toe against something hard. He cried out and clutched his foot, but when he saw the object of his pain rolling toward Junior's feet, all the pain seemed to evaporate, replaced by regret, for it was the last thing he wanted Junior to see.

But Junior saw it. He stared right into the empty sockets of the skull that appeared to be Human, and that was all he needed to launch himself up the temple steps.

"Junior, wait!" Kano hurried after him, leaving Taranis in the dust. He found more skeletons along the stairs, some burned, some twisted in pain, some reaching toward the top that they never made it to. But why had they converged on the temple? And who had they been running from?

He was about halfway up when he found his answer. It stared back at him, fixed upon one of the skeletons; not a skull, but a helmet shaped like a skull.

"Junior!" Kano ran as fast as he could and found Junior standing at the top of the temple, catatonic as he faced a pile of skulls, hundreds of them, which wrapped around the bottom of the great pillar.

"This isn't a city," said Junior, clenching his fists. "It's a tomb."

Kano drew to a halt, dumbstruck. He wanted to say something, to reassure Junior that his mother could still be alive, but he couldn't find the words in the face of the overwhelming evidence before them.

"Now do you understand why we must fight?" came Taranis's icy voice. Like a specter, he emerged behind Kano at the opportune moment.

"Can't you give him a minute?" demanded Kano, but Junior turned toward them nonetheless, rage written on his face.

"Her sacrifice was not in vain," insisted Taranis. "We are here now, despite the IDF's attempts to destroy us. Together we could—"

Junior grabbed Taranis by the throat. Kano jumped back, frightened by the sheer ferocity of the act, but Taranis did nothing to resist. He just let himself go limp as Junior guided him to the edge of the temple.

"Give me one good reason why I shouldn't kill you now," hissed Junior, the rest of the city looming some hundred feet below them.

"Because you need me for what lies ahead."

"Like my father needed you?!" Junior nudged Taranis backward. The metal boots scraped along the edge, where Taranis's toes clung for purchase.

"I was referring to a more…immediate need," said Taranis.

"What are you talking about?"

Kano had the same question. What besides Taranis did they need to fear inside this city? He looked around curiously, and immediately found his answer. "We have company!" he cried.

A ship was racing toward them, bulky as a freighter, yet fast and quiet as a stealth fighter. It had the trademark Poterian battle spikes along its hull, and a wide windscreen that stretched like a grin across its face. It swooped over their heads and lowered toward them, the wind from its phantom engines blowing their hair back.

Junior eyed Taranis carefully, unable to see his enemy's intentions through the mask.

"Junior!" called Kano over the wind. "We need him!"

"We need answers!" shouted Junior. "Who did you call?"

"I made no call," said Taranis.

The craft's liftgate lowered into a ramp as the ship touched down, and on it stood something Kano had never seen before. He raised his fists, forgetting in that moment that he had no powers, too focused on the Poterian enemy with the mechanical arm and leg making its way down the ramp.

"I told you to stay away!" barked the Poterian. He aimed his mechanical arm at Taranis. Its parts shifted, and the hand opened into a cannon that glowed with heat.

"My plan wasn't to come here," said Junior.

"He wasn't talking to you," said Taranis.

"I warned you what would happen if the gate was opened," said Sterling.

"You warned me what *could* happen," replied Taranis. "And now we must work together to prevent that from happening."

Kano shifted his gaze toward Taranis. A mistake. The cannon turned on him and pumped a stun bolt into his chest. He fell to the floor, his muscles seizing. He could only watch as Taranis grabbed Junior by the bad shoulder and vaulted over him. Junior screamed in pain, which was made only worse when Taranis threw Junior onto the ground and pressed a boot into his neck.

"But..." gasped Junior, "but you were hunting Sterling. In the castle. He was hiding from you."

"Yes," said Taranis. "Family often does that."

Chapter 22

The Next in Line

Junior watched through the porthole as the gate shrank in the distance. *Good riddance.* Sterling had stopped only to collect the spear and sword from the sand, and now they were off again to an unknown destination. Junior laid his head back against the worktable that his captors had strapped him to, his shoulder still throbbing from his encounter with Taranis. The pain had filtered to the back of his mind, though. All he could think about now were those skulls. There had been so many, and any one of them could have belonged to his mother.

"AHHH!" he cried out to no one in particular. He wanted to slam his fist against the table, but the power dampener kept his hands muzzled against his chest. It seemed a redundant measure, given he'd lost his powers when he entered Iramwerta, but Sterling was taking no chances.

Sterling. That damned Poterian had known all along how to reach the lost city. That was why Taranis had been so intent on finding him. But if he'd been hiding from Taranis before, why was he helping Taranis now?

Maybe he'd changed his mind because they were related, though Junior wasn't so sure about that detail. Even with the mask on, Junior could tell that Taranis wasn't a Poterian. It was obvious when he stood beside the much larger and huskier Sterling. However, it was clear that they shared a connection, and Junior was intent on finding what the connection was.

The ship shuddered. He heard a splash. When he checked the porthole, all he saw was water. They were in the river now. Where Sterling planned to take them, he had no idea. He turned to Kano, who laid strapped to another worktable at the other end of the room. Kano wore a power dampener too, though in his stunned state he posed even less of a threat than Junior.

"Can you move?" Junior whispered.

"Jus ma mouth," Kano got out, his tongue refusing to help him.

Junior cursed to himself and searched for something he could use. They were trapped in a storage room with plenty of tools and spare parts to choose from…if only he could reach them. He wriggled around, but the strap across his chest had no give. Oh how he wished he could just melt through it.

"Quit screwin' around," came a familiar tin-can voice.

"I'm guessing your orders are to keep me alive," said Junior, turning to find his favorite bot standing in the doorway, rifle in hand. "So don't bother threatening me with that thing."

"I will bother," said T8, cocking the rifle. "Taranis and the boss haven't decided what to do with you yet, so there's still hope for an execution."

"Sterling won't kill me. And if Taranis wants me dead, he'll do it himself."

"Damn," muttered T8, slinging the rifle over its back.

The ship shook again. Out the porthole, the water was falling away. They were rising over the valley and into the orange evening sky. Junior could tell from their trajectory that they were heading into space.

"Where's he taking us?" he demanded.

"Somewhere you won't interfere with his business."

"And what business is that? Spying on people from his little castle?"

"Don't assume you know the boss's intentions!" snapped T8.

Junior was taken aback. He'd never heard a bot get defensive before. He'd obviously pinched a nerve…figuratively speaking. But before he could respond, he noticed movement in the corner of his eye. Kano was wriggling in place, his skinny body slipping underneath the strap that was holding him down. He was almost free! But he would need a distraction.

"Your boss didn't do shit for Mogaddu!" Junior fired back. "He had leverage over the Taipa, but he didn't use it. He sat back and let us stay slaves."

"The boss wasn't here to help your people," said T8, marching closer to Junior. "He was here to make sure no one unlocked Iramwerta's power."

"Well seems like a real waste of time. Everyone keeps talking about this power but I didn't see a drop of it when I was there."

"Consider yourself lucky, then."

Hard to do when I'm strapped to a table, thought Junior. Sterling had obviously been afraid of something in Iramwerta, but how would he know what to be afraid of unless…?

"He's seen it, hasn't he?!" blurted Junior. "The Poterians unlocked the power when they took over!"

T8 drew its rifle and dug the barrel into Junior's chest. "Stop meddling in this, fleshling."

Instinct told Junior to stop talking, but he saw that Kano was now free of his restraints and tiptoeing behind T8, so he kept on. "If Sterling's so afraid of Iramwerta, then Taranis is the last person he should be helping. It was Taranis who sparked the Zoboros uprising, and attacked the fight ring, and drove us straight to the gate. He's the reason your planet is in trouble, so don't sit here and act like I'm the one who's meddling in things. I'm here because that maniac drove me here."

The light on T8's visor began pinging faster, as if the bot was processing Junior's point. "You're here because you think you're invincible." T8 tapped on Junior's bad shoulder. Junior winced at the reminder that he was, in fact, a fleshling. "You think you can take what you want from Mogaddu. But here, everything has a price. You opened the gate, now you pay for it." T8 set its finger on the trigger.

Junior gulped. He was counting on Kano now, who was just a few steps behind the bot.

"You need my help to fix it," said Junior.

"Perhaps," said T8. It spun around and fired.

"NO!" Junior struggled beneath his restraint. Kano gasped. Junior saw the smoke rising from his friend's chest…wait, not his chest. It was coming from the power dampener.

Kano stood in shock. He looked down at the machine as its lights flickered out around the hole the blaster bolt had punched into it. The pressure released from his wrists and the dampener crashed onto the floor.

"Kill Taranis for me this time, will you?" asked T8.

Kano nodded. He unlatched Junior's restraint and shut off his dampener. As it clattered on the floor, Junior felt the energy surge to his fingertips, something he hadn't felt since—

"Kano!" he exclaimed. "I think it's back."

"What's back?"

Junior snapped his finger and a flame sparked there.

"No way!" cheered Kano, letting the energy thrum back into his palms. "Wait, does that mean Taranis has his powers back, too?"

"Shit."

"We'll need backup," said Kano, his voice filled with a conviction Junior hadn't heard from him before. "T8, can you get a message to the Orlovs?"

Despite its lack of a mouth, T8 somehow gagged. "Orlovs on *my* ship! You people are more trouble than you're worth."

"Taranis and Sterling will try to go into hyperspace once they see the Orlovs on an intercept course," said Junior, heading for the door. "We need to keep them away from the controls."

"And your plan is to punch your way straight to the bridge through bot-infested halls?" asked T8.

Junior stopped at the door. "You got a better one?"

T8 pressed its hand against a pressure pad on the wall. A secret door opened beside the bot, which led into a hidden crawlspace.

"One of the many perks of a smuggler vessel," said T8.

"This might be the coolest bot I've ever seen," said Kano, seeming to forget that this same bot almost shot him a few moments ago.

"Yeah, he's a real charmer," muttered Junior. He crammed his big body into the dark and dank crawlspace. Given the odor, Junior didn't want to know what Sterling smuggled in here. He followed the narrow path, using what little light leaked in through the grates in the floor above.

Light glowed at the end of the tunnel. Junior heard voices. Two of them. He crawled faster, the exercise sending sharp stings through his shoulder, but he swallowed them down. He didn't want to miss a beat of the conversation.

He crawled in beneath the light, stopping at a grate through which he could just make out the back of Sterling's head. There were controls arranged in front of the Poterian; they were inside the bridge.

"You're the only one who's seen it and lived to tell the tale," came Taranis's low voice. "I will ask you for the last time: tell me what I need to know."

"I wouldn't tell you even if I knew where it was," said Sterling.

"But you know *what* it was, don't you? You know what the IDF created. You saw it with your own eyes before it took your arm."

"It took much more than that!" Sterling slammed his mechanical fist down. "What happened that day is but a taste of what it can do. We're lucky the whole planet wasn't lost in time, or worse."

What are they talking about? Junior's thoughts turned immediately to Iramwerta, to the projections that had come from another time. Taranis had led him to believe that Iramwerta was the cause of them, but apparently the IDF had something to do with it. Something they must have used when their Lusitani attacked. Something apparently powerful enough to destroy a planet.

Or a fleet! That was it! The secret weapon, the one that had miraculously defeated the Poterians, the one the IDF had kept shrouded in mystery for twenty cycles.

The one Kano's parents had created.

"It's the final piece I require, Sterling," continued Taranis. "Everything else is set. The gate is open; our people are on the move—"

"*Your* people, not mine."

"You don't fool me, old man. If you didn't care about the Zoboros, you wouldn't have taken me in all those cycles ago."

"When you were innocent!"

"When I was weak," snapped Taranis, sparks flickering across his gauntlet. "But you showed me my weakness. So I sought strength."

"You sought a monster."

"And now I've become one, because a monster is what my people need right now. A monster who's willing to bring change."

Sterling turned away, his mechanical footsteps clunking toward Junior, who dipped into the shadows beneath the grates.

"You think you can control this weapon, just like you think you can control the fate of the Zoboros," said Sterling. "But you can't. Greater minds have tried. You've seen their results littering the surface of Mogaddu."

"Do not be so weak-minded," hissed Taranis, his boots clunking back and forth as he paced around Sterling like a wolf. "It is more than just a weapon. It can unlock new possibilities, things we know today only in legend."

Sterling fell silent, lost in thought. Even through the grates, Junior could see temptation written on the Poterian's face.

"Tell me how to find it," whispered Taranis. "Tell me how to find Project Vortex."

Red light flooded the control room.

"What's happening?" demanded Sterling. He marched over to the controls, where bots floated at the helm.

"Interceptors," one of them answered. "They have Orlov markings!"

"Move over!" Sterling shoved the bot aside and strapped himself into the command chair. He turned the ship hard at a ninety-degree angle, causing the floor to slip out from under Junior and Kano. They tumbled through the loose grates and into the control room.

"HOW?!" demanded Taranis, who clung to a chair that was bolted to the floor as he watched his unchained prisoners roll by.

Kano answered by hurling a shockwave that blasted Taranis into the nearest window.

"You idiots! You'll cause a breach!" cried Sterling as he leveled out the ship.

Junior saw it, the growing crack in the window. It was reinforced, no doubt, but they would need to choose their attacks more carefully.

Two interceptors swept over the ship. Through the windscreen, Junior could see them angling around for another pass.

"What are you waiting for?!" barked Taranis to Sterling, keeping his hands aimed at Junior and Kano. "Get us into hyperspace!"

"The ship isn't responding!" said Sterling as he punched frantically at the controls.

Taranis cocked his head at his adversaries, knowing this was somehow their doing. "I don't have time for this," he said, placing his palm against the metal floor. He pumped electricity through it. It seized Junior; he felt all his muscles clench and suddenly he was on the floor, catatonic, Kano lying useless beside him.

Taranis marched for the controls, but the ship jerked into a sudden stop and he flew forward into the back of Sterling's chair.

"We're caught in a tractor beam," said Sterling, ripping off his restraints. "It's over."

"No it's not," said Taranis. He grabbed Sterling by the throat. "You're coming with me."

The Poterian coughed and gasped, but for some reason offered no resistance as Taranis dragged him across the floor. They passed Junior, who fought to move, but his muscles continued to spasm uselessly.

Why doesn't he fight back?! wondered Junior. He watched Taranis open the door. T8 dove through and tackled Taranis to the ground, freeing its master. Taranis grabbed the bot by the head and pumped it with electricity. The visor exploded into shards and the bot sailed back in a jet of smoke.

"Enough!" screamed Sterling, his mechanical arm now a cannon. He fired at Taranis, who dove past the shots and sprinted out the door.

"Don't let him escape!" cried Junior. He tried rising to his feet, but his knees buckled and he fell over.

A clank echoed through the ship.

"It's too late," said Sterling. "We're being boarded."

"Sir, Pod 3 has jettisoned," said one of the bots. *No surprise there.* Junior watched its firelight trail across the windscreen as Taranis made his escape. He hoped an Orlov ship would blast it out of existence, but the firelight faded into space.

He cursed. Beneath him laid T8's charred remains, and the sight sent a strange feeling through him. He'd never felt anything toward a bot before, but in this moment he felt…pity. The bot had trusted him with what would be its final wish: to stop Taranis. And he'd failed.

The other bots were still fully operational though. And they began arming themselves.

"Stand down!" ordered Sterling. He turned to Junior. "It seems T8 felt compelled to sabotage the controls. We couldn't escape even if we tried."

Junior smiled. *Godspeed, T8.*

Footsteps clattered down the hall. The cockpit door opened once again, and this time Carmichael stood there, accompanied by a young woman that Junior found vaguely familiar.

Carmichael smiled, relieved to find Kano and Junior mostly unharmed. When he turned to Sterling, however, his expression changed. He stared a moment, deciding what to do.

"Cera!" he barked.

The woman beside him launched two hands of glowing green energy. They seized Sterling and pinned him to the wall.

"It's alright!" said Junior. "Sterling was surrendering."

"Ah, so you've adopted a new name?" said Carmichael to the Poterian.

Sterling smiled despite his face being pressed against the wall. "If my eyes don't deceive me, you must be the spawn of that bastard admiral."

"You're in no position to criticize my family, General," said Carmichael dismissively.

"General?" repeated Junior.

"I told you, boy," began Sterling. "My people won't accept a cripple…no matter their status."

"And you would have had the highest status of all, wouldn't you?" said Carmichael, patting Sterling on the cheek. "As I recall, your Poterian Emperor bore no children."

Junior paled. "Who is he?" he demanded, stepping closer to Sterling. "Who are you?!"

"You're looking at General Galorin, brother to Emperor Palorex and next in line for the Poterian throne."

Chapter 23

The Reunion

The morning sun glowed upon the island palace as Sterling's ship made its descent. Kano hurried to the liftgate, eager to reunite with everyone he'd left behind. His mission may have lasted only two days, but it had felt like a lifetime given everything that happened. The journey into the desert, fighting Taranis, finding the lost city – things certainly hadn't been dull for Kano.

When the liftgate opened, Makoto was the first to rush up the ramp and embrace his older brother. He was followed closely by Jaden, who had Akio clinging to his back.

"Stealing all the action for yourself, huh?" said Jaden as he patted Kano on the shoulder.

Kano smiled. He hadn't realized just how much he would miss his friends while he was away. He did notice, however, one important absence.

"Where's Li?" he asked.

Makoto backed away at the question, leaving Jaden to answer it. "We were all worried about you," he began, "But Li…well, she was *especially* concerned."

"Concerned that I was gone or concerned that I didn't tell anyone?"

Jaden shrugged. "Bit of both?"

Kano sighed. He knew his secrecy would come with a price. "I wanted to tell you guys about the mission, I swear, but Carmichael was afraid you'd try and join if I told you."

"We are aware, boy of thunder," said Akio. He nodded down the ramp, where Chenji and Sandra were hurrying up to join them.

"You made it back!" exclaimed Kano. He rushed down and embraced them, relieved to find they only carried a few scratches and bruises from their time on Mogaddu.

"We were so worried about you!" said Sandra.

"How did you get back here so quick?!" asked Kano.

"Quick?" Chenji glanced at Sandra before continuing. "I mean, the Orlovs picked us up, but that took a few…"

Chenji trailed off, his attention zeroing in on the top of the ramp. Everyone turned. A bulking Poterian sat there in a wheelchair, its red face twisted into a scowl, its bionic arm and leg missing.

"Is— is that what I think it is?" stammered Makoto.

"I've got a name, kid," muttered Sterling as Carmichael wheeled him down the ramp.

"A fake one," added a familiar voice. Kano turned. He had been so preoccupied with his friends that he hadn't noticed Plí arrive upon a hoverpad with a small army of red guards behind her. "You've done well to hide under our noses for so long, Galorin."

Sterling spat at her feet.

"Charmed," said Plí. "We'll take him from here, captain, until we can arrange a safe and…discrete prisoner hand off with the IDF."

Carmichael paused to assess the army in front of him. "If there's one thing you people are good at, it's discretion." He passed the wheelchair over to the guards, but Kano sensed hesitation in the captain, a flicker of distrust across the captain's face that would have been imperceptible, had he not spent so much time with Carmichael over the past few weeks.

"We'll take his effects as well," said Plí, motioning toward the ship.

"I assumed you would." Carmichael stepped aside so a few guards could ascend the ramp. They pushed past Kano and company with haste, but Kano was more focused on the Poterian being carted away. He wondered what secrets Sterling – or Galorin – held, and what the IDF would do to get them. It was a troubling thought, but he didn't have time to dwell on it, for Plí was quick to address him.

"Master Kano, congratulations on your successful mission. If you'll follow me, I believe you are due for some needed rest before the party."

"Party?" Only then did Kano notice the commotion happening around the courtyard. Hundreds of servants were at work. They rushed between tables that had been set along the edges of the reflecting pool, adorning them with cloths and candles and covered trays for what he assumed to be an impending cocktail hour. Gardeners chopped away at the shrubbery, fine-tuning every detail, and decorators draped garlands and lights over the tall edges of the palace.

"Word is the Zoboros drove the Taipa and Del Clorans from Mogaddu," said Makoto excitedly. "So Danadas invited his friends and family from all over the galaxy to celebrate!"

That was fast, thought Kano. Just yesterday he'd watched the Zoboros flee from a devastating Del Cloran attack. He could still picture the bodies lying in the grass; the image made him sick. How had the Zoboros managed to turn that around in one day? The question plagued him as he followed Plí to the palace, his friends tagging along.

"So what happened after we lost you in the woods?" asked Chenji.

Kano drew a deep breath and began to weave his tale. The others clung to every word, exchanging nervous glances while he spoke, but it was at the end when they seemed most concerned. No one spoke for a while; they just stood there like they were expecting more. Kano wasn't sure why, though; he'd assumed meeting a Poterian and seeing time projections should be more than satisfactory for one mission.

"How long did it take you to reach the temple?" asked Sandra.

"An hour, maybe two," he replied. That earned him more anxious looks.

"Then how long were you unconscious on the beach?" asked Jaden.

"I don't know, but I can't imagine more than a few hours." That earned him a gasp from Sandra. Was he missing something here?

"Kano!" Junior hurried down the ramp and across the courtyard to join them, his expression even more deadly serious than usual. "Something's happened."

"Hey, the big guy's back!" exclaimed Jaden, though everyone ignored him.

Kano turned to his friends. "What's going on?"

Makoto stepped forward, a bit bashful. "Kano, we've been searching for you for over two weeks now."

The whole world stopped. *Weeks?* Impossible. His friends continued to explain, but he didn't hear them. All he could think about was waking up on that beach in front of the gate. There was no way he could've been unconscious that long.

"Kano, *Kano.*" Junior shook Kano by the shoulders and snapped him back into the present. "There's something wrong with Iramwerta. Those projections weren't the only effects."

"Effects?" repeated Kano.

"Time, Kano," said Junior. "It altered time for us. A few hours there equaled days on the outside. I'm not sure how."

Kano tried to form a question, but his head was spinning too fast. He didn't know what to make of being flung into the future. How much had they missed? And how much more would they have missed if Sterling hadn't taken them out when he did?

"Let us leave Master Kano alone," said Plí as she opened the palace doors. "He has been through an arduous few days. He deserves his rest."

The others backed off and began to disperse, but Junior stayed planted. Kano could tell by the way Junior stared at Plí that the former cadet wasn't too keen on taking orders from someone he didn't know. Or perhaps Junior, given his father's connections, did know the Orlovs, and just chose to dislike them. Either way, he soon marched away less than pleased, leaving Kano and Plí alone amid a horde of frantic servants. Whatever party preparations Kano had witnessed on the outside were tripled in here. More hands, more decorations, and more panic consumed the foyer. Plí led him deftly through the madness, unfazed by the crowded passageways as she floated along. Kano assumed that for her this sort of excitement was just another day at the palace.

"You'll be pleased to find a new suit inside your quarters," she said as she led him down a hallway. "Should you find it not to your liking, please inform me immediately and we will have other options brought to you."

"I'm sure it'll be fine," said Kano. Getting a suit he liked was the least of his concerns, and not just because Carmichael had already gifted him one on the *Dormarch*. Going to a party meant exposing himself to people. Lots of people. Unknown people. What was Danadas thinking, hosting a party while he harbored fugitives? It was a sure way to blow their cover, something they desperately needed with Taranis so close by. He'd assumed when he saw the preparations that Danadas planned to hide him and his friends somewhere, but the suit was a clear indicator that they would in fact be attending the party.

Plí motioned toward one of the doors, which Kano assumed to be his. "Ask for me should you need anything, Master Kano," she instructed, before floating away.

I need a lot of things, starting with answers, thought Kano. He reached for the door, but he stopped himself. Someone was watching him; he could sense it. He turned and found a familiar face down the hall, half-concealed beneath a hood.

"It's Warp, isn't it?" he asked.

Warp made the slightest of nods.

Kano approached her. "How did you get here?"

She pointed to Sandra, who was passing their hallway on the way to her room.

Kano nodded. He assumed Sandra had vouched for Warp when they returned, prompting the Orlovs to take her in.

"Have you met the others since you arrived?"

She waved her hand back and forth, to say, "sort of". Kano assumed that meant she'd been too shy to approach most of his friends at all. And knowing them, they'd have probably been too preoccupied to approach her. Except for one, who Kano knew was always quick to spark conversation with strangers from her cycles of bartending.

"Do you know where I can find Li?" he asked.

Warp nodded emphatically. She grabbed Kano's hand and a moment later he was standing in front of a new door.

He gulped. He hadn't expected to arrive so quickly; he still hadn't prepared his apology. He looked to Warp for support, but she just shrugged and puffed away.

Helpful, that one, he thought sarcastically. This would have been the perfect moment to compose his thoughts, but, to his horror, the door opened.

"Is that you, Warp?" asked Li. Kano stared into her green eyes, butterflies seizing his stomach as Li's face went cold.

"Li, um…I'm sorry," he said.

"Yes, I'm sure you are." She started to shut the door.

Kano caught it. "Just let me make it up to you."

She shook her head. "Did you really think you could abandon your *team* and everyone would just be fine with it?"

"It was to keep you all safe."

"Oh, so now you decide what's best for everyone? We joined this team for you. We became fugitives for you. The least we deserve is for you to be honest with us."

She slammed the door. Kano stewed in silence. He felt like an idiot. Of course his friends deserved his honesty. He'd just been afraid of putting them in danger, which now seemed like a stupid thing to be worried about. They were in danger on any given day. It wasn't an excuse to put them in the dark.

"Tough break," a high-pitched voice buzzed in his ear.

Kano jumped. A zeefly fluttered from his ear to a nearby door before morphing into a naked Chenji.

"Ah jeez," grumbled Kano. "After everything I've gone through today, the last thing I needed to see was your—"

"I have pants inside. Come in and I can explain things." Chenji entered his room. Kano hesitated before stepping inside. Thankfully, Chenji was clothed in trousers by then.

"What did you want to tell me, Chenji?"

"That you need some serious help with the female persuasion."

Kano got a little hot under the ears. "I-I don't have time for this. Apparently I just missed two weeks of my life, and now I have to go to a party even though I'm a fugitive of—"

"Sure, sure, I got ya," interrupted Chenji, opening the door for Kano to exit. "I mean, if these excuses are more important to you than Li, then who am I to waste your time?"

Now Kano was visibly red in the face. He slammed the door shut for fear of any eavesdropping. "No, it's not more important…I just don't think now's the best time to be making moves, is all."

"But we're going to a party! That's the perfect time to be making moves. There'll be music, dancing, romance… Given our line of work, who knows when we'll get another chance like this? Come on. Isn't it about time you said something to her?"

Kano shuffled where he stood. "I don't know, with Taranis out there…what if he came after us? What if he came after her to get to me?"

"You're overthinking this."

"I'm not! You saw him on Mogaddu. You saw what he can do. Him and the whole team of maniacs he's got working for him now." Kano sat down on Chenji's bed, the weight of the world pressing on his shoulders. "This whole time I've been his target. How could I put someone else in danger like that?"

"Last I checked, Li *chose* to leave Famora and join this team. She chose to put herself in danger, which you were fine with at first because you love her."

"I was not…how long have you…?" Kano stopped. His eyes narrowed on the clothes that Chenji had so hastily put on after taking the form of an insect. "Have you been spying on me?"

"Like anyone needs to spy on you to figure that one out, mate."

"Does she know?! Do you think she, you know, has feelings too?" Kano felt such a nervous excitement, like he wanted to throw up and jump for joy all at the same time.

Chenji shrugged. "Only one way to find out."

"What should I do?"

"Start with an apology. At the party. And a real one this time, not that sad one I had to witness outside. Do it the first chance you can get her in private."

"What if I freeze? I always freeze. I never know what to say."

"I can be the fly in your ear, my nervous friend. Here." Chenji grabbed Kano's wrist and tapped it. "If I land here and tap once, it means you're doing well. Two taps means dial it back. Three taps means evacuate immediately."

"Let's pray we don't get to three taps."

"Agreed. But I believe in you. I mean, you fought an intergalactic terrorist twice. I'm sure you can figure this out."

Kano knew Chenji had meant to make him feel better, but somehow that comment made him feel ten times worse. Why was this so hard for him? And why did Chenji make it look so easy? Before he could ask, Chenji was already hurrying him out the door.

"Now go get ready," said the changeling. "You've got an important mission tonight." Chenji winked and shut the door in Kano's face.

Kano sighed. He looked to Li's door and the butterflies crept back in. *What am I going to say?* From the moment he'd met her on Famora, he'd never had a clue what to say in front of her. Back when he didn't have the cloud that was Taranis hanging over him.

His fears kept him occupied all the way to his room, where he found the suit waiting for him on the largest bed he'd ever seen. He tried on the jacket first. A perfect fit. But when had the Orlovs sized him up?

"We got the measurements from Carmichael, in case you were wondering."

Kano jumped. He hadn't noticed the old man sitting in the corner, jeweled cane in hand. "H-how long have you been here?" he stammered.

"Long enough to wonder where that teleporter had taken you. Warp, is it? Such a sad story behind that one. But such is the tale of most Zoboros these days."

Kano waited for Danadas to continue, to explain why he'd been waiting here all this time, but the old man seemed content to sit in his chair and think. Didn't he have more important things to do than sit, given he had a party starting soon and the most powerful family in the galaxy to run? Kano started to suspect the man might be senile, but he pushed the thought away. Danadas was sharper than he let on – he had to be, to lead the Orlov family. There was a method to the madness. Which begged a very important question.

"Why are you throwing this party?"

Danadas smiled. "As I said, the tale of the Zoboros is a bleak one. They deserve a little light. You and your friends *deserve* a party."

"Not if it exposes us. We're fugitives after all."

"From a certain point of view."

"From every point of view!" Kano began pacing the floor, frustrated. "If we're seen here, the IDF will break down your doors and hunt every Orlov in the galaxy for questioning."

"So dramatic." Danadas rose and hobbled toward the window that overlooked the courtyard. "I thought you'd have figured out how this game is played by now."

"Game?" repeated Kano. "We're in danger. This isn't just politics anymore."

"Isn't it? The freedom of the Zoboros is on the table, and I now possess the two who have become synonymous with their movement."

So we're bargaining chips. "And your plan is to wave us in the IDF's faces?"

"No need," said Danadas as he stared out the window. "Didn't you ever wonder why your escape from the *Dormarch* was so easy?"

Kano took a step back. It *had* seemed easy. He'd assumed it was because no one had dared to question Carmichael or Cera while they wore Lusitani uniforms. But even then, there had been a distinct lack of obstacles in their escape path, which, given their team's track record, was nothing short of a miracle.

"What have you done?" he asked.

"Something the IDF cannot sanction." Danadas pulled the blinds and turned to address Kano directly. "Or rather, something Mezo refuses to sanction: turning a gang of teenagers into the face of our movement."

Kano shook his head. "Last I checked, Mezo was opposed to making us your poster children. She would never allow us to escape."

"That was before she saw your potential in the simulator. That mission on Famora was designed to break you almost immediately, but you kept going. Even when the impossible stepped in your way, you were willing to go outside the rules just to win. That is a quality that our organization respects."

"And which organization is that?"

Danadas drew a book from the shelf and handed it to Kano. On its cover was a familiar triangle with three arrows pointing inward from each of its corners toward its center.

The symbol of the Zoboros. He'd seen it before in Nobara's ancient book, and again on a pin which Hendricks had given to his son right before he died.

"You worked with Hendricks," said Kano. "You helped him smuggle Zoboros to safety."

"Hendricks did the heavy lifting. I simply backed him. How else could he afford to build all those safehouses and secret chambers?"

And an escape ship, thought Kano. Not just any ship, either, but a long-lost Poterian vessel that had been hidden deep within Famora's platforms. Taranis had stolen it in his escape, but it still begged the question: what other resources did Danadas have at his disposal? He clearly wanted to make Kano and his friends one of those resources; perhaps he thought a party would help to sweeten the deal for a "team of teenagers". But if Danadas wished to share his new team with a party crowd, it would have to be with people he trusted.

"The party…it's for people in your organization, isn't it?"

Danadas winked. "Now you're catching on."

"It's still dangerous," insisted Kano. "Taranis is close. And he's well connected. He probably already knows about the party."

"Most likely. But leave security to me. Our mission tonight is to bring the organization around your new team. You will be guests of honor, the face of our new strategy. Our new integration. And in the morning, our leaders will meet to plan our counteroffensive against our enemy. Taranis now knows where Iramwerta is, same as us. It is imperative that we prevent him from claiming it."

"Iramwerta isn't all he wants, though," said Kano. "He mentioned something else. Something called Project Vortex."

Danadas paled. He hobbled toward Kano, his cane tapping hastily against the ground. "Are you certain? Are those the exact words you heard leave his lips?"

"I'm sure," said Kano, fear bubbling up inside him at Danadas's reaction.

"I must get word to Mezo…and you must swear not to utter those words to another soul." Danadas began punching away at the communicator on his frail wrist.

"But what does it mean?" insisted Kano.

Danadas stopped typing and thought for a moment. Finally, he sighed. "What I tell you must never leave this room." He stared with a firmness Kano had never seen in the old man before. Kano nodded slowly before Danadas continued. "Project Vortex was the IDF's attempt to counter the powers of the Zoboros. Even with their dreaded Lusitani, they found themselves no match for the combined strength of the Zoboros and Poterians, so they sought a power even greater than any Zoboros could possess. A power which, once unleashed, could eradicate the Poterian armada here in the space above our little moon."

All of this was sounding familiar. Carmichael had told Kano part of the story on Famora, though his information had been severely incomplete. "My parents helped build this weapon, didn't they?"

Danadas nodded. "I tell you this now only because of my respect for them. They would want you to know what happened."

"You knew them?" asked Kano.

"I backed their research. The IDF may seem powerful now, but at the time they were desperate for resources. I provided what I could to ensure the war was won. Little did I know the true cost of my efforts.

"Your parents knew their weapon was not ready, but the IDF was near total defeat. They fought hard to prevent it from being fired, but the late Admiral Carmichael took it from them and led a small fighting force against the Poterian armada."

"What did it do?" pressed Kano. It was a question that had plagued the galaxy for twenty cycles. "What kind of power could destroy an armada?"

"A black hole. That is what your parents were attempting to generate. The thing about black holes, though, is that they require a vast amount of energy to sustain themselves, an almost inconceivable amount. But if that power level is not achieved, and the black hole fails, then the result is an explosion so great that nothing nearby will survive it."

"Which is why no one survived the battle," said Kano.

"That we know of. However, we now possess a prisoner who I expect would have intimate knowledge of what happened. One who was probably on the surface of Mogaddu at the time of the explosion, and thus protected from its most dangerous effects."

Now things were becoming clearer for Kano. Now he understood why Taranis had sought Sterling, why Danadas had been so frightened at the mention of Project Vortex, and why his parents had needed to flee after the war. But one question rose to the top of his mind. "Why would Taranis want a weapon that doesn't work? He's evil, but not suicidal."

Danadas leaned in, almost whispering. "Because he may see it as more than just a weapon. Black holes destroy, true, but their power can also create, and influence, and alter our very understanding of space and time."

There was the trigger word. Time. "I saw something in Iramwerta," Kano found himself saying. "It was like I could see through time while I was there."

"You saw the time shades, then?" asked Danadas. Kano nodded. "The lost city is more than just a home for the Zoboros. It was believed to be the source of their power, a door to forces beyond our comprehension. And some believe that door can be opened again given the right…push."

"And you think Taranis plans to use the weapon to give it that push?"

Danadas nodded. "You only know Taranis as a destroyer, but he views himself as a creator. An artist.

One who paints in blood and reveals something new. If he found a way to open the path beyond Iramwerta, he could usher in a new age for the Zoboros and the galaxy altogether, though I fear it would be a dark age indeed."

Kano gulped. Any 'age' that Taranis led would certainly be that. "How do we stop him?" he asked.

Danadas smiled. "By opening the path first."

Chapter 24

The Party

Junior watched another procession of partygoers march from their shuttles to the palace entrance. Night had fallen, but it was hard to tell with the lights blazing across the courtyard. They reflected off the marble grounds, making the space a beacon for incoming ships. And those ships just kept coming.

He glanced back from the balcony and into his room. A fresh suit waited on the bed, but he had no intention of wearing it. He'd have to be an idiot to expose himself to a crowd of strangers. He hiked up a pair of binoculars he'd "borrowed" from Sterling's ship and watched the guests enter the palace. There was a Taloan among them, her pudgy purple face familiar amidst its traditional silk robes. Junior zoomed in and the realization struck him. This party wasn't just for the Orlovs; it was for his own father's allies. Many of these people had once been guests in his old home on Famora, including the Taloan who, like most of the others, had never even acknowledged Junior's existence during her secretive visits. Junior had learned little about the purpose of those visits; all he knew for certain was that these people had been involved in the hiding of Zoboros children from the government.

Hiding *and* pacifying them.

He tossed the binoculars aside and marched into his room. These cowards didn't deserve his attention. What attention had they given him when he became a fugitive? Here they were, some of the most influential people in the galaxy, the ones "responsible" for protecting the Zoboros, yet not one of them tried to help him when he needed it. Him, the son of their leader. No, instead it had been a simple dockworker with no relationship to his father who had risked everything to get Junior safely off Famora.

He grabbed a rope he'd fashioned out of bedsheets. Let these people have their party. Let them pat themselves on the back for a Zoboros war they would never fight in. He had more important things to do.

Just as he fastened the rope around a balustrade, an Orlov serving bot floated through the balcony door. Its red eye stared at him, no doubt checking if he'd put on the suit.

"I'll wear it when I damn well feel like it," said Junior, hiding the rope behind his back.

"Is that how all fleshlings greet their friends?" asked the bot.

Junior froze. "T8?!" he blurted.

"Reuploaded and ready for action!" T8 did a little spin on its hoverpad for effect. "I do miss my legs though."

"Why are you here? How come you're an Orlov bot?"

"Did you think the boss would just let himself get captured? While everyone was focused on him, his ship was sending out a signal that programmed me into their system."

Junior glanced at the Poterian ship sitting beneath the tarp in the courtyard. Leave it to Sterling to hack in while no one suspected it. This was a carefully executed operation, which meant there was only one reason why T8 would risk exposure to come and talk to him.

"I'm not helping you break your boss out," said Junior. "In case you forgot, he's already betrayed me once."

"Suit yourself." T8 floated off the balcony. "I guess you don't want to know what really happened to your mother…"

"She's dead!" snapped Junior, leaning against the balustrades. "Don't you dare pretend you have something to offer me."

"The boss can offer you more information than you'll find on your own." T8 pointed at the rope. "I assume you've realized that this is more than just a party happening tonight."

Junior stiffened. He felt exposed, like the red eye was staring right through him. "There's nothing your boss could tell me that I'll believe."

T8 floated closer and whispered, "Believe or don't. I don't care. What I do care about is the fact that Sterling won't live through the night if we don't break him out."

"You're a liar."

"As someone with access to the Orlovs' files, I'm not the one you should be calling a liar. But go ahead. Wander through the palace aimlessly until the guards catch you." T8 floated off the balcony and toward the jungle.

Junior stood there, thinking. *Execute Sterling?* It had to be a play by T8. The Orlovs would be crazy to eliminate an asset like Sterling, who could be a wealth of information about things like the Poterian Empire, Poterian technology, the war…unless the Orlovs didn't want that information getting out. Now there was an Orlov secret he wanted the answers to.

"Meet me in the trees," T8 called back. "And do it quick. Time's almost up."

I'll come, but not to help you, thought Junior as he rappelled over the side of the railing. He had just started his descent when he heard the door to his room open.

I should've locked it! It was probably a guard or a bot coming to check on him. He looked down. He was too high up; he would need to flare fire to break the fall, but that would draw attention. It would be safer to dispose of the intruder quietly. Footsteps echoed across the balcony. Definitely a guard. It was getting closer. He readied to vault himself back over the railing and attack when a familiar face peeked over the edge.

"Did I come at a bad time?" asked Kano.

"I would say so."

"Can I tag along?"

"One of us has to face the crowd. Danadas has a place of honor for both of us. If we're both missing, they'll know we're up to something."

Kano folded his arms. "Fine…but why do you always get to do the fun stuff?"

"Because I don't ask permission." Junior continued to rappel.

"Wait!" called Kano. Junior stopped. "There's something you should know. That thing Taranis was talking about, Project Vortex, it's—"

"The weapon your parents built."

"Wow, way to steal my thunder."

"I make it a point to disappoint people." Junior reached ground level. Kano began to reel up the rope for him without him having to ask, and a pang of guilt struck Junior. He was leaving Kano to face an army of Orlovs alone, and that sounded somehow more dangerous than helping T8 free a prisoner from the palace.

"Kano, be careful in there," Junior called up. "These people…they think they're in charge of the Zoboros. Don't let them think they're in charge of you."

"I won't," said Kano. "Can I ask where you're sneaking off to?"

"You can but I won't tell you." Junior winked and headed for the trees.

"You owe me for this!"

Li adjusted her dress as she waited on the dais.

Where are they? she wondered. Two empty seats sat on either side of Danadas at the dais's center. Jaden, Makoto, Carmichael, Cera, Chenji, and Akio filled the remaining seats in a neat row that overlooked the grand dining hall. No seat had been saved for Sandra, who had reassumed her guard duties for the party, or Warp, who no one could seem to find, as usual.

To Li's surprise, the dining hall, as massive as it was, looked full to bursting. The long tables that ran to the entrance on the far side were filled with hundreds of guests, all of them talking, laughing, and stuffing their faces with hors d'oeuvres that the many servers were carrying around. Guards stood along the perimeter, spears at attention, their masked faces scanning for anyone who didn't belong, as was part of Danadas's promise to keep the team safe. But Li still had her doubts. The only reason she'd agreed to put herself on the dais for everyone to see was because she'd thought Kano, the one who their enemies always seemed to be hunting, would be here on display too. The fact that he wasn't made her infinitely more anxious.

She searched the crowd, but finding Kano seemed an impossible task given the sheer number of guests. She did, however, notice patterns. Many of the guests wore Montiquo brooches, the crest of the Orlov family, and most were Humans who bore striking resemblances to each other. A pure bloodline, something her grandmother had warned her about. Allies though they were, the Orlovs had certain traditions that made it uncomfortable for a Nurrano like herself to be in their presence. It had been a surprise when Danadas offered her a seat of honor. Even more surprising were a handful of exceptions among the crowd: a Taloan in traditional robes, a Braiman soaking up its drink through its tendrils, a Kimikan so short that the staff had to bring him a special chair. She wondered who these people were, and why the Orlovs had chosen to trust them with the knowledge that he was harboring fugitives.

Silence stole over the crowd. All the faces in it turned toward the opposite side of the dining hall. Li followed their gaze and found Kano standing there in the entrance, shuffling awkwardly with the spotlight on him. She squinted. Was he wearing a suit?

Danadas rose from his seat and applauded. The rest of the room was quick to join him, standing and cheering as Kano made his way nervously across the room. But Li stayed seated. She put on her coldest gaze and waited for Kano's wandering eyes to find her, as they often did. And when they did, she found the fear on his face immensely satisfying.

How could he have run off on a mission without telling her? After all she'd sacrificed to stay with him. To protect him. He had some nerve if he thought he could just sit here and bask in the applause of a family that should have been punished centuries ago for their greed.

As Kano climbed onto the dais, she got a good look at his suit. Black with a golden tie. And a perfect fit against his new muscles. Depending on how long they stayed at the palace, Kano might have to get used to this type of clothing. Li had no problem with that.

She noticed him whisper something to Danadas before taking his seat. She shook her head. Kano didn't see it, not yet: the Orlovs wanted something. They always did. They just hadn't revealed what it was yet.

The patriarch remained standing as he addressed the crowd in a voice surprisingly powerful for one so old. "It appears that our other guest of honor, Aaron Hendricks Jr., is indisposed as he recovers from his incredible feats on Mogaddu. But I believe we owe both him and our guest Kano our deepest gratitude for all that they have accomplished for our cause."

"TI'HA!" the crowd cheered in unison. Li flinched. There was something savage in their cry, something that made her uneasy, though she didn't know what it meant.

"For too long our family's position has withered," continued Danadas. "As a result, the Zoboros position has diminished as well. But our new friends here are helping us usher in a new age, one where Zoboros *can* return, not just to society, but to their rightful place as heroes!"

"TI'HA!" the crowd cheered again.

"Our galaxy needs heroes," continued Danadas. "For too long, it has turned its back on the Zoboros. For too long, we have ignored the gradual disappearance of our greatest gifts and left them for squalor. But starting today, we forge anew. Starting today, we tell the galaxy, 'No more.' No more hiding, no more pretending, no more weakness. Today we commit our family and its resources to the Zoboros front, not from the shadows, but publicly and unconditionally. We will shelter them, supply them, and fight for them at every opportunity. And the

Republic, which for so long has leaned on us for strength, will yield to our demands for change!”

“TI’HA!”

Li stirred in her seat. *And what do you get in return for all your goodwill, Danadas?* she wondered.

“Just as we say ‘sevas’ to things at the close, we say ‘ti’ha’ to things about to begin,” said Danadas, raising his glass. “To new friends, new alliances, and a new era for the Orlov family!”

“TI’HA!” The crowd raised their glasses and drank. The servers burst out of the kitchens on command, their trays sweeping across the tables. Roasted aivin, kreel tentacles, braised tenderloins, the food just kept coming. Li stuck to her unfinished salad, the slaughtered meats doing nothing to restore her already lost appetite. She kept an eye on Kano, whose hands shook every time he attempted to fork his food. He’d better get used to this spotlight if these were the people he wanted to take up with. All she could think about was Sandra’s sister Jacelyn, the poor Zoboros that the Orlovs had locked up in that house on Famora. An Orlov would argue that they did it for the greater good, that cutting her off from the world kept her alive, but Li disagreed. Living under someone else’s whims was no way to live.

She noticed Chenji give Kano a nudge. Kano followed it with a nervous glance in her direction. She pretended to look away. *So Chenji’s his coach now.* A step up from Jaden, but not by much.

Course after course flew by. Still, Li barely ate, and she barely returned Kano’s glances either. A band had struck up on the opposite end of the hall, and already people were getting up to dance. She paid them little mind, more focused on the several Orlov dignitaries that had stepped up to the dais to meet Kano. He exchanged few words, keeping mostly to his food, but Li could sense the people here were zeroed in on him. She sensed there was something underneath all the spectacle and politics playing out before her. Something darker behind Danadas's words of peace and—

"May I have this dance?"

She looked up, surprised to find Chenji standing over her, his shaggy hair combed back rather nicely.

"I'd sooner dance with a pig," she said, forgetting who she was talking to.

"I can arrange that."

"Please don't."

"Dance with me or you'll have to explain to a hundred Orlovs why you dressed your pet pig in a suit."

Li frowned. She looked to the crowd of strangers and then to Chenji, who she knew would keep his word.

She held out her hand. "You really know how to charm a girl."

"I can do more than charm." He took her hand and led her down from the dais.

"What talents do you possess that won't turn a girl's stomach?"

"I'm not sure," shrugged Chenji. "I never had a mother." He pulled her in close when they arrived on the dance floor. Too close. She tried squirming away when he whispered in her ear, "Relax, you're not my type."

"So you blackmailed me purely for social reasons?"

"I thought it'd make a good distraction." He nodded toward Kano on the dais.

"I'm perfectly capable of ignoring him on my own," she said as he led her into a spin.

"A distraction for me. I've been watching him flail for the past hour."

"Flail?"

"The girl near the front. You didn't see her? She hasn't taken her eyes off him since the second course."

Li tried craning her head over Chenji's shoulder for a better look, but he was too tall, even when she had her heels on.

"Relax, he's not going anywhere. I tried convincing him to dance with her but he keeps complaining that he can't—"

Li gasped as the dais came back into view. Kano was gone.

Chenji turned and, having the superior vantage point, scanned the crowd. "Hell, I think he's talking to her now. Come on, before we miss anything juicy."

Li offered no protests as she followed Chenji across the room.

◁◆▷

T8 stopped behind a line of bushes. Junior knelt beside the bot, careful not to rustle any of the loose branches that hung around them in the thicket. They were far beyond the lights of the palace proper now, but even in darkness,

327

Junior could still distinguish the two guards up ahead, their red armor twinkling ever so slightly in the starlight.

"What's your plan for them?" whispered Junior as he aimed his palm at the guards.

"Different from yours, apparently." T8 pushed Junior's arm back down with a wiry finger. "Let me handle this."

T8 burst from the bushes, its red eye flaring. The guards aimed their spears.

"Indigo, indigo!" the bot cried. "Get to the palace!"

The guards slung back their spears and ran. Once they were out of sight, Junior emerged from the bushes, impressed.

"This new body may suck," began T8, "but it does come programmed with all the Orlov emergency codes."

"How long before they realize they've been duped?"

T8 shrugged. "We'll be finished well before then."

I hope so. Junior followed the bot to a small temple submerged in the overgrowth of the jungle. Vines exploded out of every crack in its ancient stonework, leaving only its shadowy entrance visible to the outside world. A relic of the Orlovs' past, he assumed.

"How old is this place?" he asked.

"Do I look like I give a shit?" The bot floated on through the entrance and into darkness, but Junior hesitated. Walking in blind broke every one of his cadet instincts.

"Relax, there's only one lifeform inside," T8 called back.

Yeah, but he's a Poterian. Junior sparked a flame in his palm and entered the temple. The inside was mostly hollow, just a few rows of wooden pews that sat before an altar. A makeshift cage had been assembled on the altar, and Sterling was sitting inside it. Junior stared at his betrayer through the iron bars. The Poterian looked depressed without his bionic limbs, but Junior could care less. This liar deserved to suffer.

"Why didn't you tell me what happened to the Zoboros? To my mother?!" demanded Junior. He stepped up to the bars, his orange eyes staring into Sterling's soul.

"Because then you would have known Iramwerta was real." Sterling turned away.

"Hey kid," interrupted the bot as its fingers transformed into a spinning blade. "Help me get through these bars."

"Shut up." Junior turned back to Sterling. "How did she get there? Did they kill her? I know you know what happened."

Sterling stared off, shaking his head. "It was my fault," he whispered.

Junior blinked with surprise. Did Sterling seem…sad? Junior wasn't one for pity, especially with his enemies. "What was your fault?" he pressed.

Sterling waited a long time before answering, the silence filled with T8's spinning blade as it grinded through iron. "We found the gate first. It had been my brother's mission to claim the power within Iramwerta. That's why he made Mogaddu our base of operations. But the gate wouldn't open, not for us. Not for anyone we trusted to try and do it. My brother spent months obsessing over it, and while he was distracted, your late Admiral Carmichael chose to attack. My brother led his forces into the atmosphere on a counteroffensive, but I remained on the surface to…protect what we'd found." Sterling glanced at where his arm and leg had once been. "I survived, but only barely. I saw many of my people die that day. More than any being ever should. So when the Zoboros came to Mogaddu, desperate and alone, I took it upon myself to help them.

"Your mother was the strongest among them. And a natural leader. I entrusted her with the city's location, though I warned her that the gate could not be opened. But open it she did. She led her people inside to what I thought was their salvation. Little did I know I had just led them to slaughter.

"The Lusitani had been tracking them. Once the Zoboros entered a city that had only one exit point, it became the perfect time for them to strike. I tried to rescue your mother, but by the time I arrived, the gate had sealed itself, with everyone inside. I never saw her or any of those Zoboros again."

Junior stood there, speechless. He clung to the bars for support, his arms shaking. "Did any ships make it out?"

Sterling shook his head.

Rage bubbled up inside Junior, brighter than before, but not toward Sterling. This time he was angry at everyone else. At everything else. At anything that could have possibly ripped his mother from him.

"Who gave the order?!" he barked. "You have access to information everywhere. You know who ordered the execution of the Zoboros."

"Ordered?" Sterling looked up for the first time. "You don't know anything about the Lusitani, do you?"

"Their existence may be kept off the record, but my father taught me about them. He told me they secretly served the IDF. So who holds their leash?"

Sterling looked Junior in the eyes for the first time since the conversation began. "The Lusitani are *contracted* by the IDF, but that ancient cult formed long before the Republic did. The IDF only brokered a formal agreement when the Zoboros turned on their government during the war."

"Then who do they serve?"

T8's red eye began to blink. An alert.

Sterling glanced around the ancient temple. "Best start melting these bars, boy. Someone's coming."

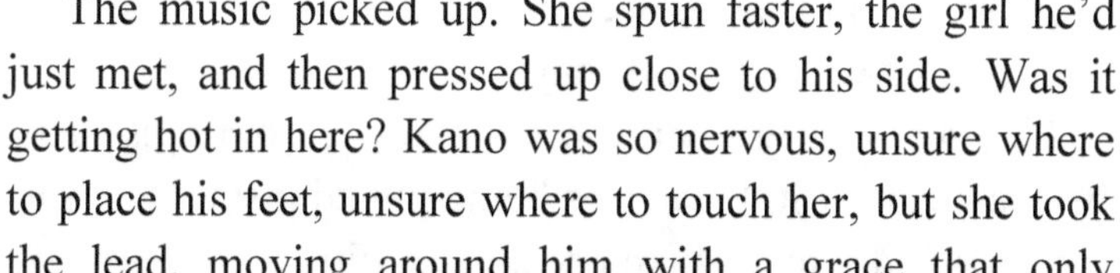

The music picked up. She spun faster, the girl he'd just met, and then pressed up close to his side. Was it getting hot in here? Kano was so nervous, unsure where to place his feet, unsure where to touch her, but she took the lead, moving around him with a grace that only heightened his feelings of incompetence.

"I heard you lost your powers," she whispered, her lips practically inside his ear.

"I-I got them back."

She smirked. "Prove it."

Kano paled. He was already nervous enough. The last thing he needed was to accidentally hurt someone in the middle of the dance floor. He glanced around and spotted Chenji dancing with Li. *Traitor*. Chenji locked eyes with him and mouthed the words, "What the hell, man?"

"It's too crowded," he told her, trying to ignore Chenji.

"What, afraid they won't come out?"

Kano blushed. "No, that's not what I—"

She grabbed his hand and rushed him off the dance floor, out the doors, and down the hallway. He wasn't sure what to do. No girl had ever given him this much attention before. And he knew Li must be inside fuming at him. Unless she didn't care at all; she'd seemed so preoccupied with—

"You better get back on that dance floor, young man!" Chenji buzzed in his ear in his zeefly form. "We had an agreement!"

"Buzz off!" Kano shouted back.

"What?" said the girl.

"Uhhh, I said where are we off to?"

"Nice save," buzzed Chenji.

The girl ripped open the door to a broom closet and before he knew it, Kano was being pulled inside. She shut the door and pressed up close against him.

"Well come on then," she said, her breath against his neck. "Show me what you can do."

Kano trembled. He didn't know what to do. Hell, he didn't even know her name yet.

"I don't think this is a good spot, either," he managed to get out.

"Really? I think it's perfect." And just like that, she was kissing him. If he'd felt out of his element on the dance floor, he felt completely blindsided now. *Close your eyes, you idiot.* He felt her hand run under his shirt and up his chest. It felt…nice. He glanced down. Her other hand had disappeared too, only he had no idea where it was. He could see her sleeve, but it just floated there without anything beneath it.

"*She can turn invisible,*" Junior echoed in his mind.

Taranis! Kano threw out his hand and blasted the girl into the wall. Her hand reappeared on impact, the stun baton inside it clattering onto the floor. Kano burst out the door and raced down the hallway.

He found Jaden by the entrance to the dining hall smacking face with an Orlov girl. Kano had to pry them apart to get his friend's attention.

"Kano, what the hell?!"

"Taranis!" gasped Kano, catching his breath. "He's here…get everyone out, now!"

Jaden turned longingly to his newfound love, thinking, then stamped his foot and ran back into the dining hall. "I hate you!" he called back.

Kano followed him inside. He looked to the dais, but Danadas had left his high seat. He needed to warn him. Kano scanned the crowd; there were hundreds of faces, but none belonged to the patriarch.

He spotted a server exiting the kitchen. *That's it!* Kano rushed through the door, much to the protest of the staff, past stoves and sinks and angry chefs, to the door of Danadas's secret study. It was wide open, its scanner busted.

Oh no. Kano raced up the steps, his powers at the ready. He expected to find Danadas either dead or at the mercy of their enemies, but instead the old man was seated comfortably behind his desk, reading a book by the fire.

"Kano!" exclaimed Danadas. "This spot is reserved for the elderly. You should be down there dancing!"

"Has anyone else come up here?!" demanded Kano, checking the corners of the room.

"My family knows to leave me in peace when I escape here."

Kano noticed the glass floor was covered, blocking off their view of the party below. *He must have really wanted to escape.*

"Sir, the party's been infiltrated," said Kano quickly. "Taranis's crew is here."

"They do work quickly, that lot," muttered Danadas. He rose from his seat but showed no urgency in his movements.

"Sir, we need to alert your guards!"

The door behind him shut. Kano turned and found there was no one around who could have shut it. He readied his powers. "Watch out, sir. One of them can turn invisible."

"Kano, wait. Don't do anything rash." The old man hobbled toward him on his cane as fast as he could.

"Stay behind me!" cried Kano, aiming his palms toward the door.

"Kano, stop!"

As the power rose to his fingertips, Kano felt a force slam against his back, so powerful it hurtled him across the room. He skidded across the glass, his senses all jumbled, as though an earthquake had just rolled over his body. When he finally stopped, he just laid there, shocked. He knew that energy, knew it intimately, but had never felt it directed on himself before.

Across the room, he saw Danadas standing with a palm aimed toward him. The invisible girl appeared beside him and stroked his back. "He came right to you grandpa, just like you said he would," she said.

"Yes he did, sweetheart. Yes he did."

Chapter 25

The Afterparty

Junior melted the bars between his palms. He reached through to help Sterling up, but the one-legged Poterian only shook his head.

"Behind you," he muttered.

Junior turned. The entrance to the temple was empty, but there was something outside among the brambles; he could sense it. He readied a fireball – an easy giveaway of his position, but there wasn't much room to hide in the enclosed space anyway.

"T8. My things," ordered Sterling.

"It might take a minute," said T8, its red eye flashing rapidly. "I'm detecting them deep inside the palace."

"Buy us some time, kid," Sterling said to Junior.

Junior kept his palms aimed at the doorway, not wasting time to wonder how Sterling planned to get his "things" all the way out here. His only concern right now was getting out of here alive.

"Can you see them?" Junior asked T8.

"They're using an EM pulse to scramble my scanners. But someone's out there."

A twig snapped. Fire swelled in Junior's palms, ready to blast through the entrance. But the doorway remained empty. All was quiet. Too quiet.

The stone wall above the entrance exploded. Blaster bolts fired through the smoldering opening. Junior dove behind one of the wooden pews and blasted fire over his head. He hadn't gotten a look at his attacker. All he knew was that the enemy had a superior vantage point.

A spear drove into the ground in front of him. An Orlov spear. Its shaft opened, its insides glowing with electricity. *An EM pulse!* He tried to vault over the pew, but blaster bolts peppered his path, trapping him. Electricity exploded from the spear. He closed his eyes, bracing for an impact, but none came. When he opened them again, he found T8 floating between him and the spear, its wiry fingers now antennae that absorbed the electricity.

"I'm gonna give you an opening, fleshling. Take it!"

T8 blasted electricity toward the hole above the entrance. Junior leaped to his feet and spotted the attacker: an Orlov guard, who dove behind one of the pews to dodge the electricity.

Junior heaved a fireball. It blasted the pew apart in a cloud of black smoke, but when the smoke cleared, the guard wasn't there.

"Above you!" barked Sterling from behind the bars.

The guard hovered over his head, suspended by a grappling hook it had fired into the ceiling. Junior dove away as the guard fired more blaster bolts from a cannon on its wrist.

Junior created a whip of fire and slashed it through the air, slicing clean through the guard's rope. The guard landed in front of him, vulnerable. He summoned fire to his fist and drove it forward in a finishing punch.

But the guard brought up its own fists. Compressed air blasted from devices on its wrists and extinguished the flames on contact, leaving Junior's fist to strike the guard's arm without any power behind it.

A counter?! Had Danadas supplied his guards with anti-Zoboros equipment? Junior had no time to think as the guard jabbed him in his bad shoulder and then kicked him over the pew.

Junior cried out in pain. He looked up at the guard, who had perched on the pew, ready to pounce. But Junior saw something the guard didn't; a bionic arm and leg rocketing through the hole that the guard had left above the doorway.

Sterling was back in the game.

Junior grabbed the wooden pews on either side of him and ignited them. The guard jumped into the aisle, flames surrounding it. Its glove sparked with electricity and the spear rushed into it on command. Junior got back on his feet and clapped his hands together, pulling the flames on either side in toward his opponent. The guard answered by striking its spear into the ground. Compressed air burst from it in all directions and snuffed the flames.

This guy's good, thought Junior. *And prepared.* The realization struck him as he dodged a jab from the spear: only Lusitani were this prepared.

He tried countering with a punch, but his bad shoulder screamed during the attempt. He drew it back, leaving himself vulnerable. The guard knew it too and drove the spear right at Junior's chest.

But a bionic arm caught it.

"Poteria sends its regards," said Sterling. The spear snapped between his metal fingers. He took the tip and, with the blast of a thruster in the back of his arm, he drove it clean through the guard's helmet. Junior looked away as the guard fell limp on the floor.

"What's the next part of your escape plan?" he asked, unwilling to show his betrayer any sort of gratitude.

"Retake my ship and get the hell out of here," replied Sterling.

"Not without the others."

"It's too late for them."

"I can get them out. You know I can."

Sterling shook his head. "We won't wait for you."

"Then don't."

<hr>

How?

Kano laid on the floor, afraid to move, afraid to breathe. How had he been so foolish to trust *anyone* after everything he'd been through, least of all an Orlov? It didn't make sense. The Orlovs had sacrificed themselves on Famora to protect him from Taranis, so why were they helping Taranis now?

The base of the jeweled cane thudded beside his face. "Rise," said Danadas.

Kano wanted to resist. He wanted to reject any command this traitor gave him. His power collected in his fists, but a sudden fear swept over him. Since Danadas had the same power, what else could he do with it? What had a lifetime of practice taught Danadas that he could use against Kano?

Danadas smiled. "I know you want to fight, Master Kano, but it will do you no good here."

The door opened behind him. Kano heard the clunk of metal boots echoing through the quiet study. He didn't need to turn to know who they belonged to.

"No sudden movements, boy." Taranis placed the tip of his sword against Kano's neck.

"Stand down," said Danadas, a hint of malice in his voice. "He knows when he's beaten."

"I wouldn't be so sure." Taranis's armor began to glow as electricity pulsed through its grooves.

"Why are you helping him?" Kano asked Danadas.

"My dear boy, Taranis is helping *me*." Danadas hobbled toward his desk. "I spent cycles planning the return of the Zoboros. The return of my family. I needed fear to spark the flame. Fear of a name, fear of a mask. And out of that fear, the people would demand heroes again. And so come you, Kano. You and your merry band of friends."

"You stay away from them!"

"They are my guests. And sooner or later you'll realize that I am the best host you will ever find in this cruel galaxy."

"But why give yourself away now?" asked Kano. "You've literally got hundreds of people downstairs on a mission to stop Taranis. When they find out you've been backing him, they'll turn against you."

"They turned against me a long time ago." Danadas stared into the fireplace, lost in memory. "When they chose the lesser path, the easier path, to hide and suppress our people for our gifts." Energy thrummed in Danadas's hand, sending vibrations through the room that chilled Kano to the bone. "I have watched my family weaken over four generations. Watched the branches split off and…interbreed. That is why our connection to the spear fails us now." He drew the spear from beneath his desk and held it tenderly. "This was our family's legacy. We are the first Zoboros family. The greatest family ever to exist. We can become this again, but measures must first be taken."

He pressed a button on his desk. The panels beneath the glass floor drew back. Kano gasped. What had once been a party below had turned to horror. Fire blazed around the edges of the dining hall. Guests screamed and ran, but guards blocked the exits, driving their spears again and again into the crowds. Bodies laid everywhere. And on the table, the Orlov Tree was covered in blood.

"What have you done?!" cried Kano. He summoned a shockwave, but Taranis zapped him into submission before he could launch it.

"Trimmed the branches," answered Danadas. "The relocation program is finished. All those with knowledge of it must be eliminated, else they might take their Zoboros charges and sneak off into the night. Only those loyal to our true cause will remain to gather the Zoboros and unite them."

"Unite them for what? War?!" hissed Kano through gritted teeth, smoke rising from his black suit.

"A dreadful thing, indeed," said Danadas. "But when it is over, the Zoboros will ascend to their rightful place in the galaxy."

"And your family with them."

Danadas knelt before Kano. "The fate of the Orlovs has always been entwined with that of the Zoboros." He let the energy thrum in his hand again, so much more controlled than Kano's. "I told you I can teach you. I can make you the face of our revolution. The face that will free millions across the galaxy."

Kano turned away. He was nauseated at the bloodshed happening right beneath him. "How many have to die for this freedom?"

"As many as it takes," said Danadas.

"I say we put a dampener on him," said Danadas's granddaughter.

"My thoughts exactly, Mila," said Danadas.

Mila marched to the desk with a smile on her face. She drew a dampener out of the drawer, one that had been prepared precisely for this moment.

"You know I'll never join you," said Kano. "So why not kill me now?"

"The gate closed with your departure," said Danadas. "That is why your powers returned to you. But I trust you and Taranis can find a way to open it again."

Kano trembled. He still didn't understand what power Iramwerta held, but if the time shades were a taste of it, then he didn't want to know what someone like Danadas could do with it. And he couldn't be the one to let him have it, either. He needed a way out, and fast. He searched the room, but with only one door and three powerful enemies surrounding him, options were limited. He needed a way to catch them by—

Something slithered beneath his sleeve. He reached for it when he felt it tap his wrist.

It tapped his wrist three times.

Chenji! Mila approached with the dampener. Kano tensed. Taranis must have sensed it, because he let a bit of electricity spark through his sword as a warning – electricity that, as Kano recalled, Taranis could use to call the blade to it upon command. Kano wondered if the same could be said for the other mystical objects that the Three Kings possessed. He looked to the spear, an idea forming. A terrible one, but easily the best that he had.

"Don't do anything stupid, Kano," said Taranis.

"And here I thought you knew me at all," replied Kano. He let the energy thrum within his hand as he reached for the spear. It sailed from Danadas's hand and landed in his own.

Danadas's eyes bugged out of his skull. "STOP HIM!" he screamed.

Kano channeled his power into the spear and drove it into the glass panel beneath him. It shattered and he fell through, the screams and cries from below now ringing in his ears. He felt the dilepede slither out from under his sleeve and up his back. The weight there became a hundred times greater – Chenji was no longer an insect. Kano felt talons clench around his shoulders and hoist him out of his freefall.

An aivin with mighty wings now carried him over the dais, but his friends were no longer on it. Instead, guards stood there, firing their rifles down into the defenseless crowd. Kano hurled a shockwave. It crumbled the dais beneath their feet and sent them toppling over each other.

"How did you know to follow me?!" Kano called up.

"I was gonna try and give you some pointers with your new girlfriend," cawed Chenji. "But after you punched her into a wall, I stuck around out of morbid curiosity."

Kano blushed. He felt violated, but also relieved that Chenji had been there to rescue him. The feeling didn't last long though, as lightning crackled past them and exploded on the table with the Orlov Tree. Kano searched frantically for an exit – all the doors were blocked, but there was a stained-glass window on the far wall.

"Chenji, our exit!"

Chenji steered them toward it. As they drew closer, Kano realized it depicted Danadas's face. How fitting. He blasted it into colorful pieces, and together he and Chenji sailed through the opening and into the night sky.

⌖

Junior burst through the brambles at breakneck speed. His shoulder throbbed without its sling, but there was no time for pain. The others were in danger. For all he knew, the fighting could have already started. *Or they could be dead.*

He spotted the palace just down the hill, still glowing like a great beacon beneath the lights, only no more ships were arriving. There were no more guests in the courtyard, either. Just guards. They were stationed at every entrance, but they didn't face the outside. For some reason, they each stared at whichever entrance they were protecting.

That's not a good sign. It appeared the Orlovs weren't as concerned with keeping people out as they were with keeping people in. It did make Junior's approach much easier, though, since no one was looking his direction. He stuck to the hedgerows in the garden for cover and sidled up near a greenhouse that was attached to the palace's east wing.

Two guards stood facing the greenhouse entrance. Junior let his energy settle in his palms and waited. He would need to be quick and quiet; if anyone else was alerted to his presence, he could expect a swarm of guards to descend upon him immediately. And if those guards were anything like the ones he'd faced in the temple, he wouldn't stand a chance.

Just as he readied to charge out and strike, one of the guards checked their communicator. Junior paused and listened.

"Dining hall is secured," she said to the other. "Lock it up."

They drew a steel bar that had been hidden behind a bush and barred the greenhouse door with it. The other guard looked around. "What about the Zoboros?"

"Secured as well. We should get out of the way."

"Don't have to tell me twice."

Secured? Junior kept low while the guards drew back through the garden. *And what are they so eager to get away from?*

A cackle echoed through the courtyard. Junior turned. He knew that voice. He knew the blue fire as it blazed across the sky.

Kazan.

Junior sprinted to the door and ripped the steel bar from it as the first fireball exploded against the roof. More and more fireballs rained down on the palace, setting whole sections ablaze as the night sky turned red. He raced through the greenhouse as the greenery began to catch fire. There was a door on the far side leading into the rest of the palace. He charged for it, the cackling growing louder in his ears. *Just a little bit closer...*

Fire exploded between himself and the door. The greenery blazed bright. Junior tried absorbing the fire, but it kept catching onto anything and everything around it with frightening speed. Amid the smoke, he smelled something even stronger: alcohol. Empty champagne bottles laid on the floor, their contents coating everything around them. *Only the Orlovs would tinder their own home*, he thought. *They didn't want anyone to survive tonight.*

He tried finding another angle, another path to the entrance, but the fire kept spreading, red and hot. Hot enough to burn him, as he'd learned in the arena. He heard a creak. The greenhouse groaned around him, its steel cage bending. *Oh no.* He smashed through the wall just as it collapsed behind him in a crash of metal and glass.

Smoke filled his lungs. He collapsed and wheezed, his head growing light from the fumes. Everywhere he looked – the palace, the gardens – it was all in flames. He felt a hand grab his shoulder. He spun around quickly, fireball at the ready, only to find Warp standing there, her hood pulled down and her face dripping with sweat.

A puff of smoke and they were standing among the trees on the hill, looking down upon the fires that consumed the mighty Orlov palace. Junior watched the flicker of light in the sky that was Kazan as it dropped more fireballs. He clenched his fists, wishing his shoulder was stronger so he could fly up and blast that demon out of the air.

Warp tugged on his arm, wishing for him to follow her deeper into the trees, but he stood firmly planted.

"We need to save them."

She shook her head and drew her finger across her neck.

"Are they dead? Do you know?!" He grabbed her by the shoulders, his orange eyes staring pleadingly into hers. She hesitated, then shook her head and pointed.

Junior looked. He saw a small army of guards crossing the courtyard toward a waiting transport ship, a group of prisoners marching between them.

"That's them! Get us down there while there's still time!" He looked to her, but she just stood there, trembling. Junior stopped himself. He had to remember that not everyone was as comfortable around fire and combat as he was. He had to rethink his approach.

"It's alright to be scared. It…happens to me all the time."

She raised an eyebrow at him, unconvinced.

"I'm serious. But I do what I do because…well, because I'd want someone to do the same for me, even if no one ever will. But those people down there; they would run into the fire for us. And that's something worth fighting for."

Warp stared into Junior's eyes. He sensed a fire rising inside her. She grabbed his hand and suddenly they were standing among the prisoners. Carmichael, Jaden, Makoto, Akio – they were all accounted for. Li and Cera too, both bound in power dampeners. Kano and the new guy with the shaggy hair were missing, but Junior had little time to worry about that, given thirty spears were now aimed at him.

"Stand down," said a young man at the head of the procession. He lacked armor or weapons; instead, he aimed his hands at Junior. *Zoboros*. Tall with baggy clothes…Junior recognized him, though he couldn't recall where.

"Careful," whispered Makoto. "That one controls gravity."

The arena! This was the Zoboros who had helped Taranis catch him before he could crawl to safety. Junior sparked a flame in either hand. "Everyone hang on to each other," he whispered. They moved to comply.

"That won't work this time, Hellfire!" shouted the enemy Zoboros. The guards stepped closer, their spear tips pressing up against the team members. "No one has to die here."

"Hundreds are dying in there already!" cried Li. "You're a murderer!"

The boy paled. "That wasn't me."

"Prove it then," said Carmichael. "You want to be a real hero? Help us."

"I...I have orders."

"So do we," said Carmichael, taking a step closer to the conflicted Zoboros.

Ristin, thought Junior. *Taranis had called him Ristin.*

"You can have new orders, Ristin," said Junior. "You don't have to serve him or anyone. Just let us go."

Ristin hesitated. Slowly, his hands began to lower, but when he looked up, fear stole across his face.

"Incoming!" he cried.

A shockwave slammed into the guards on their right and tossed them away like rag dolls. Another landed on the left. An aivin swooped overhead, Kano dangling from its talons as he fired away through his spear.

"Now *that's* an entrance!" exclaimed Makoto.

Ristin raised his palms. Junior felt weightless. His legs, *everyone's* legs, began to lift off the ground. He took aim at Ristin, but a guard beat him to it. She swung the butt of her spear into the back of Ristin's head and knocked the lights out of him. The guard ripped her helmet off so that her auburn hair could spill out.

"Come on!" shouted Sandra, pointing her spear toward the transport. "We can take it!"

The team ran toward it as fast as they could. Junior looked to the sky. The aivin weaved back and forth above them, Kano blasting away any guards who challenged them as they closed in on the—

A blue fireball slammed into the transport ship. It exploded, the force of it knocking everyone back against the hard marble floor. Junior landed on his bad shoulder and screamed. His ears rang. He felt a hand lift him off the ground. It was Carmichael. He could just make out the captain's words amid the ringing.

"Get ready for a fight."

Junior turned. Beyond the smoke and ruin, he spotted an army of guards charging out of the tree line, spears leveled in front of them. Back toward the palace, he saw the same thing.

They were trapped.

The team formed up close to each other as Kano and Chenji landed among them.

"What took you so long?!" called Junior, not realizing how loud he was.

"I was getting us a ride." Kano pointed up.

Sterling's freighter swept through the smoke, even more majestic than Chenji's aivin form. Blaster bolts fired up at it from a hundred spears, but each shot pinged harmlessly from the ship's belly.

"Everyone, lock arms!" ordered Junior. They did. Warp grabbed onto him. A puff of smoke and they were inside the cargo hold, watching through the window as the guards fired on their old positions, hitting each other instead by mistake.

"Another daring escape," said Jaden as he collapsed dramatically into the nearest chair.

"Is everyone alright?" asked Carmichael as Sterling steered them into the atmosphere.

"Over here!" said Kano.

Junior and the others hurried over to him, expecting to find Kano with a blaster scorch in his arm or something, only it wasn't Kano who was injured, nor any of their team members, but Ristin lying unconscious with a lump in the back of his head.

"What's he doing here?!" demanded Cera.

"I grabbed him right before we teleported," said Kano. "I thought we might be able to get some information out of him."

"We'll need it," said Carmichael darkly. "Akio, help me tie him down."

Junior followed the captain and the Jakari as they got to work. "Carmichael, we need to warn the IDF about Danadas. About the Orlovs."

"They won't listen to us," said Carmichael.

"What are you talking about?"

Cera stepped in. "We tried making contact, but we discovered that Danadas had already called in accusing us of the attack. The IDF is on its way, and they think he's innocent."

"That's ridiculous!" shouted Junior. "They attacked us! We can prove it."

"I'm sure we could," said Carmichael. "But until we have a case, it's our word against the IDF's biggest and most trusted benefactor."

"He's a liar!"

"Who deceived us all," said Carmichael firmly. "Our best course is to lay low. Because right now, we're the most wanted fugitives in the entire galaxy."

Chapter 26

The Mission

Shouts echoed from upstairs. Kano remained in the cargo hold, seated on the same worktable where he'd once been held prisoner. *Funny how that works*, he thought as he looked over at Ristin. Their new prisoner laid on a worktable of his own, still unconscious, his hands bound in a power dampener. He looked so young, probably not much older than Kano, and clean cut, not scarred or damaged like the people Kano would expect to follow Taranis on a revenge spree. Their brief encounter in the courtyard had been telling; Ristin had seemed so uncomfortable, like he'd never been in a fight before.

Like he didn't want to be in a fight at all.

Well, welcome to the show. Kano walked over and touched the dampener on Ristin's hands. So cold. He could feel it draining the power from Ristin as its lights pulsed. From what Kano had gathered, Sterling had plenty more of these things on standby. Just one more reason not to trust the Poterian.

Kano was still surprised that Sterling had come to their rescue at all. When he and Chenji had flagged the ship down, it had been out of desperation. Sterling was already taking off from the courtyard when they'd found him; they never expected him to start angling toward their captive friends. Did that mean Sterling actually cared about them? Or maybe the Poterian just wanted to save Junior. Kano had sensed a connection between the two of them. He'd seen Junior's reaction when Sterling betrayed them. There had been trust between them once.

Just like I had with Danadas. Kano wanted to smack himself on the head. How, after everything he'd experienced, could he let himself believe that someone was truly trying to help him? *Stupid!* He'd been so distracted by the mysteries that Danadas had laid before him that he never questioned what the patriarch's intentions were. He would never make that mistake again.

"I ain't taking my ship there!" boomed the Poterian's voice from upstairs. Kano sighed. The argument had been raging for two hours now. Carmichael wanted to take the ship into the Outer Territories where they could regroup; Sterling wanted to dump them on the nearest planet and ride off into the sunset. And Sterling would have done it too, if Cera hadn't used her powers to take the ship's controls from him. Unfortunately, only Sterling's biometrics could unlock the controls, and so that had become the stalemate.

Kano had offered to stay here and alert them when Ristin woke up, but really he just wanted to get away. A part of him hoped Ristin didn't wake up for a long time. It meant more time for him to avoid making another terrible decision. Every decision he'd made so far had brought them from bad to worse, from cheating in the

Sim, to pulling everyone into Carmichael's escape plan on the *Dormarch*, to going in search of Iramwerta. Some leader he was.

A creak echoed from across the room. Kano turned. Li stood in the doorway, unsure whether to come in or out, a coldness still orbiting around her.

"I was just checking to see if he was awake," she said. She started to leave.

"Wait!" Kano was on his feet. Li looked to him expectantly, though he had no idea what he was going to say. Desperate, he fired off a quick, "How's it going upstairs?" and was immediately disappointed in his choice of question. He knew the answer to it already, and Sterling unintentionally answered it before she could.

"How about I tie you all to the hood and give you a first-class tour of the galaxy?!"

Li shook her head. "You should be up there. The team needs you."

"I'd just make everything worse."

Li stepped tepidly into the room. "Why are you so afraid to face them?"

Let me count the ways, he thought. But with Li, he didn't need to list any of them. A look was all he needed for her to understand him.

She stepped closer, just a few tables away. "He tricked us all, Kano. It's not your fault."

"It's not just Danadas," he said. "Everywhere I go I'm being chased. No matter what I do, someone is always using me. Danadas, Taranis, Mezo, Novak, even Hendricks and Carmichael. They all have some plan for me that I can't see." He found himself saying things that he didn't know he was thinking, all while stepping closer to her. "I thought I was doing the right thing by escaping the *Dormarch,* but even *then* I was still playing into their hands. And now our allies are dead, the IDF and the Orlovs are hunting us, and our only hope is a Poterian who's desperate to get rid of us."

Kano felt exasperated. He hadn't realized that had all been pent up inside him.

"The glass is really half full with you, isn't it?" asked Li with a smirk.

"You know me so well," he muttered. He couldn't help but crack a smile. They each stepped closer, now just a worktable apart.

"We joined you for a reason, Kano. We're not going to let anyone take you away, no matter how many people come after us. Even if we have to go to the furthest edge of the galaxy. We won't stop fighting for you."

Kano choked up. He'd led his friends through complete hell these past few weeks, yet they were still here. Here and wanting more.

"I just feel like I'm always ten steps behind," he said.

"Of course we're behind," she said, stepping closer. "Our enemies have been plotting this out since we were kids. We're just now starting to play catch up."

"It feels like a little more than catch up," he said. He and Li were only inches apart now. He felt something, a warmth rising inside him. He wanted to be even closer to her. Something in her green eyes told him she wanted the same.

"Well if it makes you feel better, it can't get much worse."

This is your moment. He leaned in. She started to lean in too. It was happening.

"It can – and it does."

They turned. Their prisoner was sitting up, rubbing the lump on the back of his head, his whole body shaking.

<hr>

"For the last time, we are *not* going back to Mogaddu," said Carmichael.

"And what, you think running is going to help us?!" Junior shouted back, his throat burning after two hours of this. "It only makes us look more guilty."

"I'm with the kid on this," added Sterling.

"Only because his plan will get us off your ship faster," said Cera, her energy hands still blocking Sterling from the controls. "But we're not doing it."

"Why not?!" demanded Junior. "Mogaddu is the one place where we have protection. The Zoboros there are sympathetic to us, and the IDF won't want to engage them directly. If we linked up with them, that would give us a platform for negotiation. Then the IDF would listen to what we have to say about the Orlovs without us getting captured."

"Even if we get to the negotiation table, it won't work," said Jaden. "The Orlovs have had the government's trust for centuries. You think that would get thrown away because a group of people who were *already* fugitives pointed their fingers at them? We'd only be giving away our position to the IDF, who – need I remind you – are already in the Mogaddan atmosphere." On one of Sterling's many screens, he blew up an image of the *Dormarch* floating above the red planet.

"Besides," added Carmichael, "no one will believe that Danadas murdered his own family. Not when all the evidence has been burned. Everyone thinks he's the survivor of a horrible tragedy. It's won him the Republic's sympathy as well as the support of his surviving family members, who think they've been targeted by a rogue Zoboros cell. Until we have something concrete, we're on our own."

"He's right," said Sandra. "And my great uncle's word is worth its weight in gold in our family. Few people would think to question him."

Junior rethought his strategy. If they couldn't beat Danadas's accusations, then they would just have to beat Danadas himself. But as he looked at all the tired and frustrated faces around him, he realized this team was in no shape for another battle. These people had been running, fighting, and narrowly escaping death for weeks, just like he had. They didn't have the morale to go up against the combined strength of the Orlovs and Taranis, and certainly not when the very idea of it seemed completely hopeless. They needed their spark back.

"We can't just sit here and do nothing," he said. "Danadas's plans are just getting started, and we're the ones who're supposed to stop them. That's why you built this team, Carmichael, isn't it? To stop the galaxy's greatest threats?"

"It is," the captain answered quietly.

"But we have to be smart," said Cera. "We don't know what we're up against. We can't just go on the offensive without more intel."

"But every minute we wait, Taranis and Danadas recruit more Zoboros to their cause," said Makoto. "The fight is only going to get harder."

Junior noticed Akio nodding in the corner. The Jakari hadn't said much since the debate began; he'd just sat there sharpening his knife.

"What's your opinion, Akio?" he asked.

"My people are warriors. We believe in quick and clean strike." Akio slashed his knife in the air for emphasis. "But we must be prepared. The Orlovs have Lusitani in their pockets. I recognized their style beneath their Orlov disguises. They thought they could fool a Jakari, but a Jakari knows these things."

"Just one more reason *not* to engage," said Cera.

Junior searched the room for others with opinions. The only ones left were Chenji, who had fallen asleep in his chair an hour ago, and Warp, who never spoke. It would be up to him to keep the conversation going. And he still had one more piece of vital information.

"There's something else," he said. "Taranis is searching for something called Project Vortex, and whatever it is, millions could die if he finds it."

"He already has," announced Kano. He entered the bridge along with Li. Ristin trailed behind, shaking where he stood. Junior noticed his eyes were darting around a mile a minute.

"Wait, what's Project Vortex?" asked Jaden. "Somebody catch me up."

"It's possibly the most classified project the IDF ever pursued," answered Carmichael. "It's above even my pay grade."

"Then how do you know about it?" asked Makoto.

"Because it killed my father."

Silence swept across the room faster than Junior could blink. It was a while before Carmichael continued. "I overheard him speak of it on a few occasions when I was young. Always in riddles, but after his death their meaning became clear: he'd found a weapon he could use to defeat the Poterians, and he used it." He turned to Ristin. "Do they have the weapon yet?"

"No," said Ristin, his eye twitching. He looked pale. "They-they-they—"

"Out with it, boy!" barked Sterling. The Poterian looked anxious. The very mention of Project Vortex tended to have that effect on him.

"I-I-I need to sit down." Ristin fell into the nearest chair. He looked ready to pass out.

"What's wrong with him?" asked Makoto.

"It's the shakes," said Sterling. He reached underneath the console and pulled out a vial. "Here, take this." Sterling tilted back Ristin's head and poured the vial's contents down his throat. It took mere moments for their prisoner to stop shaking.

Junior squinted at the vial and noticed familiar traces of blue powder clinging to the glass. *Vaxum*. He'd arrested plenty of people on Famora for carrying it. Teens used it plenty, but the heavy users were typically older adults, often ones who were trying to cope with trauma. It was thus no surprise why Sterling might have some available at his workstation.

"Should we have you arrested for possession on top of war crimes?" asked Cera.

"It's a diluted amount," muttered Sterling. "For withdrawal symptoms."

Carmichael seemed uninterested in Sterling's personal habits. He approached Ristin and patted the confused boy on the shoulder. "Tell us, Ristin, what's their plan?" he asked.

"It's already happening," said Ristin, able to string together complete sentences again. "The attack on the palace was the first phase. Phase two is to intercept the weapon."

"Intercept?" asked Cera. "But who's carrying it?"

Oh no. All the pieces came together for Junior in that moment. He pointed to the big blue blot on the screen. "The *Dormarch*," he said.

"That's insane," said Cera dismissively. "That weapon killed everyone it touched the first time. Why would they keep it on their most populated ship?"

"Because it's the perfect protection," said Jaden. "Think about it: a mobile fortress filled with thousands of guards, including Lusitani? They don't even need to tell anyone on board that the weapon is inside. Everyone would just naturally protect the ship from attack. It's a perfect defense!"

"Well, if it's a perfect defense, then we know why Taranis is building a team," said Kano. "They plan to steal it."

"And with Lusitani allies inside, they could sneak in undetected," added Akio.

"But where in the ship are the IDF keeping it?" asked Junior. He turned to Ristin, who shrugged.

"I'm sure Danadas and his spies have figured that out already," said Carmichael. "They just needed to bring the *Dormarch* onto their home turf."

"Then we need to warn Mezo," said Li. "Everyone on board is in danger!"

"I am *not* sending a signal to the IDF," said Sterling, folding his arms. "They'd be all over us in minutes."

"We both know you wouldn't risk that weapon going off again," said Junior.

"If they're stupid enough to rebuild it, then they can suffer the consequences," said Sterling.

"And so would everyone on Mogaddu!" Junior fired back. "You saw what happened the last time. If you had the power to stop it then, you would have, and you know it!"

Sterling stared coldly at Junior, his fists clenched. "I am not sending that signal."

"We can't just let them take it!" said Makoto.

"No, we can't," said Kano, stepping up. Junior could see new resolve forming in his friend's eyes. "If we send a signal, they'd only come after us and leave themselves more vulnerable to attack. We know what's really happening. We have to be the ones to stop it."

"What are you suggesting?" asked Sandra, the whole room growing tense.

"I'm saying we have to break into the *Dormarch*."

"That's a suicide mission!" exclaimed Jaden.

"It's what we trained for, isn't it?" said Makoto.

Jaden paced the floor. "And how do you propose we get past the air defenses, soldiers, *and* Lusitani defending the ship?" he asked.

"That's the easy part." Kano nodded to Warp. All eyes turned to her as she tried to make herself inconspicuous in the corner.

"Can you teleport us from one ship to the other?" asked Carmichael.

She looked around anxiously, then nodded.

"In that case, let's follow your line of thinking, Kano," began Carmichael. "We've just successfully teleported past the *Dormarch*'s defenses. How do you plan to take on Taranis's team, which we can assume is better equipped than our own given they have Danadas's backing?"

Kano looked stumped, but Junior saw a way Kano's plan could work. Kano was just approaching it from the wrong angle.

"We wouldn't have to engage them," answered Junior. "Their mission is to take the weapon. All we need to do is sabotage Project Vortex so it can't be fired."

Carmichael smiled. "And how do you propose we find it?"

"The Panopticon!" exclaimed Jaden. "Most of the ship's information is stored there. I could hack into it and find where it's hidden."

A new energy began to fill the room. Everyone began looking at each other as their cogs began to click.

"Whoa, whoa, hold on a second," said Sterling, waving his bionic arm. "If you think I'm going to steer my ship toward the most powerful vessel in the IDF's fleet, you've got another thing coming."

"Warp, how close do you need to be in order to teleport inside?" asked Carmichael.

She held her hands apart to show the distance would not be great.

"More or less than a mile?" asked Sterling.

She brought her hand down to signify it was less.

"Shit," muttered Jaden.

Junior turned to the Poterian. He saw the way Sterling's eyes darted, sensed the conflict in his scowling face. Time to add pressure.

"We need you Sterling," he said. "Just like the Zoboros needed you in Iramwerta." He stepped closer; the Poterian drew back. "Just like my mother needed you. Give us a chance to destroy this thing and you'll be rid of us forever. Then you can at least know you tried to stop the weapon from being fired again."

Sterling scanned the room, over faces that now held a newfound resolve despite everything that was working against them.

"I'll give you two minutes near the *Dormarch*," said Sterling. "Not a second more."

"Then it's decided," said Carmichael, pounding his fist on Chenji's chair. The changeling awoke, drool trickling down his chin.

"What'd I miss?" Chenji asked.

Carmichael beamed. "Chenji, my boy, I believe we're breaking into the *Dormarch*."

Chapter 27

The Break In

Everything shook as Sterling's ship edged along the Mogaddan atmosphere. Kano tightened his grip on the spear. Carmichael had entrusted it to him, seeing as he could summon it on command. Why it chose to answer his call, he wasn't sure, but it offered him some small comfort as they waited for the *Dormarch* to appear in the viewport.

Once it did, their mission would begin.

Makoto and Chenji tensed beside him. Together, the three of them made up the first infiltration team. Their objective: secure the Panopticon. Once secure, Warp would teleport Jaden inside to hack into the mainframe and find the weapon's location.

Kano glanced across the bridge. Junior, Cera, and Sandra stood there with Akio clinging to Sandra's back, a pouch filled with explosives hidden under his poncho. These four made up the demo team. They would be teleported into the Sim, which Carmichael assured them would be unused and unwatched, where they would wait until Jaden had the weapon's location. Their objective: destroy the weapon.

That left Carmichael, Li, and Warp. They made up the reserve team, which would be teleported in as needed. Li had wanted to join Kano's team, but Carmichael had convinced her otherwise. Her healing powers were one of the team's biggest assets, so keeping her in reserve meant she could be sent to whichever team needed her. Kano prayed no one would need healing, but knowing their luck, she would probably be very busy aboard the *Dormarch*.

The part that concerned Kano most, however, was the teleportation. They had no idea what waited in any of the rooms they teleported to. They could land in front of an army of guards or right in the scope of a security camera. T8 had offered them some help in this department: each team carried a scrambler. Activating it blocked any comms signals, including security feed, within a large radius around them. This also meant that while any team was using a scrambler, they would be cut off from communicating with the other two teams, and so they were only to be used when necessary.

Even with the scramblers, Kano still sensed a larger issue with the mission, and that was Warp herself. Everything hinged upon her ability to teleport them in and out of danger despite her never having trained with the team before. Technically, she wasn't even a team member. She hadn't given any sign that she'd wanted to join; she was only here because the team had offered her refuge at the Orlov palace, which in hindsight had been about the worst thing for her. Now she was stuck on their most dangerous mission yet with people she barely knew and had no obligation to protect. She had a good heart, Kano knew that much, but her heart wouldn't be in this fight, and that could mean the difference between success and failure.

Between life and death.

Carmichael must have known this too, because when he caught Kano's gaze, he immediately nodded to Warp. His signal for Kano to step up and say something.

Kano took a deep breath and approached. Warp was busy staring out the viewport, her fingers drumming anxiously on a handrail. He led with a simple, "Hey," to which she jumped with surprise. Kano took a step back. This was going to be a tricky pep talk.

"I want you to know that this whole team has your back. Anything you need, just say…" he paused, remembering his audience, "…just send a signal."

He could tell by the way she rubbed her knuckles that he'd made her more nervous. Hell, he'd made himself more nervous. The whole room was tense as it was, more so than they had been for any of their other missions. He racked his brain for a mission that had seemed more impossible than this one: Mezo's test in the Sim, their escape from the *Dormarch*, their attempted escape on Famora…his eyes widened. He had an idea.

"You know, this isn't actually my first heist," he said. She looked up. Now he had her attention. "Back on Famora, we stole this firework from the—"

"Makoto and I stole that firework!" hollered Jaden from across the room. "Don't go taking credit for our heist."

Warp smiled at that comment. It was working, so Kano kept pressing. "Well 'your heist' would've been over real quick if I hadn't shown up on a speeder to rescue you."

"Whoa, whoa, whoa, I had the situation well under control," said Makoto.

"You did not," said Sandra, rubbing her temples. Kano smirked. As he recalled, Jaden had tried and failed to flirt with her as part of his "distraction" while Makoto made off with the firework.

"I don't get it," said Chenji. "What's so special about a firework?"

Jaden gasped. "This was a *golden aivin*, the greatest innovation in the pyrotechnic community! Ask Junior, he was there."

"I don't wanna talk about it," muttered Junior.

"Jaden, why are you so proud of this?" asked Sandra.

The debate continued as everyone gave their take on the story of the fabled golden aivin. Kano soaked in the laughter, the banter. For a moment, it was as if the weight of the galaxy had lifted from their shoulders. He saw Warp was laughing silently, her mouth wide open so he could see the stub of her tongue.

Someone had sliced it off.

A knot formed in his stomach, but he didn't let the surprise show. He didn't want to hurt her; not like the rest of the galaxy had. But as he looked around the room, at all these arguing outcasts who had been hurt in one way or another, he realized this was the perfect place for her.

"Welcome to the team, Warp," he said.

She smiled.

One problem down, he thought. Now all they had to do was break into the most secure ship in the galaxy and destroy the most dangerous weapon ever assembled.

And then somehow escape.

Kano looked to Sterling, who sat silent at the controls. The Poterian wouldn't be sticking around for them to teleport back to his ship, so they would need to find another way off the *Dormarch*. The team hoped to commandeer a ship from the hangar, but Carmichael had made it clear that the hangar might not be an option. Everything would go into lockdown the moment they destroyed the weapon (if they even made it that far) and leave them trapped. They hoped they could improvise something, but everyone was entering this mission knowing they may not come out of it.

While the others argued, Kano noticed Li heading for the exit. She caught his gaze before stepping through the door. She wanted to talk. Alone.

Butterflies filled his stomach. He crossed the bridge quietly, his friends too engaged in their debate to notice his departure, and found her leaned up against the wall in the hallway. He leaned up beside her.

"This is the end, isn't it?" she asked.

"I don't know," he said. Memories flooded his brain; memories he'd been pushing off since they'd decided to break into the *Dormarch*. Memories of Famora. Of spending time with Li at her grandmother's tavern. Of learning she had powers, too. Of learning he wasn't alone.

He looked into her eyes and knew she was thinking the same thing. That come the end of this mission, they might each *be* alone, if not dead altogether. They embraced so quickly he didn't have time to realize he was crying, her hug squeezing the tears right out of him.

"Just promise me you'll be safe," she sniffled.

"I can't promise any of us will—"

"*Promise* me," she repeated. "Promise that you'll call me in if you need me."

"I promise." He looked into her green eyes, knowing this may be the last time he saw them. And then, as if they'd done it a hundred times before, they kissed. Kano felt a warmth sweep over him, like his feet were rising off the floor.

"Ahem."

They pulled apart and found Cera standing in the doorway, smiling.

"Ship almost in sight. Get to your positions," she said.

Kano looked to Li. She blushed.

"Be safe," she whispered.

"You too."

They returned to the bridge. It was silent now, the room filled with anticipation as everyone stared out the viewport at the red planet rotating beneath them. Kano took his position between Chenji and Makoto, assuming no one had noticed his absence.

"How'd it go back there?" Chenji whispered in his ear. Obviously, Kano hadn't been as subtle as he'd thought. He answered with a smirk, to which Chenji beamed. "Atta boy."

"Infiltration team, get ready," announced Carmichael.

Warp stepped up behind them. Chenji and Makoto locked arms with Kano and together they rotated into a triangle formation that kept Warp at its center. Should any attack come for them in the Panopticon, better for them to take the hit than their teleporter.

"Scrambler on," ordered Carmichael.

"Scrambler on," answered Makoto, activating the device on his belt.

Everyone drew a collective breath as their big blue target appeared on the horizon, growing larger as Sterling rocketed toward it.

"Your target is the circular indent at the center," said Carmichael. Warp nodded.

Kano saw it too. The Panopticon. Clearing it will be easy, he told himself. There had only been two guards inside it the last time he'd been there, each protecting Mezo's office. The rest had been filled with analysts who doubled as Kano's personal fan club. He had a feeling he could get them to comply with their demands, though the idea of holding them hostage didn't sit well with him. But if everything went smoothly, no one would get hurt.

"You know your assignments," said Carmichael. "Let's execute and save the galaxy."

Goosebumps crawled up Kano's arms. *The entire galaxy*. No pressure or anything…

Sterling reached for the lever to idle the ship. "Your two minutes starts…*now*."

"Make the jump," ordered Carmichael.

A puff of smoke and the mission began.

Kano unlocked his arms from his teammates and raised his spear, ready for anyone who might appear before them. Guards, analysts, Lusitani…but nothing came their way. No one attacked, no one screamed, no one even moved inside the Panopticon.

The analysts just laid there in pools of blood.

"The hell is this?!" cried Chenji.

Makoto keeled over and vomited.

Kano stepped forward as if in a trance, a nightmare. Shock overtook him. He'd seen these analysts' smiling faces just days ago. Now their faces were twisted in pain and horror, their blood splashed against the windows that overlooked the rest of the ship. But no one below seemed aware of what had transpired behind the one-way glass. Kano knelt beside the body closest to him and found a gash across her abdomen.

"A sword," he said. "Taranis was here. We need to call it in." He tapped his communicator but all he got was static. "Makoto, the scrambler."

"Sorry," coughed Makoto. He switched it off, and proceeded to vomit again.

"Captain, Taranis already cleared the room. No survivors."

There was a pause before the captain spoke. "Is the room secure?"

"Yes, but it's—"

"Send Warp back for Jaden."

Kano gulped. Things already weren't going according to plan. He turned to Warp, who had pulled her hoodie in tight so she couldn't see the bodies.

"Warp. Warp, listen to me," said Kano. "I need you to return to the ship and get Jaden. Can you do that?"

Warp didn't respond. She just stood there shaking while Carmichael's voice came over the comms.

"Sixty seconds, team. Let's move!"

"Please Warp," pleaded Kano. "More people will die if you don't."

That snapped her out of her trance. She blinked, then vanished.

"I don't blame her if she doesn't come back," said Chenji. He morphed into a giant lizard with ten legs, the form that could echolocate. He sent out his signal, then snapped his eyeless head toward Mezo's office.

"Who's inside?" asked Kano.

Chenji morphed back into his Human form, his flight suit still intact from the relatively small transformation. "Just one person," he said, approaching the office. "Possibly a bot."

Jaden appeared in a puff of smoke beside them. "Holy shit!" he cried, leaping back from the trail of blood at his feet.

"Stay here," ordered Kano. "Makoto, guard him while he works." Makoto nodded, his face a bit pale, while Jaden sat at a console and got to work, his quivering fingers afraid to touch the keys with bloodstains on them.

Kano followed Chenji past Mezo's two dead guards and up the stairs. At the top, the office door was wide open.

"Why do you think it's a bot?" he asked.

"Because it's moving, but I didn't sense any footsteps," answered Chenji.

Then where's Mezo? Kano entered the office expecting to find her body. He found her chair overturned and her desk smashed down the middle, but not her.

"You shouldn't be here."

They snapped to the right, Kano aiming his spear, Chenji taking the form of a gorilla.

Plí approached them upon her hoverpad, looking as composed as ever despite the horror scene lying just outside the door. "Lord Danadas does not wish any harm to come to you here. Leave now in peace."

"If he doesn't wish us any harm, then he shouldn't have blamed us for his crimes," said Kano, his powers thrumming into the spear.

"Lord Danadas has committed no crime."

"The bodies outside would say otherwise," said Chenji in his deep gorilla voice. He stepped forward, but Kano motioned for him to hold his position.

"Step off the hoverpad, Plí," said Kano calmly.

Plí smiled and did as commanded. But when her feet touched the ground, they sprang claws that tore the straps off her heels. Her back contorted. Her body elongated and sprang fur over every inch of her skin. Her nose morphed into a snout and two long tusks stretched from her chin. Suddenly, they were no longer facing Plí, but a Kimikan hog with paws instead of feet.

"Changeling!" cried Kano. Chenji leaped at her and swung his massive fist, but she blocked it with her tusk.

With her front paws, she grabbed Chenji by the fur and heaved him through the window in a shower of glass.

"CHENJI!" Kano launched a shockwave through the spear at Plí. It sent the remains of the desk out the window, but Plí leaped over it. Kano braced, expecting her to pounce on him, but she sailed right over him and bolted through the door on all fours.

She was heading straight for their asset!

"Kannnnoooo!" cried Jaden. He and Makoto ducked under the analysts' desks as Plí bounded over the tops of them, her tusks plowing through computer monitors as she went. She stopped at Jaden's desk, reached her hairy paw underneath, and started feeling around for him.

Kano raced down the stairs and launched another shockwave. Plí dove onto the ground as it blasted everything off the tops of the desks. She turned and her vein-filled eyes landed on Jaden.

"I didn't sign up for this!" he cried, drawing his pistol. He fired at Plí, who hissed and scampered to the side, smashing computers and desks along the way. Makoto dove in behind her, a stun baton in each hand, and drove them into her back. She convulsed and let out a feral squeal that sent chills down Kano's spine. He aimed his spear at her, but he couldn't fire without hitting his brother.

"Makoto, move!" he ordered. Makoto removed his batons from Plí's back, but before he could spring clear, Plí swung her paws around and knocked him to the ground. She was on top of him in an instant, her sharp claws raised over his head.

"I'll show you Orlov hospitality," she wheezed as she brought down her claws.

"NO!" screamed Kano.

The window shattered behind Plí. Another Kimikan hog barreled through it and tackled her off Makoto before she could finish her strike.

"Oh great, there's two of them!" cried Jaden.

The hogs tumbled across the control room, smashing everything in their path in a flurry of punches and kicks and slashes until finally the new hog landed on top of Plí.

"You shouldn't have touched me, bitch!" said the hog in a wheezy voice that just barely resembled Chenji's. He swung his chin down and drove his tusks through Plí's eyes. She went limp in his arms.

"Oh please, no more blood," said Makoto, gagging.

Chenji shrunk down to his Human form again, pale and shaking, claw marks etched across his bare chest and Plí's blood splattered on his chin. It was clear he hadn't expected to do that. He'd been caught up in the heat of the moment, but now was realizing he'd just taken a life.

"Thank you, Chenji," said Kano, doing his best to mask his own revulsion. He knew if he lingered on it, Chenji and the others would do the same. Chenji had made a tough call, and they would need to make a lot more of them to survive the mission. Kano reached into his pack and tossed Chenji an extra flight suit before assessing the situation.

"Jaden, did you locate the weapon?" he asked.

"No, and I don't think I can anymore," he pointed to the wreckage that had once been the control room. Not a single computer had been spared.

"Um, guys…" Makoto pointed through the broken window, where a train loaded with troopers was entering the Panopticon.

"They know we're here," said Kano. He sprang into motion, but found his team was lagging. Chenji was still in a daze as he wriggled into his new clothes, Jaden was scrambling to find a working computer, and Makoto just stared blankly at Kano.

"We need to abort," said Jaden, kicking a dead computer. "We failed."

"There is no abort," said Kano.

"We have to tell Carmichael," insisted Jaden, reaching for his communicator. "We're in over our heads. If we call it off now there's a chance we can still catch Sterling before he ditches us."

"No!" Kano activated the scrambler on Makoto's belt before Jaden could make the call. "Sterling's already gone. There is no retreat. We need to locate Project Vortex or we're going to be arrested emptyhanded."

"Better arrested than dead," said Chenji, his eyes lingering on Plí's gored body.

"Don't say that," said Kano, pacing the floor. He couldn't panic, no matter how bad it seemed. He needed to think clearly. That was the one thing that kept them alive in the Sim; it was the only thing that would keep them alive here. "Think with me: Taranis was already here, which means he must already have the weapon's location, right?"

Everyone nodded.

"So we don't need to hack the mainframe to find it. We just need to follow the trail of bodies. That should lead us right to the weapon."

"Last I checked, bodies don't give off a traceable signal," said Makoto, strapping his stun batons back onto his belt.

"No, they don't…" said Jaden, staring at Makoto's belt. "Makoto, switch off your scrambler."

"What are you thinking?" asked Makoto as he switched it off.

Jaden pulled his datapad out of his pack and plugged his own communicator into it. "Taranis's crew must be using a scrambler too. It's the only way they've hidden from security this long."

"Won't that just make them harder to find?" asked Kano.

"Not necessarily. Scramblers create a cloud of blocked signals that's easy to trace. If I blanket the ship in messages, all we have to do is find the hole and…"

Jaden opened a map on his datapad which showed all his sent messages. A patch of red X's appeared directly beneath the Panopticon. Far beneath. He raised his communicator. "Demo team, we've got the location. Panopticon, level B82."

Muffled chatter leaked through the other line until Cera finally spoke. "That's a long way down. Are you sure?"

"Positive. Careful, hostile team is there."

"Roger that," replied Cera. "We're going in."

Chapter 28

The Demo Team

Junior stared at Carmichael's 3D map of the Panopticon. Two railway tracks ran through the middle, and eighty-two levels below that blinked their target.

"Troopers are entering from the railway," the captain explained. "Let them. Your job is to stand back and make sure that weapon doesn't leave the facility in one piece."

Stand back? thought Junior, rotating his bad shoulder. If there was a fight, he was going to make sure Taranis and Kazan didn't come out of it.

He felt Akio clamber up his shoulder. "Are you ready, spawn of Hendricks?" the Jakari whispered.

Junior nodded. Looking down from the rafters, he saw the large white room that had been the training ground for the others. His training ground had been much different, but it had prepared him all the same.

"Mogaddu has changed you," whispered Akio. "You are not same boy I was charged with on Famora."

"What am I now?" asked Junior.

"Warrior."

Junior grinned. His father had made Akio his secret protector for many cycles, so secret that Junior didn't know of Akio's existence until the attack on Famora. Since then, he'd grown strangely fond of the mysterious creature; it was a reminder that his father was hovering somewhere in the distance, watching.

"Be prepared, young Hendricks," continued Akio. "This weapon will be large. Even with detonators, we may need your powers to finish the job."

Junior nodded. He'd assumed that was why he'd been placed on the demo team, and considering an encounter with their enemies was imminent, he was happy for the appointment.

"Warp, can you get us all the way down there?" asked Cera.

Warp shook her head.

Cera thought for a moment. "If you get us behind the train, can you teleport us into the elevator as soon as it closes?"

She nodded.

"It'll be filled with troopers," said Li.

"I can handle them in close quarters," said Cera. "They won't even know what hit them."

"Music to my ears," said Akio as he adjusted the explosive pouch beneath his poncho.

Carmichael smiled. "Any questions, team?"

Cera, Sandra, Junior, and Akio all shook their heads. Carmichael opened the door. "Good luck," he said.

They locked arms. Junior felt Warp's hand on his back. A puff of smoke and they were right behind the train. The chatter of dozens of troopers filled their ears, all assembled near the elevators.

"First wave is upstairs," a trooper announced.

"Upstairs?" whispered Sandra, readying her spear. "We need to help Kano's team."

"We stick to our objective," said Cera. "They did their part, now we do ours." She pointed to the elevator as its doors opened and a second wave of troopers poured in. "Warp, get us inside as soon as the doors shut. Not a moment later."

Warp nodded. They locked arms again as the elevator doors began to slide shut.

"Intruders! Behind the train!"

The team turned. A stray sailor was pointing at them from the other side of the tracks. They heard the clatter of a hundred boots charging toward their position.

"Warp, *now!*" ordered Cera.

A puff of smoke and the railway disappeared, as did the floor beneath them. Junior fell, the wind whipping in his ears, the many doors and cables of the elevator shaft whirring by him.

"Shit, shit, shit!" he exclaimed. A green energy field appeared below him. It bent beneath his weight like a trampoline and then tossed him back in the air. The others all bounced around him, up and down until their momentum finally dissipated, watching as the elevator descended not far below them.

"We missed it," said Cera, the first to get back on her feet. "We'll have to take the stairs." She reached out and formed another green platform beneath them. Junior stepped onto it first. Unlike the platform they had landed on, this one was firm. Cera created another one below it and he continued onto it, the others following in a spiraling path that Cera created as they walked.

Warp tugged Junior's sleeve. He could tell by the look in her eyes that she was sorry.

"It's alright," he said. "We'll just be a little late to the party."

"The elevator was heading downstairs, which is a good sign," said Sandra. "The IDF must have figured out the bad guys are downstairs too."

Junior raised his communicator. "Carmichael, come in. We're in the elevator shaft. Any word on what's happening?"

"We've got two combat squads in either direction," answered Carmichael. "The first just secured the Panopticon, but our friends already cleared out. They'll rejoin the channel once it's safe to communicate. They sent a message alerting the IDF to the location of Taranis's team before evacuating their position too."

"You can thank Jaden for that one," came Kano's voice over the comms.

"Kano? Where are you?" came Li's voice.

"Don't answer that, Kano," said Carmichael. "Now that the IDF knows we're here, they're going to be looking for foreign signals to tap into. Don't give away your positions."

"Okay, then just know we're safe for now. We'll send Warp a signal when she's back in the Transitway for retrieval."

"That may be a while!" called Cera, unable to raise her communicator to her lips as she generated platforms for them to walk on. "We need her to get us to the other side of the elevator shaft!"

Shouts echoed up the shaft, followed by the pop of gunfire.

"What's that noise?" asked Carmichael.

"The IDF just engaged Taranis," answered Junior. "We need to move faster."

Cera stopped them in their tracks. She generated a platform far beneath them. "Warp!" she ordered.

Everyone locked arms. Warp teleported them to the distant platform. Cera generated another one far below, and they repeated this process, the sounds of battle growing louder with each jump, until the stopped elevator was in sight.

"What is our plan?" asked Akio, still attached to Junior's back. He'd been quiet the whole descent, but now that the action was close, he was toying with his knife excitedly.

"You stay here," ordered Cera. "We don't know what the situation looks like on the other side on the wall. We'll need to send someone in who can find us a safe place to land."

"I'll do it," said Sandra. "I'm the most expendable one here. It should be me going in."

"No one is expendable," said Cera, "but if you're willing to go, I'll give you the signal."

Sandra nodded and steadied herself. Warp placed a hand on her back.

"Bullshit," said Junior. "If she lands in the middle of a firefight, I'm gonna protect her."

"You'll stay here until we have a proper entry point," said Cera.

Junior ignored her. He saw the puff of smoke appear and snatched Warp's arm just in time. They appeared in a hallway at the elevator entrance. The battle had moved further up the hall and out of sight, but two troopers had been left behind to guard the elevator.

"Who are you?!" one of them shouted. Junior launched a fireball into the trooper's chest, slamming her into the wall. He saw the other trooper coming in the corner of his eye. Akio fired a stun bolt that made the trooper convulse and collapse.

The rest of the hallway was empty, but there were traces from the firefight. Bullet holes checkered the walls, and a few troopers laid dead along the path.

"Warp, get Cera in here please," asked Sandra. Warp vanished and appeared a moment later with a livid team leader.

"What were you thinking?!" exclaimed Cera, wasting no time in marching right into Junior's face. "I gave you a direct order."

"I'm making sure we beat Taranis," he replied coldly.

"We do that by working as a team."

"I never signed up for your IDF scam of a team," Junior shot back. "You want my help, you let me make my own calls."

Cera sneered. "We'll see how far that gets you." She raised her communicator. "Captain, any word on…?" she trailed off, realizing there was only static on the other line.

"We are inside enemy scrambler," said Akio. "We are on our own down here."

Cera nodded. "Warp, stick with us until we're out of the dead zone. We keep moving forward. *Carefully.*" They followed her down the hallway. It forked, so they took the path that was riddled with bullets, the gunfire from the battle growing louder with every step. Junior cracked his knuckles, itching for a rematch.

They rounded a corner and dove for cover as bullets zipped by. Four surviving troopers were pressed against the edges of the hallway ahead, firing at an enemy that was shooting back in the distance.

"We can't advance!" one of them shouted as bullets peppered the walls around him.

"We need to hold here for the next wave!" shouted another.

"I think one of them is invisible—" The last word was cut off, replaced by the sound of him choking. He collapsed.

"What the hell?!" cried another. A bullet zipped into his neck. He choked and fell too.

Lightning launched out of thin air and zapped the two remaining troopers until they fell to their knees. Taranis appeared alongside Mila, their arms entwined. They separated, and Taranis slashed his sword across his kneeling victims in a final blow.

Her power works through contact, just like Warp's, thought Junior. *That's how Taranis slipped past security in full armor.*

Junior and company kept their heads low as a squad of Lusitani emerged from the other side of the hallway, all reloading their weapons. Center among them was Taranis's trusted Gorv, Dimitri, its half-scarred face twisted into a smile at the sight of all the fallen troopers.

"Dimitri, you can bring her out now," said Taranis. Dimitri waved a signal and an Orlov guard emerged from the other end of the hallway, dragging Mezo in its arms.

"You'll pay for all the good men and women you killed today, Taranis," she hissed.

"Shut up," said the Orlov guard. Junior instantly recognized Kazan's voice from beneath the disguise, a disguise Mezo must have trusted to bring aboard her ship. How her friendship with Danadas had backfired.

"Let her grovel," said Taranis, leaning down so his masked face was level with Mezo's. "You were wise to have the codes changed before our arrival, but it will cost you. We will kill everyone who comes down this hallway until you provide the codes for the vault."

Mezo looked away defiantly.

"So be it," said Taranis, his normally icy voice sounding far more venomous, as if on the verge of screaming. "I'm going to enjoy this." Electricity leaped from his fingertips and danced across Mezo. The general convulsed, but never made a sound.

Cera looked away. "Warp, put us past them," she whispered. "Get us to that vault."

A puff and they were far down the adjacent hallway, their enemies out of sight. A few more puffs and the hallway widened around them. A metal door towered over their heads, sealed with an array of biometric scanners in front of it.

Junior felt a chill as he stood in its shadow. Beyond this door was the most powerful weapon ever conceived. The weapon that ended a war.

The weapon that everyone wanted.

"Finally, some action," came a voice from behind them. They spun around, powers ready, to find an Orlov guard standing there with a spear at her side.

"This one's mine," said Sandra, stepping up with her own spear ready.

The guard cocked her head. She tossed her spear aside and formed a new one in her hand made entirely of ice.

Yui! Junior ignited flames in each hand. "She's mine."

"I've been looking forward to our rematch," she replied, ripping off her Orlov helmet.

Junior stepped forward but a field of green energy blocked his path.

"Remember your mission," said Cera. "Sandra and I will take care of this one."

"No, wait!" Junior started forward, but Warp grabbed his back. A puff of smoke and the fight was gone. The vault stood before him, but he was on the other side of it now.

Which meant Project Vortex was right behind him.

He was almost afraid to turn around. He could sense the immensity of the room. And all for one weapon. He hoped between himself and Akio they had enough firepower to—

"In the name of the ancestors…" muttered Akio.

Junior turned and gasped. There was no machine behind him. No weapon. Just a white floor and white walls, like he'd seen in the Sim, only there was a bed in the corner and a table at the room's center with a few chairs around it. A woman sat in one, her back to them as she addressed them.

"What tests shall we be running today, Mezo?"

She didn't bother to turn around. She had long dark hair and wore a white uniform. Her hands were bound in a power dampener.

Project Vortex...was a Zoboros the whole time?! Junior didn't know what to do. Obviously, they couldn't blow her up. But they couldn't keep her here either. Not with Taranis banging at the gate. They had a teleporter with them. They could get her out.

"I'm not Mezo," he found himself saying. "My name is Aaron Hendricks Junior...and we're here to rescue you."

"Junior?" She turned, and Junior felt his heart leap up into his throat. He recognized everything now: her hair, her face, her eyes.

Her orange eyes.

Chapter 29

The Project

Kano checked the hallway. The lights were out, but the night vision on his binoculars let him know that no troopers were roaming the area. Or more importantly, Lusitani.

He retreated into the small office his team had taken refuge in. It was an administrative section about halfway down the Panopticon. Jaden had brought them here because the troopers would search floor by floor, going both up and down, so this spot in the middle would give them the most time to hide until Warp could retrieve them. In the meantime, Jaden had busied himself by hacking into one of the computers.

"Anything juicy?" Makoto whispered.

"Depends how much budget reports tickle your fancy," replied Jaden. "But we can always get security footage, override codes, comms channels…ah, here's something! A classified database."

"You're not going to set off any alerts by hacking it, are you?" asked Kano.

"Not if I do it right."

Chenji snickered in the corner. He was in his lizard form, using echolocation to sense any disturbances in the floors around them. Thus far, he hadn't detected anything.

That gave Kano some comfort, though Jaden sticking his nose where it didn't belong always put him on edge. He'd seen his friend make too many mistakes to trust his judgment, especially when they were deep behind enemy lines.

"Voila! We're in!" exclaimed Jaden.

"Project Vortex!" said Makoto, leaning up in front of the screen. "Look up Project Vortex!"

Jaden typed but nothing came up. "Hmmm, no files. At least none that they saved here." He started backspacing, then stopped. "That's interesting. There's a lot of other projects in here: Project Axis, Project Niskai, Project…" He trailed off.

Kano approached, his curiosity captured. "Project what?" Then he saw it on the screen, written in big bold letters that chilled him right down to his core.

PROJECT TARANIS.

◁◆▷

Junior stared in disbelief, his heart pounding. Before he knew what was happening his mother ran into his arms and pressed close to his chest, unable to hug him with her bound hands.

"I've missed you so much," she whispered. He felt her tears leak through his shirt and warm his chest.

"I missed you too," he said. A thousand emotions swept through him: shock, sadness, joy, longing. It felt as though the many cycles of wondering where she was and if she were alive were all condensing on this one moment.

Akio hopped off his shoulder and bowed beside him. "Lady Hendricks," he said humbly.

Angeline smiled as she knelt beside the Jakari. "Our little protector. I should have known you'd be at my son's side."

"I deserve no praise, Lady Hendricks," said Akio, a sadness in his voice that Junior never heard before. "I failed."

His words turned Angeline's expression cold. She knew what his failure meant.

"How did my husband die?" she asked.

"By defending your spawn to his last breath," said Akio, his head still bowed. "As I should have. As I will do if that is what it takes."

Anger flared inside of Junior. How could Mezo have kept his mother hidden from him for so long? From his father, too; the man who had trusted her with his entire operation. She didn't even have the decency to tell his mother that her husband was dead. Murdered by a maniac who was waiting just outside.

That snapped him into action. "We need to get you out of here, fast." He turned to Warp. "Get us to the others."

Angeline smiled as Warp touched her arm. "Is this a friend of yours?" she asked her son.

"Yes, Mom. Now we've gotta go."

"You have beautiful hair," she said to Warp, pulling her hood back. "You shouldn't hide it."

Warp blushed. A puff of smoke and they were on the other side of the vault. Their ears filled with the sounds of battle. Cera had two energy fields in front of her, one blocking Yui's ice, the other blocking Kazan's fire. Sandra stood behind the two fields, firing blaster bolts from her spear through the opening between them. In the distance, they could hear Taranis and the rest of his crew engaging the next wave of troopers.

"We're getting out of here," said Junior, grabbing hold of both Cera and Sandra.

"Already? I didn't hear an—" Cera paused, noticing the newcomer. "Who's this?"

"I'll explain at the rendezvous," said Junior as smoke puffed around them.

Jaden pulled up the video file. Kano kept his eyes glued to the screen as a young woman and man appeared on it, both in lab coats. A machine loomed behind them. It extended the length of their laboratory. At first, Kano thought it was a cannon, based on its shape, until he noticed what appeared to be a reactor at the end of it.

"Trial 78," announced the woman into a microphone. She sounded tired. "Bring out the next subject."

A door opened. A child was ushered in with a bag over its head and a dampener over its hands. At least, Kano assumed it was a child, because the two troopers escorting it were twice its height. It wasn't until they reached the machine that the troopers removed the dampener.

The child placed its free hands on a conduit at the back of the reactor. *Could it be?* Kano had a feeling he knew who this child was, but he didn't want to believe it.

The troopers marched back through the door and sealed it. The woman's voice came softly over the microphone, almost nervous.

"Begin."

Electricity burst from the child's hands. Kano and company gasped, their faces pressed against the screen as electricity flowed through the conduit and lit up the reactor.

"Systems are online," said the man. "But power levels are too low."

"Just a little more, sweetie," said the woman into the microphone.

The child pushed harder. The reactor began to spin, faster and faster. Junior could see the child was shaking, struggling.

"Still too low," said the man.

The woman paused. She looked to the child. "Then let's shut it down."

"And make this kid come back for another test?" said the man. "Let's run him through and be done with it."

The child shook harder. The reactor spun faster. A small voice beneath the bag began to scream. By the look on the woman's face, she couldn't take any more.

"You can stop now, sweetie!" she said into the microphone, her voice cracking beneath her nerves. But the child kept pressing. "Jeslow, why isn't he stopping?" she whispered.

Jeslow! Kano almost fell over he was leaning in so hard. *Mom and dad?* Makoto and Jaden looked to him, aware of what this meant.

"He hasn't learned how to stop!" answered Jeslow quickly, pounding his fist against the control board as the gauges all dipped into the red. "They told us he was fit for this test!"

Sparks shot not only from the child, but from the reactor now.

"We have to shut down now!" cried Jeslow.

"Abort!" Kano's mother shouted into the microphone. "I repeat, *abort*!"

The door burst open. The two troopers rushed in and each fired a stun bolt into the child's back, but the child absorbed the electricity and channeled it into the reactor.

The troopers ran to the child. A stray lightning bolt struck the first one and threw him against the wall. The second reached the child and raised his weapon.

"NO!" cried Kano's mother as the trooper swung the butt of his gun into the child's neck. The electricity ceased and the child fell limp. The reactor slowed, its lights fading. The trooper hoisted the unconscious child and carried it back through the door.

"Tr-trial complete," whispered Kano's mother. "Unsuccessful." The video stopped.

Silence filled the room. Kano stared at the blank screen, waiting for it to produce more. Waiting for some explanation as to how his parents could have been involved in something so terrible. Something that traumatized children.

Something that traumatized Taranis.

"Whelp, now we know why he hates you," said Jaden.

"Jaden!" cried Makoto.

"What?!"

"Quiet!" hissed Chenji, back in his Human form. Everyone listened as boots clattered over their heads. The troopers were getting close.

"We need Warp," said Kano, trying to distract himself from what he'd just seen. "Is Warp back in the field?" he asked into his communicator.

"Negative," came Li's voice. "They've been dark since—"

"We're on the train!" came Cera's voice. Kano checked out the window and spotted them, looking like ants as they climbed through a hatch at the top of a train car. "Warp's right behind me. We're going to—"

"No, she's behind me," interrupted Sandra in the background.

"What are you talking about?" said Cera. "I can feel her hand on my back."

There was a scream. Junior cried out. Kano saw fireballs blasting atop the train.

"What's going on?!" exclaimed Kano. "Talk to me demo team."

"Warp? Warp!" came Sandra's voice in the background.

"The invisible girl tagged us when we teleported," answered Cera. "She's stabbed Warp."

Kano took a deep breath and tried to keep his voice level. "How bad is it? Can she teleport?"

"Negative," said Cera. "She can barely stand."

"Oh shit," said Makoto. Outside, sirens blared across the Transitway.

"You need a new escape plan, teams," said Carmichael over the comms. "Get yourselves and the asset to the rendezvous point. *Now*."

"But we've got no teleporter!" cried Makoto.

"Then we improvise," said Jaden, typing away at the computer. "Demo team, hold your positions."

"Why?" asked Kano. "That whole station is crawling with troopers."

"But those troopers don't have the override codes," said Jaden, a grin spreading across his mischievous face. "We're taking the train."

Chapter 30

The Getaway

Ristin tapped Sterling on the shoulder with his power dampener. He'd spent the past hour afraid to even come near the hulking Poterian as it steered the ship, but the shakes were getting the better of him now. He could barely keep the dampener straight when he made contact. All he could think about were the vials in that drawer. Those sweet, sweet vials.

Sterling grunted something in acknowledgment and opened the drawer. Unfortunately, Ristin required a little more help than that with the dampener on his hands. He cleared his throat, to which the Poterian cursed under its breath.

"This stuff will turn your brain to mush, kid." Sterling popped open a vial and poured the contents into Ristin's mouth.

Ristin felt the screaming desire in his brain quiet to a whisper. He sat down beside the Poterian, relieved not only for the fix, but also because the Poterian didn't eat his face off.

"You have stuff like this where you come from?" he asked.

"This is chickenshit," said Sterling. "The stuff on Poteria would split your Human brain on the first dose."

Ristin leaned in, fascinated. "What's it like there? On Poteria?"

"Well for starters, the people aren't nosy." Ristin slunk back, but Sterling continued, loosening some of the edge from his voice. "We're much more civilized than people here think."

"Then why do you eat the faces off your enemies?" blurted Ristin. He'd heard about it a hundred times in school, but he felt ashamed to say it now to an actual Poterian.

Sterling frowned. "Some of our weapons are strong enough to melt faces off. The whole 'eating faces' thing was just propaganda that your government started."

"Weapons that melt faces don't sound very civilized, either."

"Given your people created Project Vortex, I don't think you have much room to talk. But I understand how you feel. My brother took my people in a...unique direction." He stared off through the viewport, as if something out there in the void of space was staring back at him. "We had been peaceful for a long time, but there was an anger beneath the surface. An anger about how your people handled things on this side of the Rift. My brother stoked that anger, and my people paid dearly for it."

"So did ours," muttered Ristin. He stared off through the viewport, a pain rising from deep inside. A pain no amount of vaxum could ever quiet.

Sterling watched him for a long time. "Who did you lose?"

"My father," he said, his own voice sounding strange to him. He never talked about this. Not to his friends or his fans or even to his own mother, who the Poterians had made a widow before he was born. "He died in the Battle of Mogaddu. Taranis promised me we would find the people responsible. Had I known he was planning to use the weapon, I would never have joined him. I would be out there helping the others stop him. I owe that much, at least."

Sterling looked out the viewport again, drumming his fingers on the throttle.

"Dammit, kid."

<hr/>

"Stay with me, Warp," whispered Junior. He had her slung over his good shoulder as he carried her down the hatch and into the train, her blood trickling down his arm. *Damn that invisible bitch!*

He set her down on one of the seats. The color had drained from her face, her eyes opening and closing as she dipped in and out of consciousness. He pressed his palms against the knife wound in her side and applied pressure. It was treatable, but only if they could get her to Li in time. He pounded his fist against the wall. Without Warp, they were stuck without a medic.

"I'll take care of her." His mother swooped in beside him and placed her dampener over the wound. Warp shifted from the cold touch of the metal. "It's going to be alright, sweetie. I need you to take a deep breath for me. Can you do that?"

Warp did, then relaxed her body. Junior was shocked. All it had taken was a few words from his mother to ease her pain.

"Let me get that thing off you," he said, warming his hands as he reached for the dampener. "They'll slide right off once I fry the circuits."

"No!" barked his mother, her tenderness suddenly gone. He jumped back with surprise, but then she calmed. "I'll let you know if your friend needs more attention."

Junior nodded, confused. Was she so afraid of her powers that she *preferred* the dampener? He didn't want to believe that, but he also didn't know the extent of her power. There was so much they had to catch up on. So much he wanted to learn.

But they needed to make it off the *Dormarch* first.

Boots clattered outside. Troopers hurried along the railway on either side of their train car and aimed their rifles. Everyone ducked, Junior using his own body to shield his mother and Warp as bullets shattered the windows above them.

Cera generated shields over the broken windows, her face straining as bullets pounded against them.

"I don't think she can hold them," said Sandra.

"No, she cannot," said Akio, readying the explosives in his pouch.

"Wait!" said Angeline. She pointed out the window with her dampener. Chenji was swooping down from the

Panopticon in bird form, Kano clenched in his talons, once again launching shockwaves through his spear.

Cera gasped with relief as the troopers were knocked from the railway. "Where's the rest of the infiltration team?" she asked into her communicator.

Makoto answered with a cheer, not through the communicator, but out in the open, his voice echoing in through the broken windows. Junior spotted him surfing on the head of a floating bot, Jaden cradled in the bot's wiry arms, their combined weight pulling the bot down toward the train from the middle of the tower.

Typical. Junior reopened the hatch above and received them both, Jaden looking much paler than the enthusiastic Makoto as they climbed inside.

"Never again," Jaden muttered as he passed Junior, trembling.

Kano and Chenji were last to enter. Now everyone was assembled, four infiltration members along with Junior, Sandra, Cera, Akio, Angeline, and an injured Warp.

"How do we get this train moving?" asked Cera.

"Already on it," replied Jaden, punching a few keys on his datapad, his fingers still shaking from his ten-story descent. Everyone grabbed the handrails as the train lurched forward.

"Can't the IDF override the train's controls?" asked Sandra.

"Not anymore," said Jaden with a smile, waving his datapad. "At least, not remotely. But they can still manually stop it if they take the controls at either end of the train.”

“Then that’s where we need to go,” said Cera. “Two teams.”

“I’ll lead one,” said Kano, to which Makoto and Chenji formed up behind him. “We can take the back of the train.”

“Good, because that’s the side the troopers are chasing,” said Jaden, showing security footage on his datapad of troop transports pursuing the tail end of the train.

Junior stepped up. “I’ll lead a team to the front. If the IDF’s smart, they’ll have a team waiting up ahead to catch us.”

Akio was first to join Junior, eagerly loading his pistol.

“Cadets stick together, right?” asked Sandra as she joined them.

“That they do,” said Junior, recalling their time on Famora. It had only been a few weeks ago, yet something about being chased by the army they once swore to uphold as cadets made it seem so long ago.

“I’ll stay here and protect the train car,” said Cera, nodding toward Jaden on her left, who was busy running interference on his datapad, and a semi-conscious Warp on her right who Angeline was attending to. “This will be home base until we reach the hangar. How long is the train ride?”

“About eight minutes,” answered Jaden.

“A lot can happen in eight minutes,” said Makoto.

"Then we better move," said Cera.

Junior nodded and led his team out the door. They sped through each train car, careful to check for any remaining IDF agents along the way, but they found it a straight shot to the front. When they arrived and looked through the windshield, though, it became clear why the path had been so clear: two transports were lowering a massive crab bot onto the tracks, its head of reinforced steel tilted toward the incoming train, its six legs reaching to clamp around the rails.

"I suggest we get back a couple of cars," said Sandra.

"Agreed."

They had started back when something bright flashed outside. They turned as a blue fireball impacted one of the transports. The light from it hit them faster than the shockwave, which blasted the windshield into little beads and threw all three of them into the next train car.

Junior groaned on the floor. His ears rang. When he looked out, the burning transport was veering off-course, pulling the crab bot with it away from the railway. The train's path was clear, but the controls were now a smoldering mess of broken parts and sparking wires.

"Well, that's one problem out of the way," said Junior, igniting a flame in his hand as the blue flare in the sky angled toward their position. "But now we have a bigger one."

Kano cheered as another troop transport spiraled away from the train. Chenji cawed above him – a signal that another one was approaching. He took aim with his spear and blasted the transport sideways, the troops inside all shouting and cursing as they skidded to a stop at a nearby station. Down on the roof of the train, he spotted Makoto making short work of the IDF troopers who had already landed there, each one feeling the sting of his dual stun batons.

"Kano, come in," came Carmichael's voice through the comms.

"Yes sir?"

"New problem. Taranis's team wants to keep your train in motion."

"I'm not sure how that's a problem, sir."

"It will be when we try to stop," came Jaden's voice. "They've got speeders heading straight for our car. We think their plan is to take Junior's mom and leave us to crash."

"Then we're coming back for you!" said Kano.

"Negative!" said Carmichael. "You need to protect the brakes in the back in case Jaden or his datapad is taken. If we can't stop the train, the entire team is compromised."

"Then we should pool all our assets and protect Jaden so he can stop the train remotely," Kano fired back.

"Leave Jaden to me. Carmichael out."

Kano gulped. His instincts told him to race back and protect his best friend, but Carmichael clearly had a larger plan in mind; the worst thing he could do was go against it and create more confusion. He took a deep breath and tried to tune out his nerves.

"Makoto, Chenji, we need to get to the back of the train," he said into his comms.

Chenji cawed and swooped onto the roof beside Makoto.

"I don't know what you're worried about," said Makoto as he zapped the final trooper out of consciousness. "I got the whole thing handled."

Not for long, thought Kano. Taranis was coming, along with Kazan, Yui, and—

"Mila!" he cried. "She was already on the train when she stabbed Warp!" He turned to Chenji, who morphed into his lizard form to use his echolocation. When he morphed back to his Human form, he had a grave look on his face.

"She's at the controls," he said.

They raced through the top hatch and into the last car, but saw no one at the controls. Kano and Makoto stayed in the doorway and kept their weapons trained, knowing she was somewhere, while Chenji morphed back into a lizard behind them.

"We know you're here," said Kano. "Show yourself and we won't hurt you."

"I don't think so," said Mila. They each aimed their weapons in the direction of her voice. "You've caught me rigging this thing to blow. A little premature, but I'm sure there's enough explosives here to kill all four of us."

"We both know you don't want to do that," said Kano.

"I could be persuaded," she replied. Kano could tell by her voice that she was getting closer to him. "But I'd hate for you to die without getting a second kiss."

"What's she talking about?" asked Makoto.

"Ignore her," said Kano, raising his spear.

"Ah, ah, ah," she said, her voice drawing back. "Kano, we both know you wouldn't risk setting off this detonator. Not with your friends in the room."

Kano clenched the spear tighter, though he knew he wouldn't fire it. She'd called his bluff.

"Let me pass," she said, "and no one has to die."

Kano lowered the spear. He nudged Chenji, who begrudgingly morphed back into his Human form. Then he looked to Makoto, who had his eyes closed. *Accepting defeat*, Kano assumed, stepping aside.

"Smart boys, all of you," said Mila. "But don't get any ideas. This detonator is still primed and—"

Makoto stuck out his baton and struck Mila right in the chest. Kano knew because she appeared on contact, all her muscles seizing, her finger unable to squeeze the detonator in her hand. Makoto snatched it from her with his free hand and then kicked her over.

"Nice try," he said, switching off the detonator. "But a Nurrano always knows his surroundings."

"Great work, Makoto," said Kano, beaming.

"LOOK OUT!" cried Chenji. He tackled them both as lightning zapped over their heads and struck the controls. The bombs Mila had attached to it exploded on impact and threw them all out the doorway and right to Taranis's feet.

"There'll be no stopping this train," muttered the masked man. He zapped the three of them with a stream of electricity from his fingertips.

Kano screamed as all the familiar places convulsed from Taranis's power. For a moment, it was so intense that he almost wished for death, but then the electricity ceased. He groaned. Everything ached. Everything burned. Beside him, Mila laid unconscious, a lump rising from her head from something she'd struck when the explosions went off.

Taranis knelt beside him. "Danadas thinks you're needed to open the gate. I disagree, but I won't have him think it was my hand that killed you. I'll let the train do that." He hoisted Mila over his shoulder and marched toward the next car.

Kano wanted to get up, wanted to fight, but everything hurt too much. He knew if he tried now, he'd only open him and his teammates up to more electricity.

But Chenji didn't know that. The changeling crawled past Kano, hissing through his gritted teeth.

"Wait, Chenji!" said Kano.

Chenji started to transform into a serpent when Taranis spun around and struck him with electricity in mid-transformation. Chenji shrieked and convulsed, his body morphing into a serpent, then a lizard, then a frog, then a monkey.

"No, no, no!" cried Kano, crawling over as his friend switched from animal to animal without any control.

"He should have stayed down," said Taranis as the door to the next car shut between them.

"We're almost there," said Junior into his communicator as he ran through the train cars, Akio on his shoulder, Sandra right behind, her spear in hand. He checked out the windows. The speeders were arriving at the middle car, Lusitani leaping from them and onto the roof of the train. He picked up the pace, fire rising to his palms. He'd waited this long to be reunited with his mother. He wasn't going to let anyone take that away.

"Fireball!" cried Akio. It impacted side of the train car and blasted the windows to bits. Everyone dove to the ground, shattered glass raining around them. Junior clenched his fists tight.

Kazan.

Feet pattered on the roof. Junior followed the sound and threw a fireball at the source. It punched a hole in the ceiling, letting the wind whip into the car as the train thundered along.

But Kazan wasn't there.

A fireball blasted through the roof a few feet away and landed near Junior's feet. He dove back and collided with Sandra. Together they collapsed, Akio tumbling off his shoulder and into a nearby seat.

"What a cute little Jakari you have!" shouted Kazan from the roof. He threw another fireball right at Akio.

"No!" Junior reached out and absorbed the fireball before it could hit Akio or the explosives he was carrying.

"He called me cute," said Akio, drawing his knife. "He must die."

"Wait," said Junior, blocking the Jakari from the hatch that led to the roof. "I'll go. You can do more damage from down here."

Akio pondered that for a moment. "Yes. Yes, I believe I could."

Junior drew a deep breath and climbed out the hatch for his rematch. The wind whipped at his face and threatened to tip him over the edge of the train. He found the Morabani standing across from him, eyes wide and eager for blood.

"How's the shoulder?" he hissed, blue flames glowing against his coal-black skin.

"Better than you'll be when I'm finished," said Junior. He sparked a flame in his hand, but the wind blew it away.

Oh shit.

Junior ducked as a fireball sailed overhead, the wind doing nothing to snuff Kazan's flames. "Akio!" he called into his comms. "Two meters ahead of the hole he made."

"Two meters!" the Jakari replied through the comms. An explosion erupted beneath Kazan's feet. The Morabani screamed and fell into the train car. Junior hurried through the hatch. By the time he was inside, the Morabani was already on its bare feet, aiming its palms for Akio and Sandra.

"You will pay for that!" cried Kazan.

Sandra and Akio dove behind the seats. Akio pressed his detonator and two more bombs exploded on either side of Kazan. The force threw him forward.

Junior raced toward his opponent, absorbing the flames from the explosives as he went, and drove all the fire down at Kazan.

The door ahead flung open. Yui burst through and fired a jet of icy wind. It snuffed Junior's flames and threw him back before he could reach Kazan. He laid on the ground, shivering.

We don't have time for this, he thought. Sandra must have been thinking the same thing as she drove her spear for Yui's chest, but the Ice Queen caught it in mid-thrust.

"You should leave this fight to the Zoboros," said Yui.

"Why? Are you scared?" Sandra pushed a button on her spear and looked away as the tip flashed a bright light in Yui's face.

Yui screamed, shielding her eyes, and stumbled back where Akio was there to trip her.

"Come on!" said Junior. He stepped over Kazan's back as the Morabani attempted to stand up and led his team through the train cars. "Cera, what's your status?"

"Not good," she said. "They're breaching from the roof. My shields can't hold!"

Junior stopped halfway through the next train car and ripped open the hatch. "Everyone up!" he cried. His team followed him out and over the tops of the train cars. Everything felt shaky, like a sudden bump from the train was all they needed to get flung off, but Junior accepted the risk. He had his mother to save.

He counted six Lusitani ahead, each drilling through the roof and into Cera's shield. He could hear Cera screaming on the other side as she strained – the Lusitani must have found drills effective against her powers. They wouldn't need anything special to counter Junior's powers, though; the train was already doing that.

"Sandra, Akio, get behind me and be ready for my signal." They did as he commanded, his body big enough to shield them from view. The skull helmets began turning toward him, locking on to their next Zoboros target.

"That's right, look at me," he said under his breath. He held his hand close to his chest and readied a flame there. Any further out and the wind would blow it away, but the Lusitani didn't know that. Not yet.

The Lusitani abandoned their drills and rose, readying whatever weapons they planned to use against him. Compressed air, he assumed.

"Aim for their wrists," he whispered, a chill washing over him as he stared down these Zoboros killers. Killers who thought they could dispose of him like they'd done to so many others.

They were wrong.

Junior dove onto his belly. Akio and Sandra opened fire, Akio from his pistol and Sandra from her spear. Their blaster bolts burst on the Lusitani's wrist devices. The Lusitani stumbled back, surprised. Vulnerable. Junior smiled. They had them.

Until a bolt of lightning exploded between them.

Oh great.

Two speeders landed between them and the Lusitani, one carrying Dimitri the Gorv, the other carrying Taranis.

"It's over, Hendricks," announced Taranis. "Project Vortex is mine."

"She has a name!" blurted Junior, fire flaring in his palm.

"So she does." Taranis nodded to his Gorv, who opened the hatch to find a shield blocking him.

"Cera!" called Taranis over his shoulder, aiming his sword at Junior. "Lower your shields or your friends die. Starting with Angeline's son."

"How about you come down here and face me?" said Cera. "One on one."

"I'm afraid I don't have time for that," said Taranis, sparking electricity in his sword.

"Wait!" cried Angeline. There was silence for a while until finally the shield disappeared and the hatch opened. Dimitri reached in and pulled her out. She offered no resistance.

"Mom, no!" shouted Junior. He stepped forward, but Taranis sent sparks leaping in his direction. A warning.

"I'll go," said Angeline. "Just please don't hurt him."

"Finally, someone with some sense," came Yui's voice. Junior turned. She and Kazan had formed up behind his team. They were trapped.

Angeline approached Taranis, who snatched her arm in his gauntlet. That made Junior clench his fists even tighter.

"I'll be fine, Junior," she said. "It's okay."

Taranis looked from Angeline to Junior. "It looks like your luck favors me now, Hendricks." He turned to Dimitri and the Lusitani. "Take the boy alive. He's a useful motivator. Kill the rest."

Junior raised his fists. Akio and Sandra formed up close behind him. If they were going down, they would go down fighting.

That's when Junior noticed something happening beside them. They were passing a train on the opposite railway, but the train was accelerating to match their speed. Taranis aimed his sword at it, ready for however many IDF troopers would come pouring out of it, but Junior saw no one in the windows.

Why would they catch up with us without bringing any reinforcements?

Vines burst from the windows of the opposite train. They snapped around the Lusitani and flung them off the roof.

"Someone need an assist?!" came Li's voice through the comms.

"Great timing!" said Junior, wasting no time in charging toward Taranis, who was too busy cleaving vines with his sword to notice him. Akio vaulted from Junior's shoulder, knife drawn, ready to pierce the masked man's armor.

Taranis snapped around and zapped Akio in midair. The Jakari cried out as he sailed over the edge of the train and toward the surface far beneath the raised railway.

"AKIO!" cried Junior. Looking back, he saw Sandra holding off Yui, her spear versus Yui's spear of ice, while Kazan flew between the trains, burning away Li's vines.

When he turned back toward his mother, Dimitri was standing there to kick him in the chest with its massive foot. He skated back toward Sandra as she broke Yui's spear clean in two and brought the tip of her own spear to Yui's neck.

"Don't make me kill you," said Sandra.

"Then you should've done it already," replied Yui. Sandra gasped. Junior screamed. A broken half of the ice spear protruded from Sandra's belly. She fell to her knees while Yui smiled.

Junior lunged and punched Yui in the face with all the force he could muster. The impact threw her clear off the train, and Junior watched from above as she formed a ramp of ice beneath her feet and slid safely away.

He ran to Sandra's side as she gasped for breath. "Stay with me. You're gonna be okay."

Sandra shook her head. "We're not cadets anymore." She looked at the spear lodged in her gut. "This is real."

He cupped her head in his hand, his eyes searching for someone who could help, but the whole train was in chaos, a blitz of fire and smoke and vines. And no one was coming for them; no one except the Gorv.

"Keep fighting Junior," whispered Sandra. "You need to find my sister for me."

"No, Sandra, don't…" but the life left her eyes before Junior could say any more. He rested her head against the train as the Gorv's shadow fell over him.

"You're going to pay for this," said Junior. The Gorv only laughed at him. It laughed until a vine whipped around the side of the train, carrying a little blue creature upon it. There was the flash of a blade as it passed Dimitri, and then Akio landed beside Junior, his knife coated in black blood.

"Never count a Jakari out," said Akio. The Gorv gripped its neck, blood oozing between its fingertips. The creature fell over the side and into the rails, its black blood splattering against the train on impact.

"DIMITRI!" screamed Taranis. He tossed Angeline aside and sparked electricity around him in a frantic web, more electricity than Junior had ever seen him produce. Junior braced, knowing he had nowhere to turn, nowhere to run atop this train. Taranis drew back his sword, the voltage all surging into the blade. Angeline screamed. Junior closed his eyes.

There was a thunderclap, but Junior felt nothing. He opened his eyes. He was still atop the train, vines whipping around him, chaos everywhere, but the electricity wasn't flying toward him. Instead, *Taranis* was flying toward him, the electricity misfiring into the railway beneath them.

What the hell? Junior searched and spotted the source of the thunderclap standing a few train cars away, spear aimed.

Got him. Kano smiled as he watched Taranis fly forward, caught in the center of the shockwave he'd just launched across the top of the train. His enemy's electricity still shot out, but into the railway rather than into his friend's chest.

Sparks exploded along the magnetic tracks. One after the other, their generators overloaded. Kano's smile vanished. The magnets gave out and the train slammed down onto the rails beneath it, the metal screaming as the train skated along.

Oops.

Kano stumbled forward, the train tipping left and right, his friends onboard all teetering close to the edge with nothing to grab onto. Li's vines came grasping for them. He saw Jaden, Cera, and Warp being pulled from the middle car and into the opposite train. He glanced over his shoulder; Makoto was far behind him, carrying an unconscious Chenji on his back, when a vine scooped both of them as well. Another vine was coming for him, but Taranis was rising ahead.

"Li, save me for last!" he called into his comms. "I'm still in this fight."

"Kano, the train is *literally* going to crash!" came her voice.

"I know what I'm doing."

"No, you don't."

"You know me so well." He sprinted forward. The vines stayed away, leaving him a clear path to Taranis, who was busy cleaving any vine that came for Angeline. Junior was rushing Taranis from the opposite side, Akio upon his back; Li had thankfully left them on the train for backup. He would need it.

Kano aimed his spear, but the train tipped left and his feet slipped from under him. He slid across the surface and grabbed onto the edge, his feet dangling over a forty-foot drop. The train scraped along the railings – the only thing keeping it from tipping completely – while the railings groaned and bent. They couldn't hold.

"KAZAN!" Taranis screamed into his communicator. The Morabani flew in, grabbed the side of the train, and blasted a jet of blue flame that began to push the train upright. Kano's eyes met Kazan's as he pulled himself over the edge, a clear understanding that they wouldn't engage. Not yet.

Kano spotted a riderless speeder coming for Taranis and charged for it as the train leveled beneath his feet.

"Kano, come in," came Carmichael's voice.

"I see it," answered Kano. "I'm going to try and take it out."

"Negative. The IDF is converging on your location. The ship is in lockdown. Taranis won't make it out. You and Akio have a new objective: terminate the asset."

Everything went silent for Kano. The fighting, the train, it was as though all his senses zeroed in on Angeline, standing there helpless in Taranis's gauntlet as the speeder rolled in beside them.

"Sir, that's Junior's mother."

"And if she survives, Danadas will send others to capture her. We can't afford to let that happen. Understood?"

Kano looked to Junior, who was sprinting to save his mother. The mother who could destroy an entire planet if Taranis got hold of her.

"Understood." Kano aimed his spear at Angeline, though everything inside him told him not to. She was innocent. She was good. And she was his friend's mother; a friend who had searched the galaxy to find her. He knew he would have to make tough calls, but this was different. This call held millions of lives in the balance.

And also his friendship.

Kano turned his spear and sent the shockwave roaring out. It thundered over the top of the train and slammed into the speeder just as Taranis was reaching for it, flipping it over the edge and smashing it against the railway.

Kano smiled as Taranis turned toward him, electricity flowing through the grooves of his mask. Beneath that mask, Kano knew his enemy was furious.

"It's over, Taranis!" he shouted.

"Never." Taranis charged, sword drawn, and swung. Kano blocked it with the spear, sparks bursting between the two weapons as their energy collided. Kano skated back, but Taranis was on him, slashing and stabbing, Kano barely able to keep up with the strikes as they came in. He saw Junior running in from behind Taranis, but not fast enough.

The blade caught underneath his spear and wrenched it from his hands. *No!* Kano reached out to summon it, but Taranis snatched it from the air, his electricity pulsing through it.

Taranis aimed the sword at Kano, the spear behind him at Junior, who skidded to a stop. They both braced, expecting to be electrocuted, but the electricity didn't come.

"We three found Iramwerta," said Taranis. "Your friends are gone. The IDF is upon us. Help me clear them out and we can escape together."

Kano looked. The other train was far ahead now, while their dead train scraped to a pitiful stop against the railway. Dozens of transports were racing in, far more than they could take on alone. And where was Carmichael in all this? Had the captain left them for dead? Fighting alongside Taranis seemed a sure way to get themselves killed.

"Don't fight," said Angeline. "Please don't. They will kill you if you try."

"We have to try, Mom," said Junior, flames sparking in each hand.

Kazan joined them atop the train, focused on the oncoming horde of IDF troops. "To the death, then?" he asked.

Kano noticed someone was missing. *Where's Akio?* He scanned and spotted the Jakari off to the side, its knife drawn, pain in its bulbous eyes.

Kano froze. The knife was aimed for Angeline.

"Wait, don't!" he cried, starting forward. Taranis mistook his sudden movement for an attack and zapped him with lightning. He fell flat on his back, groaning as the knife careened through the air. Junior, realizing what was happening, cried out, and Taranis zapped him too out of panic, unaware of the knife heading toward his hostage.

Angeline gasped. She looked down. The knife was lodged in the dampener, its lights flickering out. She saw her son convulsing on the floor. Her expression changed. She turned to the masked man responsible, a darkness falling over.

"How dare you," she said, but her voice was different. It sounded like a thousand voices pressed into one. The dampener fell to the floor. A strange mass orbited around her hands, black and irregular, rising and writhing like an animal trying to escape a cage. She threw her hands forward and the mass shot out in a beam that traced the surface of the train toward Taranis. He dove out of the way, the beam just grazing his chest plate, and landed beside Kano.

The beam kept slicing. Angeline's hands shook; she seemed to have no control over her power as it lasered along the distant walls of the Transitway and eventually flickered out. Kano followed the trail she'd created. Her power had left a clean cut in the train, but there was something strange about it. It was...moving. He looked closer, watching as the cut expanded, the metal of the train slowly flaking away.

"What is this?!" cried Taranis. He threw off his chest plate. It clunked against the ground, shrinking, dissolving, until there was nothing more.

Kano stepped back. Kazan brushed past him, his eyes wide with fright.

"The demon plight!" he screamed. He leaped off the train, fire flaring, and flew far away.

Demon plight? Kano started to panic. Red lights flooded the Transitway. A new siren sounded, its wail piercing Kano's ears.

"Anti-matter breach," came a voice over the *Dormarch*'s intercom. "Abandon ship."

Abandon ship? This was the biggest ship in the fleet. How could they just—?

When he looked again, the breach in the train had expanded to triple its size, and it was growing by the second.

Taranis scrambled back, the sword and spear clattering out of his shaking hands as Angeline marched toward him, the mass still floating around her hands.

"Please, please don't," he whispered. Some of his mask began to dust away. He ripped it off. Kano gasped. The face he saw was Human, but with small tusks along his chin and an indent in his forehead.

Half Poterian, Kano realized. Even Angeline stopped with surprise. Kano braced, unsure if she would go for the kill, when Akio swept in and struck Taranis in the back of the head with the hilt of his knife. The light left Taranis's eyes and he slumped back, unconscious.

"It is over, Lady Hendricks," he said, bowing. "Your spawn is safe."

The mass slowly faded around Angeline's hands. She fell to her knees, winded and dazed. Kano looked to the troop transports in the distance. They were all veering off, headed for the hangar, headed for escape, but one kept steering toward them. Kano grabbed up the spear, ready to fight, when a voice came through his communicator.

"Someone need a ride?" asked Carmichael.

Kano saw the captain waving from the driver's seat of the transport. It pulled up and the hatch opened. All his teammates waited inside, Li tending to Warp, Chenji still unconscious. Junior led his mother onboard, Akio trailing right behind, but Kano hesitated. He looked to the unconscious Taranis lying helpless on the train. He started for the transport but stopped himself.

"Kano, what are you waiting for?!" called Cera.

He turned and scooped up Taranis in his arms. He was so heavy with all the armor that Kano struggled to even lift him up. Suddenly, he felt the weight alleviate. He looked, and two green energy hands were supporting Taranis from underneath.

"Just get inside, quickly!" barked Cera, levitating Taranis into the transport. Kano jumped in after them and the transport raced off.

Carmichael drove them into the hangar. Thousands were running through it, piling into ships, clamoring for a space. The ships that were taking off struggled to lift beneath the weight of all their passengers.

The transport landed and the team poured out. No one from the IDF seemed the least bit concerned about stopping them; the sailors and troopers were all too focused on catching a ride.

"This way!" called Carmichael. He dropped from the driver's seat and ran toward an open space on the hangar floor where there were no ships.

"Why *there*?!" called Makoto. Everyone was confused by Carmichael until a familiar Poterian freighter swooped into the hangar. It didn't land, but hovered above the space Carmichael had marked. Its ramp lowered in midair and Ristin stood upon it, his hands aimed and free of their dampener. Kano felt himself lifting off the ground.

"Now this is a getaway!" exclaimed Jaden as they floated off the hangar floor and into the freighter. Li clung close to Warp while Jaden and Makoto held Chenji between them. Kano stayed close to the unconscious Taranis, who no one wanted to touch. Once they were all inside, Ristin pounded the release button and the hydraulic door sealed behind them.

"We're clear!" Ristin shouted up the ship.

Sterling jammed on the throttle. The ship zipped out of the hangar and into the void of space while the team watched the mighty *Dormarch* sever in two in the distance.

Epilogue

"This will pinch a little."

Kano grimaced as Li slid the giant needle beneath his skin. *Not as bad as it looked*, he realized. He wasn't sure why it had freaked him out; given everything they had just been through, a needle was nothing.

He looked around the cargo hold, which they had converted into a makeshift infirmary. Chenji laid on the bed beside him (which was just a worktable they had covered in cushions). The changeling had made a solid recovery over the past two days. No permanent damage that Li could find; at this point the only lingering effect was a migraine, though Kano hadn't seen him attempt to change form yet. He suspected Chenji was afraid to.

The next bed held the one everyone was worried about: Warp. Li had her stabilized, but Warp's wound leaked blood every day – blood she needed replenished. Hence the needle in Kano's arm.

Li dodged Kano's glance and pretended to busy herself with the blood bags from the other team members.

"Are we going to talk?" he asked.

"There isn't much to say."

Kano drummed his fingers nervously. Romance was hard.

"I thought if we both survived we could, I don't know, pick up where we left off before the mission?"

"Pick up what, Kano?" she snapped.

He flushed, unsure what to say. He wasn't even sure why he kept talking. It might have been the blood loss. "I thought we were going to, I don't know…be something."

"Be something?!" Li leaned forward and lowered her voice. "I gave you a chance to get off that train and you stayed."

"I had a mission to—"

"You *stayed*."

Kano drew a deep breath. "This is our life now, Li. We have to make tough choices."

"Then I don't want to be there when you make the choice that gets you killed." She pulled the needle from his arm and jammed an alcohol rag against the puncture wound.

"Ow!" he yelped, but Li was already out the door. He turned to Chenji, who had his eyes closed. "Did you hear anything?"

"Nope," replied Chenji, smiling.

Kano sighed. He could've abandoned the train on the *Dormarch*, but that would have meant abandoning the mission. Staying was the right thing to do. At least, that's what he told himself.

Junior appeared in the doorway. His infirmary bed had been empty most of the day despite the team encouraging him to rest his shoulder. He hadn't interacted much with anyone since their mission; Kano suspected Junior was still struggling with the loss of Sandra. They all were.

Junior just carried a much darker look on his face than the others.

He was wearing that dark look when he nodded for Kano to come meet him outside.

Wonderful. Kano climbed off the bed, wishing he'd pretended to be asleep like Chenji, and met Junior in the empty hallway.

"I have a question for you," muttered Junior.

Kano nodded, sensing this was a sensitive subject.

"Akio won't give me a straight answer, but I wanted to hear it from you." Junior checked over his shoulder before continuing. "Did Carmichael put a kill order on my mother?"

Kano gulped. How had Junior figured that out? As a friend, Kano felt compelled to tell him the truth, but as a part of this team, he felt compelled to lie. The team needed to trust in Carmichael; if they knew the order he'd given, if *Junior* knew the order he'd given, that trust would be lost forever. And without their leader, the team would crumble.

"He didn't give that order," whispered Kano.

Junior's eyes narrowed. He studied Kano for a while before muttering, "Ok then." He marched off without another word.

Kano sighed. Junior wasn't convinced. He wasn't sure Junior ever could be convinced. But after seeing what Junior's mother could do, Kano couldn't entirely fault Carmichael for making that call. One burst of her powers had been enough to cripple the largest ship in the galaxy.

Taking her with them was an awful risk, especially with so many of their enemies hunting her.

He started down the hallway when he heard her voice leak through one of the doors.

"We shouldn't discuss this," she whispered.

"I don't *want* to discuss this. I want you to discuss it with your son." *Sterling*. Kano could recognize that gruff voice anywhere.

"The less he knows the better," said Angeline.

"I kept your secret because it wasn't mine to tell," said Sterling, "but sooner or later he will discover what he truly is. And when he does, you'll want him to be on your side."

"The truth would destroy him, Sterling." Angeline paused for a long time. "And it would turn him from my side regardless."

"Do what you please then," said Sterling angrily. Kano heard the clunk of the Poterian's bionic leg and hurried through an adjacent door, watching through the crease in the door as Sterling stormed his way down the hallway. It wasn't until the Poterian was out of sight that Kano let out the breath he'd been holding.

"An unexpected visit, to be sure," came a voice like ice.

Kano froze. He'd been so set on hiding that he hadn't realized he'd chosen *that* room to do it in. He turned slowly and found Taranis standing behind iron bars that T8 had drilled in specifically for their new prisoner, who looked so much smaller without his armor, without his mask. Yet still Kano felt a chill in the half-Poterian's presence.

"We have nothing to discuss." Kano turned to walk away.

"You're afraid, aren't you Kano?"

"Not of you," he called back.

"But you are afraid of what's coming. The Orlovs. The IDF. They will rip this galaxy apart to find you. To find *her*."

"We can take them," said Kano, stepping out the door.

Taranis laughed. "You look to the stars and see your enemies, Kano. But there's something else. Something worse. And it's staring you in the face, though you fail to see it."

Kano stopped. "And what's that, Taranis?"

"Your team. They're frightened. They're vulnerable. And they serve a man who brought them together with a lie. It's only a matter of time before your team breaks completely."

"That won't happen."

"Really?" Taranis pressed against the bars. "Because it sounded like it's already begun."

Kano clenched his fists. Taranis had heard his conversation with Junior, and perhaps Angeline's conversation about Junior, whatever she'd meant. It didn't matter. This team was stronger than Taranis thought; his words were only meant to scare him.

"You lost Taranis. Accept it."

Taranis smiled. "For now."

Kano marched out the door, a part of him regretting that he had saved his enemy. He wasn't sure why he'd done it; after seeing that security footage of his parents, of Taranis as a tortured child, Kano felt some strange responsibility toward him. Like there was more to his enemy, even if no one else saw it.

Hell, he was having a hard time seeing it too.

He rejoined the others, who had assembled in the bridge – Carmichael, Sterling, Cera, Li, Makoto, Akio, Jaden, T8, and Junior. Looking around, both Li and Junior dodged his glance, and that was enough to make Taranis's warning echo in his head.

"It's been two days," said Jaden. "We can't keep sitting around. We need a plan. We need a place to go."

"There aren't any places where the IDF and the Orlovs won't hunt us," said Li.

"Thanks for the backup, Li," said Jaden. She stuck her tongue out at him.

"There is one place, for those of us bold enough to go," said Carmichael. He nodded to Sterling, who grunted as he pulled up a map. Kano got a chill as he watched the Poterian work. For some reason, he felt like he knew where this conversation was going.

And he didn't like it.

"Your captain and I have spoken for a while," said Sterling. "Given our limited options, I've agreed to take you out of IDF jurisdiction. However, the journey will be dangerous. In fact, so dangerous that they'd be foolish to try and follow us."

"Just like we'd be foolish for going," muttered T8.

"And where exactly are we going?" asked Makoto.

Kano tensed. He noticed Junior doing the same. They both knew the answer without anyone having to say it.

Carmichael smiled. "Poteria."

Michael Ciccarelli-Walsh lives in Tallahassee, Florida, where he attended Florida State University for both his undergraduate and graduate degrees (Go Noles!). He is also the author of *Trouble in the Floating City*, the first novel in the Zoboros series.

ciccarelliwalsh.com

www.ingramcontent.com/pod-product-compliance
Lightning Source LLC
Chambersburg PA
CBHW062108290726
48975CB00001B/149